KING PENGUIN

16/14.   £2-50
PB

THE OLD FOREST

Peter Taylor was born in 1919. He has taught at Harvard and at the University of North Carolina and is now a professor at the University of Virginia. He is the author of several previous collections of stories, the last of which was *In the Miro District* (1977), a novel and two books of plays. He has received the American National Academy Award for Fiction, the Gold Medal for Fiction and Fulbright, Guggenheim and Rockefeller grants, and he was made a member of the American Academy of Arts and Letters in 1983.

D1150211

PETER TAYLOR

—

THE
OLD FOREST

A KING PENGUIN
PUBLISHED BY PENGUIN BOOKS

Penguin Books Ltd, Harmondsworth, Middlesex, England
Viking Penguin Inc., 40 West 23rd Street, New York, New York 10010, U.S.A.
Penguin Books Australia Ltd, Ringwood, Victoria, Australia
Penguin Books Canada Ltd, 2801 John Street, Markham, Ontario, Canada L3R 1B4
Penguin Books (N.Z.) Ltd, 182–190 Wairau Road, Auckland 10, New Zealand

First published by Chatto & Windus · The Hogarth Press 1985
Published in Penguin Books 1987

The following stories were originally published in *The New Yorker*:
'The Gift of the Prodigal'; 'The Old Forest'; 'Promise of Rain'; 'Bad Dreams';
'The Little Cousins'; 'Porte Cochere'; 'Two Ladies in Retirement'.
'A Friend and Protector' and 'Allegiance' originally appeared in
The Kenyon Review.
'A Walled Garden' originally appeared in *The New Republic*.
'A long Fourth'; 'Rain in the Heart'; and 'The Death of a Kinsman'
originally appeared in *Sewanee Review*.
'The Scoutmaster' originally appeared in *The Partisan Review*.

Printed and bound in Great Britain by
Cox & Wyman Ltd, Reading

CONTENTS

THE
OLD
FOREST

THE GIFT
OF THE PRODIGAL

THERE'S RICKY down in the washed river gravel of my driveway.
I had my yardman out raking it before 7 A.M.—the driveway. It
looks nearly perfect. Ricky also looks nearly perfect down there.
He looks extremely got up and cleaned up, as though he had
been carefully raked over and smoothed out. He is wearing a
three-piece linen suit, which my other son, you may be sure,
wouldn't be seen wearing on any occasion. And he has on an
expensive striped shirt, open at the collar. No tie, of course. His
thick head of hair, parted and slicked down, is just the same tan
color as the gravel. Hair and gravel seem equally clean and in
order. The fact is, Ricky looks this morning as though he belongs
nowhere else in the world but out there in that smooth spread of
washed river gravel (which will be mussed up again before noon,
of course—I'm resigned to it), looks as though he feels perfectly
at home in that driveway of mine that was so expensive to install
and that requires so much upkeep.

Since one can't see his freckles from where I stand at this
second-story window, his skin looks very fair—almost transpar-
ent. (Ricky just misses being a real redhead, and so never lets
himself get suntanned. Bright sunlight tends to give him skin
cancers.) From the window directly above him, I am able to get

the full effect of his outfit. He looks very masculine standing down there, which is no doubt the impression his formfitting clothes are meant to give. And Ricky *is* very masculine, no matter what else he is or isn't. Peering down from up here, I mark particularly that where his collar stands open, and with several shirt buttons left carelessly or carefully undone, you can see a triangle of darker hair glistening on his chest. It isn't hard to imagine just how recently he has stepped out of the shower. In a word, he is looking what he considers his very best. And this says to me that Ricky is coming to me *for* something, or *because of* something.

His little sports car is parked in the turnaround behind this house, which I've built since he and the other children grew up and since their mother died. I know of course that, for them, coming here to see me can never really be like coming home. For Rick it must be like going to see any other old fellow who might happen to be his boss and who is ailing and is staying away from the office for a few days. As soon as I saw him down there, though, I knew something was really seriously wrong. From here I could easily recognize the expression on his face. He has a way, when he is concerned about something, of knitting his eyebrows and at the same time opening his eyes very wide, as though his eyes are about to pop out of his head and his eyebrows are trying to hold them in. It's a look that used to give him away even as a child when he was in trouble at school. If his mother and I saw that expression on his face, we would know that we were apt to be rung up by one of his teachers in a day or so or maybe have a house call from one of them.

Momentarily Ricky massages his face with his big right hand, as if to wipe away the expression. And clearly now he is headed for the side door that opens on the driveway. But before actually coming over to the door he has stopped in one spot and keeps shuffling his suede shoes about, roughing up the smooth gravel, like a young bull in a pen. I almost call out to him not to *do* that, not to muss up my gravel, which even his car wheels haven't disturbed—or not so much as he is doing with his suede shoes. I *almost* call out to him. But of course I don't really. For Ricky is a man twenty-nine years old, with two divorces already and no doubt another coming up soon. He's been through all that, besides a series of live-ins between marriages that I don't generally speak of, even.

For some time before coming on into the house, Ricky remains there in that spot in the driveway. While he stands there, it occurs to me that he may actually be looking the place over, as though he'd never noticed what this house is like until now. The old place on Wertland Street, where he and the other children grew up, didn't have half the style and convenience of this one. It had more room, but the room was mostly in pantries and hallways, with front stairs and back stairs and third-floor servants' quarters in an age when no servant would be caught dead living up there in the attic—or staying anywhere else on the place, for that matter. I am not unaware, of course, how much better that old house on Wertland was than this one. You couldn't have replaced it for twice what I've poured into this compact and well-appointed habitation out here in Farmington. But its neighborhood had gone bad. Nearly all of Charlottesville proper has, as a matter of fact, either gone commercial or been absorbed by the university. You can no longer live within the shadow of Mr. Jefferson's Academical Village. And our old Wertland Street house is now a funeral parlor. Which is what it ought to have been five years before I left it. From the day my wife, Cary, died, the place seemed like a tomb. I wandered up and down the stairs and all around, from room to room, sometimes greeting myself in one of Cary's looking glasses, doing so out of loneliness or out of thinking *that* couldn't be *me* still in my dressing gown and slippers at midday, or fully dressed— necktie and all—at 3 A.M. I knew well enough it was time to sell. And, besides, I wanted to have the experience at last of making something new. You see, we never built a house of our own, Cary and I. We always bought instead of building, wishing to be in an established neighborhood, you know, where there were good day schools for the girls (it was before St. Anne's moved to the suburbs), where there were streetcars and buses for the servants, or, better still, an easy walk for them to Ridge Street.

My scheme for building a new house after Cary died seemed a harebrained idea to my three older children. They tried to talk me out of it. They said I was only doing it out of idleness. They'd laugh and say I'd chosen a rather expensive form of entertainment for myself in my old age. That's what they *said*. That wasn't all they *thought*, however. But I never held against them what they thought. All motherless children—regardless of age—have such thoughts. They had in mind that I'd got notions of marrying again. Me! Why, I've never looked at another woman since the day I married. Not to this very hour. At any rate, one night when we were having dinner and they were telling me how they worried about me, and making it plainer than usual what they thought my plans for the future were or might be, Ricky spoke up—Ricky who never gave a thought in his life to what happened to anybody except himself—and he came out with just what was on the others' minds. "What if you should take a notion to marry again?" he asked. And I began shaking my head before the words were out of his mouth, as did all the others. It was an unthinkable thought for them as well as for me. "Why not?" Ricky persisted, happy of course that he was making everybody uncomfortable. "Worse things have happened, you know. And I nominate the handsome Mrs. Capers as a likely candidate for bride."

I *think* he was referring to a certain low sort of woman who had recently moved into the old neighborhood. You could depend upon Rick to know about her and know her name. As he spoke he winked at me. Presently he crammed his wide mouth full of food, and as he chewed he made a point of drawing back his lips and showing his somewhat overlarge and overly white front teeth. He continued to look straight at me as he chewed, but looking with only one eye, keeping the eye he'd winked at me squinched up tight. He looked for all the world like some old tomcat who's found a nasty morsel he likes the taste of and is not going to let go of. I willingly would have knocked him out of his chair for what he'd said, even more for that common look he was giving me. I knew he knew as well as the others that I'd never looked at any woman besides his mother.

Yet I laughed with the others as soon as I realized they were laughing. You don't let a fellow like Ricky know he's got your goat—especially when he's your own son, and has been in one bad scrape after another ever since he's been grown, and seems always just waiting for a chance to get back at you for something censorious you may have said to him while trying to help him out of one of his escapades. Since Cary died, I've tried mostly just to keep lines of communication open with him. I think that's the thing she would have wanted of me—that is, not to shut Rick out, to keep him talking. Cary used to say to me, "You may be the only person he can talk to about the women he gets involved with. He can't talk to me about such things." Cary always thought it was the women he had most on his mind and who got him into scrapes. I never used to think so. Anyway, I believe that Cary would have wished above all else for me to keep lines open with Rick, would have wanted it even more than she would have wanted me to go ahead in whatever way I chose with schemes for a new house for my old age.

The house was *our* plan originally, you see, hers and mine. It was something we never told the children about. There seemed no reason why we should. Not talking about it except between ourselves was part of the pleasure of it, somehow. And that night when Ricky came out with the speculation about my possibly marrying again, I didn't tell him or the others that actually I had already sold the Wertland Street house and already had blueprints for the new house here in Farmington locked away in my desk drawer, and even a contractor all set to break ground.

Well, my new house was finished the following spring. By that time all the children, excepting Rick, had developed a real enthusiasm for it. (Rick didn't give a damn one way or the other, of course.) They helped me dispose of all the superfluous furniture in the old house. The girls even saw to the details of moving and saw to it that I got comfortably settled in. They wanted me to be happy out here. And soon enough they saw I was. There was no more they could do for me now than there had been in recent years. They had their good marriages to look after (that's what

Cary would have wished for them), and they saw to it that I wasn't left out of whatever of their activities I wanted to be in on. In a word, they went on with their busy lives, and my own life seemed busy enough for any man my age.

What has vexed the other children, though, during the five years since I built my house, is their brother Ricky's continuing to come to me at almost regular intervals with new ordeals of one kind or another that he's been going through. They have thought he ought not to burden me with his outrageous and sometimes sordid affairs. I think they have especially resented his troubling me here at home. I still go to the office, you see, two or three days a week—just whenever I feel like it or when I'm not playing golf or bridge or am not off on a little trip to Sarasota (I stay at the same inn Cary and I used to go to). And so I've always seen Ricky quite regularly at the office. He's had every chance to talk to me there. But the fact is Rick was never one for bringing his personal problems to the office. He has always brought them home.

Even since I've moved, he has always come *here*, to the house, when he's really wanted to talk to me about something. I don't know whether it's the two servants I still keep or some of the young neighbors hereabouts who tell them, but somehow the other children always know when Ricky has been here. And they of course can put two and two together. It will come out over Sunday dinner at one of their houses or at the Club—in one of those little private dining rooms. It is all right if we eat in the big dining room, where everybody else is. I know I'm safe there. But as soon as I see they've reserved a private room I know they want to talk about Ricky's latest escapade. They will begin by making veiled references to it among themselves. But at last it is I who am certain to let the cat out of the bag. For I can't resist joining in when they get onto Rick, as they all know very well I won't be able to. You see, often they will have the details wrong—maybe they get them wrong on purpose—and I feel obliged to straighten them out. Then one of them will turn to me, pretending shocked surprise: "How ever did you know about it? Has *he* been bringing his troubles to *you* again? At his age you'd think he'd be ashamed to! Someone ought to remind him he's a grown man now!" At that point one of the girls is apt to rest her hand on mine. As they go on, I can hear the love for me in their voices and see it in their eyes. I know then what a lucky man I am. I want to say to them that their affection makes up for all the unhappiness Ricky causes me. But I have never been one to make speeches like that. Whenever I have managed to say such things, I have somehow always felt like a hypocrite afterward. Anyway, the talk will go on for a while till I remember a bridge game I have an appointment for in the Club lounge, at two o'clock. Or I recall that my golf foursome is waiting for me in the locker room.

I've never tried to defend Rick from the others. The things he does are really quite indefensible. Sometimes I've even found myself giving details about some escapade of his that the others didn't already know and are genuinely shocked to hear—especially coming from me. He was in a shooting once that everybody in Farmington and in the whole county set knew about—or knew about, that is, in a general way, though without knowing the very thing that would finally make it a public scandal. It's an ugly story, I warn you, as, indeed, nearly all of Ricky's stories are.

He had caught another fellow in bed with a young married woman with whom he himself was running around. Of course it was a scandalous business, all of it. But the girl, as Rick described her to me afterward, was a real beauty of a certain type and, according to Rick, as smart as a whip. Rick even showed me her picture, though I hadn't asked to see it, naturally. She had a tight little mouth, and eyes that—even in that wallet-sized picture—burned themselves into your memory. She was the sort of intense and reckless-looking girl that Ricky has always gone for. I've sometimes looked at pictures of his other girls, too, when he wanted to show them to me. And of course I know what his wives have looked like. All three of his wives have been from good families. For, bad as he is, Ricky is not the sort of fellow who would embarrass the rest of us by *marrying* some slut. Yet even his wives have tended to dress themselves in a way that my own daughters wouldn't. They have dressed, that is to say, in clothes that seemed designed to call attention to their female forms and not, as with my daughters, to call attention to the station and the affluence of their husbands. Being the timid sort of man I am, I used to find myself whenever I talked with his wife—whichever one—carefully looking out the window or looking across the room, away from her, at some inanimate object or other over there or out there. My wife, Cary, used to say that Ricky had bad luck in his wives, that each of them turned out to have just as roving an eye as Ricky himself. I can't say for certain whether this was true for each of them in the beginning or whether it was something Ricky managed to teach them all.

Anyway, the case of the young married woman in whose bed —or apartment—Ricky found that other fellow came near to causing Ricky more trouble than any of his other escapades. The fellow ran out of the apartment, with Rick chasing him into the corridor and down the corridor to a door of an outside stairway. It was not here in Farmington, you see, but out on Barracks Road, where so many of Rick's friends are—in a development that's been put up on the very edge of where the horse farms begin. The fellow scurried down the outside stairs and across a parking lot toward some pastureland beyond. And Rick, as he said, couldn't resist taking a shot at him from that upstairs stoop where he had abandoned the chase. He took aim just when the fellow reached the first pasture fence and was about to climb over. Afterward, Rick said that it was simply too good to miss. But Rick rarely misses a target when he takes aim. He hit the fellow with a load of rat shot right in the seat of the pants.

I'll never know how Rick happened to have the gun with him. He told me that he was deeply in love with the young woman and would have married her if her husband had been willing to give her a divorce. The other children maintain to this day that it was the husband Rick meant to threaten with the gun, but the husband was out of town and Rick lost his head when he found that other fellow there in his place. Anyhow, the story got all over town. I suppose Ricky himself helped to spread it. He thought it all awfully funny at first. But before it was over, the matter came near to getting into the courts and into the paper.

And that was because there was something else involved, which the other children and the people in the Barracks Road set didn't know about and I did. In fact, it was something that I worried about from the beginning. You see, Rick naturally took that fellow he'd blasted with the rat shot to a doctor—a young doctor friend of theirs—who removed the shot. But, being a friend, the doctor didn't report the incident. A certain member of our judiciary heard the details and thought perhaps the matter needed looking into. We were months getting it straightened out. Ricky went out of town for a while, and the young doctor ended by having to move away permanently—to Richmond or Norfolk, I think. I only give this incident in such detail in order to show the sort of low company Ricky has always kept, even when he seemed to be among our own sort.

His troubles haven't all involved women, though. Or not primarily. And that's what I used to tell Cary. Like so many people in Charlottesville, Rick has always had a weakness for horses. For a while he fancied himself a polo player. He bought a polo pony and got cheated on it. He bought it at a stable where he kept another horse he owned—bought it from the man who ran the stable. After a day or so, he found that the animal was a worthless, worn-out nag. It couldn't even last through the first chukker, which was humiliating of course for Ricky. He daren't try to take it onto the field again. It had been all doped up when he bought it. Ricky was outraged. Instead of simply trying to get his money back, he wanted to have his revenge upon the man and make an even bigger fool of *him*. He persuaded a friend to dress himself up in a turtleneck sweater and a pair of yellow jodhpurs and pretend just to be passing by the stall in the same stable where the polo pony was still kept. His friend played the role, you see, of someone only just taking up the game and who thought he *had* to have that particular pony. He asked the man whose animal it was, and before he could get an answer he offered more than twice the price that Rick had paid. He even put the offer into writing—using an assumed name, of course. He said he was from up in Maryland and would return in two days' time. Naturally, the stableman telephoned Ricky as soon as the stranger in jodhpurs had left the stable. He said he had discovered, to his chagrin, that the pony was not in as good condition as he had thought it was. And he said that in order that there be no bad feeling between them he was willing to buy it back for the price Ricky had paid.

Ricky went over that night and collected his money. But when the stranger didn't reappear and couldn't be traced, the stableman of course knew what had happened. Rick didn't return to the stable during the following several days. I suppose, being Ricky, he was busy spreading the story all over town. His brother and sisters got wind of it. And I did soon enough. On Sunday night, two thugs and some woman Ricky knew but would never identify—not even to me—came to his house and persuaded him to go out and sit in their car with them in front of his house. And there they beat him brutally. He had to be in the hospital for five or six days. They broke his right arm, and one of them—maybe it was the woman—was trying to bite off the lobe of his left ear when Ricky's current wife, who had been out to some party without the favor of his company, pulled into the driveway beside the house. The assailants shoved poor Ricky, bruised and bleeding and with his arm broken, out onto the sidewalk. And then of course they sped away down the street in their rented car. Ricky's wife and the male friend who was with her got the license number, but the car had been rented under an assumed name—the same name, actually, as some kind of joke, I suppose, that Ricky's friend in jodhpurs had used with the stablekeeper.

Since Ricky insisted that he could not possibly recognize his two male assailants in a lineup, and since he refused to identify the woman, there was little that could be done about his actual beating. I don't know that he ever confessed to anyone but me that he knew the woman. It was easy enough for me to imagine what *she* looked like. Though I would not have admitted it to Ricky or to anyone else, I would now and then during the following weeks see a woman of a certain type on the streets downtown —with one of those tight little mouths and with burning eyes— and imagine that she might be the very one. All we were ever able to do about the miserable fracas was to see to it finally that

that stable was put out of business and that the man himself had to go elsewhere (he went down into North Carolina) to ply his trade.

There is one other scrape of Ricky's that I must mention, because it remains particularly vivid for me. The nature and the paraphernalia of this one will seem even more old-fashioned than those of the other incidents. Maybe that's why it sticks in my mind so. It's something that might have happened to any number of rough fellows I knew when I was coming along.

Ricky, not surprising to say, likes to gamble. From the time he was a young boy he would often try to inveigle one of the other children into making wagers with him on how overdone his steak was at dinner. He always liked it very rare and when his serving came he would hold up a bite on his fork and, for a decision on the bet, would ask everyone what shade of brown the meat was. He made all the suggestions of color himself. And one night his suggestions got so coarse and vile his mother had to send him from the dining room and not let him have a bite of supper. Sometimes he would try to get the other children to bet with him on the exact number of minutes the parson's sermon would last on Sunday or how many times the preacher would use the word "Hell" or "damnation" or "adultery." Since he has got grown, it's the races, of course, he likes—horse races, it goes without saying, but also such low-life affairs as dog races and auto races. What catches his fancy above all else, though, are the chicken fights we have always had in our part of the country. And a few years ago he bought himself a little farm a dozen miles or so south of town where he could raise his own game chickens. I saw nothing wrong with that at the time. Then he built an octagonal barn down there, with a pit in it where he could hold the fights. I worried a little when he did that. But we've always had cockfights hereabouts. The birds are beautiful creatures, really, though they have no brains, of course. The fight itself is a real spectacle and no worse than some other things people enjoy. At Ricky's urging, I even went down to two or three fights at his place. I didn't bet, because I knew the stakes

were very high. (Besides, it's the betting that's illegal.) And I
didn't tell the other children about my going. But this was after
Cary was dead, you see, and I thought maybe she would have
liked my going for Ricky's sake, though she would never have
acknowledged it. Pretty soon, sizable crowds began attending the
fights on weekend nights. Cars would be parked all over Ricky's
front pasture and all around the yard of the tenant house. He
might as well have put up a sign down at the gate where his farm
road came off the highway.

The point is, everyone knew that the cockfights went on. And
one of his most regular customers and biggest bettors was one of
the county sheriff's right-hand men. I'm afraid Rick must have
bragged about that in advertising his fights to friends—friends
who would otherwise have been a little timid about coming. And
during the fights he would move about among the crowd, winking at people and saying to them under his breath, "The
deputy's here tonight." I suppose it was his way of reassuring
them that everything was all right. I don't know whether or not
his spreading the word so widely had anything to do with the
raid, but nevertheless the deputy was present the night the federal officers came stealing up the farm road, with their car lights
off and with search warrants in their pockets. And it was the
deputy who first got wind of the federal officers' approach. He
had one of his sidekicks posted outside the barn. Maybe he had
somebody watching out there every night that he came. Maybe
all along he had had a plan for his escape in such an emergency.
Rick thought so afterward. Anyhow, the deputy's man outside
knew at once what those cars moving up the lane with their
lights off meant. The deputy got the word before anyone else,
but, depend upon Ricky, he saw the first move the deputy made
to leave. And he was not going to have it. He took out after him.

The deputy's watchman was prepared to stay on and take his
chances. (He wasn't even a patrolman. He probably only worked
in the office.) I imagine he was prepared to spend a night in jail
if necessary, and pay whatever fine there might be, because his
presence could explain one of the sheriff's cars' being parked in
the pasture. But the deputy himself took off through the back-

woods on Ricky's property and toward a county road on the back
of the place. Ricky, as I've said, was not going to have that. Since
the cockfight was on his farm, he knew there was no way out of
trouble for himself. But he thought it couldn't, at least, do him
any harm to have the deputy caught along with everybody else.
Moreover, the deputy had lost considerable amounts of money
there at the pit in recent weeks and had insinuated to Ricky that
he suspected some of the cocks had been tampered with. (I,
personally, don't believe Ricky would stand for that.) Ricky
couldn't be sure there wasn't some collusion between the deputy
and the feds. He saw the deputy's man catch the deputy's eye
from the barn doorway and observed the deputy's departure. He
was right after him. He overtook him just before he reached the
woods. Fortunately, the deputy wasn't armed. (Ricky allowed no
one to bring a gun inside the barn.) And fortunately Ricky
wasn't armed, either, that night. They scuffled a little near the
gate to the woods lot. The deputy, being a man twice Rick's age,
was no match for him and was soon overpowered. Ricky dragged
him back to the barn, himself resisting—as he later testified—all
efforts at bribery on the deputy's part, and turned in both himself and his captive to the federal officers.

Extricating Ricky from that affair and setting matters aright
was a long and complicated undertaking. The worst of it really
began for Ricky after the court proceedings were finished and all
fines were paid (there were no jail terms for anyone), because
from his last appearance in the federal courthouse Ricky could
drive his car scarcely one block through that suburb where he
lives without receiving a traffic ticket of some kind. There may
not have been anything crooked about it, for Ricky is a wild sort
of driver at best. But, anyhow, within a short time his driving
license was revoked for the period of a year. Giving up driving
was a great inconvenience for him and a humiliation. All we
could do about the deputy, who, Ricky felt sure, had connived
with the federal officers, was to get him out of his job after the
next election.

The outcome of the court proceedings was that Rick's fines
were very heavy. Moreover, efforts were made to confiscate all

the livestock on his farm, as well as the farm machinery. But he was saved from the confiscation by a special circumstance, which, however, turned out to produce for him only a sort of Pyrrhic victory. It turned out, you see, that the farm was not in Ricky's name but in that of his young tenant farmer's wife. I never saw her, or didn't know it if I did. Afterward, I used to try to recall if I hadn't seen some such young woman when I was down watching the cockfights—one who would have fitted the picture in my mind. My imagination played tricks on me, though. I would think I remembered the face or figure of some young girl I'd seen there who could conceivably be the one. But then suddenly I'd recall another and think possibly it might be she who had the title to Ricky's farm. I never could be sure.

When Ricky appeared outside my window just now, I'd already had a very bad morning. The bursitis in my right shoulder had waked me before dawn. At last I got up and dressed, which was an ordeal in itself. (My right hip was hurting somewhat, too.) When finally the cook came in, she wanted to give me a massage before she began fixing breakfast even. Cary would never have allowed her to make that mistake. A massage, you see, is the worst thing you can do for my sort of bursitis. What I wanted was some breakfast. And I knew it would take Meg three quarters of an hour to put breakfast on the table. And so I managed to get out of my clothes again and ease myself into a hot bath, groaning so loud all the while that Meg came up to the door twice and asked if I was all right. I told her just to go and get my breakfast ready. After breakfast, I waited till a decent hour and then telephoned one of my golf foursome to tell him I couldn't play today. It's this damp fall weather that does us in worst. All you can do is sit and think how you've got the whole winter before you and wonder if you'll be able to get yourself off to someplace like Sarasota.

While I sat at a front window, waiting for the postman (he never brings anything but circulars and catalogs on Saturday; besides, all my serious mail goes to the office and is opened by someone else), I found myself thinking of all the things I couldn't do and all the people who are dead and that I mustn't think about. I tried to do a little better—that is, to think of something cheerful. There was lots I *could* be cheerful about, wasn't there? At least three of my children were certain to telephone today—all but Ricky, and it was sure to be bad news if he did! And a couple of the grandchildren would likely call, too. Then tomorrow I'd be going to lunch with some of them if I felt up to it. Suddenly I thought of the pills I was supposed to have taken before breakfast and had forgotten to: the Inderal and the potassium and the hydrochlorothiazide. I began to get up from my chair and then I settled down again. It didn't really matter. There was no ailment I had that could really be counted on to be fatal if I missed one day's dosage. And then I wholeheartedly embraced the old subject, the old speculation: How many days like this one, how many years like this one lay ahead for me? And finally, irresistibly, I descended to lower depths still, thinking of past times not with any relish but remembering how in past times I had always *told* myself I'd someday look back with pleasure on what would seem good old days, which was an indication itself that they hadn't somehow been good enough—not good enough, that is, to stand on their own as an end in themselves. If the old days were so damned good, why had I had to think always how good they would someday seem in retrospect? I had just reached the part where I think there was nothing *wrong* with them and that I ought to be satisfied, had just reached that point at which I recall that I loved and was loved by my wife, that I love and am loved by my children, that it's not them or my life but *me* there's something wrong with!—had just reached that inevitable syllogism that I always come to, when I was distracted by the arrival of Saturday morning's late mail delivery. It was brought in, it was handed to me by a pair of black hands, and of course it had nothing in it. But I took it upstairs to my sitting room. (So that even the servant wouldn't see there was nothing worth having in it.) I had just closed my door and got out my pills when I heard Ricky's car turn into the gravel driveway.

He was driving so slowly that his car wheels hardly disturbed the gravel. That in itself was an ominous phenomenon. He was approaching slowly and quietly. He didn't want me to know ahead of time what there was in store for me. My first impulse was to lock my door and refuse to admit him. I simply did not feel up to Rick this morning! But I said to myself, "That's something I've never done, though maybe ought to have done years ago no matter what Cary said. He's sure to send my blood pressure soaring." I thought of picking up the telephone and phoning one of the other children to come and protect me from this monster of a son and from whatever sort of trouble he was now in.

But it was just then that I caught my first glimpse of him down in the driveway. I had the illusion that he was admiring the place. And then of course I was at once disillusioned. He was only hesitating down there because he dreaded seeing me. But he was telling himself he *had* to see me. There would be no other solution to his problem but to see his old man. I knew what he was thinking by the gesture he was making with his left hand. It's strange how you get the notion that your children are like you just because they have the same facial features and the same gestures when talking to themselves. None of it means a thing! It's only an illusion. Even now I find myself making gestures with my hands when I'm talking to myself that I used to notice my own father making sometimes when we were out walking together and neither of us had spoken a word for half an hour or so. It used to get on my nerves when I saw Father do it, throwing out his hand almost imperceptibly, with his long fingers spread apart. I don't know why it got on my nerves so. But, anyhow, I never dreamed that I could inherit such a gesture—or much less that one of my sons would. And yet there Ricky is, down in the driveway, making the same gesture precisely. And there never were three men with more different characters than my father and me and my youngest child. I watch Ricky make the gesture several times while standing in the driveway. And now suddenly he turns as if to go back to his car. I step away from the window, hoping he hasn't seen me and will go on off. But, having once seen him down there, I can't, of course, do that. I have to receive him and hear him out. I open the sash and call down to him, "Come on up, Ricky."

He looks up at me, smiles guiltily, and shrugs. Then he comes on in the side entrance. As he moves through the house and up the stairs, I try to calm myself. I gaze down at the roughed-up gravel where his suede shoes did their damage and tell myself it isn't so bad and even manage to smile at my own old-maidishness. Presently, he comes into the sitting room. We greet each other with the usual handshake. I can smell his shaving lotion. Or maybe it is something he puts on his hair. We go over and sit down by the fireplace, where there is a fire laid but not lit in this season, of course. He begins by talking about everything under the sun except what is on his mind. This is standard procedure in our talks at such times. Finally, he begins looking into the fireplace as though the fire were lit and as though he were watching low-burning flames. I barely keep myself from smiling when he says, "I've got a little problem—not so damned little, in fact. It's a matter that's got out of hand."

And then I say, "I supposed as much."

You can't give Ricky an inch at these times, you see. Else he'll take advantage of you. Pretty soon he'll have shifted the whole burden of how he's to be extricated onto your shoulders. I wait for him to continue, and he is about to, I think. But before he can get started he turns his eyes away from the dry logs and the unlit kindling and begins looking about the room, just as he looked about the premises outside. It occurs to me again that he seems to be observing my place for the very first time. But I don't suppose he really is. His mind is, as usual, on himself. Then all at once his eyes do obviously come to focus on something over my shoulder. He runs his tongue up under his upper lip and then under his lower lip, as though he were cleaning his teeth. I, involuntarily almost, look over my shoulder. There on the library table behind me, on what I call my desk, are my cut-glass tumbler and three bottles of pills—my hydrochlorothiazide, my Inderal, and my potassium. Somehow I failed to put them back in my desk drawer earlier. I was so distracted by my morbid thoughts when I came upstairs that I forgot to stick them away in the place where I keep them out of sight from everybody. (I don't even like for the servants to see what and how much medicine I take.) Without a word passing between us, and despite the pains in my shoulder and hip, I push myself up out of my chair and sweep the bottles, and the tumbler, too, into the desk drawer. I keep my back to Ricky for a minute or so till I can overcome the grimacing I never can repress when these pains strike. Suddenly, though, I do turn back to him and find he has come to his feet. I pay no special attention to that. I ease myself back into my chair saying, "Yes, Ricky." Making my voice rather hard, I say, "You've got a problem?" He looks at me coldly, without a trace of the sympathy any one of the other children would have shown—knowing, that is, as he surely does, that I am having pains of some description. And he speaks to me as though I were a total stranger toward whom he feels nothing but is just barely human enough to wish not to torture. "Man," he says— the idea of his addressing *me* that way!—"Man, you've got problems enough of your own. Even the world's greatest snotface can see that. One thing sure, you don't need to hear *my* crap."

I am on my feet so quick you wouldn't think I have a pain in my body. "Don't you use that gutter language with me, Ricky!" I say. "You weren't brought up in some slum over beyond Vinegar Hill!" He only turns and looks into the fireplace again. If there were a fire going I reckon he would have spat in it at this point. Then he looks back at me, running his tongue over his teeth again. And then, without any apology or so much as a by-your-leave, he heads for the door. "Come back here, Ricky!" I command. "Don't you dare leave the room!" Still moving toward the closed door, he glances back over his shoulder at me, with a wide, hard grin on his face, showing his mouthful of white teeth, as though my command were the funniest thing he has ever heard. At the door, he puts his big right hand on the glass knob, covering it entirely. Then he twists his upper body, his torso, around—seemingly just from the hips—to face me. And simultaneously he brings up his left hand and scratches that triangle of dark hair where his shirt is open. It is like some kind of dirty gesture he is making. I say to myself, "He really is like something not quite human. For all the jams and scrapes he's been in, he's never suffered any second thoughts or known the meaning of remorse. I ought to have let him hang," I say to myself, "by his own beautiful locks."

But almost simultaneously what I hear myself saying aloud is "Please don't go, Rick. Don't go yet, son." Yes, I am pleading with him, and I mean what I say with my whole heart. He still has his right hand on the doorknob and has given it a full turn. Our eyes meet across the room, directly, as they never have before in the whole of Ricky's life or mine. I think neither of us could tell anyone what it is he sees in the other's eyes, unless it is a need beyond any description either of us is capable of.

Presently Rick says, "You don't need to hear my crap."

And I hear my bewildered voice saying, "I do . . . I do." And "Don't go, Rick, my boy." My eyes have even misted over. But I still meet his eyes across the now too silent room. He looks at me in the most compassionate way imaginable. I don't think any child of mine has ever looked at me so before. Or perhaps it isn't really with compassion he is viewing me but with the sudden, gratifying knowledge that it is not, after all, such a one-sided business, the business between us. He keeps his right hand on the doorknob a few seconds longer. Then I hear the latch click and know he has let go. Meanwhile, I observe his left hand making that familiar gesture, his fingers splayed, his hand tilting back and forth. I am out of my chair by now. I go to the desk and bring out two Danlys cigars from another desk drawer, which I keep locked. He is there ready to receive my offering when I turn around. He accepts the cigar without smiling, and I give it without smiling, too. Seated opposite each other again, each of us lights his own.

And then Ricky begins. What will it be this time, I think. I am wild with anticipation. Whatever it will be, I know it is all anyone in the world can give me now—perhaps the most anyone has ever been able to give a man like me. As Ricky begins, I try to think of all the good things the other children have done for me through the years and of their affection, and of my wife's. But it seems this was all there ever was. I forget my pains and my pills, and the canceled golf game, and the meaningless mail that morning. I find I can scarcely sit still in my chair for wanting Ricky to get on with it. Has he been brandishing his pistol again? Or dragging the sheriff's deputy across a field at midnight? And does he have in his wallet perhaps a picture of some other girl with a tight little mouth, and eyes that burn? Will his outrageous story include her? And perhaps explain it, leaving her a blessed mystery? As Ricky begins, I find myself listening not merely with fixed attention but with my whole being. . . . I hear him beginning. I am listening. I am listening gratefully to all he will tell me about himself, about any life that is not my own.

THE OLD FOREST

I WAS ALREADY formally engaged, as we used to say, to the girl I was going to marry. But still I sometimes went out on the town with girls of a different sort. And during the very week before the date set for the wedding, in December, I was in an automobile accident at a time when one of those girls was with me. It was a calamitous thing to have happen—not the accident itself, which caused no serious injury to anyone, but the accident plus the presence of that girl.

As a matter of fact, it was not unusual in those days—forty years ago and a little more—for a well-brought-up young man like me to keep up his acquaintance, until the very eve of his wedding, with some member of what we facetiously and somewhat arrogantly referred to as the Memphis demimonde. (That was merely to say with a girl who was not in the Memphis debutante set.) I am not even sure how many of us knew what the word "demimonde" meant or implied. But once it had been applied to such girls, it was hard for us to give it up. We even learned to speak of them individually as demimondaines—and later corrupted that to demimondames. The girls were of course a considerably less sophisticated lot than any of this sounds, though they were bright girls certainly and some of them even highly intelligent. They read books, they looked at pictures, and they were apt to attend any concert or play that came to Memphis. When the old San Carlo Opera Company turned up in town, you could count on certain girls of the demimonde being present in their block of seats, and often with a score of the opera in hand. From that you will understand that they certainly weren't the innocent, untutored types that we generally took to dances at the Memphis Country Club and whom we eventually looked forward to marrying.

These girls I refer to would, in fact, very frequently and very frankly say to us that the MCC (that's how we always spoke of the Club) was the last place they wanted to be taken. There was one girl in particular, not so smart as some of the others perhaps and certainly less restrained in the humor she sometimes poked at the world we boys lived in, an outspoken girl, who was the most vociferous of all in her disdain for the Country Club. I remember one night, in one of those beer gardens that became popular in Memphis in the late thirties, when this girl suddenly announced to a group of us, "*I* haven't lost anything at the MCC. That's something you boys can bet your daddy's bottom dollar on." We were gathered—four or five couples—about one of the big wooden beer-garden tables with an umbrella in its center, and when she said that, all the other girls in the party went into a fit of laughter. It was a kind of giggling that was unusual for them. The boys in the party laughed, too, of course, but we were surprised by the way the girls continued to giggle among themselves for such a long time. We were out of college by then and thought we knew the world pretty well; most of us had been working for two or three years in our fathers' business firms. But we didn't see why this joke was so very funny. I suppose it was too broad for us in its reference. There is no way of knowing, after all these years, if it was too broad for our sheltered minds or if the rest of the girls were laughing at the vulgar tone of the girl who had spoken. She was, you see, a little bit coarser than the rest, and I suspect they were laughing at the way she had phrased what she said. For us boys, anyhow, it was pleasant that the demimondaines took the lighthearted view they did about not going to the MCC, because it was the last place most of us would have wished to take them. Our *other* girls would have known too readily who they were and would not willingly or gracefully have endured their presence. To have brought one of those girls to the Club would have required, at any rate, a boy who was a much bolder and freer spirit than I was at twenty-three.

To the liberated young people of today all this may seem a corrupting factor in our old way of life—not our snobbery so much as our continuing to see those demimonde girls right up until the time of marriage. And yet I suspect that in the Memphis of today customs concerning serious courtship and customs concerning unacknowledged love affairs have not been entirely altered. Automobile accidents occur there still, for instance, the reports of which in the newspaper do not mention the name of the driver's "female companion," just as the report of my accident did not. If the driver is a "scion of a prominent local family" with his engagement to be married already announced at an MCC party, as well as in the Sunday newspaper, then the account of his automobile collision is likely to refer to the girl in the car with him only as his "female companion." Some newspaper readers might, I know, assume this to be a reference to the young man's fiancée. That is what is intended, I suppose—*for* the general reader. But it would almost certainly not have been the case—not in the Memphis, Tennessee, of 1937.

The girl with me in my accident was a girl whose origins nobody knew anything about. But she was a perfectly decent sort of girl, living independently in a respectable rooming house and working at a respectable job. That was the sort of girl about whom the Memphis newspapers felt obliged to exercise the greatest care when making any reference to her in their columns. It was as though she were their special ward. Such a girl must be protected from any blaze of publicity. Such a girl must not suffer from the misconduct of any Memphis man or group of men— even newspaper publishers. That was fine for the girl, of course, and who could possibly resent it? It was splendid for her, but I, the driver of the car, had to suffer considerable anguish just because of such a girl's presence in the car and suffer still more because of her behavior afterward. Moreover, the response of certain older men in town to her subsequent behavior would cause me still further anguish and prolong my suffering by several days. Those men were the editors of the city's two newspapers, along with the lawyers called in by my father to represent me if I should be taken into court. There was also my father himself, and the father of my fiancée, *his* lawyer (for some reason or other), and, finally, no less a person than the mayor of Memphis, all of whom one would ordinarily have supposed to be indifferent to the caprices of such a girl. They were the civic leaders and merchant princes of the city. They had great matters on their minds. They were, to say the least, an imposing group in the eyes of a young man who had just the previous year entered his father's cotton-brokerage firm, a young man who was still learning how to operate under the pecking order of Memphis's male establishment.

The girl in question was named Lee Ann Deehart. She was a quite beautiful, fair-haired, hazel-eyed girl with a lively manner, and surely she was far from stupid. The thing she did which drew attention from the city fathers came very near, also, to changing the course of my entire life. I had known Lee Ann for perhaps two years at the time, and knew her to be more levelheaded and more reserved and self-possessed than most of her friends among the demimondaines. It would have been impossible for me to predict the behavior she was guilty of that winter afternoon. Immediately after the collision, she threw open the door on her side of the car, stepped out onto the roadside, and fled into the woods of Overton Park, which is where the accident took place. And from that time, and during the next four days, she was unheard from by people who wished to question her and protect her. During that endless-seeming period of four days no one could be certain of Lee Ann Deehart's whereabouts.

The circumstances of the accident were rather complicated. The collision occurred just after three o'clock on a very cold Saturday afternoon—the fourth of December. Although at that time in my life I was already a member of my father's cotton firm, I was nevertheless—and strange as it may seem—enrolled in a Latin class out at Southwestern College, which is on the north side of Overton Park. (We were reading Horace's *Odes!*) The class was not held on Saturday afternoon, but I was on my way out to the college to study for a test that had been scheduled for Monday. My interest in Latin was regarded by my father and mother as one of my "anomalies"—a remnant of many "anomalies" I had annoyed them with when I was in my teens and was showing some signs of "not turning out well." It seemed now of course that I had "turned out well" after all, except that nobody in the family and nobody among my friends could understand why I went on showing this interest in Latin. I was not able to explain to them why. Any more than I was able to explain why to myself. It clearly had nothing to do with anything else in my life at that period. Furthermore, in the classroom and under the strict eye of our classics professor, a rotund, mustachioed little man hardly four feet in height (he had to sit on a large Latin dictionary in order to be comfortable at his desk), I didn't excel. I was often embarrassed by having to own up to Professor Bartlett's accusation that I had not so much as glanced at the assigned odes before coming to class. Sometimes other members of the class would be caught helping me with the translation, out in the hallway, when Professor Bartlett opened his classroom door to us. My real excuse for neglecting the assignments made by that earnest and admirable little scholar was that too many hours of my life were consumed by my job, by my courtship of the society girl I was going to marry, and by my old, bad habits of knocking about town with my boyhood cronies and keeping company with girls like Lee Ann Deehart.

Yet I had persisted with my Horace class throughout that fall (against the advice of nearly everyone, including Professor Bartlett). On that frigid December afternoon I had resolved to mend my ways as a student. I decided I would take my Horace and go out to Professor Bartlett's classroom at the college and make use of his big dictionary in preparing for Monday's test. It was something we had all been urged to do, with the promise that we would always find the door unlocked. As it turned out, of course, I was destined not to take the test on Monday and never to enter Professor Bartlett's classroom again.

It happened that just before I was setting out from home that afternoon I was filled suddenly with a dread of the silence and the peculiar isolation of a college classroom building on a weekend afternoon. I telephoned my fiancée and asked her to go along with me. At the other end of the telephone line, Caroline Braxley broke into laughter. She said that I clearly had no conception of all the things she had to do within the next seven days before we were to be married. I said I supposed I ought to be helping in some way, though until now she had not asked me so much as to help address invitations to the wedding. "No indeed," said my bride-to-be, "I want to do everything myself. I wouldn't have it any other way."

Caroline Braxley, this capable and handsome bride-to-be of mine, was a very remarkable girl, just as today, as my wife, she seems to me a very remarkable woman of sixty. She and I have been married for forty-one years now, and her good judgment in all matters relating to our marriage has never failed her—or us. She had already said to me before that Saturday afternoon that a successful marriage depended in part on the two persons' developing and maintaining a certain number of separate interests in life. She was all for my keeping up my golf, my hunting, my fishing. And, unlike my own family, she saw no reason that I shouldn't keep up my peculiar interest in Latin, though she had to confess that she thought it almost the funniest thing she had ever heard of a man of my sort going in for.

Caroline liked any sort of individualism in men. But I already knew her ways sufficiently well to understand that there was no use trying to persuade her to come along with me to the college. I wished she would come with me, or maybe I wished even more she would try to persuade me to come over to her house and help her with something in preparation for the wedding. After I had put down the telephone, it even occurred to me that I might simply drive over to her house and present myself at her front door. But I knew what the expression on her face would be, and

I could even imagine the sort of thing she would say: "No man is going to set foot in my house this afternoon, Nat Ramsey! *I'm* getting married next Saturday, in case the fact has slipped your mind. Besides, you're coming here for dinner tonight, aren't you? And there are parties every night next week!"

This Caroline Braxley of mine was a very tall girl. (Actually taller than she is nowadays. We have recently measured ourselves and found that each of us is an inch shorter than we used to be.) One often had the feeling that one was looking up at her, though of course she wasn't really so tall as that. Caroline's height and the splendid way she carried herself were one of her first attractions for me. It seems to me now that I was ever attracted to tall girls—that is, when there was the possibility of falling in love. And I think this was due in part to the fact that even as a boy I was half in love with my father's two spinster sisters, who were nearly six feet in height and were always more attentive to me than to the other children in the family.

Anyhow, only moments after I had put down the telephone that Saturday, when I still sat with my hand on the instrument and was thinking vaguely of rushing over to Caroline's house, the telephone underneath my hand began ringing. Perhaps, I thought, it was Caroline calling back to say that she had changed her mind. Instead, it was Lee Ann Deehart. As soon as she heard my voice, she began telling me that she was bored to death. Couldn't I think of something fun she and I could do on this dreary winter afternoon? I laughed aloud at her. "What a shameless wench you are, Lee Ann!" I said.

"Shameless? How so?" she said with pretended innocence.

"As if you weren't fully aware," I lectured her, "that I'm getting married a week from today!"

"What's that got to do with the price of eggs in Arkansas?" She laughed. "Do you think, old Nat, *I* want to marry you?"

"Well," I explained, "I happen to be going out to the college to cram for a Latin test on Monday."

I could hear her laughter at the other end. "Is your daddy going to let you off work long enough to take your Latin test?"

she asked with heavy irony in her voice. It was the usual way those girls had of making fun of our dependence on our fathers.

"Ah, yes," I said tolerantly.

"And is he going to let you off next Saturday, too," she went on, "long enough to get married?"

"Listen," I said, "I've just had an idea. Why don't you ride out to the college with me, and fool around some while I do my Latin?" I suppose I didn't really imagine she would go, but suddenly I had thought again of the lonely isolation of Dr. Bartlett's classroom on a Saturday afternoon. I honestly wanted to go ahead out there. It was something I somehow felt I had to do. My preoccupation with the study of Latin poetry, ineffectual student though I was, may have represented a perverse wish to experience the isolation I was at the same time dreading or may have represented a taste for morbidity left over from my adolescence. I can allow myself to speculate on all that now, though it would not have occurred to me to do so at the time.

"Well," said Lee Ann Deehart presently, to my surprise and delight, "it couldn't be more boring out there than sitting here in my room is."

"I'll pick you up in fifteen minutes," I said quickly. And I hung up the telephone before she could possibly change her mind. Thirty minutes later, we were driving through Overton Park on our way to the college. We had passed the Art Gallery and were headed down the hill toward the low ground where the Park Pond is. Ahead of us, on the left, were the gates to the Zoo. And on beyond was the point where the road crossed the streetcar tracks and entered a densely wooded area which is actually the last surviving bit of the primeval forest that once grew right up to the bluffs above the Mississippi River. Here are giant oak and yellow poplar trees older than the memory of the earliest white settler. Some of them surely may have been mature trees when Hernando de Soto passed this way, and were very old trees indeed when General Jackson, General Winchester, and Judge John Overton purchased this land and laid out the city of Memphis. Between the Art Gallery and the pond there used to be, in my day, a little spinney of woods which ran nearly all the way back to what was left of the old forest. It was just when I reached this spinney, with Lee Ann beside me, that I saw a truck approaching us on the wrong side of the icy road. There was a moderately deep snow on the ground, and the park roads had, to say the least, been imperfectly cleared. On the ice and the packed snow, the driver of the truck had clearly lost control of his vehicle. When he was within about seventy-five feet of us, Lee Ann said, "Pull off the road, Nat!"

Lee Ann Deehart's beauty was of the most feminine sort. She was a tiny, delicate-looking girl, and I had noticed, when I went to fetch her that day, in her fur-collared coat and knitted cap and gutta-percha boots she somehow seemed smaller than usual. And I was now struck by the tone of authority coming from this small person whose diminutive size and whose role in my life were such that it wouldn't have occurred to me to heed her advice about driving a car—or about anything else, I suppose. I remember feeling something like: This is an ordeal that I must, and that I want, to face in my own way. It was as though Professor Bartlett himself were in the approaching truck. It seemed my duty not to admit any weakness in my own position. At least I *thought* that was what I felt.

"Pull off the road, Nat!" Lee Ann urged again. And my incredible reply to her was "He's on *my* side of the road! Besides, trucks are not allowed in the park!" And in reply to this Lee Ann gave only a loud snicker.

I believe I did, in the last seconds, try to swing the car off onto the shoulder of the road. But the next thing I really remember is the fierce impact of the two vehicles' meeting.

It was a relatively minor sort of collision, or seemed so at the moment. Since the driver of the truck, which was actually a converted Oldsmobile sedan—and a rather ancient one at that— had the good sense not to put on his brakes and to turn off her motor, the crash was less severe than it might have been. Moreover, since I *had* pulled a little to the right it was not a head-on meeting. It is worth mentioning, though, that it was sufficiently bad to put permanently out of commission the car I was driving, which was not my own car (my car was in the shop, being refurbished for the honeymoon trip) but an aging Packard limousine of my mother's, which I knew she would actually be happy to see retired. I don't remember getting out of the car at all and I don't remember Lee Ann's getting out. The police were told by the driver of the truck, however, that within a second after the impact Lee Ann had thrown open her door, leaped out onto the snow-covered shoulder, jumped the ditch beyond, and run up the incline and into the spinney. The truck driver's account was corroborated by two ice skaters on the pond, who also saw her run through the leafless trees of the spinney and on across a narrow stretch of the public golf course which divides the spinney from the old forest. They agreed that, considering there was a deep snow on the ground and that she was wearing those gutta-percha boots, she traveled at a remarkable speed.

I didn't even know she was out of the car until I got around on the other side and saw the door there standing open and saw her tracks in the snow, going down the bank. I suppose I was too dazed even to follow the tracks with my eyes down the bank and up the other side of the ditch. I must have stood there for several seconds, looking down blankly at the tracks she had left just outside the car door. Presently I looked up at the truck driver, who was standing before me. I know now his eyes must have been following Lee Ann's progress. Finally he turned his eyes to me, and I could tell from his expression that I wasn't a pleasant sight. "Is your head hurt bad?" he asked. I put my hand up to my forehead and when I brought it down it was covered with blood. That was when I passed out. When I came to, they wouldn't let me get up. Besides the truck driver, there were two policemen and the two ice skaters standing over me. They told me that an ambulance was on the way.

At the hospital, the doctor took four stitches in my forehead; and that was it. I went home and lay down for a couple of hours, as I had been told to do. My parents and my two brothers and my little sister and even the servants were very much concerned about me. They hovered around in a way I had never before seen them do—not even when somebody was desperately sick. I suppose it was because a piece of violence like this accident was a very extraordinary thing in our quiet Memphis life in those years. They were disturbed, too, I soon realized, by my silence as I lay there on the daybed in the upstairs sitting room and particularly by my being reticent to talk about the collision. I had other things on my mind. Every so often I would remember Lee Ann's boot tracks in the snow. And I would begin to wonder where she was now. Since I had not found an opportunity to telephone her, I could only surmise that she had somehow managed to get back to the rooming house where she lived. I had not told anyone about her presence in the car with me. And as I lay there on the daybed, with the family and servants coming and going and making inquiries about how I felt, I would find myself wondering sometimes how and whether or not I could tell Caroline Braxley about Lee Ann's being with me that afternoon. It turned out the next day—or, rather, on Monday morning—that the truck driver had told the two policemen and then, later, repeated to someone who called from one of the newspapers that there had been a girl with me in the car. As a matter of fact, I learned that this was the case on the night of the accident, but as I lay there in the upstairs sitting room during the afternoon I didn't yet know it.

Shortly before five o'clock Caroline Braxley arrived at our house, making a proper sick call but also with the intention of taking me back to dinner with her parents and her two younger sisters. Immediately after she entered the upstairs sitting room, and almost before she and I had greeted each other, my mother's houseboy and sometime chauffeur came in, bringing my volume of Horace. Because Mother had thought it might raise my spirits, she had sent him down to the service garage where the wrecked car had been taken to fetch it for me. Smiling sympathetically, he placed it on a table near the daybed and left the room. Looking at the book, Caroline said to me with a smile that expressed a mixture of sympathy and reproach, "I hope you see now what folly your pursuit of Latin poetry is." And suddenly, then, the book on the table appeared to me as an alien object. In retrospect it seems to me that I really knew then that I would never open it again.

I went to dinner that night at Caroline's house, my head still in bandages. The Braxley family treated me with a tenderness equal to that I had received at home. At table, the servingman offered to help my plate for me, as though I were a sick child. I could have enjoyed all this immensely, I think, since I have always been one to relish loving, domestic care, if only I had not been worrying and speculating all the while about Lee Ann. As I talked genially with Caroline's family during the meal and immediately afterward before the briskly burning fire at the end of the Braxleys' long living room, I kept seeing Lee Ann's boot tracks in the snow. And then I would see my own bloody hand as I took it down from my face before I fainted. I remember still having the distinct feeling, as I sat there in the bosom of the Braxley family, that it had not been merely my bloody hand that had made me faint but my bloody hand plus the tracks in the deep snow. In a way, it is strange that I remember all these impressions so vividly after forty years, because it is not as though I have lived an uneventful life during the years since. My Second World War experiences are what I perhaps ought to remember best—those, along with the deaths of my two younger brothers in the Korean War. Even worse, really, were the deaths of my two parents in a terrible fire that destroyed our house on Central Avenue when they had got to be quite old, my mother leaping from a second-story window, my father asphyxiated inside the house. And I can hardly mention without being overcome with emotion the accidental deaths that took two of my and Caroline's children when they were in their early teens. It would seem that with all these disasters to remember, along with the various business and professional crises I have had, I might hardly be able to recall that earlier episode. But I think that, besides its coming at that impressionable period of my life and the fact that one just does remember things better from one's youth, there is the undeniable fact that life *was* different in those times. What I mean to say is that all these later, terrible events took place in a world where acts of terror are, so to speak, all around us—everyday occurrences—and are brought home to us audibly and pictorially on radio and television almost every hour. I am not saying that some of these ugly acts of terror did not need to take place or were not brought on by what our world was like in those days. But I am saying that the context was different. Our tranquil, upper-middle-class world of 1937 did not have the rest of the world crowding in on it so much. And thus when something only a little ugly did crowd in or when we, often unconsciously, reached out for it, the contrasts seemed sharper. It was not just in the Braxleys' household or in my own family's that everything seemed quiet and well ordered and unchanging. The households were in a context like themselves. Suffice it to say that though the Braxleys' house in Memphis was situated on East Parkway and our house on Central Avenue, at least two miles across town from each other, I could in those days feel perfectly safe, and *was* relatively safe, in walking home many a night from Caroline's house to our house at two in the morning. It was when we young men in Memphis ventured out with the more adventurous girls of the demimonde that we touched on the unsafe zones of Memphis. And there were girls still more adventurous, of course, with whom some of my contemporaries found their way into the very most dangerous zones. But we did think of it that way, you see, thought of it in terms of the girls' being the adventurous ones, whom we followed or didn't follow.

Anyhow, while we were sitting there before the fire, with the portrait of Caroline's paternal grandfather peering down at us from above the mantel and with her father in his broad-lapelled, double-breasted suit standing on the marble hearth, occasionally poking at the logs with the brass poker or sometimes kicking a log with the toe of his wing-tipped shoes, suddenly I was called to the telephone by the Negro servingman who had wanted to help my plate for me. As he preceded me the length of the living room and then gently guided me across the hall to the telephone in the library, I believe he would have put his hand under my elbow to help me—as if a real invalid—if I had allowed him to. As we passed through the hall, I glanced through one of the broad, etched sidelights beside the front door and caught a glimpse of the snow on the ground outside. The weather had turned even colder. There had been no additional snowfall, but even at a glance you could tell how crisply frozen the old snow was on its surface. The servingman at my elbow was saying, "It's your daddy on the phone. I'd suppose he just wants to know how you'd be feeling by now."

But I knew in my heart it wasn't that. It was as if that glimpse of the crisp snow through the front-door sidelight had told me what it was. When I took up the telephone and heard my father's voice pronouncing my name, I knew almost exactly what he was going to say. He said that his friend the editor of the morning paper had called him and reported that there had been a girl in the car with me, and though they didn't of course plan to use her name, probably wouldn't even run the story until Monday, they would have to *know* her name. And would have to assure themselves she wasn't hurt in the crash. And that she was unharmed after leaving the scene. Without hesitation I gave my father Lee Ann Deehart's name, as well as her address and telephone number. But I made no further explanation to Father, and he asked me for none. The only other thing I said was that I'd be home in a little while. Father was silent a moment after that. Then he said, "Are you all right?"

I said, "I'm fine."

And he said, "Good. I'll be waiting up for you."

I hung up the telephone, and my first thought was that before I left Caroline tonight I'd have to tell her that Lee Ann had been in the car with me. Then, without thinking almost, I dialed Lee Ann's rooming-house number. It felt very strange to be doing this in the Braxleys' library. The woman who ran the rooming house said that Lee Ann had not been in since she left with me in the afternoon.

As I passed back across the wide hallway and caught another glimpse of the snow outside, the question arose in my mind for the first time: *Had* Lee Ann come to some harm in those woods? More than the density of the underbrush, more than its proximity to the Zoo, where certain unsavory characters often hung out, it was the great size and antiquity of the forest trees somehow and the old rumors that white settlers had once been ambushed there by Chickasaw Indians that made me feel that if anything had happened to the girl, it had happened there. And on the heels of such thoughts I found myself wondering for the first time if all this might actually lead to my beautiful, willowy Caroline Braxley's breaking off our engagement. I returned to the living room, and at the sight of Caroline's tall figure at the far end of the room, placed between that of her mother and that of her father, the conviction became firm in me that I would have to tell her about Lee Ann before she and I parted that night. And as I drew nearer to her, still wondering if something ghastly had happened to Lee Ann there in the old forest, I saw the perplexed and even suspicious expression on Caroline's face and presently observed similar expressions on the faces of her two parents. And from that moment began the gnawing wonder which would be with me for several days ahead: What precisely would Caroline consider sufficient provocation for breaking off our engagement to be married? I had no idea, really. Would it be sufficient that I had had one of those unnamed "female companions" in the car with me at the time of the accident? I knew of engagements like ours which had been broken with apparently less provocation. Or would it be the suspicious-seeming circumstances of Lee Ann's leaping out of the car and running off through the snow? Or might it be the final, worst possibility—that of delicate little Lee Ann Deehart's having actually met with foul play in that infrequently entered area of underbrush and towering forest trees?

Broken engagements were a subject of common and considerable interest to girls like Caroline Braxley. Whereas a generation earlier a broken engagement had been somewhat of a scandal—an engagement that had been formally announced at a party and in the newspaper, that is—it did not necessarily represent that in our day. Even in our day, you see, it meant something quite different from what it had once meant. There was, after all, no written contract and it was in no sense so unalterably binding as it had been in our parents' day. For us it was not considered absolutely dishonorable for either party to break off the plans merely because he or she had had a change of heart. Since the boy was no longer expected literally to ask the father for the girl's hand (though he would probably be expected to go through the form, as I had done with Mr. Braxley), it was no longer a breach of contract between families. There was certainly nothing like a dowry any longer—not in Memphis—and there was only rarely any kind of property settlement involved, except in cases where both families were extraordinarily rich. The thought pleased me —that is, the ease with which an engagement might be ended. I suppose in part I was simply preparing myself for such an eventuality. And there in the Braxleys' long living room in the very presence of Caroline and Mr. and Mrs. Braxley themselves, I found myself indulging in a perverse fantasy, a fantasy in which Caroline had broken off our engagement and I was standing up pretty well, was even seeking consolation in the arms, so to speak, of a safely returned Lee Ann Deehart.

But all at once I felt so guilty for my private indiscretion that actually for the first time in the presence of my prospective in-laws I put my arm about Caroline Braxley's waist. And I told her that I felt so fatigued by events of the afternoon that probably I ought now to go ahead home. She and her parents agreed at once. And they agreed among themselves that they each had just now been reflecting privately that I looked exhausted. Mrs. Braxley suggested that under the circumstances she ought to ask Robert to drive me home. I accepted. No other suggestion could have seemed so welcome. Robert was the same servingman who had offered to help my plate at dinner and who had so gently guided me to the telephone when my father called. Almost at once, after I got into the front seat of the car beside him—in his dark chauffeur's uniform and cap—I fell asleep. He had to wake me when we pulled up to the side door of my father's house. I remember how warmly I thanked him for bringing me home, even shaking his hand, which was a rather unusual thing to do in those days. I felt greatly refreshed and restored and personally grateful to Robert for it. There was not, in those days in Memphis, any time or occasion when one felt more secure and relaxed than when one had given oneself over completely to the care and protection of the black servants who surrounded us and who created and sustained for the most part the luxury which distinguished the lives we lived then from the lives we live now. They did so for us, whatever their motives and however degrading our demands and our acceptance of their attentions may have been to them.

At any rate, after my slumber in the front seat beside Robert I felt sufficiently restored to face my father (and his awareness of Lee Ann's having been in the car) with some degree of equanimity. And before leaving the Braxleys' house I had found a moment in the hallway to break the news to Caroline that I had not been alone in the car that afternoon. To my considerable surprise she revealed, after a moment's hesitation, that she already knew that had been the case. Her father, like my father, had learned it from one of the newspaper editors—only he had learned it several hours earlier than my father had. I was obliged to realize as we were saying good night to each other that she, along with her two parents, had known all evening that Lee Ann had been with me and had fled into the woods of Overton Park—that she, Caroline, had as a matter of fact known the full story when she came to my house to fetch me back to her house to dinner. "Where is Lee Ann now?" she asked me presently, holding my two hands in her own and looking me directly in the eye. "I don't know," I said. Knowing how much she knew, I decided I must tell her the rest of it, holding nothing back. I felt that I was seeing a new side to my fiancée and that unless I told her the whole truth there might be something of this other side of her that wouldn't be revealed to me. "I tried to telephone her after I answered my father's call tonight. But she was not in her room and had not been in since I picked her up at two o'clock." And I told Caroline about Lee Ann's telephoning me (after Caroline and I had talked in the early afternoon) and about my inviting her to go out to the college with me. Then I gave her my uncensored version of the accident, including the sight of Lee Ann's footprints in the snow.

"How did she sound on the telephone?" she asked.

"What do you mean by that?" I said impatiently. "I just told you she wasn't home when I called."

"I mean earlier—when she called you."

"But why do you want to know that? It doesn't matter, does it?"

"I mean, did she sound depressed? But it doesn't matter for the moment." She still held my hands in hers. "You do know, don't you," she went on after a moment, "that you are going to have to *find* Lee Ann? And you probably are going to need help."

Suddenly I had the feeling that Caroline Braxley was someone twenty years older than I; but, rather than sounding like my parents or her parents, she sounded like one or another of the college teachers I had had—even like Dr. Bartlett, who once had told me that I was going to need outside help if I was going to keep up with the class. To reassure myself, I suppose, I put my arm about Caroline's waist again and drew her to me. But in our good-night kiss there was a reticence on her part, or a quality that I could only define as conditional or possibly probational. Still, I knew now that she knew everything, and I suppose that was why I was able to catch such a good nap in the car on the way home.

Girls who had been brought up the way Caroline had, in the Memphis of forty years ago, knew not only what was going to be expected of them in making a marriage and bringing up a family there in Memphis—a marriage and a family of the kind their parents had had—they knew also from a fairly early time that they would have to contend with girls and women of certain sorts before and frequently after they were married: with girls, that is, who had no conception of what it was to have a certain type of performance expected of them, or girls of another kind (and more like themselves) who came visiting in Memphis from Mississippi or Arkansas—pretty little plantation girls, my mother called them—or from Nashville or from the old towns of West Tennessee. Oftentimes these other girls were their cousins, but that made them no less dangerous. Not being on their home ground—in their own country, so to speak—these Nashville or Mississippi or West Tennessee or Arkansas girls did not bother to abide by the usual rules of civilized warfare. They were marauders. But girls like Lee Ann Deehart were something else again.

They were the Trojan horse, more or less, established in the very citadel. They were the fifth column, and were perhaps the most dangerous of all. At the end of a brilliant debutante season, sometimes the most eligible bachelor of all those on the list would still remain uncommitted, or even secretly committed to someone who had never seen the inside of the Memphis Country Club. This kind of thing, girls like Caroline Braxley understood, was not to be tolerated—not if the power of moral woman included the power to divine the nature of any man's commitment and the power to test the strength and nature of another kind of woman's power. Young people today may say that that old-fashioned behavior on the part of girls doesn't matter today, that girls don't have those problems anymore. But I suspect that in Memphis, if not everywhere, there must be something equivalent even nowadays in the struggle of women for power among themselves.

Perhaps, though, to the present generation these distinctions I am making won't seem significant, after all, or worth my bothering so much about—especially the present generation outside of Memphis and the Deep South. Even in Memphis the great majority of people might say, Why is this little band of spoiled rich girls who lived here forty years ago so important as to deserve our attention? In fact, during the very period I am writing about it is likely that the majority of people in Memphis felt that way. I think the significant point is that those girls took themselves seriously—girls like Caroline—and took seriously the forms of the life they lived. They imagined they knew quite well who they were and they imagined that that was important. They were what, at any rate, those girls like Lee Ann were not. Or they claimed to be what those girls like Lee Ann didn't claim to be and what very few people nowadays claim to be. They considered themselves the heirs to something, though most likely they could not have said what: something their forebears had brought to Memphis with them from somewhere else—from the country around Memphis and from other places, from the country towns of West Tennessee, from Middle Tennessee and East Tennessee, from the Valley of Virginia, from the Piedmont, even from the

Tidewater. Girls like Caroline thought they were the heirs to something, and that's what the other girls didn't think about themselves, though probably they were, and probably the present generation, in and out of Memphis—even the sad generation of the sixties and seventies—is heir to more than it thinks it is, in the matter of manners, I mean to say, and of general behavior. And it is of course because these girls like Caroline are regarded as mere old-fashioned society girls that the present generation tends to dismiss them, whereas if it were their fathers we were writing about, the story would, shocking though it is to say, be taken more seriously by everyone. Everyone would recognize now that the fathers and grandfathers of these girls were the sons of the old plantation South come to town and converted or half-converted into modern Memphis businessmen, only with a certain something held over from the old order that made them both better and worse than businessmen elsewhere. They are the authors of much good and much bad in modern Memphis—and modern Nashville and modern Birmingham and modern Atlanta, too. The good they mostly brought with them from life in cities elsewhere in the nation, the thing they were imitating when they constructed the new life in Memphis. And why not judge their daughters and wives in much the same way? Isn't there a need to know what they were like, too? One thing those girls did know they were heirs to was the old, country manners and the insistence upon old, country connections. The first evidence of this that comes to mind is the fact that they often spoke of girls like Lee Ann as "city girls," by which they meant that such girls didn't usually have the old family connections back in the country on the cotton farms in West Tennessee, in Mississippi, in Arkansas, or back in Nashville or in Jonesboro or in Virginia.

When Robert had let me out at our side door that night and I came into the house, my father and mother both were downstairs. It was still early of course, but I had the sense of their having waited up for me to come in. They greeted me as though I were returning from some dangerous mission. Each of them asked me how the Braxleys "seemed." Finally Mother insisted upon examining the stitches underneath the bandage on my forehead. After that, I said that I thought I would hit the hay. They responded to that with the same enthusiasm that Mr. and Mrs. Braxley had evidenced when I told them I thought I should go ahead home. Nothing would do me more good than a good night's sleep, my parents agreed. It was a day everybody was glad to have come to an end.

After I got upstairs and in my room, it occurred to me that my parents both suddenly looked very old. That seems laughable to me now almost, because my parents were then ten or fifteen years younger than I am today. I look back on them now as a youngish couple in their early middle age, whose first son was about to be married and about whose possible infidelity they were concerned. But indeed what an old-fashioned pair they seem to me in the present day, waiting up for their children to come in. Because actually they stayed downstairs a long while after I went up to bed, waiting there for my younger brothers and my little sister to come in, all of whom were out on their separate dates. In my mind's eye I can see them there, waiting as parents had waited for hundreds of years for their grown-up children to come home at night. They would seem now to be violating the rights of young individuals and even interfering with the maturing process. But in those times it seemed only natural for parents to be watchful and concerned about their children's first flight away from the nest. I am referring mainly to my parents' waiting up for my brothers and my sister, who were in their middle teens, but also as I lay in my bed I felt, myself, more relaxed knowing that they were downstairs in the front room speculating upon what Lee Ann's disappearance meant and alert to whatever new development there might be. After a while, my father came up and opened the door to my room. I don't know how much later it was. I don't think I had been to sleep, but I could not tell for sure even at the time—my waking and sleeping thoughts were so much alike that night. At any rate, Father stepped inside the room and came over to my bed.

"I have just called down to the police station," he said, "and they say they have checked and that Lee Ann has still not come back to her rooming house. She seems to have gone into some sort of hiding." He said this with wonderment and with just the slightest trace of irritation in his voice. "Have you any notion, Nat, why she *might* want to go into hiding?"

The next day was Sunday, December 5. During the night it had turned bitterly cold, the snow had frozen into a crisp sheet that covered most of the ground. At about nine o'clock in the morning another snow began falling. I had breakfast with the family, still wearing the bandage on my forehead. I sat around in my bathrobe all morning, pretending to read the newspaper. I didn't see any report of my accident, and my father said it wouldn't appear till Monday. At ten o'clock, I dialed Lee Ann's telephone number. One of the other girls who roomed in the house answered. She said she thought Lee Ann hadn't come in last night and she giggled. I asked her if she would make sure about it. She left the phone and came back presently to say in a whisper that there was no doubt about it: Lee Ann had not slept in her bed. I knew she was whispering so that the landlady wouldn't hear. . . . And then I had a call from Caroline, who wanted to know how my head was this morning and whether or not there had been any word about Lee Ann. After I told her what I had just learned, we were both silent for a time. Finally she said she had intended to come over and see how I was feeling but her father had decreed that nobody should go out in such bad weather. It would just be inviting another automobile wreck, he said. She reported that her parents were not going to church, and I said that mine weren't either. We agreed to talk later and to see each other after lunch if the weather improved. Then I could hear her father's voice in the background, and she said that he wanted to use the telephone.

At noon the snow was still falling. My father stood at a front window in the living room, wearing his dark smoking jacket. He predicted that it might be the deepest snowfall we had ever had in Memphis. He said that people in other parts of the country didn't realize how much cold weather came all the way down the Mississippi Valley from Minneapolis to Memphis. I had never heard him pay so much attention to the weather and talk so much about it. I wondered if, like me, he was really thinking about the old forest out in Overton Park and wishing he were free to go out there and make sure there was no sign of Lee Ann Deehart's having come to grief in those ancient woods. I wonder now if there weren't others besides us who were thinking of the old forest all day that day. I knew that my father, too, had been on the telephone that morning—and he was on it again during a good part of the afternoon. In retrospect, I am certain that all day that day he was in touch with a whole circle of friends and colleagues who were concerned about Lee Ann's safety. It was not only the heavy snow that checked his freedom—and mine, too, of course—to go out and search those woods and put his mind at rest on the possibility at least. It was more than just this snow, which the radio reported as snarling up and halting all traffic. What prevented him was his own unwillingness to admit fully to himself and to others that this particular danger was really there; what prevented him and perhaps all the rest of us was the fear that the answer to the gnawing question of Lee Ann's whereabouts might really be out there within that imme-morial grove of snow-laden oaks and yellow poplars and hickory trees. It is a grove, I believe, that men in Memphis have feared and wanted to destroy for a long time and whose destruction they are still working at even in this latter day. It has only re-cently been saved by a very narrow margin from a great highway that men wished to put through there—saved by groups of women determined to save this last bit of the old forest from the axes of modern men. Perhaps in old pioneer days, before the plantation and the neoclassic towns were made, the great forests seemed woman's last refuge from the brute she lived alone with in the wilderness. Perhaps all men in Memphis who had any sense of their past felt this, though they felt more keenly (or perhaps it amounts to the same feeling) that the forest was wom-an's greatest danger. Men remembered mad pioneer women, driven mad by their loneliness and isolation, who ran off into the forest, never to be seen again, or incautious women who allowed themselves to be captured by Indians and returned at last so

mutilated that they were unrecognizable to their husbands or
who at their own wish lived out their lives among their savage
captors. I think that if I had said to my father (or to myself),
"What is it that's so scary about the old forest?", he (or I) would
have answered, "There's nothing at all scary about it. But we
can't do anything today because of the snow. It's the worst snow
in history!" I think that all day long my father—like me—was
busily not letting himself believe that anything awful had happened to Lee Ann Deehart, or that if it had it certainly hadn't
happened in those woods. Not just my father and me, though.
Caroline's father, too, and all their friends—their peers. And the
newspapermen and the police. If they waited long enough, it
would come out all right and there would be no need to search
the woods even. And it turned out, in the most literal sense, that
they—we—were right. Yet what guilty feelings must not everyone have lived with—lived with in silence—all that snowbound
day.

At two o'clock, Caroline called again to say that because of
the snow, her aunt was canceling the dinner party she had
planned that night in honor of the bride and groom. I remember
as well as anything else that terrible day how my mother and
father looked at each other when they received this news. Surely
they were wondering, as I had to also, if this was but the first
gesture of withdrawal. There was no knowing what their behavior or the behavior of any of us that day meant. The day simply
dragged on until the hour when we could decently go to bed. It
was December, and we were near the shortest day of the year,
but that day had seemed the longest day of my life.

On Monday morning, two uniformed policemen were at our
house before I had finished my breakfast. When I learned they
were waiting in the living room to see me, I got up from the
table at once. I wouldn't let my father go in with me to see
them. Mother tried to make me finish my eggs before going in,
but I only laughed at her and kissed her on the top of the head as
I left the breakfast room. The two policemen were sitting in the
very chairs my parents had sat in the night before. This some-

how made the interview easier from the outset. I felt initially that they were there to help me, not to harass me in any way. They had already, at the break of dawn, been out to Overton Park. (The whole case—if case it was—had of course been allowed to rest on Sunday.) And along with four other policemen they had conducted a full-scale search of the old forest. There was no trace of Lee Ann Deehart there. They had also been to her rooming house on Tutwiler Avenue and questioned Mrs. Troxler, whose house it was, about all of Lee Ann's friends and acquaintances and about the habits of her daily life. They said that they were sure the girl would turn up but that the newspapers were putting pressure on them to explain her disappearance and—more particularly—to explain her precipitate flight from the scene of the accident.

I spent that day with the police, leaving them only for an hour at lunchtime, when they dropped me off at my father's office on Front Street, where I worked. There I made a small pretense of attending to some business for the firm while I consumed a club sandwich and milk shake that my father or one of my uncles in the firm had had sent up for me. At the end of the hour, I jogged down the two flights of steep wooden stairs and found the police car waiting for me at the curb, just outside the entrance. At some time during the morning, one of the policemen had suggested that they might have a bulldozer or some other piece of machinery brought in to crack the ice on the Overton Park Pond and then drag the pond for Lee Ann's body. But I had pointed out that the two skaters had returned to the pond after the accident and skated there until dark. There was no hole in the ice anywhere. Moreover, the skaters had reported that when the girl left the scene she did not go by way of the pond but went up the rise and into the wooded area. There was every indication that she had gone that way, and so the suggestion that the pond be dragged was dismissed. And we continued during the rest of the morning to make the rounds of the rooming houses and apartments of Lee Ann's friends and acquaintances, as well as the houses of the parents with whom some of them lived. In the afternoon we planned to go to the shops and offices in which some of the girls worked and to interview them there concerning Lee Ann's whereabouts and where it was they last had seen her. It seemed a futile procedure to me. But while I was eating my club sandwich alone in our third-floor walkup office I received a shocking telephone call.

Our offices, like most of the other cotton factors' offices, were in one of the plain-faced, three- and four-story buildings put up on Front Street during the middle years of the last century, just before the Civil War. Cotton men were very fond of those offices, and the offices did possess a certain rough beauty that anyone could see. Apparently there had been few, if any, improvements or alterations since the time they were built. All the electrical wiring and all the plumbing, such as they were, were "exposed." The wooden stairsteps and the floors were rough and splintery and extremely worn down. The walls were whitewashed and the ceilings were twelve or fourteen feet in height. But the chief charm of the rooms was the tall windows across the front of the buildings—wide sash windows with small windowlights, windows looking down onto Front Street and from which you could catch glimpses of the brown Mississippi River at the foot of the bluff, and even of the Arkansas shoreline on the other side. I was sitting on a cotton trough beside one of those windows, eating my club sandwich, when I heard the telephone ring back in the inner office. I remember that when it rang my eyes were on a little stretch of the Arkansas shoreline roughly delineated by its scrubby trees and my thoughts were on the Arkansas roadhouses where we often went with the demimonde girls on a Saturday night. At first I thought I wouldn't answer the phone. I let it ring for a minute or two. It went on ringing—persistently. Suddenly I realized that a normal business call would have stopped ringing before now. I jumped down from my perch by the window and ran back between the cotton troughs to the office. When I picked up the receiver, a girl's voice called my name before I spoke.

"Yes," I said. The voice had sounded familiar, but I knew it wasn't Caroline's. And it wasn't Lee Ann's. I couldn't identify it exactly, though I did say to myself right away that it was one of the city girls.

"Nat," the voice said, "Lee Ann wants you to stop trying to trail her."

"Who is this?" I said. "Where is Lee Ann?"

"Never mind," the girl on the other end of the line said. "We're not going to let you find her, and you're making her very uncomfortable with your going around with the police after her and all that."

"The police aren't 'after her,' " I said. "They just want to be sure she's all right."

"She'll be all right," the voice said, "if you'll lay off and stop chasing her. Don't you have any decency at all? Don't you have a brain in your head? Don't you know what this is like for Lee Ann? We all thought you were her friend."

"I am," I said. "Just let me speak to Lee Ann."

But there was a click in the telephone, and no one was there any longer.

I turned back into the room where the cotton troughs were. When I saw my milk-shake carton and the sandwich paper up by the window, and remembered how the girl had called my name as soon as I picked up the telephone, I felt sure that someone had been watching me from down in the street or from a window across the way. Without going back to my lunch, I turned quickly and started down the stairs toward the street. But when I looked at my watch, I realized it was time for the policemen to pick me up again. And there they were, of course, waiting at the entrance to our building. When I got into the police car, I didn't tell them about my call. And we began our rounds again, going to the addresses where some of Lee Ann's friends worked.

Lee Ann Deehart and other girls like her that we went about with, as I have indicated, were not literally ladies of any Memphis demimonde. Possibly they got called that first by the only member of our generation in Memphis who had read Marcel Proust, a literary boy who later became a college professor and who wanted to make his own life in Memphis—and ours—seem more interesting than it was. Actually, they were girls who had gone to the public high schools, and more often than not to some school other than Central High, which during those Depression years had a degree of acceptance in Memphis society. As anyone could have observed on that morning when I rode about town with the policemen, those girls came from a variety of backgrounds. We went to the houses of some of their parents, some of whom were day laborers who spoke in accents of the old Memphis Irish, descendants of the Irish who were imported to build the railroads to Texas. Today some of the girls would inevitably have been black. But they were the daughters also of bank clerks and salesmen and of professional men, too, because they made no distinction among themselves. The parents of some of them had moved to Memphis from cities in other sections of the country or even from Southern small towns. The girls were not interested in such distinctions of origin, were not conscious of them, had not been made aware of them by their parents. They would have been highly approved of by the present generation of young people. Like the present generation in general, these girls —Lee Ann included—tended to be bookish and artistic in a middlebrow sort of way, and some of them had real intellectual aspirations. They did not care who each other's families were or where they had gone to school. They met and got to know each other in roadhouses, on double dates, and in the offices and stores where they worked. As I have said, they tended to be bookish and artistic. If they had found themselves in Proust's Paris, instead of in our Memphis of the 1930s, possibly they would have played some role in the intellectual life of the place. But of course this is only my ignorant speculation. It is always impossible to know what changes might have been wrought in people under circumstances of the greatest or slightest degree of difference from the actual.

The girls we saw that afternoon at their places of work were generally more responsive to the policemen's questions than to my own. And I became aware that the two policemen—youngish men in their late thirties, for whom this special assignment was somehow distasteful—were more interested in protecting these girls from any embarrassment than in obtaining information about Lee Ann. With all but one of the half-dozen girls we sought out, the policemen sent me in to see the girl first, to ask her if she would rather be questioned by them in her place of business or in the police car. In each case the girl treated my question concerning this as an affront, but always she finally sent word back to the policemen to come inside. And in each case I found myself admiring the girl not only for her boldness in dealing with the situation (they seemed fearless in their talk with the police and refused absolutely to acknowledge close friendship with Lee Ann, insisting—all of them—that they saw her only occasionally at night spots, sometimes with me, sometimes with other young men, that they had no idea who her parents were or where she came to Memphis from) but also for a personal, feminine beauty that I had never before been fully aware of. Perhaps I saw or sensed it now for the first time because I had not before seen them threatened or in danger. It is true, I know, that the effect of all this questioning seemed somehow to put them in jeopardy. Perhaps I saw now how much more vulnerable they were than were the girls in the set my parents more or less intended me to travel in. There was a delicacy about them, a frailty even, that didn't seem to exist in other girls I knew and that contrasted strangely—and disturbingly—with the rough surroundings of the roadhouses they frequented at night and the harsh, businesslike atmosphere of the places where they worked. Within each of them, moreover, there seemed a contrast between the delicate beauty of their bodies, their prettily formed arms and legs, their breasts and hips, their small feet and hands, their soft natural hair—hair worn so becomingly, groomed, in each case, on their pretty little heads to direct one's eyes first of all to the fair or olive complexion and the nicely proportioned features of the face—a contrast, that is to say, between this physical beauty and a bookishness and a certain toughness of mind and a boldness of spirit which were unmistakable in all of them.

The last girl we paid a call on that afternoon was one Nancy Minnifee, who happened to be the girl who was always frankest and crudest in making jokes about families like my own and who had made the crack that the other girls had laughed at so irrepressibly in the beer garden: "I haven't lost anything at the MCC." Or it may not have been that she just happened to be the last we called on. Perhaps out of dread of her jokes I guided the police last of all to the farm-implement warehouse where Nancy was a secretary. Or perhaps it wasn't so much because of her personality as because I knew she was Lee Ann's closest friend and I somehow dreaded facing her for that reason. Anyway, at the warehouse she was out on the loading platform with a clipboard and pencil in her hands when we drove up.

"That's Nancy Minnifee up there," I said to the two policemen in the front seat. I was sitting in the backseat alone. I saw them shake their heads. I knew that it was with a certain sadness and a personal admiration that they did so. Nancy was a very pretty girl, and they hated the thought of bothering this lovely creature with the kind of questions they were going to ask. They hated it without even knowing she was Lee Ann's closest friend. Suddenly I began seeing all those girls through the policemen's eyes, just as next day, when I would make a similar expedition in the company of my father and the newspaper editor, I'd see the girls through their eyes. The worst of it, somehow, for the policemen, was that the investigation wasn't really an official investigation but was something the newspapers had forced upon the police in case something had happened which they hadn't reported. The girl hadn't been missing long enough for anyone to declare her "officially" missing. Yet the police, along with the mayor's office and the newspaper editor, didn't want to risk something's having happened to a girl like Lee Ann. They—all of them—thought of such girls, in a sense, as their special wards. It would be hard to say why they did. At any rate, before the police car had fully stopped I saw Nancy Minnifee up there on the platform. She was wearing a fur-collared overcoat but no hat or gloves. Immediately she began moving along the loading platform toward us, holding the clipboard up to shield her eyes from the late-afternoon winter sun. She came down the steps to the graveled area where we were stopped, and when the policeman at the wheel of the car ran down his window she bent forward and put her arm on his door. The casual way she did it seemed almost familiar—indeed, almost provocative. I found myself resenting her manner, because I was afraid she would give the wrong impression. The way she leaned on the door reminded me of the prostitutes down on Pontotoc Street when we, as teenage boys, used to stop in front of their houses and leave the motor running because we were afraid of them.

"I've been expecting you two gentlemen," Nancy said, smiling amiably at the two policemen and pointedly ignoring my presence in the backseat. The policemen broke into laughter.

"I suppose your friends have been calling ahead," the driver said. Then Nancy laughed as though he had said something very funny.

"I could draw you a map of the route you've taken this afternoon," she said. She was awfully polite in her tone, and the two policemen were awfully polite, too. But before they could really begin asking her their questions she began giving them her answers. She hadn't seen Lee Ann since several days before the accident. She didn't know anything about where she might be. She didn't know anything about her family. She had always understood that Lee Ann came from Texas.

"That's a big state," the policeman who wasn't driving said.

"Well, I've never been there," she said, "but I'm told it's a mighty big state."

The three of them burst into laughter again. Then the driver said quite seriously, "But we understand you're her best friend."

"I don't know her any better than most of the other girls do," she said. "I can't imagine who told you that." Now for the first time she looked at me in the backseat. "Hello, Nat," she said. I nodded to her. I couldn't imagine why she was lying to them. But I didn't tell her, as I hadn't told the other girls or the police, about the call I had had in the cotton office. I knew that she must know all about it, but I said nothing.

When we had pulled away, the policeman who was driving the car said, "This Lee Ann must be all right or these girls wouldn't be closing ranks so. They've got too much sense for that. They're smart girls."

Presently the other policeman turned his head halfway around, though not looking directly at me, and asked, "She wouldn't be pregnant by any chance, would she?"

"Uh-uh," I said. It was all the answer it seemed to me he deserved. But then I couldn't resist echoing what he had said. "They've got too much sense for that. They're smart girls." He looked all the way around at me now and gave me what I am sure he thought was a straight look.

"Damn right they are," said the driver, glancing at his colleague with a frown on his forehead and speaking with a curled lip. "Get your mind out of the gutter, Fred. After all, they're just kids, all of them."

We rode on in silence after that. For the first time in several hours, I thought of Caroline Braxley, and I wondered again whether or not she would break our engagement.

When the policemen let me off at my office at five o'clock, I went to my car and drove straight to the apartment house at Crosstown where Nancy Minnifee lived. I was waiting for Nancy in the parking lot when she got home. She invited me inside, but without a smile.

"I want to know where Lee Ann is," I said as soon as she had closed the door.

"Do you imagine I'd tell you if I knew?" she said.

I sat myself down in an upholstered chair as if I were going to stay there till she told me. "I want to know what the hell's going on," I said with what I thought was considerable force, "and why you told such lies to those policemen."

"If you don't know that now, Nat," she said, sitting down opposite me, "you probably won't ever know."

"She wouldn't be pregnant by any chance, would she?" I said, without really having known I was going to say it.

Nancy's mouth dropped open. Then she laughed aloud. Presently she said, "Well, one thing's certain, Nat. It wouldn't be any concern of yours if she were."

I pulled myself up out of the big chair and left without another word's passing between us.

Lee Ann Deehart and Nancy Minnifee and that whole band of girls that we liked to refer to as the girls of the Memphis demimonde were of course no more like the ladies of the demimonde as they appear in French literature than *they* were like some band of angels. And I hardly need say—though it does somehow occur to me to say—their manners and morals bore no resemblance whatsoever to those of the mercenary, filthy-mouthed whores on Pontotoc Street. I might even say that their manners were practically indistinguishable from those of the girls we knew who had attended Miss Hutchison's School and St. Mary's and Lausanne and were now members of the debutante set. The fact is that some of them—only a few perhaps—were from families that were related by blood, and rather closely related, to the families of the debutante set, but families that, for one reason or another, now found themselves economically in another class from their relatives. At any rate, they were all freed from old restraints put upon them by family and community, liberated in each case, so it seems to me, by sheer strength of character, liberated in many respects, but above all else—and I cannot say how it came about—liberated sexually. The most precise thing I can say about them is that they, in their little band, were like hordes of young girls today. It seems to me that in their attitude toward sex they were at least forty years ahead of their time. But I cannot say how it came about. Perhaps it was an individual thing with each of them—or partly so. Perhaps it was because they were the second or third generation of women in Memphis who were working in offices. They were not promiscuous—not most of them—but they slept with the men they were in love with and they did not conceal the fact. The men they were in love with were usually older than we were. Generally speaking, the girls merely amused themselves with us, just as we amused ourselves with them. There was a wonderful freedom in our relations which I have never known anything else quite like. And though I may not have had the most realistic sense of what their lives were, I came to know what I did know through my friendship with Lee Ann Deehart.

She and I first met, I think, at one of those dives where we all hung out. Or it may have been at some girl's apartment. I suspect we both would have been hard put to it to say where it was or exactly when. She was simply one of the good-looking girls we ran around with. I remember dancing with her on several occasions before I had any idea what her name was. We drifted into our special kind of friendship because, as a matter of fact, she was the good friend of Nancy Minnifee, whom my own close friend Bob Childress got very serious about for a time. Bob and Nancy may even have been living together for a while in Nancy's apartment. I think Bob, who was one of six or eight boys of approximately my background who used to go about with these girls, would have married Nancy if she'd consented to have him. Possibly it was at Nancy's apartment that I met Lee Ann. Anyway, we did a lot of double dating, the four of us, and had some wonderful times going to the sort of rough night spots that we all liked and found sufficiently exciting to return to again and again. We would be dancing and drinking at one of those places until about two in the morning, when most of them closed. At that hour most of us would take our girls home, because we nearly all of us had jobs—the girls and the boys, too—which we had to report to by eight or nine in the morning.

Between Lee Ann and me, as between most of the boys and their girls, I think, there was never a serious affair. That is, we never actually—as the young people today say—"had sex." But in the car on the way home or in the car parked outside her rooming house or even outside the night spot, as soon as we came out, we would regularly indulge in what used to be known as "heavy necking." Our stopping at that I must attribute first of all to Lee Ann's resistance, though also, in part, to a hesitation I felt about insisting with such a girl. You see, she was in all respects like the girls we called "nice girls," by which I suppose we really meant society girls. And most of us accepted the restriction that we were not to "go to bed" with society girls. They were the girls we were going to marry. These girls were not what those society girls would have termed shopgirls. They had much better taste in their clothes and in their general demeanor. And, as I have said, in the particular group I speak of there was at least an intellectual strain. Some of them had been to college for as much as a year or two, whereas others seemed hardly to have finished high school. Nearly all of them read magazines and books that most of us had never heard of. And they found my odd addiction to Latin poetry the most interesting thing about me. Most of them belonged to a national book club, from which they received a new book each month, and they nearly all bought records and listened to classical music. You would see them sometimes in groups at the Art Gallery. Or whenever there was an opera or a good play at the city auditorium they were all likely to be there in a group—almost never with dates. If you hadn't known who they were, you might easily have mistaken them for some committee from the Junior League or for an exceptionally pretty group of schoolteachers—from some fashionable girls' school probably.

But mostly, of course, one saw them with their dates at one of the roadhouses, over in Arkansas or down in Mississippi or out east on the Bristol Highway, or yet again at one of the places we called the "town joints." They preferred going to those road-houses and town joints to going to the Peabody Hotel Roof or the Claridge—as I suppose nearly everyone else did, really, including society girls like Caroline. You would, as a matter of fact, frequently see girls like Caroline at such places. At her request, I had more than once taken Caroline to a town joint down on Adams Street called The Cellar and once to a roadhouse called The Jungle, over in Arkansas. She had met some of the city girls there and said she found them "dead attractive." And she once recognized them at a play I took her to see and afterward expressed interest in them and asked me to tell her what they were like.

The fact may be that neither the roadhouses nor the town joints were quite as tough as they seemed. Or they weren't as tough as for the demimonde girls, anyway. Because the propri-etors clearly had protective feelings about them. At The Jungle, for instance, the middle-aged couple who operated the place, an extremely obese couple who were forever grinning in our direc-tion and who were usually barefoot (we called them Ma and Pa), would often come and stand by our table—one or the other of them—and sing the words to whatever was playing on the jukebox. Often as not, one of them would be standing there during the entire evening. Sometimes Ma would talk to us about her two little daughters, whom she kept in a private school in Memphis, and Pa, who was a practicing taxidermist, would talk to us about the dogs whose mounted heads adorned the walls on every side of the dimly lit room. All this afforded us great privacy and safety. No drunk or roughneck would come near our table while either Ma or Pa was close by. We had similar protection at other places. At The Cellar, for instance, old Mrs. Power was the sole proprietor. She had a huge goiter on her neck and was never known to smile. Not even in our direction. But it was easy to see that she watched our table like a hawk, and if any other patron lingered near us even momentarily she would begin moving slowly toward us. And whoever it was would catch one glimpse of her and move on. We went to these places quite regularly, though some of the girls had their favorites and dislikes among them. Lee Ann would never be taken to The Cellar. She would say only that the place depressed her. And Caroline, when I took her there, felt an instant dislike for The Jungle. She would shake her head afterward and say she would never go back and have those dogs' eyes staring down through the darkness at her.

On the day after I made the rounds with the policemen, I found myself following almost the same routine in the company of my father and the editor of the morning paper, and, as a matter of fact, the mayor of Memphis himself. The investigation or search was, you see, still entirely unofficial. And men like my father and the mayor and the editor wanted to keep it so. That's why after that routine and off-the-record series of questionings by the police they preferred to do a bit of investigation themselves rather than entrust the matter to someone else. As I have said, that generation of men in Memphis evidenced feelings of responsibility for such girls—for "working girls of a superior kind," as they phrased it—which I find somewhat difficult to explain. For it wasn't just the men I drove about town with that day. Or the dozen or so men who gathered for conference in our driveway before we set out—that is, Caroline's father, his lawyer, the driver of the other vehicle, his lawyer, my father's lawyer, ministers from three church denominations, the editor of the afternoon newspaper, and still others. That day, when I rode about town with my father and the two other men in our car, I came as near as I ever had or ever would to receiving a satisfactory explanation of the phenomenon. They were a generation of American men who were perhaps the last to grow up in a world where women were absolutely subjected and under the absolute protection of men. While my father wheeled his big Cadillac through the side streets on which some of the girls lived and then along the wide boulevards of Memphis, they spoke of the changes they had seen. In referring to the character of the life girls like Lee Ann led—of which they showed a far greater awareness than I would have supposed they possessed—they agreed that this was the second or third generation there of women who had lived as independently, as freely as these girls did. I felt that what they said was in no sense as derogatory or critical as it would have been in the presence of their wives or daughters. They spoke almost affectionately and with a certain sadness of such girls. They spoke as if these were daughters of dead brothers of their own or of dead companions-in-arms during the First World War. And it seemed to me that they thought of these girls as the daughters of men who had abdicated their authority and responsibility as fathers, men who were not strangers or foreign to them, though they were perhaps of a different economic class. The family names of the girls were familiar to them. The fathers of these girls were Americans of the great hinterland like themselves, even Southerners like themselves. I felt that they were actually cousins of ours who had failed as fathers somehow, had been destined to fail, even required to do so in a changing world. And so these men of position and power had to act as surrogate fathers during a transitional period. It was a sort of communal fatherhood they were acting out. Eventually, they seemed to say, fathers might not be required. I actually heard my father saying, "That's what the whole world is going to be like someday." He meant like the life such girls as Lee Ann were making for themselves. I often think nowadays of Father's saying that whenever I see his prediction being fulfilled by the students in the university where I have been teaching for twenty years now, and I wonder if Father did really believe his prediction would come true.

Yet while he and the other two men talked their rather sanguine talk that day, I was thinking of a call I had had the night before after I came back from seeing Nancy Minnifee. One of the servants answered the telephone downstairs in the back part of the house, and she must have guessed it was something special. Because instead of buzzing the buzzer three times, which was the signal when a call was for me, the maid came up the backstairs and tapped gently on my door. "It's for you, Nat," she said softly. "Do you want to take it downstairs?"

There was nothing peculiar about her doing this, really. Since I didn't have an extension phone in my room, I had a tacit understanding with the servants that I preferred to take what I considered my private calls down in that quarter of the house. And so I followed the maid down the back stairway and shut myself in the little, servants' dining room that was behind the great white-tiled kitchen. I answered the call on the wall phone there.

A girl's voice, which wasn't the same voice I had heard on the office telephone at noon, said, "Lee Ann doesn't want another day like this one, Nat."

"Who is this?" I said, lowering my voice to be sure even the servants didn't hear me. "What the hell is going on?" I asked. "Where is Lee Ann?"

"She's been keeping just one apartment or one rooming house ahead of you all day."

"But why? Why is she hiding this way?"

"All I want to say is she's had about enough. You let up on pursuing her so."

"It's not me," I protested. "There's nothing I can do to stop them."

Over the phone there came a contemptuous laugh. "No. And you can't get married till they find her, can you?" Momentarily I thought I heard Lee Ann's voice in the background. "Anyhow," the same voice continued, "Lee Ann's had about as much as she can take of all this. She was depressed as it was when she called you in the first place. Why else do you think she would call you, Nat? She was desperate for some comic relief."

"Relief from what?"

"Relief from her depression, you idiot."

"But what's she depressed about?" I was listening carefully to the voice, thinking it was that of first one girl and then another.

"Nat, we don't always have to have something to be depressed about. But Lee Ann will be all right, if you'll let her alone."

"But what is she depressed about?" I persisted. I had begun to think maybe it was Lee Ann herself on the phone, disguising her voice.

"About life in general, you bastard! Isn't that enough?" Then I knew it wasn't Lee Ann, after all.

"Listen," I said, "let me speak to Lee Ann. I want to speak to Lee Ann."

And then I heard whoever it was I was talking with break off the connection. I quietly replaced the receiver and went upstairs again.

In those days I didn't know what it was to be depressed—not, anyway, about "life in general." Later on, you see, I did know. Later on, after years of being married, and having three children, and going to grown-up Memphis dinner parties three or four times a week, and working in the cotton office six days a week, I got so depressed about life in general that I sold my interest in the cotton firm to a cousin of mine (my father and uncles were dead by then) and managed to make Caroline understand that what I needed was to go back to school for a while so that we could start our life all over. I took degrees at three universities, which made it possible for me to become a college professor. That may be an awful revelation about myself—I mean to say, awful that what decided me to become a teacher was that I was so depressed about life in general. But I reasoned that being an English professor—even if I was relegated to teaching composition and simpleminded survey courses—would be something useful and would throw us in with a different kind of people. (Caroline tried to persuade me to go into the sciences, but I told her she was just lucky that I didn't take up classics again.) Anyway, teaching has made me see a lot of young people over the years, in addition to my own children, and I think it is why, in retrospect, those Memphis girls I'm writing about still seem interesting to me after all these many years.

But the fact is I was still so uneasy about the significance of both those calls from Lee Ann's friends that I was unwilling to mention them to Caroline that night. At first I thought I would tell her, but as soon as I saw her tall and graceful figure in her white, pleated evening dress and wearing the white corsage I had sent, I began worrying again about whether or not she might still break off the engagement. Besides, we had plenty of other matters to discuss, including the rounds I had made with the two policemen that day and her various activities in preparation for the wedding. We went to a dinner that one of my aunts gave for us at the Memphis Country Club that night. We came home early and spent twenty minutes or so in her living room, telling each other how much we loved each other and how we would let nothing on earth interfere with our getting married. I felt reassured, or I tried to feel so. It seemed to me, though, that Caroline still had not really made up her mind. It worried me that she didn't have more to say about Lee Ann. After I got home, I kept waking all night and wondering what if that had not been Lee Ann's voice I had heard in the background and what if she never surfaced again. The circumstances of her disappearance would have to be made public, and that would certainly be too embarrassing for Caroline and her parents to ignore.

Next day, I didn't tell my father and his two friends, the editor and the mayor, about either of the two telephone calls. I don't know why I didn't, unless it was because I feared they might begin monitoring all my calls. I could not tolerate the thought of having them hear the things that girl said to me.

In preference to interviewing the girls whose addresses I could give them, those three middle-aged men seemed much more interested in talking to the girls' rooming-house landladies, or their apartment landlords, or their mothers. They did talk to some of the girls themselves, though, and I observed that the girls were so impressed by having these older men want to talk to them that they could hardly look at them directly. What I think is that the girls were *afraid* they would tell them the truth. They would reply to their questions respectfully, if evasively, but they were apt to keep their eyes on me. This was not the case, however, with the mothers and the landlords and the landladies. There was an immediate rapport between these persons and the three men. There hardly needed to be any explanation required of the unofficial nature of the investigation or of the concern of these particular men about such a girl as Lee Ann. One woman who told them that Lee Ann had roomed with her for a time described her as being always a moody sort of girl. "But lots of these girls living on their own are moody," she said.

"Where did Miss Deehart come from?" my father asked. "Who were her people?"

"She always claimed she came from Texas," the woman said. "But she could never make it clear to me where it was in Texas."

Later the mayor asked Lee Ann's current landlady, Mrs. Troxler, where she supposed Lee Ann might have gone. "Well," Mrs. Troxler said, "a girl, a decent girl, even among these modern girls, generally goes to her mother when there's trouble. Women turn to women," she said, "when there's real trouble."

The three men found no trace of Lee Ann, got no real clue to where she might have gone. When finally we were leaving the editor at his newspaper office on Union Avenue, he hesitated a moment before opening the car door. "Well," he began, but he sat for a moment beating his leg thoughtfully with a newspaper he had rolled up in his hand. "I don't know," he said. "It's going to be a matter for the police, after all, if we can't do any better than this." I still didn't say anything about my telephone calls. But the calls were worrying me a good deal, and that night I told Caroline.

And when I had told her about the calls and told her how the police and my father and his friends had failed to get any information from the girls, Caroline, who was then sitting beside me

on the couch in her living room, suddenly took my hand in hers
and, putting her face close to mine and looking me directly in
the eye, said, "Nat, I don't want you to go to work at all tomorrow. Don't make any explanation to your father or to anybody.
Just get up early and come over here and get me. I want you to
take me to meet some of those girls." Then she asked me which
of the girls she might possibly have met on the rare occasions
when I had taken her dancing at The Jungle or at The Cellar.
And before I left that night she got me to tell her all I knew
about "that whole tribe of city girls." I told her everything,
including an account of my innocent friendship with Lee Ann
Deehart, as well as an account of my earlier relations, which
were not innocent, with a girl named Fern Morris. When, next
morning, I came to fetch Caroline for our expedition, there were
only three girls that she wanted to be taken to see. One of the
three was of course Fern Morris.

There was something that had happened to me the day before, when I was going about Memphis with my father and his
two friends, that I could not tell Caroline about. You see, I had
been imagining, each place we went, how as we came in the
front door Lee Ann was hurriedly, quietly going out the back.
This mental picture of her in flight I found not merely appealing
but strangely exciting. And it seemed to me I was discovering
what my true feelings toward Lee Ann had been during the past
two years. I had never dared insist upon the occasional advances
I had naturally made to her, because she had always seemed too
delicate, too vulnerable, for me to think of suggesting a casual
sexual relationship with her. She had seemed too clever and too
intelligent for me to deceive her about my intentions or my
worth as a person. And I imagined I relished the kind of restraint
there was between us because it was so altogether personal and
not one placed upon us by any element or segment of society, or
by any outside circumstances whatever. It kept coming to my
mind as we stood waiting for an answer to the pressure on each
doorbell that she was the girl I ought and wanted to be marrying.
I realized the absolute folly of such thoughts and the utter im-
possibility of any such conclusion to present events. But still such

feelings and thoughts had kept swimming in and out of my head all that day. I kept seeing Lee Ann in my mind's eye and hearing her soft, somewhat husky voice. I kept imagining how her figure would appear in the doorway before us. I saw her slender ankles, her small breasts, her head of ash-blond hair, which had a way of seeming to fall about her face when she talked but which with one shake of her head she could throw back into perfect place. But of course when the door opened there was the inevitable landlady or mother or friend. And when the next day came and I saw Caroline rolling up her sleeves, so to speak, to pitch in and settle this matter once and for all, then my thoughts and fantasies of the day before seemed literally like something out of a dream that I might have had.

The first two girls Caroline had wanted to see were the two that she very definitely remembered having met when I had taken her—"on a lark"—to my favorite night spots. She caught them both before they went to work that morning, and I was asked to wait in the car. I felt like an idiot waiting out there in the car, because I knew I'd been seen from some window as I gingerly hopped out and opened the door for Caroline when she got out—and opened it again when she returned. But there was no way around it. I waited out there, playing the car radio even at the risk of running down the battery.

When she came back from seeing the first girl, whose name was Lucy Phelan, Caroline was very angry. She reported that Lucy Phelan had pretended not to remember ever having met her. Moreover, Lucy had pretended that she knew Lee Ann Deehart only slightly and had no idea where she could be or what her disappearance meant. As Caroline fumed and I started up the car, I was picturing Lee Ann quietly tiptoeing out the backdoor of Lucy's rooming house just as Lucy was telling Caroline she scarcely knew the girl or while she was insisting that she didn't remember Caroline. As Caroline came back down the walk from the big Victorian house to the car, Lucy, who had stepped out onto the narrow porch that ran across the front of the house and around one corner of it, squatted down on her haunches at the top of the wooden porch steps and waved to me from behind Caroline's back. Though I knew it was no good, I pretended not to see her there. As I put the car into second gear and we sped away down the block, I took a quick glance back at the house. Lucy was still standing on the porch and waving to me the way one waves to a little child. She knew I had seen her stooping and waving moments before. And knew I would be stealing a glance now.

For a short time Caroline seemed undecided about calling on the second girl. But she decided finally to press on. Lucy Phelan she remembered meeting at The Cellar. The next girl, Betsy Morehouse, she had met at The Jungle and at a considerably more recent time. Caroline was a dog fancier in those days and she recalled a conversation with Betsy about the mounted dogs' heads that adorned the walls of The Jungle. They both had been outraged. When she mentioned this to me there in the car, I realized for the first time that by trying to make these girls acknowledge an acquaintance with her she had hoped to make them feel she was almost one of them and that they would thus be more likely to confide in her. But she failed with Betsy Morehouse, too. Betsy lived in an apartment house—an old residence, that is, converted into apartments—and when Caroline got inside the entrance-hall door she met Betsy, who was just then coming down the stairs. Betsy carried a purse and was wearing a fur coat and overshoes. When Caroline got back to the car and told me about it, I could not help feeling that Betsy had had a call from Lucy Phelan and even perhaps that Lee Ann was hiding in her apartment, having just arrived there from Lucy's. Because Betsy didn't offer to take Caroline back upstairs to her apartment for a talk. Instead, they sat down on two straight-backed chairs in the entrance hall and exchanged their few words there. Betsy at once denied the possibility of Caroline's ever having met her before. She denied that she had, herself, ever been to The Jungle. I knew this to be a lie, of course, but I didn't insist upon it to Caroline. I said that perhaps both she and I were mistaken about Betsy's being there on the night I had taken Caroline. As soon as Caroline saw she would learn nothing from Betsy, she got up and began to make motions of leaving.

Betsy followed her to the door. But upon seeing my car out at the curb—so Caroline believed—she turned back, saying that she had remembered a telephone call she had to make. Caroline suspected that the girl didn't want to have to face me with her lie. That possibly was true. But my thought was that Betsy just might, also, have a telephone call she wanted to make.

There was now no question about Caroline's wanting to proceed to the third girl's house. This was the girl I had told her about having had a real affair with—the one I had gone with before Lee Ann and I had become friends. Caroline knew that she and Fern Morris had never met, but she counted on a different psychology with Fern. Most probably she had hoped it wouldn't be necessary for her to go to see Fern. She had been sure that one of those two other girls would give her the lead she needed. But as a last resort she was fully prepared to call on Fern Morris and to take me into the house with her.

Fern was a girl who still lived at home with her mother. She was in no sense a mama's girl or even a home-loving girl, since she was unhappy unless she went out on a date every night of her life. Perhaps she was not so clever and not so intellectual as most of her friends—if reading books, that is, on psychology and on China and every new volume of Andre Maurois indicated intellectuality. And though she was not home-loving, I suppose you would have to say she was more domestic than the other girls were. She had never "held down" a job. Rather, she stayed at home in the daytime and kept house for her mother, who was said to "hold down" a high-powered job under Boss Crump down at City Hall. Mrs. Morris was a very sensible woman, who put no restrictions on her grown-up daughter and was glad to have her as a housekeeper. She used to tell me what a good cook and housekeeper Fern was and how well fixed she would leave her when she died. I really believe Mrs. Morris hoped our romance might end in matrimony, and, as a matter of fact, it was when I began to suspect that Fern, too, was entertaining such notions that I stopped seeing her and turned my attentions to Lee Ann Deehart.

Mrs. Morris still seemed glad to see me when I arrived at their bungalow that morning with Caroline and when I proceeded to introduce Caroline to her as my fiancée. Fern herself greeted me warmly. In fact, when I told her that Caroline and I were going to be married (though she must certainly have already read about it in the newspaper) she threw her arms about my neck and kissed me. "Oh, Natty," she said, "I'm so happy for you. Really I am. But poor Lee Ann." And in later life, especially in recent years, whenever Caroline has thought I was being silly about some other woman, usually a woman she considers her mental and social inferior, she has delighted in addressing me as "Natty." On more than one such occasion I have even had her say to me, "I am so happy for you, Natty. Really I am."

The fact is, Mrs. Morris was just leaving the house for work when we arrived. And so there was no delay in Caroline's interview with Fern. "I assume you know about Lee Ann's disappearance?" Caroline began as soon as we had seated ourselves in the little front parlor, with which I was very familiar.

"Of course I do," said Fern, looking at me and laughing gleefully.

"You think it's a laughing matter, then?" Caroline asked.

"I do indeed. It's all a big joke," Fern said at once. It was as though she had her answers all prepared. "And a very successful joke it is."

"Successful?" both Caroline and I asked. We looked at each other in dismay.

"It's only my opinion, of course. But I think she only wants to make you two suffer."

"Suffer?" I said. This time Caroline was silent.

Fern was now addressing me directly. "Everybody knows Caroline is not going to marry you until Lee Ann turns up safe."

"Everybody?" Both of us again.

"Everybody in the world practically," said Fern.

Caroline's face showed no expression. Neither, I believe, did mine.

"Fern, do you know where Lee Ann is?" Caroline asked gently.

Fern Morris, her eyes on me, shook her head, smiling.

"Do you know where her people are?" Caroline asked. "And whether she's with them or hiding with her friends?"

Fern shook her head again, but now she gazed directly at Caroline. "I'm not going to tell you anything!" she asserted. But after a moment she took a deep breath and said, still looking at Caroline, "You're a smart girl. I think you'll likely be going to Lee Ann's room in that place where she lives. If you do go there, and if you are a smart girl, you'll look in the left-hand drawer of Lee Ann's dressing table." Fern had an uneasy smile on her face after she had spoken, as if Caroline had got her to say something she hadn't really meant to say, as if she felt guilty for what she had just done.

Caroline had us out of there in only a minute or so and on our way to Lee Ann's rooming house.

It was a red-brick bungalow up in north Memphis. It looked very much like the one that Fern lived in but was used as a rooming house. When Mrs. Troxler opened the front door to us, Caroline said, "We're friends of Lee Ann's, and she wants us to pack a suitcase and bring it to her."

"You know where she is, then?" Mrs. Troxler asked. "Hello, Nat," she said, looking at me over Caroline's shoulder.

"Hello, Mrs. Troxler," I said. I was so stunned by what I had just heard Caroline say that I spoke in a whisper.

"She's with her mother—or with her family, at least," Caroline said. By now she had slipped into the hallway, and I had followed without Mrs. Troxler's really inviting us in.

"Where are her family?" Mrs. Troxler asked, giving way to Caroline's forward thrust. "She never volunteered to tell me anything about them. And I never think it's my business to ask."

Caroline nodded her head at me, indicating that I should lead the way to Lee Ann's room. I knew that her room was toward the back of the house and I headed in that direction.

"I'll have to unlock the room for you," said Mrs. Troxler. "There have been a number of people coming here and wanting to look about her room. And so I keep it locked."

"A number of people?" asked Caroline casually.

"Yes. Nat knows. There were the police. And then there were

some other gentlemen. Nat knows about it, though he didn't come in. And there were two other girls. The girls just seemed idly curious, and so I've taken to locking the door. Where do her people live?"

"I don't know," said Caroline. "She's going to meet us downtown at the bus station and take a bus."

When Mrs. Troxler had unlocked the door she asked, "Is Lee Ann all right? Do you think she will be coming back here?"

"She's fine," Caroline said, "and I'm sure she'll be coming back. She just wants a few things."

"Yes, I've wondered how she's been getting along without a change of clothes. I'll fetch her suitcase. I keep my roomers' luggage in my storage closet down the hall." We waited till she came back with a piece of plaid luggage, and then we went into the room and closed the door. Caroline went to the oak dresser and began pulling things out and stuffing them in the bag. I stood by, watching, hardly able to believe what I saw Caroline doing. When she had closed the bag, she looked up at me as if to say, "What are you waiting for?" She had not gone near the little mahogany dressing table, and I had not realized that was going to be my part. I went over and opened the left-hand drawer. The only thing in the drawer was a small snapshot. I took it up and examined it carefully. I said nothing to Caroline, just handed her the picture. Finally I said, "Do you know who that is? And where the picture was taken?" She recognized the woman with the goiter who ran The Cellar. The picture had been taken with Mrs. Power standing in one of the flower beds against the side of the house. The big cut stones of the house were unmistakable. After bringing the snapshot up close to her face and peering into it for ten seconds or so, Caroline looked at me and said, "That's her family."

By the time we had stopped the car in front of The Cellar, I had told Caroline all that I knew about Lee Ann's schooling and about how it was that, though she had a "family" in Memphis, no one had known her when she was growing up. She had been to one boarding school in Shreveport, Louisiana, to one in East Texas, and to still another in St. Charles, Missouri. I had heard her make references to all of those schools. "They kept her away from home," Caroline speculated. "And so when she had finished school she wasn't prepared for the kind of 'family' she had. That's why she moved out on them and lived in a rooming house."

She reached that conclusion while I was parking the car at the curb, near the front entrance to the house. Meanwhile, I was preparing myself mentally to accompany Caroline to the door of the old woman's living quarters, which were on the main floor and above The Cellar. But Caroline rested her hand on the steering wheel beside mine and said, "This is something I have to do without you."

"But I'd like to see Lee Ann if she's here," I said.

"I know you would," said Caroline. "Of course you would."

"But, Caroline," I said, "I've made it clear that ours was an innocent—"

"I know," she said. "That's why I don't want you to see her again." Then she took Lee Ann's bag and went up to the front entrance of the house.

The main entrance to The Cellar was to the side of and underneath the high front stoop of the old house. Caroline had to climb a flight of ten or twelve stone steps to reach the door to the residence. From the car I saw a vague figure appear at one of the first-floor windows. I was relatively certain that it was Lee Ann I saw. I could barely restrain myself from jumping from the car and running up that flight of steps and forcing myself past Caroline and into the house. During the hundred hours or so since she had fled into the woods of Overton Park, Lee Ann Deehart had come to represent feelings of mine that I didn't try to comprehend. The notion I had had yesterday that I was in love with her and wanted to marry her didn't really adequately express the emotions that her disappearance had stirred in me. I felt that I had never looked at her really or had any conception of what sort of person she was or what her experience in life was like. Now it seemed I would never know. I suddenly realized—at that early age—that there was experience to be had in life that I might never know anything about except through hearsay and through books. I felt that this was my last moment to reach out and understand something of the world that was other than my own narrow circumstances and my own narrow nature. When, nearly fifteen years later, I came into a comfortable amount of money—after my father's death—I made my extraordinary decision to go back to the university and prepare myself to become a teacher. But I knew then, at thirty-seven, that I was only going to try to comprehend intellectually the world about me and beyond me and that I had failed somehow at some time to reach out and grasp direct experience of a larger life which no amount of intellectualizing could compensate for. It may be that the moment of my great failure was when I continued to sit there in the car and did not force my way into the house where the old woman with the goiter lived and where it now seemed Lee Ann had been hiding for four days.

I was scarcely aware of the moment when the big front door opened and Caroline was admitted to the house. She was in there for nearly an hour. During that time I don't know what thoughts I had. It was as though I ceased to exist for the time that Lee Ann Deehart and Caroline Braxley were closeted together. When Caroline reappeared on the high stone stoop of the house, I was surprised to see she was still carrying Lee Ann's suitcase. But she would soon make it all clear. It *was* Lee Ann who received her at the door. No doubt she had seen that Caroline was carrying her own piece of luggage. And no doubt Caroline had counted on just that mystification and its efficacy, because Caroline is an extremely clever psychologist when she sets her mind to it. At any rate, in that relatively brief interview between them Caroline learned that all she had surmised about Lee Ann was true. Moreover, she learned that Lee Ann had fled the scene of the accident because she feared that the publicity would reveal to everyone who her grandmother was.

Lee Ann had crossed the little strip of snow-covered golf course and had entered the part of the woods where the old-forest trees were. And something had made her want to remain there for a while. She didn't know what it was. She had leaned against one of the trees, feeling quite content. It had seemed to her that she was not alone in the woods. And whatever the other presences were, instead of interfering with her reflections they seemed to wish to help her clear her thoughts. She stood there for a long time—perhaps for an hour or more. At any rate, she remained there until all at once she realized how cold she had grown and realized that she had no choice but to go back to the real world. Yet she wasn't going back to her room or to her pretty possessions there. That wasn't the kind of freedom she wanted any longer. She was going back to her grandmother. But still she hoped to avoid the publicity that the accident might bring. She decided to go, first of all, and stay with some of her friends, so that her grandmother would not suppose she was only turning to her because she was in trouble. And while making this important change in her life she felt she must be protected by her friends. She wanted to have an interval of time to herself and she wanted, above all, not to be bothered during that time by the silly society boy in whose car she had been riding.

During the first days she had gone from one girl's house to another. Finally she went to her grandmother. In the beginning she had, it was true, been mightily depressed. That was why she had telephoned me to start with, and had wanted someone to cheer her up. But during these four days she had much time for thinking and had overcome all her depression and had no other thought but to follow through with the decision to go and live openly with her old grandmother in her quarters above The Cellar.

Caroline also, in that single interview, learned other things about Lee Ann which had been unknown to me. She learned that Lee Ann's own mother had abandoned her in infancy to her grandmother but had always through the years sent money back for her education. She had had—the mother—an extremely successful career as a buyer for a women's clothing store in Lincoln, Nebraska. But she had never tried to see her daughter and had never expressed a wish to see her. The only word she ever sent was that children were not her dish, but that she didn't want it on her conscience that, because of her, some little girl in Memphis, Tennessee, had got no education and was therefore the domestic slave of some man. When Caroline told me all of this about the mother's not caring to see the daughter, it brought from her her first emotional outburst with regard to the whole business. But that was at a later time. The first thing she had told me when she returned to the car was that once Lee Ann realized that her place of hiding could no longer be concealed, she was quickly and easily persuaded to speak to the newspaper editor on the telephone and to tell him that she was safe and well. But she did this only after Caroline had first spoken to the editor herself, and obtained a promise from him that there would be no embarrassing publicity for Lee Ann's grandmother.

The reason Caroline had returned with Lee Ann's suitcase was that Lee Ann had emptied it there in her grandmother's front parlor and had asked that we return to her rooming house and bring all of her possessions to her at her grandmother's. We obliged her in this, making appropriate, truthless explanations to her landlady, whom Lee Ann had meanwhile telephoned and given whatever little authority Mrs. Troxler required in order to let us remove her things. It seemed to me that the poor woman scarcely listened to the explanations we gave. Another girl was already moving into the room before we had well got Lee Ann's things out. When we returned to the grandmother's house with these possessions in the car, Caroline insisted upon making an endless number of trips into the house, carrying everything herself. She was firm in her stipulation that Lee Ann and I not see each other again.

The incident was closed then. I could be certain that there would be no broken engagement—not on Caroline's initiative. But from that point—from that afternoon—my real effort and my real concern would be to try to understand why Caroline had not been so terribly enraged or so sorely wounded upon first discovering that there had been another girl with me in the car at the time of the accident, and by the realization that I had not immediately disclosed her presence, that she had not at least once threatened to end the engagement. What her mental processes had been during the past four days, knowing now as I did that she was the person with whom I was going to spend the rest of my life, became of paramount interest to me.

But at that age I was so unquestioning of human behavior in general and so accepting of events as they came, and so without perception or reflection regarding the binding and molding effect upon people of the circumstances in which they are born, that I actually might not have found Caroline's thoughts of such profound interest and so vitally important to be understood had not Caroline, as soon as we were riding down Adams Street and were out of sight of The Cellar and of Mrs. Power's great stone house above it, suddenly requested that I drive her out to the Bristol Highway, and once we were on the Bristol Highway asked me to drive as fast and as far out of town as I could or would, to drive and drive until she should beg me to turn around and take her home; and had she not, as soon as we were out of town and beyond city speed limits, where I could press down on the accelerator and send us flying along the three-lane strip of concrete which cut through the endless expanse of cotton fields and swamps on either side, had she not then at last, after talking quietly about Lee Ann's mother's sending back the money for her education, burst into weeping that began with a kind of wailing and grinding of teeth that one ordinarily associates more with a very old person in very great physical pain, a wailing that became mixed almost immediately with a sort of hollow laughter in which there was no mirth. I commenced slowing the car at once. I was searching for a place where I could pull off to the side of the road. But through her tears and her harsh, dry laughter she hissed at me, "Don't stop! Don't stop! Go on. Go on. Go as far and as fast as you can, so that I can forget this day and put it forever behind me!" I obeyed her and sped on, reaching out my right hand to hold her two hands that were resting in her lap and were making no effort to wipe away her tears. I was not looking at her—only thinking thoughts of a kind I had never before had. It was the first time I had ever witnessed a victim of genuine hysteria. Indeed, I wasn't to hear such noises again until six or seven years later, during the Second World War. I heard them from men during days after a battle, men who had stood with great bravery against the enemy—particularly, as I remember now, men who had been brought back from the first onslaught of the Normandy invasion, physically whole but shaken in their souls. I think that during the stress of the four previous days Caroline Braxley had shed not a tear of self-pity or of shame and had not allowed herself a moment of genuine grief for my possible faithlessness to her. She had been far too busy with thinking—with thinking her thoughts of how to cope with Lee Ann's unexplained disappearance, with, that is, its possible effect upon her own life. But now the time had come when her checked emotions could be checked no longer.

The Bristol Highway, along which we were speeding as she wept hysterically, was a very straight and a very wide roadway for those days. It went northeast from Memphis. As its name implied, it was the old road that shot more or less diagonally across the long hinterland that is the state of Tennessee. It was the road along which many of our ancestors had first made their way from Virginia and the Carolinas to Memphis, to settle in the forest wilderness along the bluffs above the Mississippi River. And it occurred to me now that when Caroline said go as fast and as far as you can she really meant to take us all the way back into our past and begin the journey all over again, not merely from a point of four days ago or from the days of our childhood but from a point in our identity that would require a much deeper delving and a more radical return.

When we had got scarcely beyond the outskirts of Memphis, the most obvious signs of her hysteria had abated. Instead, however, she began to speak with a rapidity and in tones I was not accustomed to in her speech. This began after I had seen her give one long look over her shoulder and out the rear window of the car. Sensing some significance in that look and sensing some connection between it and the monologue she had now launched upon, I myself gave one glance into the rearview mirror. What met my eye was the skyline of modern Memphis beyond the snow-covered suburban rooftops—the modern Memphis of 1937, with its two or three high-rise office buildings. It was not clear to me immediately what there was in that skyline to inspire all that followed. She was speaking to me openly about Lee Ann and about her own feelings of jealousy and resentment of the girl —of *that* girl and of all those other girls, too, whose names and personalities and way of life had occupied our thoughts and had seemed to threaten our future during the four-day crisis that had followed my accident in the park.

"It isn't only Lee Ann that disturbs me," she said. "It began with her, of course. It began not with what she might be to you but with her freedom to jump out of your car, her freedom *from* you, her freedom to run off into the woods—with her capacity, which her special way of living provided her, simply to vanish, to remove herself from the eyes of the world, literally to disappear from the glaring light of day while the whole world, so to speak, looked on."

"You would like to be able to do that?" I interrupted. It seemed so unlike her role as I understood it.

*"Any*body would, wouldn't they?" she said, not looking at me but at the endless stretch of concrete that lay straight ahead. *"Men* have always been able to do it," she said. "In my own family, for as many generations back as our family stories go, there have been men who seemed to disappear from the face of the earth just because they wanted to. They used to write 'Gone to Texas' on the front door and leave the house and the farm to be sold for taxes. They walked out on dependent old parents and on sweethearts or even on wives and little children. And though they were considered black sheep for doing so, they were something of heroes, too. It seemed romantic to the rest of us that they had gone Out West somewhere and got a new start or had begun life over. But there was never a woman in our family who did that! There was no way it could happen. Or perhaps in some rare instance it did happen and the story hasn't come down to us. Her name simply isn't recorded in our family annals or reported in stories told around the fire. The assumption of course is that she is a streetwalker in Chicago or she resides in a red-plush whorehouse in Cheyenne. But with girls like Lee Ann and Lucy and Betsy it's all different. They have made their break with the past. Each of them had had the strength and intelli-

gence to make the break for herself. But now they have formed a sort of league for their own protection. How I do admire and envy them! And how little you understand them, Nat. How little you understand Lee Ann's loneliness and depression and bravery. She and all the others are wonderful—even Fern. They occupy the real city of Memphis as none of the rest of us do. They treat men just as they please. And not the way men are treated in *our* circles. And men like them better for it. Those girls have learned to enjoy life together and to be mutually protective, but they enjoy a protection also, I hope you have observed, a kind of communal protection, from men who admire their very independence, from a league of men, mind you, not from individual men, from the police and from men like my father and your father, from men who would never say openly how much they admire them. Naturally we fear them. Those of us who are not like them in temperament—or in intelligence, because there is no use in denying it—we must fear them and find a means to give delaying action. And of course the only way we know is the age-old way!"

She became silent for a time now. But I knew I was going to hear what I had been waiting to hear. If I had been the least bit impatient with her explanation of Lee Ann and her friends, it was due in part to my impatience to see if she would explain *herself* to me. We were now speeding along the Bristol Highway at the very top speed the car would go. Except when we were passing through some crossroad or village I consciously kept the speed above ninety. In those days there was no speed limit in Tennessee. There were merely signs placed every so often along the roadside saying "Speed Limit: Please Drive Carefully." I felt somehow that, considering Caroline's emotional state and my own tension, it would be altogether unreasonable, it would constitute careless and unsafe driving, for me to reduce our speed to anything below the maximum capability of the car. And when we did of necessity slow down for some village or small town it was precisely as though we had arrived at some at once familiar and strange point in the past. And on each occasion I think we both experienced a sense of danger and disappointment. It was as though we expected to experience a satisfaction in having gone so far. But the satisfaction was not to be had. When we had passed that point, I felt only the need to press on at an even greater speed. And so we drove on and on, at first north and east through the wintry cotton land and cornland, past the old Orgill Plantation, the mansion house in plain view, its round brick columns on which the plaster was mostly gone, and now and then another white man's antebellum house, and always at the roadside or on the horizon, atop some distant ridge, a variety of black men's shacks and cabins, each with a little streamer of smoke rising from an improvised tin stovepipe or from an ill-made brick chimney bent away from the cabin at a precarious angle.

We went through the old villages of Arlington and Mason and the town of Brownsville—down streets of houses with columned porticoes and double galleries—and then we turned south to Bolivar, whose very name told you when it was built, and headed back to Memphis through Grand Junction and La Grange. (Mississippi towns really, though north of the Tennessee line.) I had slowed our speed after Bolivar, because that was where Caroline began her second monologue. The tone and pace of her speech were very different now. Her speech was slow and deliberate, her emotions more under control than usual, as she described what she had felt and thought in the time since the accident and explained how she came to reach the decision to take the action she had—that is, action toward searching out and finding Lee Ann Deehart. Though I had said nothing on the subject of what she had done about Lee Ann and not done about our engagement, expressed no request or demand for any explanation unless it was by my silence, when she spoke now it was almost as though Caroline were making a courtroom defense of accusations hurled at her by me. "I finally saw there was only one thing for me to do and saw why I had to do it. I saw that the only power in the world I had for saving myself lay in my saving you. And I saw that I could only save you by 'saving' Lee Ann Deehart. At first, of course, I thought I would have to break our engagement, or at least postpone the wedding for a year. That's what *every*body thought, of course—everybody in the family."

"Even your father and mother?" I could not help interjecting. It had seemed to me that Caroline's parents had—of all people —been most sympathetic to me.

"Yes, even my mother and father," she went on, rather serenely now. "They could not have been more sympathetic to you personally. Mother said that, after all, you were a mere man. Father said that, after all, you were only human. But circumstances were circumstances, and if some disaster had befallen Lee Ann, if she was murdered or if she was pregnant or if she was a suicide or whatever other horror you can conjure up, and it all came out, say, on our wedding day or came out afterward, for that matter—well, what then? *They* and *I* had to think of that. On the other hand, as I kept thinking, what if the wedding *was* called off? What then for me? The only power I had to save myself was to save you, and to save you by rescuing Lee Ann Deehart. It always came to that, and comes to that still. Don't you see, it was a question of how very much I had to lose and how little power I had to save myself. Because *I* had not set *my*self free the way those other girls have. One makes that choice at a much earlier age than this, I'm afraid. And so I knew already, Nat, and I know now what the only kind of power I can ever have must be."

She hesitated then. She was capable of phrasing what she said much more precisely. But it would have been indelicate, somehow, for her to have done so. And so I said it for her in my crude way: "You mean the power of a woman in a man's world."

She nodded and continued. "I had to protect *that*. Even if it had been *I* that broke our engagement, Nat, or even if you and I had been married before some second scandal broke, still I would have been a jilted, a rejected girl. And some part of my power to protect myself would be gone forever. Power, or strength, is what everybody must have some of if he—if she—is to survive in any kind of world. I have to protect and use whatever strength I have."

Caroline went on in that voice until we were back in Memphis and at her father's house on East Parkway. She kissed me before we got out of the car there, kissed me for my silence, I believe. I had said almost nothing during the whole of the long ride. And I think she has ever since been grateful to me for the silence I kept. Perhaps she mistook it for more understanding than I was capable of at the time. At any rate, I cannot help believing that it has much to do with the support and understanding—rather silent though it was—which she gave me when I made the great break in my life in my late thirties. Though it clearly meant that we must live on a somewhat more modest scale and live among people of a sort she was not used to, and even meant leaving Memphis forever behind us, the firmness with which she supported my decision, and the look in her eyes whenever I spoke of feeling I must make the change, seemed to say to me that she would dedicate her pride of power to the power of freedom I sought.

PROMISE OF RAIN

UNDERSTAND, there was never anything *really* wrong with Hugh
Robert. He was a well-built boy, strong and quick and bursting
with vitality. That, at least, was the impression of himself he
managed to give people. I guess he did it just by carrying himself
well and never letting down in front of anyone. Actually, he was
no better built than my other boys. And how is one really to
know about a person's vitality? He had a bright look in his blue
eyes, a fresh complexion, and a shock of black curly hair on a
head so handsomely shaped that everybody noticed it. It was the
shape of his head, I imagine, that made people feel Hugh was so
much better-looking than his older brothers. All the girls were
crazy about him. And even if I am his father, I have to say that
he was a boy who seemed fairly crazy about himself.

When Hugh was sixteen, I kept a pretty close watch on him—
closer than I ever had time to keep on the others. I observed how
he seldom left for school in the mornings without stopping a
moment before the long gilt-framed mirror in the front hall.
Sometimes he would seem to be looking at himself with painful
curiosity and sometimes with pure admiration. Either way it was
unbecoming of him. But still I wasn't too critical of the morning
looks he gave himself. I did mind, however, his doing the same

thing again when he got home from school in the afternoons. Many a winter's afternoon I would already be home when he came in, and from where I sat in the living room, or in the library across the hall, I could tell by his footsteps that he was stopping to see himself in that great expanse of looking glass.

For Hugh's own good I used, some afternoons, to let him catch me watching him at the mirror. I thought it might break him of the habit. But his eyes would meet mine without the least shame and he would say something he didn't mean, like "I'm not much to look at, am I, Mr. Perkins?" And he continued to stop there and ogle himself in the mirror whenever it suited him to. He would often call me Mr. Perkins like that, and call his mother Mrs. Perkins. We could never be quite sure how it was meant, and I don't think he intended us to be. When he was being outright playful, he was apt to call us Will and Mary.

Hugh kept his schoolbooks in a compartment of the cupboard in the downstairs hall. The cupboard I speak of was a big oak, antique thing, a very expensive piece of furniture, which Hugh's mother had bought in Europe during our 1924 trip—ten years before. Hugh's schoolbooks seldom got farther into the house than the hall cupboard. If I complained about this to Mary, she would refer me to his report card, with its wall of straight A's. If I carried my attack further and mentioned the silly kinds of subjects he was taking, she would sigh and blame it on his having to go to the public school. As though I *wanted* Hugh to go to the public school! And as though I wanted to be home those afternoons when he came in from school! It was just that Hugh Robert grew up during bad times for us, which, as I see it, was no more my fault than it was his. Those were years when it seemed that my business firm might have to close its doors almost anytime. I couldn't *afford* to keep a boy in private school. And as for myself, I just couldn't bear to hang around the office all of those long, dead winter afternoons at the bottom of the Depression.

I can see Hugh now in his corduroy jacket and sheepskin collar stooping down to slip his books always in the same corner of the same compartment of the hall cupboard. He was orderly and systematic about everything like that. His older brothers had never measured up to him in this respect. In an instant he could tell you the whereabouts of any of his possessions. He had things stashed away—ice skates, baseball gloves, and other athletic equipment, as well as sets of carpentry tools, car tools, and radio parts—had them pushed neatly away in nooks and shelves and drawers all over the house. They were all things he had been very much excited about at one time or another. Hugh would plague us to buy him something, and then when we did and he didn't get the satisfaction out of it he had expected, he would brood about it for weeks. Finally, he would put it away somewhere. If it was something expensive and we asked him what became of it, he would say it was just one of his "mistakes" and that we needn't think he had forgotten it. Sometimes when I was looking for something I had misplaced, I would come on one of those nests of "mistakes" and know at once it was Hugh's. I remember its occurring to me once that it wouldn't take Hugh Robert thirty seconds to lay his hands on anything he owned, and that he would be able in ten minutes' time to assemble *everything* he owned and be on his way, if ever that notion struck him. It wasn't a thought that would ever have occurred to me in connection with the other children.

Our daughter and two older boys were married and gone from the house by this time, but when they were home with their spouses on a Sunday they'd say we were still babying Hugh, and say that they knew what would have happened to *them* if they had ever tried calling us by our first names. I suppose you really can't help babying the youngest, in one way or another, and favoring him a little over the others, especially when he comes along as a sort of trailer after the others are already up in school. But to Hugh's mother it was very annoying to have the older children point this out, and she would deny it hotly. If on a Monday morning, after the others had been there on Sunday, Hugh came down to breakfast and began that first-name or Mr.-and-Mrs. business, Mary was likely to try to talk to him as she used to talk to the other children, and tell him that it was not very respectful of him. It never did any good, though, and she would say afterward that I never supported her in these efforts. I don't know. I do know, though, that disrespectful is hardly the word for my son Hugh Robert Perkins—not when he was sixteen, not when he was younger than that, not even nowadays, when he favors us with one of his rare visits and sits around the house for three days talking mostly about himself and about how broke I was when he was growing up. Mary says he's the only person who can remind me, nowadays, of how hard up we were then without making me mad. If that is so, it is because he seems to take such innocent pleasure in remembering it. He talks about it in a way that makes you feel he is saying, "I owe *everything* to that!"

It got to be the fashion in those days for high-school boys to wear the knee bands of their golf knickers unfastened, letting the baggy pants legs hang loose down to their ankles. They went to school that way, and it looked far worse to me than even the shirttail-out fashion that came along after the war. I had never seen Hugh wearing his own plus fours that way, but I remarked to him one day that I regarded it as the ugliest, sloppiest, most ungentlemanly habit of dress I had ever encountered. And I asked him what in the world possessed those boys to make them do it. I think he took this as a nasty slam against his classmates. "I don't know why they do it," he said, with something of a sneer, "but I could find out for you, Mr. Perkins." I told him never mind, that I didn't want to know.

Next day Hugh appeared at breakfast with his knickers hanging down about his ankles. He lunged into the room with his buckles on his knee bands jangling like spurs. Naturally, I was supposed to blow up and tell him to fasten them. But I pretended not even to notice, and I wouldn't let Mary mention it to him. He wore them that way for a couple of days, and then seeing he wasn't going to get a rise out of me, he stopped. He seemed dispirited and rather gloomy for a day or so. Then, finding me at home after school one afternoon, he said out of the clear, "I made a discovery for you, Dad."

"What's that?" I said. I really didn't know what he meant.

"I found out why those fellows wear their plus fours drooping down. I tried wearing my own that way for a couple of days, though you didn't even notice it." And he had the cheek to wink at me in the hall mirror.

"Well?" I said noncommittally. I remembered I had said I didn't want to know why. But I didn't remind him, because I knew he remembered, too.

He had already put his books away, and he was about to take his jacket to the closet behind the stair. He stood running one finger along the ribbing of the corduroy jacket, which he had thrown over his arm, and he had a dejected look on his face. "It makes them feel kind of reckless and devil-may-care and as if they don't give a darn for what anybody thinks of how they look." This he volunteered, mind you. I had only said, "Well?"

I thought he would continue, but when he didn't I asked, "You don't recommend it? You didn't like the feeling?"

"It didn't make *me* feel that way. It only made me understand how it makes *them* feel. I didn't get any kick out of it. I don't blame them too much, though. Those guys don't have much to make them feel important."

I had to bite my tongue to keep from asking the boy what he had to make him feel important. But I let it go at that, because I saw what he was getting at. I realized I was supposed to feel pretty cheap for having criticized the people he went to school with.

Hugh didn't have any duties at home. We weren't people who lived in any do-it-yourself world in those days, no matter how bad business was. I still kept me a yardman in summer and a furnaceman in winter. I can't help saying that in that respect I did as well by Hugh as by his older brothers. When he came home in the afternoon and had stuck his books in the cupboard he was *free*—free as a bird. He might have looked at himself in the mirror all afternoon if he had wanted to. Or he might have been out on the town with a bunch of the high-school rough-necks. But Hugh wasn't a ruffian, and he wasn't an idler, either; not in the worst sense. He was vain and self-centered, but you knew that while he stood before that looking glass unbuckling his corduroy jacket he was trying to make judgments and decisions about himself; he was checking something he had thought about himself during the day.

In the mirror Hugh's blue eyes would seem to study their own blueness for a time, and then, not satisfied, they would begin to explore the hall—the hall, that is, as reflected in the glass, and with himself, of course, always in the foreground. If I had purposely planted myself in the library doorway, that's when his eyes would light on me. He would look at me curiously for a split second—before he let his eyes meet mine—look at me as he did at everything else in view. The first time it happened, I thought the look meant he was curious and resentful about my being home from the office so early. Next time, I saw that this wasn't so and that he was merely fitting me into his picture of himself. I remember very well what he said to me on one of these occasions: "Mr. Perkins, even among mirrors there's a difference! Especially the big ones. They all give you different ideas of how you look." He rambled on, seemingly without any embarrassment. "I saw myself in a big one downtown one day and there was a second when I couldn't place where I'd seen that uncouth, unkempt, uncanny individual before. And at school there's a huge one in the room where we take typing—don't ask me what it's there for. It makes me look like everybody else in the class, with all of us pecking away at typewriters. We all look so much alike I can hardly find myself in it." When Hugh finished that spiel, I found myself blushing—blushing for him. I hated so to think of the boy gaping at himself in mirrors all over town the way he did in that one in my front hall.

During the summer after Hugh turned seventeen I had the misfortune to learn, firsthand, something about his habits away from home—that is, when he did take a notion to use his freedom differently and go out on the town with his cronies from the high school. I am not speaking of nightlife, though there was beginning to be some of that, too, but of the hours that young people have to kill in the daytime. The city of Chatham, which is where we have always lived, is not the biggest city in our state. Since the Second World War it has grown substantially, and the newspapers claim that there are now half a million people in the "municipal area," by which they mean almost the whole county. But twenty-five years ago people didn't speak of it as being more than half that size. For me to encounter my son Hugh downtown or riding along Division Boulevard couldn't really be thought a great coincidence—especially not since, almost without knowing it, I had developed the habit of keeping an eye out for that head of his.

I would catch a glimpse of him on the street and, with my mind still on some problem we had at the office, wouldn't know right away what it was I had seen. Often I had to turn around and look to be sure. There Hugh would be, his dark head moving along in a group of other youthful heads—frequently a girl's head for every boy's—out under the boiling July sun, in a section of the city that they couldn't possibly have had any reason for being in. There was at least one occasion when I was certain that Hugh saw me, too. I was in the backseat of the car, and when I turned and looked out the rear window, Hugh was waving. But I was crowded in between two hefty fellows—two of my men from the office—and couldn't have returned his wave even if I had tried. On that occasion, we were riding through a section of town that used long ago to be called the Irish Flats. The men with me were both of them strictly Chatham Irish, and as we rode along I commenced teasing them about how tough that section used to be and how when I was a boy a "white man" didn't dare put foot in that end of town.

Perkins Finance Company, which was the name of our firm before we reorganized in 1946, used to make loans on small properties all over Chatham. Since the boys took over—my two older boys and my daughter's husband—they haven't wanted to deal much in that kind of thing. We have bigger irons in the fire now, and the boys have even put a cable address on the company stationery, along with the new name: Perkins, Hodgeson Investments. (The Hodgeson's for my daughter's husband.) But our small loans were what saved us in the Depression. The boys weren't with me in the firm then, of course. When they came back from college up East, just at the time of the Crash, I

wouldn't let them come in with me. I got them jobs in two
Chatham banks which I *knew* weren't going to fail. They were
locked up down there in their cages all day and went home to
their young wives at night without ever having any notion of the
kind of hide-and-seek games Hugh and I were playing in our
idleness. What I would often do—when I didn't go home in the
afternoon—was to ride around town with some of my men and
look at the property we had an interest in. Aside from any business reason, it did something for me—more than going home
did, more than a round of golf, or going to the ball game even. It
did something for me to get out and look at the town, to see how
it had stopped building and growing. The feeling I got from it
was that Time itself had stopped and was actually waiting for me
instead of passing me by and leaving me behind just when I was
in my prime. At the time, I already had a son-in-law and two
daughters-in-law, but I wasn't an old man. I had just turned fifty.
In the hot summertime of the Depression I could sometimes
look at Chatham and feel about it that it was a big, powerful,
stubborn horse that wouldn't go. I was still in the saddle, it
seemed—or I had just dismounted and had a tight grip on the
reins near the bit and was meaning to remount. Perhaps I even
had in mind beating the brute somehow, to make it go; for I was
young enough then to be impatient and to feel that I just
couldn't wait for the town to begin to move again. I knew I had
to have my second chance. Hugh could take whatever pleasure
and instruction he would from exploring the city as it was in
those days and getting to know different kinds of people. It
corresponded to something in his makeup. Or it answered some
need of his temperament. Anyway, he seemed to be born for it.
But, as for me, I could hardly wait for things to begin to move
again and to be the way they had been before.

Yet I was a man old enough to take a certain reasonable satisfaction in everything's suddenly stopping still the way it did in
the Depression and giving me the chance to look at the city the
way I could then. It has a beauty, a town like Chatham does.
Even with things getting mighty shabby, as they were in 1933,
Division Boulevard was a magnificent street with handsome

stone and tile-faced office buildings and store buildings downtown, with the automobile showrooms taking up beyond the
overpass at the Union Station—a cathedral of a building!—and
after that a half mile of old mansions from the last century, most
of them long since turned into undertaking parlors, all of them
so well built that no amount of abuse or remodeling seemed to
alter them much; and then almost a mile of small apartment
houses, and after that the clinics and the State Medical Center
and the two big hospitals.

Beyond the hospitals, Division Boulevard runs right through
Lawton Park. On one side you get a glimpse among the trees of
the Art Gallery; farther along on that side, there is the bronze
monument to the doughboy. On the other side is a mound with
Lawton Park spelled out in sweet alyssum and pinks and ground
myrtle; and away over on that side you can see among the treetops the glass dome of the birdhouse at the zoo. It's a handsomely kept park—was all the way through the Depression even
—and when you come out at the other end, there before your
eyes is the beginning of Singleton Heights!

From Singleton Heights on out past the Country Club to the
Hunt and Polo Grounds it's all like a fairyland. Great stucco and
stone houses, and whitewashed brick, acres upon acres of them.
All of them planted round with evergreens and flowering fruit
trees, with wide green lawns—the sprinklers playing like foun-
tains all summer long—lawns that are really meadows, stretching
off to low stone walls or rustic fences or even a sluggish little
creek with willow trees growing along its banks in places. It's the
sort of thing that when you've been off to New York, or maybe
to Europe for the summer, and come back to it, the very prettiness of it nearly breaks your heart.

But I ought to say, before speaking of Hugh again, that Singleton Heights and the Country Club area beyond are not the only
fine neighborhoods in Chatham and it is not of those sections of
Chatham that I think when I'm up at the lake in the summer or
away on a business trip. My own house, for instance, is in one of
the gated-off streets that were laid out just north of Lawton Park
at the turn of the century. The houses there are mostly big three-

story houses. There's a green parkway down the center of the street, and we have so many forest trees you would think you were in the middle of Lawton Park itself. But, actually, it's not even the Lawton Park area that's most typical of Chatham, any more than Singleton Heights or the Country Club area. And, in my mind, it is certainly not the new do-it-yourself ranch-house district that means Chatham to me. . . . It is the block after block of modest two-story houses, built thirty to forty years ago now, that seem most typical and give me a really comfortable feeling. It was the people in those houses who managed to keep paying something on their loans in the Depression. Whenever I think of Chatham when Mary and I go away in the summer and think of how pleasant it can be to be there despite the awful heat, I think first of those bungalows built of good wire-cut brick, with red and orange tile roofs and big screened porches, of the little privet hedges that divide their sixty-foot lots, and of the maples and oaks and sycamores whose summer shade their front yards share.

The summer Hugh was seventeen I must have seen him hoofing it along the sidewalk or standing at the curb of every block of Division Boulevard. I could never be certain that the men with me recognized him, and once I asked Joe McNary, "What were those kids doing back there on the curb?"

"They're hitchhiking, Will," he said.

"Hitchhiking?" I had never heard the term before, but I knew at once what it meant. "Where are they going?" I said.

"Nowhere. They're just doing the town. There's no harm in it, I guess."

I guess he was right. Hugh never got into any trouble that I know of, except over a car that he and his buddies made a down payment on, one time. They put down seven dollars on an old Packard touring car and drove it around town till it ran out of gas. They had bought the car in Hugh's name, and so when the police found it parked at the roadside out near the Polo Club, they gave me a ring. I told them just to take it back to the dealer and that I'd pay whatever fine it was. But they were pretty inquisitive, and I had to go down to the police station and answer a lot of questions. It was an embarrassing experience for me, because I had to confess that I hadn't known of Hugh's part in the adventure and didn't know the names of the other boys who went in on it with him. From the police station I had to get Hugh on the telephone at the high school and find out the names of the other boys. He didn't want to tell me. And we had to argue it out right then, which was the bad part, with him talking from the principal's office and with me at the sergeant's desk at the police station. Hugh ended by giving me the boys' names, and we never heard any more about it from the police, though I did have to pay the used-car dealer something to make him forget the whole business.

Hugh Robert was in the dumps for a couple of weeks afterward. Instead of excusing himself from the dinner table, as he had always done when his mother and I sat dawdling over our coffee, he would sit there pretending to listen to what we had to say, or he would just gaze despairingly up into the glass prisms of the chandelier above the table. One night when I felt I couldn't stand his black mood any longer, I gave his mother a sign to leave us alone. At first she frowned and refused to do it. Finally though, when I grew as silent as Hugh, she invented a reason to have to go to the kitchen. As soon as I heard her and the cook's voices out there, I said, "What's the matter, Hugh. What are you thinking about?"

He said, "I was thinking about how sorry I am. I really am, Dad."

"What's this?" I said.

"I'm sorry you had to pay that money on the car."

"Is that all?"

"No. Worse than that was their having you down at the station. I know you hated that worse than paying the money." Right away, you see, he was making me out as some kind of pantywaist.

"I didn't give a hoot in hell about going to the police station," I said. "But it was a damn-fool idea you boys had."

"You don't have to tell me that," he said. "It was the stupidest idea I've ever had. It was an awful mistake."

What could you say to such a boy? I wanted to ask him where they would have gone if they had had more gas, but his mother came bustling back from the kitchen then, followed by Lucy May, the cook, who began pressing Hugh to have a second helping of chocolate pie, which, if I remember correctly, he did.

One other time, when I was out with another group of men, and in another part of town, I asked, "What do you suppose those kids are doing out here?"

"*Out* here?" one of them said, and I could tell from his lack of interest that he hadn't recognized Hugh. But I think the fellow who was driving the car that day must have known that what I meant was: What was a son of mine doing so far from home?

"Oh," he said, "I can guess pretty well what they're doing. They've heard there's a drugstore in this end of town that sells milk shakes for a nickel. It's something like that; you can just count on it." We were in a perfectly decent neighborhood out on the south side, where a lot of the rich Germans used to live. It's a nice section and didn't get too awfully run-down during the Depression. I could hardly have told the difference between it and my own section if I hadn't known Chatham well.

Still another time, we had parked the car and were crossing the street toward a little Italian grocery store and lunchroom, a place just west of Court Square and near the old canal. It was a pretty rough and slummy part of town. (Not long afterward FDR had the whole area demolished and put one of his housing projects there.) But the little joint, which was called Baccalupo's Quick Lunch & Grocery, was getting to be well known for its rye and prosciutto and its three-point-two draft beer. As we headed across the street, I saw Hugh and two other boys running out of the place, with Tony Baccalupo, a swarthy little dwarf of a man, after them. I watched Tony overtake them and snatch some fruit away from them. Then the boys went off laughing together at Tony, who stood shouting something in Italian at the top of his voice. Tony was himself a sort of half-wit, I suppose. He was not the proprietor but the proprietor's younger brother—or older brother. When we got inside, I found the opportunity to ask him about the boys who had gone out just before we came in.

"They jelly beans," he said. "They just-a jelly beans. They think they plenty smart and I see 'em making the fun of me, winking in the mirror over the counter. But they got no money, got no jobs, not even know how to make-a the real trouble. They steal them grapefruit just-a to make-a me hafta run out in the street and get a sweat." He spat in the sawdust on the floor, and began taking our orders.

It got so, instead of watching for Hugh, I tried not to see him. All summer, he was wandering about town, hitchhiking from one point to another, never with any real destination, sometimes driving my old Pierce-Arrow, when his mother didn't need it. He didn't really like to take the car, however; it was an old limousine with a glass between the front and back seats, and used too much gas. He and his friends drifted about town, not ever knowing where they were, really, because to them the different parts of the city didn't mean anything. I would be riding in the backseat of a car or walking on the sidewalk, aware only of how all business and progress had bogged down, wondering if and when we could ever get it going again, searching for the first sign of a comeback. Hugh and his gang were searching for something, too, you might say. Searching for mirrors to admire themselves in. Or that's how it seemed. Every time I saw them, I would think of Tony's word: jelly beans.

One night when I got up from the dinner table, Hugh was just coming in from one of his days of wandering about town. We met in the dining-room doorway. "I hope you're making the most of your freedom, son," I said.

He looked at me for a moment, almost squinting. Then he opened his eyes wide, and turned his blue gaze on the room in general, blinking his eyelids two or three times as though they were camera shutters, his eyes registering everything, including the black cook; Mary had buzzed for her when she heard Hugh shut the front door, and Lucy May was now holding the swinging door a little way open. Finally he squinted at me again—

squinted so that you couldn't have told the color of his eyes. And I repeated, "I hope you're making the most of your freedom."

"I wonder if I *am*," he said, smiling, with a tinge of contempt in his smile and in his voice, I thought.

I looked over my shoulder at his mother, and she shook her head, meaning for me not to say anything more.

It was as though Hugh and I were drifting about through two different cities that were laid out on the very same tract of land. I used to feel we were even occupying two different houses built upon one piece of ground—houses of identical dimensions and filling one and the same area of cubic space. It was just a feeling I had. It first came to me one afternoon when I watched Hugh looking at himself in the mirror. I imagined that the interior that Hugh and I saw there wasn't the same as the one I stood in. That's all there was to it. But probably even to mention that feeling of mine is carrying things too far. I don't want to be misleading about this mirror business. I don't think the mirror-gazing itself was any real fetish with Hugh. In the first place, he didn't *always* make for the mirror as soon as he came in. Sometimes he would slip his books into the hall cupboard and go straight to the telephone; he was a great one for the telephone.

And what a lot of common talk we had to listen to on the telephone: "Did he say that? . . . I saw her looking at me and I wondered what she thought. . . . 'What do you mean?' I mean what she thought about *me*. . . ."

Always himself. Often as not, one of his girls would call him.

There was a girl named Ida, who nearly drove us all crazy. In the beginning, Hugh was mightily smitten by her. Of that I am quite certain. She was the belle of the class when Hugh entered the tenth grade at the high school, and throughout most of that year it seemed as though he looked for excuses to mention Ida Thomas's name at the dinner table. We didn't get much notion of her except that she was "a gorgeous redhead" and that she had so many admirers that Hugh "couldn't get near her with a ten-foot pole." Nevertheless, he clearly liked for us to tease him about her, though he would always insist that "she didn't know

he existed." But at last—and after considerable effort, I gather—
he managed to make Ida aware of his existence. From that day
the girl gave him no peace.

She would telephone him two or three times in one evening:
She was a brash little thing and would engage Hugh's mother in
conversation if she answered the telephone, or even me, if I
answered it: "How are *you*, Mr. Perkins? . . . How's Mrs. Perkins? . . . And how's that good-looking son of yours—your
pride and joy, so they tell me?" Hugh had a time shaking her, I
guess. He got so he wouldn't come to the telephone if Mary or I
answered and recognized Ida's voice, and he would never answer
it himself. She took to writing him letters at home and finally
tended to embarrass the boy with his family. One card said,
"Roses are red, violets are blue. Sugar's sweet and so is Hugh."
Another said, "Someday I'll ride in your Pierce-Arrow, Hugh
Robert Perkins."

One Sunday, I got Hugh to go for a walk with me while his
mother was at church, and I asked him outright why he put up
with so much nonsense from the girl. "I feel sorry for her," he
said. As though that were any kind of an excuse.

"She's not as popular as she used to be?" I asked.

"Certainly she is!" he said.

"Oh," I said. "Then you feel sorry for her because she has all
the other fellows but *not* you?"

He laughed aloud. "I never thought of it that way, Mr. Perkins," he said, as if he thought I was only joking.

So I laughed, too, and took the opportunity to ask another
question. "Tell me, son," I said, "what turned you against her?
Was it the telephone calls?"

"No. Not exactly. You see, it wasn't even *me* she was interested in. She was impressed by your old Pierce-Arrow. And still
more by our living in West Vesey Place."

"But you didn't exactly like those telephone calls. And what
about those postcards, Hugh?"

"Why, she didn't know any better, Dad!" For a minute he
stopped there on the street on Sunday morning and looked at me
as though it was I who didn't have good sense about such things.

"That's why I had to put up with it. That's why I felt sorry for her."

He was very cagey, and I didn't bother him any further about Ida, since it was all over by then anyway. But judging from the gloom he dwelt in for several months, he must have considered Ida one of his worst mistakes.

Hugh wouldn't study, and he wasn't really too hot an athlete, although certainly for a while he thought he was going to be. He made several of his "mistakes" in the athletic line, and would, of course, fall into a black mood each time he was dropped from a team or was even kept on the sidelines. His mother said he couldn't excel in athletics because he had to compete with the big, tough fellows who went out for sports at Chatham West High. And she said that the schoolwork at the public school was too easy and didn't occupy him. Maybe she was right. I know that when his two brothers had finished at Chatham Academy they had had trigonometry and Latin and even some Greek. Both of them passed the College Board examinations with flying colors and had a summer in Europe before starting college. Hugh wouldn't even *talk* about going to college—not to any local college that I could afford to send him to. Since the war, of course, he has gotten himself some kind of degree at Columbia University on the G.I. Bill. But during high school, when we mentioned college to him, he only laughed at the idea. One Sunday in his senior year, when the other children were at the house and the subject came up, he said, "Why, I've already been to the best college in our part of the country, the College of William and Mary"—meaning his mother and me, of course. "I've been studying diplomacy, and next June I'll be ready for the foreign service."

The others took this as a joke, but it made me realize how soon he might be gone from us to wherever he had in mind going. I was only half through my meal, but involuntarily I began searching my pockets for my pipe and a match. It's hard having your youngest be the one who disappoints you. I sat there searching for my pipe, thinking that I could just imagine how the letter he would leave would look on the library table, or how he would come down to breakfast one morning and say he had written off and gotten himself a job somewhere away from us—away from Chatham! I suppose it was rather simpleminded and old-fashioned of me to think about it the way I did.

In his senior year, Hugh actually began to show an interest in his schoolwork—in a certain part of it, in a part I wouldn't have called work. You would just hardly believe the things they offered in the curriculum of that school. But anyway, the first indication I had of what was stirring was Hugh's coming to me one morning with a very odd sort of request. From some neat, dark, and no doubt carefully protected corner of the house, known only to himself, he had pulled out an old dictation machine—a Dictaphone—which I had given him as a little fellow. It was an old model that I had brought home from the office and let him use as a plaything. I had forgotten about it. It had been seven or eight years since he had asked me to take the wax cylinders downtown and have them scraped so he could use them again. But he came to me after breakfast one morning, when he was all ready to leave for school, carrying the case of cylinders that came with the Dictaphone. He looked a little shamefaced, I must say, like any big boy caught playing with one of his old toys. I was touched to see that he had hung on to something I had given him so long ago. He handed the case to me and as I examined it I remarked silently that it seemed to be in as good condition as on the day I gave it to him. "Where did you resurrect this from, Hugh?" I asked.

"I've had it put by against a rainy day," he said.

"Do you still have the machine itself?" I asked.

"Oh yes, of course," he said.

I held the case of cylinders and then I said, "You intend to sell it, I suppose—the whole outfit?"

"Why no, Mr. Perkins. I want you to have these cylinders scraped for me."

"You know it costs something to have it done?" It occurred to me that as a child he mightn't have realized that.

"Oh, certainly. I'll pay for it. I have some *money* put by, too," he said, giving me one of his quick winks, "against the same rainy day." He was no spendthrift, to be sure. I doubt that there was ever a week when he spent the whole of the small allowance his mother gave him.

I set the case of cylinders on the floor beside me and picked up the paper I had been reading when he came in. "What are you going to use them for?" I said from behind the paper.

"In connection with one of my classes," he said. "A readings course."

I looked at him over my paper. He was still standing before me and was clearly willing for me to pursue the subject. "A reading course?"

"Oral readings," he explained. "A class in oral readings, for additional speech credit." He was in dead earnest. He said they were graded according to some kind of point system and that it had been wonderful help for him to be able to hear himself on the Dictaphone, that he had already made terrific progress.

"You've already been using the Dictaphone, then?" I inquired. "The cylinders were clean when you got them out?"

"Yes," he said. "Don't you remember, I got you to have them scraped before I ever put them away?"

"No, I didn't remember," I said. "It's been a pretty long time, Hugh."

Now I found myself wondering how many nights had he already been up there in his room listening to his own voice on the Dictaphone. I went back to my paper again, because I knew I didn't want to hear any more about this business. Sooner or later, I thought, he will see it as just another of his mistakes.

But for some months to come, Hugh's concern with his voice was all we did hear about. My theory was that the boy had been trying a long while to decide what it was about himself that charmed him most. And at last he thought he knew. All that winter he was as busy as a beaver with his "speech lessons" and "exercises." I would bring home the set of cylinders freshly scraped, and they wouldn't last him much more than a week. Finally, I guess he wore them out because well before spring he quit asking me to take them. But his interest didn't stop there.

He continued to engage me now and then in discussions of his current "problems" in speech, as openly and seriously as though he were talking about math or history. And first thing his mother and I knew, he was on the debating team, was trying out for a part in the class play, was even getting special instructions from the teacher in "newscasting."

It occurred to me once during this time that maybe Hugh had fallen in love with his speech teacher, Miss Arrowood. In recent months his mother had complained of a tendency in him to resent any questions about the girls he was having dates with on the weekends. If, under pressure, he mentioned the name of a particular girl, it wasn't a name that his mother knew. I couldn't explain such a business to Mary—there was no use in it—but I think I understood pretty well what Hugh was going through in that respect. And I could remember that a boy, hating himself for his own fallen and degraded state, is apt at such times to begin idealizing some attractive, sympathetic woman who is enough older than himself to seem quite beyond his aspiration— particularly if she is even vaguely the intellectual type. I didn't ask Hugh how old Miss Arrowood was or what she looked like. I just dropped by the school one afternoon in March when I knew there was to be a rehearsal of the class play.

It wasn't even necessary for me to go inside the auditorium to see what I had come to see. Through a glass panel in one of the rear doors I could see the whole stage. The play they were practicing for was one of those moronic things that they give big grown-up boys and girls to act in. (They did it even in the private schools when my older children were coming along.) This one was called *Mr. Hairbrain's Confession: A Comedy*. I read the title in a notice on the bulletin board beside the auditorium door.

After two seconds I spotted Miss Arrowood, who was giving directions from a position at the side of the stage, and I knew that my conjecture had been a false one. I say "after two seconds" because for about two seconds I mistook that lady to be one of the cast and already in costume and makeup. Her bosom was of a size and shape that one of the youngsters might have

effected with a bed pillow. Her orange-colored hair may really
have been a wig. On the far end of her unbelievable nose rode
the inevitable pince-nez. The woman's every gesture had just the
exaggeration that you could expect from any member of the cast
on the night of the performance.

I realized who she was when she started giving some directions
to Hugh, who was now posturing in the center of the stage. No,
she wasn't directing him, after all; she was applauding something
he had already done or said. Hugh, like his fellow actors, was
reading his lines from the book. Every time he opened his mouth
or so much as turned his dark head or struck a new position, she
either nodded approval or shook with laughter. She hardly took
her eyes off him. Hugh no doubt had a comic role, but I knew
that nothing in that play was so funny or so interesting as Miss
Arrowood's conduct would have led me to believe. I can't say
exactly how long I stood watching, lost in my own damned
thoughts. When finally I did leave it was because someone in the
cast—not Hugh—saw me and called Miss Arrowood's attention
to my presence. At once she began motioning to me to go away,
waving her book in the air and shooing me with her other hand.
She didn't know who I was and didn't care. Miss Arrowood
knew only that she wasn't going to have any interruption of the
pleasure she took from watching Hugh.

There was no more to it than that. Miss Arrowood was just
another old-maid schoolteacher with a crush on one of her
pupils. I doubt very much that Hugh's experience with her had
any influence on his finally going into the theater the way he has.
Quite naturally she must nowadays imagine herself to have been
his first great influence and inspiration, but if Miss Arrowood has
ever gotten to New York and found her way over to the East
Side, to that little cubbyhole of a theater where my son Hugh
Robert directs plays, I'll bet she doesn't understand the kind of
plays he puts on any better than I do. At any rate, she didn't
succeed in turning him into any radio announcer or even into an
actor, thank God. I doubt that she hoped to, even; for in my
opinion Hugh Robert didn't have any better voice than any of
the rest of the family. Physically he is very much like the rest of

us. But it is my opinion also that the lady tried to play upon Hugh's vanity for that year, for the sake of keeping him near her. And it must certainly have been she who arranged for a certain phonograph record, which he made on a machine at school, to be put on the local radio. This happened one miserable Sunday afternoon in May. It capped everything else that had happened.

Hugh rose early that Sunday morning in order to plug in the charger to the batteries of the radio. Our set was an old battery-type table model, one that I had paid a lot of money for when it was new. Hugh was fond of giving it a big thump and saying in his best smart-aleck voice, "They don't make 'em like that anymore." But he would have been the first to admit—especially on the Sunday I'm speaking of—that there are times when the electricity goes off just as you want to hear some program. I hung on to my battery set all through the Depression, just the way I did my Pierce-Arrow. And it is true, of course, that we did sometimes find, when a favorite program was due to come on, that we had forgotten to charge the batteries.

But the batteries didn't need charging at all that Sunday in May, and Hugh knew they didn't. He simply wasn't taking any chances. When I came down to breakfast, I saw the ugly little violet light burning in the charger at the end of the living room. I observed Hugh coming in there to check on them off and on all morning. Apparently when the idea of charging the batteries first struck him, he had jumped out of bed and thrown on some clothes without bothering to comb his hair or put on his shoes. He came down wearing his old run-over bedroom slippers, his everyday corduroy pants, and a wrinkled shirt that he must have pulled out of the clothes hamper. He wandered around the house like that all morning. When his mother was leaving for church at ten-thirty, I asked her if she didn't think she ought to remind him to get properly dressed before the other children came for dinner. But either she forgot to, or she decided against it, or she just "hated to" and didn't.

During the two hours his mother was gone, I could hear Hugh moving about all over the house. First he would be in the basement, then at the closet in the back hall, then upstairs somewhere, even on the third floor. Every so often he would come back to the living room to have a look at the batteries. He would sit down and try to get interested in some section of the Sunday paper. But he couldn't stay still except for short intervals. Every time he got up, the first thing he did was to go and look out one of the living-room windows. I suspect that during his wandering through the house he must now and then have stopped and looked out windows in most of the other rooms, too. To him, that day, the weather outside was the most important matter in the world.

And in spite of its being May, the weather outside was quite wintry and nasty. Rain fell during most of the morning, and there was occasional thunder, with streaks of lightning away off across town. We had been having a series of electrical storms, which generally come to us a month earlier than they did that year. This bad weather was what Hugh had pinned his hopes on. The understanding was that if the ball game—the third of the season—was called that Sunday, then Station WCM was going to fill in the first ten minutes or so of the time with a recorded reading Hugh had made of "A Message to Garcia." Though I had been unaware of it before, it seems that the station made a practice of devoting such free periods to activities of the public schools. Hugh managed that Sunday to make us all keenly aware of the fact.

I seldom missed listening to the Chatham Barons' home games. When it was a good season, I even used to go out to Runnymede Park and watch the games. The Barons, however, hadn't had such a season in almost a decade. The last time they had won their league's pennant was in 1925. But, even so, I have never been one to go running off to Cincinnati or St. Louis to see big-league games when we have a team right in Chatham to support and root for. It happened that this year the Barons had won their first two games, and I was hopeful. In particular, I hoped to be listening to the broadcast of a third game in what might turn into a winning streak. I knew why Hugh kept looking out the windows, and soon I was looking out windows, too. The rain came down pretty steady all morning and only began to let up about noon. I found I was pitting my hopes against his. I was, at least, until I saw how awfully worked up the boy was. Then I tried my best to hope with him. But I don't think I ever before had such mixed feelings about so small a thing as whether or not a ball game would be rained out.

Hugh's mother returned from church at twelve-thirty. The other children came for dinner just before one. Hugh was off upstairs when the others arrived, and had to be called to come to the table. I supposed that he had finally gone up to get himself dressed, but he came down in the same state of undress, with his hair still uncombed, and I saw at once that it offended his brothers and his sister. I saw Sister trying to signal her mother, indicating that Hugh ought at least to go and comb his hair. But her mother's eye was not to be caught that day.

Hugh was unusually silent during the meal, and his silence was contagious. From time to time I saw every member of the family taking a glance out the window to see how the weather was. After raining all morning, the skies seemed to be clearing. It was mostly bright while we sat there, with only an occasional dark interval. During those dark intervals, Hugh ate feverishly; otherwise he only picked at his food. I'm afraid that with the rest of us the reverse was true.

Once, while Lucy May was passing around a dish, I even saw her turn her black face toward a sunlit window at Hugh's back. Just as she did so, there came from outside the clear chirping of a redbird, which brought a beautiful smile to her face. The others were making a show of keeping up the conversation while a servant was in the room, and so when she offered Hugh the dish she was able to mumble to him without their taking notice, "You hear that redbird, don't you, Hugh! He say, 'To wet! To wet!' That's a promise of rain, honey!" Hugh may or may not have heard the redbird. But he paid no more attention to Lucy May's encouraging words than he had to the encouragement and applause of Miss Arrowood.

The very instant we rose from the table, there was a flash of lightning so close to us that it brightened the windows. And there followed a deafening crack of thunder. Hugh galloped across the hall into the living room and commenced disconnecting the batteries from the charger and hooking them up to the radio. The rest of us followed, just as if there were no other room in the house we could have gone to. By the time I got in there, Hugh was tuning in on WCM. There was a roar of static, and then, as the static receded, the announcer's voice came through saying, "The next voice you hear will be that of Hugh Robert Perkins," and went on to tell who Hugh's parents were, to give his street address, and to say that he was a senior at West High and a member of Miss Arrowood's class in oral readings. Outside, a sheet of rain was falling, and there was more thunder and lightning than there had been all morning.

Through the loudspeaker the voice of Hugh Robert Perkins began with some introductory remarks, telling us how, why, when, and by whom "A Message to Garcia" had been written. It didn't sound especially like Hugh's voice, but even at the outset the static was so bad that I missed about every third word. After the first half minute of the "Message" itself, it seemed hopeless to try to listen. Yet we had to sit there, all of us—and without any assistance from Miss Arrowood or Lucy May—and suffer through the awful business with Hugh. At least, it seemed to us we had to; and we *thought* that's what we were doing.

Hugh never once looked around from the radio. His eyes were glued to the loudspeaker, which was placed on top of the set. He had pulled up a straight chair, and he sat with his legs crossed and his hands clasped over one knee. He held his neck as straight and stiff as a board and didn't move his head to left or right during the entire ten minutes. The storm and static got worse every second, and he didn't even try to improve the reception. He didn't touch the dials. Toward the very end, I saw his mother raise her eyebrows and tighten her mouth the way she does when she's about to cry, and I shook my head vigorously at her, forbidding it. I knew what she was feeling well enough; we were all feeling it: Poor boy had endured his uncertainty, had for days been pinning his hopes on the chance of rain, and now had to hear himself drowned out by the static on our old radio. I thought it might be more than flesh and blood could bear. I thought that at any moment he might spring up and begin kicking that radio set to bits. But I knew, too, that his mother's tears wouldn't help matters.

What a fortunate thing for us all that I stopped her. Because not ten seconds after I did, the reading was finished and Hugh was on his feet and facing us with a broad grin of satisfaction. I saw at once that for him there had been no static. Or, rather, that he had heard the clear, sweet, reassuring tones of his own voice calling to him through and above the static, and that his last doubts about the kind of glory he yearned for had been swept away. He ran his hand through his tangled hair self-consciously. His blue eyes shone. "There!" he said. And after a moment he said it again, "There!" And I felt as strongly then as I feel it now that that was the real moment of Hugh's departure from our midst. He tried to fix his gaze on me for a second, but it was quite beyond his powers to concentrate on any one of us present. "It's a shame . . ." he began rather vaguely, "it's a shame you had to listen to my sorry voice instead of hearing the game. But maybe the game will come on later. . . . Did you hear the place where my voice cracked? That was the worst part of all, wasn't it? I'm glad it's over with." He gave a deep sigh, and then he said, in a voice full of wonder and excitement and confidence, "Gosh!"

At once, he went upstairs and dressed himself in his Sunday clothes and left the house, saying that he had a date, or maybe it was that he was going to meet some of his cronies somewhere. I didn't bother to listen. I knew that he would be back for supper that night and that he wasn't really going to leave us for some time yet. And I knew it wouldn't be a matter of a letter on the breakfast table when he did go, because it couldn't any longer be a matter of a boy running away from home. While the other children were laughing over what had happened and were talking about what a child Hugh still was, I was thinking to myself that Hugh Robert Perkins hadn't many more of his "mistakes" ahead of him. I felt certain that this afternoon he had seen his way ahead clear, and I imagined that I could see it with him.

The other children left the house soon after lunch that Sun-

day. Mary went upstairs to take a nap, as she often did when we
had been through something that there was no use talking about.
I wandered through the downstairs rooms, feeling not myself at
all. Once, I looked out a window in the library and saw that the
weather had cleared, and I didn't go and turn on the radio. And
I had a strange experience that afternoon. I was fifty, but suddenly I felt very young again. As I wandered through the house I
kept thinking of how everything must look to Hugh, of what his
life was going to be like, and of just what he would be like when
he got to be my age. It all seemed very clear to me, and I
understood how right it was for him. And because it seemed so
clear I realized the time had come when I could forgive my son
the difference there had always been between our two natures. I
was fifty, but I had just discovered what it means to see the
world through another man's eyes. It is a discovery you are lucky
to make at any age, and one that is no less marvelous whether
you make it at fifty or fifteen. Because it is only then that the
world, as you have seen it through your own eyes, will begin to
tell you things about yourself.

BAD DREAMS

THE OLD NEGRO MAN had come from somewhere in West Tennessee, though certainly not from the Tollivers' hometown. Mr. James Tolliver had simply run across him in downtown St. Louis and had become obligated or attached to him somehow. For two or three years, Mr. James had kept him as a hand around his office there, no doubt believing every day he would discover some real use for him. Then one evening, without a word to his wife or to anybody else, he brought the old fellow home with him and installed him in an empty room above the garage.

Actually, this was likely to make little difference to Mrs. James Tolliver, whom everybody called Miss Amy. It would concern Miss Amy hardly at all, since the old fellow was clearly not the house-servant type. He might do for a janitor (which was Mr. James's plan) or even a yardman (under Mr. James's close supervision), and he could undoubtedly pick up odd jobs in the neighborhood. But his tenure of the room above the garage was bound to go almost unnoticed by Miss Amy and by her three half-grown sons and two elderly female relatives. They would hardly know he was on the place. They hardly knew the room he would occupy was on the place. Yet during the first few minutes after his arrival the old Negro must have supposed that Miss Amy was a nervous and exacting fussbudget and that every member of the family had a claim on that unoccupied servant's room above the garage.

The Tollivers' garage, having been designed originally as a carriage house and stable, was of remarkable amplitude. When the Tollivers' two Lincolns were in their places at night, there was space enough for two more cars of the same wonderful length and breadth. And on the second floor, under the high mansard roof, the stairway opened onto an enormous room, or area, known as the loft room, in one end of which there was still a gaping hay chute, and from the opposite end of which opened three servant's rooms. The Tollivers' housemaid, Emmaline, and her husband, Bert, shared with their infant daughter a suite of two rooms and bath. The third room had been unoccupied for several years and was furnished only with an iron bedstead and a three-legged chest of drawers.

It happened that Emmaline was in her quarters on that late afternoon in October when Mr. James arrived with the old Negro. Her husband, who was houseboy and butler, was in the house setting the table for dinner, and she herself had just hurried out for one reassuring glance at their four-month-old baby, for whom they had not yet agreed upon a name. When the sounds of Mr. James's car reached her ears, Emmaline was in the room with the sleeping baby. She had no idea that anything unusual was astir, but at the first sound of the Lincoln motor she began moving away from the baby bed and toward the door to the loft room. It was almost dark, but, craning her neck and squinting her eyes, she gave a last loving and protective look toward the dark little object in its cagelike bed. Then she went out, closing the door behind her. She had taken only two steps across the rough flooring of the wide, unlighted loft room when she saw Mr. James ascending the stairs, followed by an old Negro man whom she had never seen before.

The Negro man halted at the top of the steps to get his breath, and, catching the sight of Emmaline, he abruptly jerked the tattered felt hat from his head. Emmaline, at the same moment, commenced striding with quickened step toward him and Mr. James.

"Is that somebody you aim to put up out here, Mr. James?" she asked in a loud and contentious whisper as she approached the two men.

"Is there no electric light in this room?" Mr. James said sternly.

He had heard Emmaline's question distinctly enough, and she knew that he was not pretending he had not. Mr. James was, after all, Emmaline and Bert's landlord, the master of the house where they worked, and a Tolliver of the preeminent Tolliver family of Thornton, Tennessee, where she and Bert were born; and this was merely his way of saying that he did not desire to have any conversation with her about the old fellow. But why didn't he? What could it be, Emmaline asked herself. Then the truth about the whole situation came to her, and as she recognized the true picture of what was happening now and of what, indeed, had been happening for several months past, she began uttering a volley of objections that had no relation to any truth: Why, now, Mr. James ought to have given Miss Amy some warning of this, oughtn't he? Miss Amy was going to be right upset, wasn't she, being taken by surprise, with Mr. James's moving somebody or other into her good storeroom where she was planning to put the porch furniture any week now? And besides, weren't the two old aunts expecting some of their antiques sent up from Tennessee? And where else *could* the aunts store their antiques? And wasn't it a shame, too, how crazy about playing in that room James, Jr., and little Landon always had been? Why, the room was half full of basketballs and bows and arrows and bowie knives this minute unless the boys had moved them this very day!

She was addressing this collection of untruths not to Mr. James but frankly to the old Negro, who stood with his hat in one hand and a knotty bundle of clothes under the other arm. The old man gave no sign either that he recognized Emmaline's hostility or that he really believed his moving in would cause a great stir in the family. He stood at the top of the steps gazing with respect at the great, dark, unceiled loft room, as though it might be a chapel of some kind. So little, his manner seemed to say, such a one as he knew about even the loft rooms of the rich.

Mr. James, in the meantime, was walking heavily across the floor in the direction of the empty servant's room. Suddenly Emmaline turned and ran on tiptoe after him. "Mr. James!" she whispered rather frantically.

Mr. James stopped and did a soldierly about-face. "Emmaline," he said, "I want some light in this place."

In a single moment, total darkness seemed to have overcome the loft room. And at that same moment came the waking cry of Bert and Emmaline's baby. With her next step Emmaline abandoned her tiptoeing and began stabbing the floor with her high heels. As she passed Mr. James, she reached one arm into the empty room to switch on a light and said, "Now that's what I been afraid of—that we would go and wake that baby of mine before I help Bert serve supper."

"In here," Mr. James said to the old Negro, and gestured toward the room. "And we'll have you a stove of some sort before winter sets in."

The weak light from inside the bedroom doorway only made the wide loft room seem darker. Mr. James remained completely beyond the reach of the light. "Is there no electrical outlet in this loft room, Emmaline?" he said.

The baby had set up a steady, angry wailing now. "No, sir," Emmaline replied softly.

"In here," Mr. James's voice repeated. This time the words came plainly as an order for the old man to advance. At once there was the sound of the old man's shambling across the rough flooring, and presently there was the sound of Mr. James's heavy footsteps as he went off toward the stairs. Somewhere in the darkness the two men passed each other, but Emmaline knew they made no communication as they passed. She heard Mr. James's firm footsteps as he descended the dark stairs, but still she didn't go to the baby, who was crying now in a less resentful manner. She waited by the open door until the old man came into the light.

"Who are you, old fellow?" she asked when he shuffled past her into the room. "Who are you?" As though who he was were not the thing Emmaline knew best in the world at this moment. As though guessing who the old fellow was hadn't been what gave her, a few minutes before, the full, true picture of what was now happening and what had been happening for several months past. Ever since the baby came, and before too, she had been trying to guess how the Tollivers felt about her and Bert's living here on the place with a baby. Did they want them to get rooms somewhere else? Did they want her to take the baby down to her mama's, in Tennessee, and leave her there? She had talked to Miss Amy about the first plan and then the second, hoping thus to find out just what the Tollivers thought. But Miss Amy had always put her off. "We'll talk about it later, Emmaline, after Mr. James decides what he thinks is best," she would say, or, "I'll have to discuss it with Mr. James some more." Day after day Emmaline had wondered how much talk there had already been about it and what had been said. For some reason it had all seemed to depend on Mr. James.

And now she knew why. Mr. James had been waiting to spring *this* on them. It would be all right about the baby if she and Bert would take on this old granddaddy to look after for as long as they lived. Ah, she and Bert hadn't thought of that! They had known about the old fellow ever since Mr. James first found him, and Bert had seen him a good many times, had even talked to him on various occasions at Mr. James's office. But he was such a dirty, ignorant old fellow that Bert had sheered away from much conversation or friendliness with him. Both Bert and Emmaline had even sheered away from any talk with Mr. James *about* him. They didn't like to have Mr. James connecting them in his mind with such a dirty old ignoramus just because they happened to be colored people.

But here the dirty, ignorant old fellow was, standing in the very room that Emmaline had come to think of as her baby's future nursery. Here he had come—himself to be nursed and someday, no doubt, to die on her hands. She studied the room for a moment, mocking her earlier appraisals of it as a possible nursery. What mere trash all her thoughts had been. When she had not even *known* that she could keep the two rooms she had, she had been counting on a third. She had been going to make the room that the baby slept in now into a sort of living room. Oh, the window-shopping she had already done for living-room furniture! For some reason, the piece she had set her heart on pictured the baby's room, as it would have been—painted the same pink as the old nursery in the Tollivers' house!

Emmaline looked at the room more realistically now than she ever had done before. There was no door connecting it with her and Bert's room, as there was between their room and the baby's. There was but the one door and one small window, and it really wasn't finished nearly so well as the two other servant's rooms. The walls were of rough sheathing, not plaster, and it would be harder to heat. In the neighborhood, there was a German washwoman who had been washing for people hereabouts since long before the Tollivers bought their place, and she had told Emmaline how the coachman used to sleep in this room and how the very finest carriage harness had always hung on the walls there under his protection. The massive hooks, which evidently had held the harness, were still on the walls and they caught Emmaline's eye momentarily. They were the hardware of a barn.

She and Bert were still living, after all, in a barn. And yet she had named this room a nursery. It was the plaster on the walls of her own two rooms that had deceived her. She realized that now, and realized that those rooms might never look the same to her again, just as her life here with Bert and the baby would hardly be the same while this old Tennessee hobo was present to be a part of it—to eat with them in the house (it was bad enough eating with the grouchy, complaining, overpaid cook, Nora Belle) and to share their bathroom (he would have to pass through her very own bedroom to reach the bathroom; she resolved that instant to make him use a chamber and to permit him to empty it only once a day). The ill-furnished bedroom and the old man standing in the center of it, now dropping his bundle on the lumpy mattress, brought back to her all the poverty and nigger life she had known as a girl in Tennessee, before the

Tollivers had sent back for her. And this unwashed and ragged old man was like the old uncles and cousins whom she had been taught to respect as a little girl but whom she had learned to despise before she ever left home. While she stared at him, the old man replaced and then removed his hat at least three or four times. Finally, he hung the hat over one of the big harness hooks.

The hat hanging on the wall there seemed an all too familiar sight to Emmaline, and the uncovered head and the whole figure of the man seemed just as infuriatingly familiar. Perhaps she had thought she would never set eyes again on such a shiftless and lousy-looking creature. Certainly she had thought she would never again have to associate such a one with herself and with the place she lived in. His uncut and unkempt white hair was precisely like a filthy dust mop that ought to be thrown out. Even the whites of his eyes looked soiled. His skin was neither brown nor black but, rather (in this light, at least), the same worn-out gray as his overcoat. Though the evening was one in early autumn, and warm for the season, the old fellow wore a heavy overcoat that reached almost to his ankles. One of the coat's patch pockets was gone; the other was torn but was held in place with safety pins and was crammed full of something— probably his spare socks, and maybe his razor wrapped in a news- paper, or a piece of a filthy old towel. God knew what all. The coat was buttonless and hung open, showing the even more dis- reputable rags he wore underneath. For a moment Emmaline wondered if it was really likely that Mr. James had let the old fellow hang around his office for two or three years looking like that. And then she reflected that it was a fact, and characteristic of Mr. James.

But now the old Negro was hers, hers and Bert's. Miss Amy wouldn't so much as know he was on the place. It was Miss Amy's policy not to know janitors and yardmen existed. And Mr. James—he, too, was out of it now. The final sound of Mr. James's footsteps on the stairs seemed to echo in her ears. The old fellow was nobody's but hers and Bert's.

The baby continued to wail monotonously, and rather dispassionately now, as though only to exercise her lungs. Suddenly, Emmaline said to the old man, "That's *my* baby you hear crying in there." The old man still had not spoken a word. Emmaline turned away from him abruptly. She went first to the door of the room where she and Bert slept, and then to that of the baby's room. She opened each door slightly, fumblingly took the key from the inside, and then closed and locked the door from the loft side. When she had locked both doors and tried them noisily and removed the keys, and while the baby cried on, Emmaline took her leave. She went down the steps, through the garage, and across the yard toward the house. Just before she reached the back porch, she began hurrying her steps. Bert would be wondering what had kept her so long, and she could hardly wait to tell him.

It was nine o'clock. Emmaline had made a half-dozen trips back to see about the baby. At seven-thirty she had offered her breast, and the baby had fed eagerly for several minutes and then dozed off. It was not unusual that Emmaline should make so many trips when the baby was fretful, except that she could usually persuade Bert to go for her at least once or twice to the foot of the steps and listen. Tonight, however, Bert had seemed incapable of even listening to her reports on how the baby was crying— whether "whining sort of puppy-like" or "bawling its lungs out." When she first came in from the garage, he had asked her in his usual carefree, good-natured way if "that little old sweet baby was cutting up." But when she told him about the old fellow's being out there, all the good cheer and animation habitual to Bert seemed to go out of him for a while. In the dining room, he was as lively and foolish-talking as ever when one of the boys said something to him, but in the pantry he listened only absentmindedly to what she said about the old fellow and not at all to her reports on the baby. Then, as soon as dinner was over and the dishes were brought out, he took off his white coat and, without stopping to eat any supper, lit into the washing of the table dishes in the pantry sink.

At nine o'clock, the two of them went up the steps into the

loft room. There was no sound from the baby. They crossed in the darkness to the door of the room where they slept. Emmaline was turning the key in the lock when the door to the old man's room opened. In his undershirt and galluses, and barefoot, he showed himself in the doorway. Presently, he made a noise like "psst" and beckoned with one hand. Bert went over to him. There was a brief, whispered exchange between them, and Bert returned to where Emmaline was waiting. He told her that the old fellow wanted to use the toilet. Emmaline stepped inside the room and switched on the light. With her finger still on the switch she looked searchingly into Bert's eyes. But his eyes told her nothing. She would have to wait a little longer to learn exactly what was going on in his head.

Then, upon hearing the old man's bare feet padding over the floor of the loft, Emmaline stepped to the door that joined her room to the baby's room, opened it softly, and went in there and waited in the dark, listening to the baby's breathing. She did this not out of any delicacy of feeling but because she felt she could not bear another sight of the dirty old man tonight. When he had been to the toilet and she had heard him go away again, Emmaline went back into their bedroom. She found Bert seated on the bed with one shoe already removed and his fingers casually unlacing the string of the other.

"Is *that* all you care?" she said belligerently. He seemed to be preparing for bed as though nothing extraordinary had happened.

"Just what you mean 'care'?" Bert answered in a whisper.

Emmaline's eyes widened. When Bert whispered, it wasn't for the baby's sake or for anybody else's but because he was resenting something some white person had said or done. It was a satisfaction to her to know he was mad, yet at the same time it always roiled her that he whispered at times when her impulse would be to shout. Bert would whisper even if the nearest white person was ten blocks away, and in his mind he always set about trying to weasel out of being mad. She regarded him thoughtfully for a moment. Then she pretended to shift the subject. "Didn't the old fellow ask you for nothing to eat?" she asked. "I

thought he would be looking for you to bring him something."
She had made herself sound quite casual. Now she moved to the
door to the loft room, opened it, took the key from outside, and
fitted it into the lock from the inside.

"No use locking that door," Bert said, still in a whisper. "The
old fellow says he's got to go to the toilet two or three times
before morning, and he don't have any chamber."

Emmaline turned around slowly. "You sound right mad about
things, Bert," she said with affected calm.

"What you mean 'mad'?" Bert said, clearing his throat.

He began to smile, but well before he smiled, Emmaline could
see that he was no longer mad, that he really hadn't been mad
since before they left the house, that his whispering was only a
sort of leftover frog in his throat from his having been mad when
she first told him.

He proceeded now to pull off his other shoe. He arranged the
two highly polished black shoes side by side and then, with the
heel of his right foot, pushed them carefully under the bed. And
now, since Bert was pigeon-toed, he sat there with the heels of
his sock feet nearly a foot apart and his big toes almost touching.
Before leaving the house, he had slipped on his white coat again,
as protection against the mildly cool night air, because Bert was
ever mindful of dangers to his health from the cold. He was
perhaps even more mindful of dangers from uncleanliness. The
socks on his feet, the sharply creased whipcord trousers, the
starched shirt underneath the white coat, all bespoke a personal
cleanliness that the symbolic whiteness of the butler's coat could
never suggest. "Well, I'll tell you," he said presently, in his naturally loud and cheerful voice. "I *was* mad about it, Emmaline,
but I'm not no more."

"*Was* mad about it?" she said, taking a step toward him. The
emphasis of his "no more" was somehow irksome to her. "I tell
you I *am* mad about it," she said. "And I aim to stay mad about
it, Bert. I'm not going to have it."

"Why, no use being mad about it," Bert said. He dropped his
eyes to his feet and then looked up again. "No use my being mad
about it and no use your getting that crazy-woman look in your

eyes about it. Ever since you came over in the house for supper, Emmaline, you been acting your crazy-woman worst." He began laughing deep in his throat. Then he got up from the bed. "Like this," he said. He trotted clownishly about the room, bent forward at the waist, with his eyes sort of popped out. "You been walking around like this." He could nearly always make Emmaline laugh by mimicking her and saying she was a crazy woman. "You been walking around like 'Stracted Mag."

But Emmaline refused to laugh. "It's not so, Bert," she said. "You know it ain't." She didn't want to give in to his resolute cheerfulness. At a time like this, she found his cheerfulness a trial to her soul.

"Why, you been your 'Stracted Mag worst tonight," he said. He went up to her and pretended to jabber wildly in her face. The 'Stracted Mag to whom he referred had been a poor, demented old Negro woman wandering the streets of their hometown when Bert and Emmaline were children, jabbering to everyone, understood by no one, but credited by all with a fierce hatred of the white race.

"Not me," Emmaline said very seriously, backing away from him. "You're the 'Stracted Mag here." It seemed downright perverse of him to be making jokes at such a time, but it was like him. Whenever he was put out of humor, whenever he quarreled with her—usually about the occasional failure to keep their rooms in order, or to keep his clothes in order and clean—or when he complained about some particularly dirty piece of work Miss Amy had set him to, he was always bound and compelled to get around at last to some happy, self-mollifying view of the matter. He could no more tolerate protracted gloom on any subject, from himself or from anyone else, than he could go for more than an hour without washing his hands. Not, that is, except when he was awakened in the middle of the night. Then Bert wasn't himself. Right now, Emmaline could tell from the way he was acting that he either considered the situation too hopeless to be taken seriously or had already decided what was to be done. Anyhow, he had cooked up some way of looking at it cheerfully.

But Emmaline was not yet ready to accept a cheerful view. She pretended to resent his calling her 'Stracted Mag. "Who *you* to be calling anybody 'Stracted Mag. In *my* day she was giddy and foolish like you, not pop-eyed wild." Emmaline was nearly six years older than Bert and actually they had known each other only slightly in Thornton, their courtship and marriage having taken place after they had come here to work for the Tollivers. "In *my* day," Emmaline said, "she was simple foolish, not wile-eyed crazy."

"Naw! Naw!" Bert said in utter astonishment. "How can you say so?" Her contradiction of the picture he carried of that old Negro woman left Bert absurdly shaken. "How can you say so, Emmaline, when I seen her one time fighting a dog in the street?"

"Oh, I don't reckon you did, sure enough," Emmaline said in a tone she would have used with a child.

"You know I did!" Bert said. "Down on her all fours, in the horse manure, fighting and scrapping with that old spotted dog of Miss Patty Bean's. And it was just because she hated Miss Patty and all them Beans so."

"Well, not in my day," Emmaline insisted, stubbornly and purposefully. She stared straight into Bert's eyes. "In my day, she didn't mix with man nor dog. She muttered and mumbled and kept all to herself." Emmaline evidently knew the exact effect her contradiction was having upon Bert. Like the names of other characters in Thornton, 'Stracted Mag's name was on their lips almost daily and had ceased to be a mere proper noun for her and Bert. It had become a word whose meaning neither of them could have defined, though it was well established between them —a meaning that no other words in their vocabulary could express.

Bert looked at Emmaline reproachfully. He could hardly believe that she would thus tamper with the meaning of a single one of their stock of Thornton words, or even pretend to do so. He felt as he would have felt if she had threatened to deprive him of his sight or hearing by some sort of magic. She could so easily snatch this word from his vocabulary and render him even less able than he was to express his feelings about things in the world. He saw that in order to stop her, he must tell her at once how easy it was going to be to get rid of the old man. Still sitting on the bed, he reached forth and took Emmaline by the arm, just above the wrist. "Come sit down on the bed," he said urgently. "I aim to tell you about the old fellow."

Emmaline took two steps and sat down beside him. With his hand still on her forearm, he felt the tension of her muscles. She *was* her 'Stracted Mag worst tonight! He often told her in a joking way that she was like old Mag, but it was really no joke at all. He knew that many a time Emmaline would have left the Tollivers' service or said something out of the way to one of the old aunts if it had not been for him. Emmaline was a good, hardworking, smart sort of a woman—smarter than most anyone gave her credit for, but at a moment's notice she could get a look so bughouse-wild in her face that you felt you had to talk fast if you were going to keep her calm. Bert's mother had been that sort of woman, too. In fact he felt that most of the women he had ever had much to do with had been that sort; he felt that he had spent no small part of his life keeping Negro women from blurting out their resentment at white people. Emmaline was more easily handled than some, but it was because, after all, she used more sense about what she expected to get out of life than most of her sort did. Like him, she had no illusions about someday leaving domestic service. She accepted as good enough for her the prospect of spending her life in the service of such a family as the Tollivers, provided she did not have to live in the leaking, lean-to-kind of shack she had been brought up in, and provided that in her comfortable quarters she might at the same time be raising a family of her own. She and Bert saw eye to eye on that. Emmaline was smart and she was not an unhandsome woman. She was tall and, though she was a little stooped, her figure was slender and well formed, and proportions of her head and her rather long neck were decidedly graceful. Yet when excited, as she had been tonight, her eyes seemed actually to swell from their sockets, her nostrils would spread until her nose seemed completely flattened, and her heavy lower lip would protrude above her upper lip; at those times her shoulders appeared more stooped than usual, her arms longer, her brown skin darker.

"Look here," Bert was saying. "We going to get shed of that old man. You know that, don't you?"

"What you mean get shed of him?" she asked. There was contention in her voice, but already her eyes showed her satisfaction with what he said.

"I mean he can't stay here with us."

"Who says he can't, Bert?"

"You and me won't let him."

"What we got to do with it, Bert? All I know is we ain't going to stay if he does. Is that what you mean?"

"No!" Bert exclaimed—so loud that the baby stirred in her bed in the next room. "That ain't what I mean. You think we going to vacate here for *him?* Quit the best me or you either has ever had or is like to have?"

Emmaline said, "There's other people in this here very block we could work for—mighty good places, Bert."

"And bring Baby with us?" Because they had not given the baby a name, Bert used "Baby" as a name. "And you know it wouldn't be like working with folks from Thornton."

Emmaline's eyes seemed to swell again. She asked, almost begged, him to tell her. "What we going to do, Bert? He's nasty and ignorant, and living so close. I tell you this—just as sure as Mr. James is a Thornton white man, that old fellow is a Thornton sort of nigger. Maybe where one is there's got to be the other."

"We going to run him off!" Bert said. He had released her arm, but he took it again, and at the same time he began grinning at her. "We going to run him off." He said it with a carefree kind of enthusiasm, as though he were playing a game, said it in a loud voice, as though he were trying to make the old man hear. "Why, we going to run him off just by telling him we don't want him. He'll know what we mean. He'll think we mean worser than we do, and he'll git. And nobody will care."

"Mr. James will care," Emmaline warned.

"Nobody will care enough to stop us. I studied it out while I was washing dishes," he said. "Mr. James has done done all he's about to do for that old man. He allows he's fixed things so we'll be afraid *not* to look after the old man and keep him. But Mr. James's not going to do no more than that. I can tell by the way you said he walked off across the floor of the loft room. Mr. James is through and done with the old fellow. He can say to himself now that he done what he could. But both him and Miss Amy thinks heaps more of us and having us wait on them than to be letting us go because we run off such as him. Oh, Lord, we'll run him off all right."

Emmaline felt fully reassured, and her eyes seemed to have sunk back into their sockets. But she asked quietly, "How?" She could hear the old man snoring in his room and she could hear the baby beginning to whimper. But before she got up to go to the baby, she repeated, "How?"

Bert laughed under his breath. "We'll just tell him to git, and he'll git."

"When, Bert?"

"Well, tomorrow," Bert said thoughtfully. "And not the day after, either. We'll scare him off while we're new to him, and he'll think we're worser than we know how to be. He's lived hard, and with harder folks than you and me, Emmaline."

When Emmaline brought the baby in on her shoulder a few minutes later, her features were composed again, and Bert was humming softly to himself. He had removed his white coat and his shirt and had hung them on hangers in the big wardrobe beside the bed. At the sight of the baby, he commenced talking a baby talk that was incomprehensible even to Emmaline. But Emmaline beamed and let him snatch the baby from her in mock roughness. Uttering a steady stream of almost consonant-less baby talk, he first threw the baby a few inches in the air, and then danced about the room with her—in his sock feet, whip-cord trousers, and gleaming-white undershirt. Finally, the baby's dark, screwed-up little face relaxed into the sweetest of smiles.

"Don't wake her up no more than need be, Bert," Emmaline protested feebly. "She ain't slept half her due all day."

Bert let himself fall across the bed on his back, holding the baby at arm's length above him. Now with his muscular brown arms he was bringing the baby down to his face and then raising her again like a weight. Each time her laughing little face touched his own, Bert would say, "Timmy-wye-ea! Timmy-wye-ea!" And the meaning of this Emmaline, for sufficient reason, did understand. It was Bert's baby talk for "Kiss me right here."

Later on, after the baby had fed at Emmaline's breast and had been sung to sleep on her shoulder, she was put down in her own bed in the dark room. Then Bert and Emmaline were not long in retiring. After their light was out, they lay in bed talking for a while, though not once mentioning the old man, whose intermittent snoring they heard from the next room. As they so often did, they went to sleep debating what name they should give the baby. They could never agree (probably the baby would be called Baby all her life), but neither did they ever fully disagree about the appropriateness of the various possible names. They went off to sleep pronouncing softly to one another some of the possibilities: Amy Amelia, Shirley Elizabeth, Easter May, Rebecca Jane.

They were awakened by a terrible shrieking—a noise wild enough to be inhuman, and yet unmistakably human. Emmaline sprang from her bed and ran through the darkness to the baby's crib. So swift and unfaltering were her steps that as she reached her hands into the crib, she imagined that Bert mightn't yet be fully awake. She even muttered to herself, "I pray God he ain't." Yet in the next awful moment, when she would have caught up the baby—except that she found no baby there—the thought that Bert might be still asleep seemed the worst, last terror her heart could ever know. Searching the empty crib with her hands, she screamed Bert's name. Her voice came so shrill and loud it caused a painful sensation in her own ears.

And Bert, who all the while stood in the darkness only a few inches from her, and with the baby in his arms, raged forth at her out of the darkness, "God, woman! Goddamn, woman! You want to make your baby deaf? You yell at me like that again, woman, and I'll knock you flat on the floor." It was Bert in his worst midnight temper.

His own movements had been swifter than Emmaline's. He had even had to open the door between the rooms, yet had arrived so far ahead of Emmaline that he was holding the baby in his arms by the time her hands began searching the crib. Perhaps he had awakened a moment before she had. It seemed to both of them that they were already awake when the baby cried out, and at first neither had believed it could be *their* baby making such a noise. The two of them had come, as on one impulse, simply to make sure about the baby. All of this, of course, they revealed to each other much later; at the moment they stood in the dark cursing each other.

"You'll knock *who* flat on the floor?" Emmaline cried in a voice only a trifle less shrill and less loud than that in which she had called Bert's name. "Give me that baby of mine!" she demanded. She felt about for the light switch. When she found it, she was asking, "You'll knock who flat on the floor, you bastardy, black son of Ham?" But when the light came on, her voice and her words changed, and so, no doubt, did her whole face. She saw Bert, clad in his immaculately white pajamas, holding on his shoulder the tiny, woolly-headed baby, clad in its white cotton nightgown. Beads of sweat shone on the brown skin of Bert's forehead. His wide, brown hands held firmly to the little body that was squirming incessantly on his shoulder. And in the first moment of light, Emmaline saw Bert throwing his head back in order to look into the baby's face.

Emmaline moved toward Bert with outstretched arms. "Honey," she said in a new voice, "hand me m'baby. Let me have her, Bert."

Bert let her take the baby from him. He, too, seemed to have been changed by the light. "Something's wrong with her," he said. "She ain't made a sound since I picked her up." His eyes were now fixed on the little face. "Look at her eyes, Emmaline!" The baby's dark eyes were fairly bulging from her head, and she was gasping tearfully for breath. "I think your baby's dying, Emmaline," Bert said.

Emmaline seized the baby and began patting her gently up and down the spine. This soon restored the baby's breath somewhat and allowed her to begin shrieking again. Emmaline walked from one room to the other, and then back again. Back and forth she walked, talking quietly to the baby, patting her between the shoulder blades or sometimes gently stroking her little body. Meanwhile, Bert followed at Emmaline's heels, trying to peer over her shoulder into the baby's face. At last the baby left off shrieking, and began crying in a more normal way.

At this change, Bert went to the bathroom and washed his face and hands in cold water. When he returned, he said impatiently, "What's got in her?"

"She's sick somehow, Bert," Emmaline said. Though the baby had stopped shrieking, still she was crying passionately and with no hint of abatement.

"Maybe she's hungry," Bert suggested in a voice of growing impatience.

"I just tried her while you was in the bathroom and she wouldn't take it," Emmaline said. Then she said, "Oh, Lord," and by this she meant to say it was bad enough worrying over the baby without Bert's having one of his real fits of midnight anger. She thought of stories she had heard, as a girl, of men whipping their babies when they cried at night, whipping them to death sometimes. "Let him try!" she said to herself, but it didn't quiet her fears. Also, she now thought she heard sounds coming from the old man's room. She had forgotten his presence there until now. What if he should take this time to go to the toilet? . . . Bert would kill him.

All at once she knew for a certainty that the old man *would* come in. Oh, Bert would kill him when he came! Or there would be such an awful fight somebody would hear them in the house and Mr. James would come out and maybe shoot Bert with that little pistol he kept on his closet shelf. All she could see before her eyes was blood. And all the time she was pacing the floor, from the baby's room, where the light was on, to her and Bert's room, where there was no light except that which came through the open doorway.

"Someway you've got to stop her," Bert said, putting his hands over his ears. He nearly always woke when the baby cried at night, but the crying had never been like this before, had never begun so suddenly or with such piercing shrieks.

"I *is* trying to stop her, Bert, but I can't," Emmaline said excitedly. "You go on back to bed, Bert."

He sat down on the side of the bed and watched Emmaline walking and listened to the baby's crying. Once he got up and went to the dresser to peer at the face of the alarm clock. It was a quarter to one. "Aw, she's hungry and don't know it," he said after a while. "You *make* her take something. It's time she's fed."

Emmaline sat down in the big wicker rocking chair in the baby's room, slipped off the strap of her nightgown, and tried to settle the baby to her breast. But the baby pushed away and commenced thrashing about, throwing her head back and rolling her eyes in a frightening way. Now Emmaline began to sob. "The baby's sick, Bert," she said. "She's afire with fever, she is."

"Let me walk her some," Bert said, coming into the lighted room.

"Oh, don't hurt her, Bert," Emmaline pleaded. "Don't hurt her."

"Why, I ain't going to hurt no little baby," Bert said, frowning. "I ain't going to hurt Baby. You know that, Emmaline." As he took the baby, his wife saw the look of concern in his eyes. He was no longer in his midnight temper—not for the time being at least. Or, anyway, he was out of the depths of it.

But Emmaline sat in the rocking chair sobbing while Bert walked with the baby from one room to the other. Finally, he stopped before her and said, "You cut out your crying—she ain't got much fever I can feel. Something's ailing her, and she's sick all right, but your carrying on don't help none."

In the far room Emmaline could hear the old man knocking about, as though he were in the dark. He was looking for the light, she thought. And she thought, Bert can hear him too. Suddenly she wailed, "If the baby's sick, Bert, then why ain't you gone to the house to get somebody to—"

"To get somebody?" Bert shouted back at her. "What in hell do you mean?"

"To get some of them to call a doctor, Bert."

"Go wake Mr. James to call a doctor?" Now the baby began shrieking as at the outset, but Bert shouted above the shrieking. "On top of him sending that old fellow—"

"Then go out and find a doctor. Get dressed and go out and find us a doctor somewheres." She was on her feet and wresting the baby from Bert.

Bert stood nodding his head, almost smiling, in a sudden bewilderment. Then he went into the other room and took his shirt off the coat hanger. He was leaning over the dresser drawer to get out clean underwear when Emmaline heard the unmistakable sound of their door from the loft room opening. The sound came at a moment when the baby had completely lost her breath again. Emmaline commenced shaking the baby violently. "Oh, Lord! Oh, Lord God!" she cried out. She was standing in the doorway between the two rooms. Bert looked over his shoulder. She thought at first he was looking at her, but then she saw he was looking at the shadowy figure in the other doorway.

Now the baby's gasping for breath claimed Emmaline's attention again. But even so, the shadow of a question fell across her mind: Did Bert keep his knife in the drawer with his underwear? It was a needless question she asked herself, however.

She could see that Bert was smiling at the old man. "Our baby's sick." But at the moment the words meant nothing to her. There, in her arms, the baby seemed to be gagging. And then Emmaline felt her baby being jerked away from her. It happened so quickly that she could not even try to resist. She saw Bert springing to his feet. Then she beheld the dirty old man holding the baby upside down by her feet, as he would have held a chicken. Among the shadows of the room he was somehow like another shadow. Barefoot and shirtless, he gave the effect of being totally naked except for some rather new-looking galluses that held up his dark trousers. A naked-looking, gray figure, he stood holding the baby upside down and shaking her until her nightgown fell almost over her head, exposing her white diaper and her black, heaving little stomach.

Emmaline felt all the strength go out of her body, and it

seemed to her that she was staggering blindly about, or falling. Indistinctly, as though from a great distance, she heard the voices of the two men. The old man's voice was very deep and— she resisted such a thought—was a voice fraught with kindliness. Presently, Emmaline realized that Bert was standing by her with his arm about her waist, and the baby was crying softly in the old man's arms.

"But something *sure* must be ailing her," Bert was saying quietly. He was talking about the baby and didn't seem to realize that though Emmaline had remained on her feet, she had lost consciousness for a moment. "She don't yell like that, and she *woke up* yelling bloody murder," Bert said.

The old man smiled. He was gap-toothed, and the few teeth he had were yellow-brown. "Bad dreams," he said. "Bad dreams is all. I reckon he thought the boogeyman after him."

Bert laughed good-naturedly. "I reckon so," he said, looking at Emmaline. He asked her if she was all right, and she nodded. "How come we didn't suppose it was bad dreams?" he asked, smiling. "It just didn't come to us, I reckon. But what could that little baby have to dream about?" He laughed again, trying to imagine what the baby could have to dream about.

Emmaline stared at Bert. At some point, he had woken up all the way and had become himself as he was in the daytime. She had a feeling of terrible loss for a moment, and the next moment was one of fear.

What if Bert *had* straightened up and turned away from the dresser drawer with his knife in his hand? Yet it wasn't that question that frightened her. It was another. Why had she tried to start Bert on his way to get a doctor? She wasn't sure, and she knew she would never be sure, whether it was really to get a doctor, or to get him away before the old man came into the room, or to get him to that drawer where he kept his knife before the old man came in. Now, in a trembling voice, she said, "Let me have the baby."

The baby had stopped crying altogether. All signs of hysteria were gone. She sniffled now and then and caught her breath, but she had forgotten her nightmare and forgotten how frightened and quarrelsome her parents' voices had sounded a short while before. In the half-darkness of the room, her eyes were focused on the buckle of one of the old man's galluses.

Emmaline came forward and took the baby, who, though she seemed sorry to leave the old man, was now in such a happy frame of mind that she made not a whimper of objection. On Emmaline's shoulder, she even made soft little pigeonlike speeches.

It was during this time, while the baby cooed in her mother's arms, that Bert and Emmaline and the old man stood staring at one another in silence, all three of them plainly absorbed in thoughts of their own. It was only for a moment, for soon the old man asked to be allowed to hold the baby again. Emmaline felt that she could not refuse him. She told him that the baby was not a boy but a girl, that they had not yet named her, but that Bert usually just called her plain Baby; and then she let the baby go to the old man. Whatever other thoughts she and Bert were having, they both were so happy to have found the baby wasn't the least bit sick, after all, that they were content to stand there awhile contemplating the good spirits the old man had put her in. The baby changed hands several times, being passed to Bert, then to Emmaline, and then back to the old man. Finally, she began to fret.

"Now she's hungry," the old man said with authority.

There could be no doubt that that was what this sort of fretting meant. Emmaline automatically stepped up and took the baby from him. She went into the lighted room where the crib was and closed the door. As she sat down in the wicker rocking chair and gave the baby her breast, she could hear the old fellow still talking to Bert in the next room. It occurred to her then that all the while they had stood there passing the baby back and forth and delighting in the baby's good spirits, the old man had been talking on and on, as though he didn't know how to stop once he had begun. Emmaline hadn't listened to him, but as she now heard his bass voice droning on beyond the closed door, she began to recollect the sort of thing he had been saying. Off his tongue had rolled all the obvious things, all the unnecessary things, all the dull things—every last thing that might have been left unsaid: He guessed he had a way with children; they flocked to him in the neighborhood where he lived, and he looked after them and did for them. Along with the quality of kindliness in his voice was a quality that could finally make you forget kindliness, no matter how genuine. Why, he didn't mind doing for children when their folks ought to go out and have their good time of it before they got like him, "a decrepited and lonesome old wreck on time's beach." What Bert and Emmaline needed was some of their old folks from Tennessee—or the likes of them —to show them something about raising children, so they wouldn't go scaring themselves to death and worrying where they needn't. Tears of pity came into Emmaline's eyes—pity for herself. It would be like that from now on. She heard the old man's voice going on and on in the next room even after she had heard Bert letting himself down on the bed. She even thought she heard the old man saying that if they didn't want him to stay, he would leave tomorrow. That's what he *would* say, anyhow. He would be saying it again and again for years and years because he knew that Bert would not have the heart, any more than she would, to run him off after tonight.

She got up and turned off the light, and then, with the baby in her arms, found her way to the rocking chair. She continued to sit there rocking long after the old man had talked himself out for this time and had, without shutting the bathroom door, used the toilet and finally gone off to his own room. She went on rocking even long after she knew the baby was asleep and would be dead to the world until morning. During the time she and Bert and the old man had stood in the shadowy room in silence, each absorbed in his own thoughts, she had been remembering that the baby's shrieking had awakened her from a nightmare of her own. She had not been able to remember at the time what the nightmare was, but now she did. There wasn't much to the dream. She was on the Square in Thornton. Across the courthouse yard she spied old 'Stracted Mag coming toward her. The old woman had three or four cur dogs on leash, and she was walking between two Thornton white ladies whom Emmaline recognized. As the group drew near to Emmaline, she had the impulse to run forward and throw her arms about old Mag and tell her how she admired her serene and calm manner. But when she began to run she saw old Mag unleash the dogs, and the dogs rushed upon her growling and turning back their lips to show their yellow, tobacco-stained teeth. Emmaline tried to scream and could not. And then she did manage to scream. But it was the baby shrieking, of course, and she had woken from her nightmare.

As she rocked in the dark with her sleeping baby, she shook her head, trying to forget the dream she had just remembered. Life seemed bad enough without fool dreams to make it worse. She would think, instead, about the old man and how she would have to make him clean himself up and how she would have to train him to do for the baby when the baby got older. She even tried to think kindly of him and managed to recall moments of tenderness with her old granddaddy and her uncles in Thornton, but as she did so, tears of bitterness stung her eyes—bitterness that out of the past, as it seemed, this old fellow had come to disrupt and spoil her happy life in St. Louis.

In the next room, Bert, in his white pajamas, lay on their bed listening to the noise that the rocking chair made. It went "quat-plat, quat-plat," like any old country rocking chair. He knew the baby must be asleep by now, but he didn't want Emmaline to come back to bed yet. For while he and Emmaline and the old man had stood together in the brief silence, Bert, too, had realized that the baby had awakened *him* from a nightmare. He had thought he was a little boy in school again, in the old one-room Negro grade school at Thornton. He was seated at the back of the room, far away from the stove, and he was cold. It seemed he had forgotten to go to the privy before he left home, as he so often used to forget, but he could not bring himself to raise his hand and ask to go now. On top of all this, the teacher was asking him to read, and he could not find the place on the page. This was a dream that Bert often had. It could take one of several endings—all of them equally terrible to him. Sometimes the teacher said, "Why can't you learn, boy?" and commenced beating him. Sometimes he ran past the teacher (who sometimes was a white man) to the door and found the door locked. Sometimes he got away and ran down to the school privy, to find indescribable horrors awaiting him there.

As he lay in bed tonight, he could not or would not remember how the dream had ended this time. And he would not let himself go back to sleep, for fear of having the dream again. There had been nights when he had had the dream over and over in all its variations. Why should he go back to sleep now and have that dreadful dream when he could stay awake and think of pleasant things?—or the pleasanter duties ahead of him tomorrow, of polishing the silver, of scouring the tile floor in the pantry, perhaps of washing Miss Amy's car if she didn't go out in the afternoon. He stayed awake for a long time, but without thinking of the old man at all, without even thinking of what could be keeping Emmaline in the next room.

And while Bert lay there carefully not thinking of his bad dream and not thinking of the old man and wept bitterly because of him, wasn't it likely that the old man himself was still awake—in the dark room with the three-legged chest of drawers, the unplastered walls, and the old harness hooks? If so, was it possible that he, too, had been awakened from a bad dream tonight? Who would ever know? Bert and Emmaline would tell each other in the morning about their dreams—their loneliness was only of the moment—and when Baby grew up, they would tell her about themselves and about their bad dreams. But who was there to know about *his?* Who is there that can imagine the things that such a dirty, ignorant, old tramp of a Negro thinks about when he is alone at night, or dreams about while he sleeps? Such pathetic old tramps seem, somehow, to have moved beyond the reach of human imagination. They are too unlike us, in their loneliness and ignorance and age and dirt, for us even to guess about them as people. It may be necessary for us, when we meet them in life or when we encounter them in a story, to treat them not as people but as symbols of something we like or dislike. Or is it possible to suppose, for instance, that their bad dreams, after all—to the very end of life, and in the most hopeless circumstances—are only like Bert's and Emmaline's. Is it possible that this old fellow had been awakened tonight from a miserable dream of his own childhood in some little town or on some farm in that vague region which the Tollivers called West Tennessee? Perhaps, when he returned from the toilet, he sat up in bed, knowing that at his age he wasn't likely to get back to sleep soon, and thought about a nightmare he had remembered while standing in that shadowy room with Bert and Emmaline. It might even be that the old fellow smiled to himself and took comfort from the thought that anyway there were not for him so many nightmares ahead as there were for Bert and for Emmaline, and certainly not so many as for their little woolly-headed baby who didn't yet have a name.

A FRIEND
AND PROTECTOR

FAMILY FRIENDS would always say how devoted Jesse Munroe was to my uncle. And Jesse himself would tell me sometimes what he would do to anybody who harmed a hair on "that white gentleman's head." The poor fellow was much too humorless and lived much too much in the past—or in some other kind of removal from the present—to reflect that Uncle Andrew no longer had a hair on his head to be harmed. While he was telling me the things he would do, I'd often burst out laughing at the very thought of my uncle's baldness. Or that was what I told myself I was laughing about. At any rate, my outbursts didn't bother Jesse. He always went right ahead with his description of the violence he would do Uncle Andrew's assailant. And I, watching his obscene gestures and reminding myself of all the scrapes he had been in and of the serious trouble my uncle had got him out of twenty years back, I could almost believe he would do the things he said. More than one time, in fact, his delineations became so real and convincing it took my best fit of laughter to conceal the shudders he sent through me.

He was a naturally fierce-looking little man with purplish black skin and thick wiry hair, which he wore not clipped short like most Negro men's hair but long and bushed up on his head. It was intended to give him height, I used to suppose. But it contributed instead to a general sinister effect, just as his long, narrow sideburns did; and my Uncle Andrew would always insist that it was this effect Jesse strived for. He wasn't, actually, such a little man. He was of medium height. It was because he was so stoop-shouldered and was so often seen beside my Uncle Andrew that we, my aunt and I, thought of him as little. He *was* extremely stoop-shouldered, though, and his neck was so short that the lobes of his overlarge ears seemed to reach almost to the collar of his white linen jacket. Probably it was this peculiarity along with his bushy hair and his perpetually bloodshot eyes that made me say at first he was naturally fierce-looking.

He wasn't *naturally* fierce-looking. My Uncle Andrew was right about that. It was something he had achieved. And according to my uncle, the scrapes he was always getting into didn't really amount to much. My Aunt Margaret, however—my "blood aunt," married to Uncle Andrew—used to shake her head bitterly and say that Negroes could get away with anything with Uncle Andrew and that his ideas of "much" were very different from hers. "Jesse Munroe can disappear into the bowels of Beale Street," she would say in Jesse's presence, "knowing that when he comes out all he did there will be a closed chapter for 'Mr. Andrew.'" Jesse would be clearing the table or laying a fire in the living room, and while such talk went on he would keep his eyes lowered except to steal a glance now and then at my aunt.

I was a boy of fifteen when I used to observe this. I was staying there in Memphis with my uncle and aunt just after Mother died. The things Aunt Margaret said in Jesse's presence made me feel very uncomfortable. And it seemed unlike her. I used to wish Jesse would look at Uncle Andrew instead of at her and spare himself the sight of the expression on her face at those moments.

But it was foolish of me to waste sympathy on Jesse Munroe, and even at the time I knew it was. For one thing, despite all the evenings we spent talking back in the pantry during the two years I lived there, he never seemed to be really aware of me as a person. Each time we talked it was almost as though it was the first time. There was no getting to know him. Two years later when I had finished high school and was not getting along with my uncle and aunt as well as at first, I didn't live at their house anymore. But I would sometimes see Jesse at my uncle's Front Street office where I then had a job and where Jesse soon came to work as my uncle's special flunky. Uncle Andrew was a cotton broker, and it wasn't unusual for such a successful cotton man as he was to keep a factotum like Jesse around the office. I would see Jesse there, and he wouldn't even bother to speak to me. I am certain that if nowadays he is in a condition to remember anyone he doesn't remember me. I appeared on the scene too late. By the time I came along Jesse's escapades and my uncle's and aunt's reactions to them had become a regular pattern. It was too well established, over too many years, for my presence or my sympathy one way or the other to make any difference. It was the central and perhaps the only reality in Jesse's life. It had been so since before I was born and it would continue to be so, for a while at least, after I left the house.

My uncle and aunt had brought Jesse with them to Memphis when Uncle Andrew moved his office there from out at Braxton, which is the country town our family comes from. He was the only local Negro they brought with them, and since this was right after Jesse had received a suspended sentence for an alleged part in the murder of Aunt Margaret's washwoman's husband, it was assumed in Braxton that there had been some sensible understanding arrived at between Andrew Nelson and the presiding judge. Jesse was to have a suspended sentence; Uncle Andrew was to get him out of Braxton and keep him out. . . . Be that as it may, Jesse came away with them to Memphis and during the first year he hardly set foot outside their house and yard.

He was altogether too faithful and too hardworking to be tolerated by any of the trifling servants Aunt Margaret was able to hire in Memphis. For a while she couldn't keep a cook on the place. Then one finally came along who discovered how to get Jesse's goat, and this one stayed the normal time for a Memphis cook—that is, four or five years. She was Jesse's ruin, I suppose. She discovered the secret of how to get his goat, and passed it on to the maid and the furnace boy and the part-time chauffeur that Uncle Andrew kept. And they passed it on to those who came after them. They teased him unmercifully, made life a misery for him. What they said to him was that he was a country boy in the city, scared to go out on the street. Now, there is a story, seemingly known to all Negro citizens of Memphis, of a Mississippi country boy who robs his old grandmother and comes to town prepared to enjoy life. He takes a hotel room and sits in the window looking down at the crowds. But he can't bring himself to go down and "mix with 'em." The story has several versions, but usually it ends with the boy's starving to death in his room because he is scared to go down and take his chances on Beale Street. And this was how they pictured Jesse. They went so far, even, as to ridicule him that way in front of my aunt and uncle.

As a matter of fact, Jesse couldn't have been much more than a boy in those days. And his nature may really have been a timid one. Whatever other reasons there were for his behavior, probably it was due partly to his being a timid country boy. There was always something of the puritan in him, too. I could see this when I was only fifteen. I never once heard him use any profanity, or any rough language at all except when he was indicating what he would do to my uncle's imaginary attacker—and then it was more a matter of gestures than of words. When the cook my aunt had during the time I was there would sometimes make insinuating remarks about the dates I began having and about the hours I kept toward the end of my stay, Jesse would say, "You oughtn't talk that way before this white boy." If I sometimes seemed to enjoy the cook's teasing and even egged her on a little, he would get up and leave the room. Perhaps the most old-fashioned and country thing about him was that he still wore his long underwear the year round. On Mondays, when he generally had a terrible hangover and was tapering off from the weekend, he would work all day in the garden. I would see him out there even on the hottest July day working with his shirt off but still wearing his long-sleeved undershirt. The other servants took his long underwear as another mark of his primness, and whenever they talked about the light he kept burning in his room all night they would say he never put it out except once a week when he took his bath and changed his long johns.

Yet no matter how much fun they made of him to his face, when Jesse wasn't present the other servants admitted they would hate to run into him while he was off on one of his sprees, and they assured me that *they* didn't hang around the kind of places that he did. And laugh at him though they did, they respected him for the amount of work he could turn out and for the quality of it. He was a perfectionist in his work both in the house and in the yard, and especially in my uncle's vegetable garden.

The cook who found out how to get Jesse's goat shouldn't be blamed too much. She couldn't have known the harm she was doing. And surely Jesse couldn't have gone on forever never leaving the house. The time had to come. And once that teasing had started, Jesse had to *show* them. He didn't tell anyone when he first began going out. The other servants didn't live on the place regularly, and my uncle only discovered Jesse's absence by chance late one night when he wanted him for some trifle. He went out in the backyard and called up to his room above the garage. The light was on, but there was no answer. Uncle climbed the rickety outside stairs that went up to the room and banged the door to wake him. Then he came down the stairs again and went in the house and conferred with Aunt Margaret. They were worried about Jesse, thinking something might have happened to him, and so Uncle Andrew went up and forced the lock on the door to Jesse's room.

The light was burning—a little twenty-watt bulb on a cord hanging in the middle of the room—and the room was as neat as a pin. But there was no Jesse. My aunt, who can always remember every detail of a moment like that, said that from the back-door she could hear Uncle Andrew's footstep out there in the room above the garage. For a time that was all she heard. But then finally she heard Uncle Andrew break out into a kind of laughter that was characteristic of him. It expressed all the good nature in his being and at the same time a certain hateful spirit, too. From her description I am sure it was just like his laughter when he caught you napping at Russian bank or checkers or when he saw he had you beaten and began slapping down his cards or pushing his kings around.

Presently he came out on the stoop at the head of the stairs and, still chuckling in his throat, called down to Aunt Margaret, "Our chick has left the nest." Then, closing the door, he took out his pocketknife and managed to screw the lock in place again. When he joined Aunt Margaret at the kitchen door he told her not to say anything about the incident to Jesse, that it was none of their business if he wanted a night out now and again.

Aunt Margaret could never get Jesse to tell her when he was planning an evening out, and later when he began taking an occasional Sunday off he never gave advance warning of that either. Sunday morning would come and he would simply not be on the place. It was still the same when I came there to live. After a Sunday's absence without leave, Jesse would be working my uncle's garden all day Monday. It was a big country vegetable garden right on Belvedere Street in Memphis. I have seen my aunt stand for a long period of time at one of the upstairs windows watching Jesse at work down there on a Monday morning, herself not moving a muscle until he looked up at her. Then she would shake her head sadly—exaggerating the shake so that he couldn't miss it—and turn her back to the window. When my uncle came home in the evening on one of those Mondays he would go straight to the garden and exclaim over the wonderful weeding and chopping the garden had had. Later, in the house, he would say it was worth having Jesse take French leave now and then in order to get that good day's work in the garden from him.

His real escapades and the scrapes he got into were in a different category from his occasional weekends. In the first place, they lasted longer. When he had already been missing for three or four days or even a week there would be a telephone call late at night or early some morning. Usually it would be an anonymous call, sometimes a man's voice, sometimes a woman's. If a name were given it was one that meant nothing to Uncle Andrew, and when Jesse had been rescued he invariably maintained he had never heard the name of the caller before. He would say he just wished he knew who it was, and always protested that he hadn't wanted Uncle Andrew to be bothered. The telephone call usually went about like this: "You Mr. Andrew Nelson at Number 212 Belvedere Street?"

"Yes."

"Yo friend Jesse's in jail and he needs yo help."

Then the informer would hang up or, if questioned in time by Uncle Andrew, would give a name like "Henry White" or "Mary Jones" along with some made-up street number and a street nobody ever heard of. One time the voice said only, "Yo friend Jesse's been pisened. He's in room Number 9 at the New Charleston Hotel." Uncle Andrew had gone down to the New Charleston with a policeman, and they found Jesse seriously ill and out of his head—probably from getting hold of bad whiskey. They took him to the John Gaston Hospital where he had to stay for nearly a week.

Usually, though, it wasn't just a matter of his being on a drunk. According to my aunt, he got into dreadful fights in which he slashed other Negroes with a knife and got cut up himself, though I never saw any of his scars. Probably they were all hidden beneath his long underwear. And besides, by the time I came along they would have been old scars since by then his scrapes had, for a long time, been of a different kind. There had been a number of years when his troubles were all with women. There were women who fought over him, women who fought *him*, women who got him put in jail for bothering them, and women who got him put in jail for not helping support their children. Then, after this phase, he was involved off and on for several years in the numbers racket and the kind of gang warfare that goes along with that. Uncle Andrew would have to get the police and go down and rescue him from some room above a pool hall where the rival gang had him cornered.

My account of all this came of course from my aunt since my uncle never revealed the nature of Jesse's troubles to anyone but Aunt Margaret. She dragged it out of him because she felt she had a right to know. She may have exaggerated it all to me. But I used to think two of the points she made about it were good ones. She pointed out that the nature of his escapades grew successively worse, so that it was harder each time for Uncle Andrew to intervene. And she suspected that that gave Jesse considerable satisfaction. She also said that from the beginning all of Jesse's degrading adventures had had one thing in common: He never was able or willing to get out of any jam on his own. He would let any situation run on until there was no way he could be saved except through Uncle Andrew's intervention. "All he seems to want," she said, "is to have something worse than the time before for his 'Mr. Andrew' to save him from and dismiss as a mere nothing."

I felt at the time that this was very true, and it tended to make me agree with Uncle Andrew that Jesse Munroe's scrapes were not very important in themselves, and, in that sense, didn't "amount to much." In fact, my aunt's observation seemed so obviously true that it was hard to think of Jesse as anything but a spoiled child, which, I suppose, is the way Uncle Andrew did think of him.

The murder that Jesse had gotten mixed up in back in Braxton was as nasty a business as you hear about. Uncle Andrew would not have had a white man living about his garage who had had any connection with such a business. When *I* finally gave up my room at his house and went to live at the "Y," it was more because of *his* disapproval of my friends (and of the hours I kept) than it was because of my aunt's. And though I couldn't have said so to a living soul that I knew when I was a boy, I used to wish my uncle could have been half as tolerant of my own father, who was a weak man and got into various kinds of trouble, as he was of Jesse. My father was killed in an automobile crash when I was only a little fellow, but, for several years before, Uncle Andrew had refused to have anything to do with him personally, though he would always help him get jobs as long as they were away from Braxton and, always, on the condition that my mother and I would continue to live in Braxton with my grandparents. I was taught to believe that Uncle Andrew was right about all of this, and I still believe that he was in a way. Jesse hadn't, after all, had the advantages that my father had, and he may have been a victim of circumstances. But my father was a victim of circumstances, too, I think—as who isn't, for that matter? Even Uncle Andrew and Aunt Margaret were, in a way.

In that murder of Aunt Margaret's washwoman's husband I believe Jesse was accused of being an accessory after the fact. I don't think anyone accused him of having anything to do with the actual killing. The washwoman and a boyfriend of hers named Cleveland Blakemore had done in her husband without help from anyone. They did it in a woods lot behind a roadhouse on the outskirts of town, where the husband found them together. At the trial I think the usual blunt instrument was produced as the murder weapon. Then they had transported the body to the washwoman's house where they dismembered it and attempted to burn the parts in the chimney. But it was a rainy night and the flue wouldn't draw. They ended by pulling out the charred remains and burying them in a cotton patch behind the washwoman's house, not in one grave but in a number of graves scattered about the cotton patch. (You may wonder why I bring in these awful details of the murder, and I wonder myself. I tell them out of some kind of compulsion and because I have known them ever since I was a small child in Braxton. I couldn't have told the story without somehow bringing them in. I find I have only been waiting for the right moment. And it seems to me now that I would never have had the interest I did in Jesse except that he was someone connected with those gory details of a crime I had heard about when I was very young and which had stuck in my mind during all the years when I was growing up in the house with my pretty, gentle mother and my aged grandparents.) At any rate, it was on a rainy winter morning just a few weeks after the murder that a Negro girl, hurrying to work, took a shortcut through that cotton patch. In her haste she stumbled and fell into a hole where the pigs had rooted up what was left of the victim's left forearm and hand.

In the trial it was proved that Jesse had provided the transportation for the corpse from the woods lot to the washwoman's house. His defense contended that he just happened to be at the roadhouse that night, driving a funeral car which he had borrowed, without permission, from the undertaker's parlor where he worked as janitor, and sometimes as driver. (You can hear the voice of the prosecution: "It was the saddest funeral that car ever went to.") He was paid in advance for the trip, and it was represented to him (according to his defense) that the washwoman's husband was only dead drunk.

It was never proved conclusively that Jesse had any part in the dismemberment or in the efforts at burning. Witnesses who testified they had seen *two* men coming and going from the house to the cotton patch (in the heavy rain on that autumn night) were not reliable ones. Yet the testimony that Jesse's borrowed car was parked in front of the house during most of the night was given by Negro men and women of the highest character. Even Jesse's defense never denied his presence in there. But to me it seems quite as likely that, as his defense maintained, he was kept there at knife's point, or at least by the fear that if he attempted to go he might meet the same fate that the washwoman's husband had, as that he willingly took part in what went on. My uncle of course felt that there was no question about it, that Jesse was an innocent country boy drawn into the business by the washwoman and her friend, Cleveland Blakemore (who no doubt guessed he had taken the undertaker's car without permission), and that he wasn't to be blamed. Uncle Andrew even served as a character witness for Jesse at the trial, because he had known him before the murder when Jesse was janitor at his office as well as at the undertaker's.

I never heard any talk about the murder from Uncle Andrew and Aunt Margaret themselves. In private Aunt Margaret would tell me about some of the other troubles Jesse had been in and about how narrowly he had escaped long jail sentences. Only Uncle Andrew's ever widening connections among influential people in Memphis had been able to prevent those sentences. She said that my uncle was such a modest man that he naturally minimized Jesse's scrapes so as not to put too much importance on the things he was able to do to get him out of them.

But my uncle knew his wife well enough to know what she would have told me. Without ever giving me his version of any of the incidents he would say to me now and then that Aunt Margaret was much too severe and that she set too high standards for Jesse. And I did find it painful to hear the way she spoke to Jesse and to see the way she looked at him even after one of his milder weekends. In those days, so soon after my mother died, Aunt Margaret was always so kind and so considerate of my feelings and of my every want that it seemed out of character for her to be harsh and severe with anyone. Before that day I packed my things and moved out of her house, however, I came to doubt that it was so entirely out of character. If I had stayed there a day longer, I might have had even greater doubts. I think it is fortunate I left when I did. Our quarrel didn't amount to a lot. It was about my staying out all night one time without ever being willing to explain where I was. As soon as I was a little older and began to settle down to work and behave myself we made it up. Nowadays I'm on the best of terms with her and Uncle Andrew. And whenever I'm over at their place for a meal things seem very much the way they used to. Even the talk about Jesse goes very much the way it did when he was on the scene and in easy earshot.

When they talked about him together in the old days, especially when there was company around, it was all about his loyalty and devotion to Uncle Andrew. I agreed with every word they said on the subject, and if someone had said to me then that it was Aunt Margaret whom Jesse was most dependent upon and whose attention he most needed I would have said that person was crazy. How could anyone have supposed such a thing? And if I should advance such a theory nowadays to my uncle and aunt or to their friends they would imagine that I was expressing some long-buried resentment against Uncle Andrew. Any new analysis made in the light of what happened to Jesse after he went to work in my uncle's Front Street office would not interest them. They wouldn't be able to reverse a view based upon the impressions of all those years when Jesse was with them, a view based upon impressions received before any of them ever knew Jesse, impressions inherited from their own uncles and aunts and parents and grandparents.

I used to watch the expression on his black face when he was waiting on Uncle Andrew at table or was helping him into his overcoat when Uncle Andrew left for his office in the morning. His careful attention to my uncle's readiness for his next sleeve or for the next helping of greens made you feel he considered it a privilege to be doing all these little favors for a man who had done so many large ones for him. His attentions to my uncle impressed everyone who came to the house. If there was a party, he couldn't pass through the room, even with a tray loaded with glasses, without stopping before Uncle Andrew to nod and mutter respectfully, "Mr. Andrew." This itself was a memorable spectacle, and often was enough to stop the party talk of those who witnessed it: Uncle Andrew, so tall and erect, so bald and clean-shaven, so proudly beak-nosed, and yet with such a benign expression in those gray eyes that focused for one quick moment upon Jesse. And Jesse, stooped and purple-black and bushy-headed and red-eyed, clad in his white vestment and all but genuflecting while he held the tray of glasses perfectly steady for my uncle. It lasted only a second, and then Jesse's eyes would dart from one to another of the men standing nearest Uncle Andrew as though looking for some Cassius among them—some Judas. (And perhaps thinking all the time only that my aunt's eyes were upon him, denouncing him not merely as a sycophant and hypocrite but as a man who would have to answer for his manifold sins before the dread seat of judgment on the Last Day.) When he had moved on with his tray, some guest who had not been to the house before was apt to comment on what a wicked-looking fellow he was. My uncle would laugh heartily and say that nothing would please Jesse more than to think this was the impression he gave. "He gets himself up to look awful mean and he likes to think of himself as a devil. But actually he's as harmless as that boy standing there," Uncle Andrew would say, pointing of course to me.

I would laugh self-consciously, not really liking to have my own harmlessness pointed out. And I wonder if Jesse, already on the other side of the room, sometimes heard my laughter then and detected a certain hollowness in it that was also there when he told me the things he would do to my uncle's imaginary assailant. Because often, when I stood looking at the guest made uncomfortable by Jesse's glance, I could not help thinking of those things. In my mind's eye I would see his gestures, see him seizing his throat, rolling his eyes about, making as if to slice off his ears and nose, and indicating an even more debilitating operation. It may seem strange that I never imagined that those threats might be directed toward me personally, since I was my father's son and might easily have been supposed to bear a grudge against my uncle. But I felt that Jesse made it graphically clear that it was some Negro man like himself he had in mind as my uncle's assailant. When he was going through his routine he would usually be in the pantry and he would have placed himself in such relation to the mirror panel beside the swinging door there that, by rolling his eyes, he could be certain to see the black visage of this man he was mutilating.

It was another coincidence, like their moving to Memphis just when Jesse had to be gotten out of Braxton, that my aunt and uncle decided to give up the house and move to an apartment at just the time when it was no longer feasible for them to have Jesse Munroe working at their house. Uncle Andrew was nearly seventy years old at the time. He was spending less time at his office, and he and Aunt Margaret wanted to be free to travel. During the two years I was with them, there were three occasions when Jesse was missing from the house for about a week and had to be rescued by my uncle. I didn't know then exactly what his current outside activities were. Even Aunt Margaret preferred not to discuss it with me. She would say only that in her estimation it was worse than anything before. Later I learned that he had become a kind of confidence man and that—as in the numbers racket—his chief troubles came from his competitors. He specialized, for a time, in preying upon green country boys who had come to Memphis with their little wads of money. After I had left the house he went to something still worse. He was delivering country girls whom he picked up on Beale Street into the hands of the Pontotoc Street madams.

It was the authorities from neighboring counties in West Tennessee and Mississippi who finally began to put pressure on the police. They threatened, so I have been told, to come in and take care of Jesse themselves. Uncle Andrew moved him to a little room on the top floor of the ramshackle old building that his cotton company was in. Jesse lived up there and acted as a kind of butler and bartender in my uncle's private office, which was a paneled, air-conditioned suite far in the rear of and very different-looking from the display rooms where the troughs of cotton samples were. The trouble was that his "Mr. Andrew" was not at the office very much anymore for Jesse to wait on. And so most of the time he stayed up in his little cubbyhole on the top floor, and of course he got to drinking up my uncle's whiskey. He never left the building, never came down below the third floor, which Uncle Andrew's offices were on, and he never talked to the other Negroes who worked there. I would pass him in the hallway sometimes and speak to him, but he wouldn't even look at me. At last, of course, he went crazy up there in my uncle's office. It may have been partly from drinking so much whiskey, but at least this time we knew it wasn't bad whiskey. . . . When the office force came and opened up that morning they found him locked up in Uncle Andrew's air-conditioned, sound-proofed suite and they could see through the glass doors the wreck he had made of everything in there. He had slashed the draperies and cut up the upholstery on the chairs. There were big spots and gashes on the walls where he had thrown things—mostly bottles of whiskey and gin, which of course had been broken and left lying all about the floor. He had pushed over the bar, the filing cabinets, the refrigerator, the electric watercooler, and even the air-conditioning unit. For a while nobody could tell where Jesse himself was. It wasn't till just before I got there that they spotted him crouched under Uncle Andrew's mahogany desk. From the beginning, though, they could hear him moaning and praying and calling out now and then for help. And even before I arrived someone had observed that it wasn't for Uncle Andrew but for Aunt Margaret he was calling.

I was parking my car down in the alley when one of the secretaries who had already been up there rushed up to me and told me what had happened. I hurried around to the street side of the building and went up the stairs so fast that I stumbled two or three times before I got to the third floor. They made a place for me at the glass door and told me that if I would stoop down I could see him back in the inner office crouched under the desk. I saw him there, and what I noticed first was that he didn't have on his white jacket or his shirt but was still wearing his long-sleeved winter underwear.

Fortunately, it happened that Uncle Andrew and Aunt Margaret were not on one of their trips at the time. Everyone at the office knew this, and they knew better than to call the police. They would have known better even if Uncle Andrew had not been in town. They waited for me to come in and telephone Uncle Andrew. I went up into the front display room and picked up the telephone. It was only eight-thirty, and I knew that Uncle Andrew would probably still be in bed. He sounded half asleep when he answered. I blurted out, "Uncle Andrew, Jesse's cracked up pretty bad down here at the office and has himself locked in your rooms."

"Yes," said Uncle Andrew, guardedly.

"He's made a mess of the place and is hiding under your desk. He has a knife, I suppose. And he keeps calling for Aunt Margaret. Do you think you'll come down, or—"

"Who is it speaking?" Uncle Andrew said, as though anyone else at the office ever called him "uncle." He did it out of habit. But it gave me an unpleasant feeling. I was tempted to give some name like "Henry White" and hang up, but I said nothing. I just waited. Uncle Andrew was silent for a moment. Then I heard him clear his throat, and he said, "Do you think he'll be all right till I can get down there?"

"I think so," I said. "I don't know."

"I'll get Fred Morley and be down there in fifteen minutes," he said.

I don't know why but I said again, "He keeps calling for Aunt Margaret."

"I heard you," Uncle Andrew said. Then he said, "We'll be down in fifteen minutes."

I didn't know whether his "we" meant himself and Fred Morley, who was the family doctor, or whether it included Aunt Margaret. I don't know yet which he meant. But when he and Dr. Morley arrived, my aunt was with them, and I don't think I was ever so glad to see anyone. I kissed her when she came in.

I came near to kissing Uncle Andrew too. I was touched by how old he had looked as he came up the stairs—he and Aunt Margaret, and Dr. Morley, too—how old and yet how much the same. And I was touched by the fact that it hadn't occurred to any of the three not to come. However right or wrong their feelings toward Jesse were they were the same as they would have been thirty years before. In a way this seemed pretty wonderful to me. It did at the moment. I thought of the phrase my aunt was so fond of using about people: "true blue."

The office force, and two of the partners by now, were still bunched around the glass door peering in at Jesse and trying to hear the things he was saying. I stood at the top of the stairs watching the three old people ascend the two straight flights of steps that I had come stumbling up half an hour earlier—two flights that came up from the ground floor without a turn or a landing between floors. I thought how absurd it was that in these Front Street buildings, where so much Memphis money was made, such a thing as an elevator was unknown. Except for adding the little air-conditioned offices at the rear, nobody was allowed to do anything there that would change the old-fashioned, masculine character of the cotton man's world. This row of buildings, hardly two blocks long, with their plaster facade and unbroken line of windows looking out over the brown Mississippi River were a kind of last sanctuary—generally beyond the reach of the ladies and practically beyond the reach of the law.

When they got to the top of the stairs I kissed my aunt on her powdered cheek. She took my arm and stood a moment catching her breath before we moved out of the hallway. I thought to myself that she had put more powder on her face this morning than was usual for her. No doubt she had dressed in a great hurry, hardly looking in her glass. But I observed that underneath the powder her face was flushed from the climb, and her china blue eyes shone brightly. Instead of seeming older to me now, I felt she looked younger and prettier and more feminine than I had ever before seen her. It must have been just seeing her there in a Front Street office for the first time. . . . But I still remember the delicate pressure of her hand as she leaned on my arm.

Uncle Andrew went straight to the door of his office and shooed everyone else away. I don't know whether I saw him do this or not, but I know that's how it was. Presently I found myself in the middle display room standing beside Aunt Margaret while Dr. Morley made pleasantries to her about how the appearance of cotton offices never changed. He hadn't been inside one in more than a decade, and he wondered how long it had been for her. Uncle Andrew, meanwhile, in order to be sure that Jesse heard him through the glass door and above his moaning had to speak in a voice that resounded all over the third floor of the building. Yet he didn't seem to be shouting, and he managed to put into his voice all the reassurance and forgiveness that must have been there during their private interchanges in years past. It was like hearing a radio soap opera turned on unbearably loud in a drugstore or in some other public place. "Come open the door, Jesse. You know I'm your friend. Haven't I always done right by you? It doesn't matter about the mess you've made in there. I have insurance to cover everything, and I'm not going to let anybody harm you."

It didn't do any good, though. Even in the middle room we could hear Jesse calling out—more persistently now—for Aunt Margaret to help him. Yet Aunt Margaret still seemed to be listening to Dr. Morley. I couldn't understand it. I wanted to interrupt and ask her if she didn't hear Jesse? Why had she come if she wasn't even going in there and look at him through the glass door? Didn't she feel any compassion for the poor fellow? Surely she would suddenly turn her back on us and walk in there. That seemed how she would do it.

Then for a moment my attention was distracted from Aunt Margaret to myself—to how concerned I was about whether or not she would go to him, to how very much I cared about Jesse's suffering and his need to have my aunt come and look at him! I took my eyes off Aunt Margaret and was myself resolutely trying to observe what a Front Street cotton office was really like when I felt her hand on my arm again. Looking at her I saw that underneath the powder her color was still quite high. While Dr. Morley talked on she gazed at me with moist eyes which made her look still prettier than before. And now I perceived that she had been intending all the time to go to Jesse and give the poor brute whatever comfort she could. But I saw too that there were difficulties for her which I had not imagined. Suddenly she did as she *would* do. Without a word she turned her back on us and went back there and showed herself in the glass door.

That was all there was to it really. Or for Jesse it was. It seemed to be all the real help he needed or could accept. He didn't come out and open the door, but he was relatively quiet afterward, even after Aunt Margaret was finally led away by Uncle Andrew and Dr. Morley, and even after Dr. Morley's two men came and broke the glass in the door and went in for him. When Aunt Margaret had been led away it seemed to be my turn again, and so I went back there and stood watching him until the men came. Now and then he would start to crawl out from under the desk but each time would suddenly pull back and try to hide himself again, and then again the animal grunts and groans would begin. Obviously, he was still seeing the things he had thought were after him during the night. But though he made some feeble efforts at resistance, I think he had regained his senses sufficiently to be glad when Dr. Morley's men finally came in and took him.

That was the end of it for Jesse. And this is where I would like to leave off. It is the next part that it is hardest for me to tell.

But the whole truth is that my aunt did more than just show herself to Jesse through the glass door. While she remained there her behavior was such that it made me understand for the first time that this was not merely the story of that purplish-black, kinky-headed Jesse's ruined life. It is the story of my aunt's pathetically unruined life, and my uncle's too, and even my own. I mean to say that at this moment I understood that Jesse's outside activities had been not only *his,* but *ours* too. My Uncle Andrew, with his double standard or triple standard—whichever it was—had most certainly forced Jesse's destruction upon him, and Aunt Margaret had made the complete destruction possible and desirable to him with her censorious words and looks. But they did it because they had to, because they were so dissatisfied with the pale *un*ruin of their own lives. They did it because something would not let them ruin their own lives as they wanted and felt a need to do—as I have often felt a need to do, myself. As who does not sometimes feel a need to do? Without knowing it, I think, Aunt Margaret wanted to see Jesse as he was that morning. And it occurs to me now that Dr. Morley understood this at the time.

The moment she left us to go to Jesse, the old doctor became silent. He and I stood on opposite sides of one of the troughs of cotton, each of us fumbling with samples we had picked up there. Dr. Morley carefully turned his back on the scene that was about to take place in the room beyond. I could not keep myself from watching it.

I think I had never seen my aunt hurry before. As soon as she had passed into the back display room she began running on tiptoe. Uncle Andrew heard her soft footfall. As he turned around, their eyes must have met. I saw Uncle's face and saw, or imagined I saw, the expression in his gray eyes—one of utter dismay. Yet I don't think this had anything to do with Aunt Margaret. It was Jesse who was on his mind. He could not believe that he had failed to bring Jesse to his senses. I suspect that when Aunt Margaret looked into his eyes she got the impression that her husband didn't at that moment know who in the world she was. Maybe at that moment *she* couldn't have said who *he* was. I imagine their eyes meeting like the eyes of strangers, perhaps two white people passing each other on some desolate back street in the toughest part of niggertown, each wondering what dire circumstances could have brought so nice-looking a person as the other to this unlikely neighborhood. . . . At last, when Aunt Margaret drew near the glass door, Uncle Andrew stepped aside and moved out of my view.

For a time she stood before the glass panel in silence. She was peering about the two rooms inside, looking for Jesse. At last, without ever seeing where he was, I suppose, she began speaking to him. Her words were not audible to me and almost certainly they weren't so to Jesse, who continued for some time to keep on with his moaning and praying, though seeing that she had come he didn't go on calling out for her. The voice she spoke to him in was utterly sweet and beautiful. I think she was quoting scripture to him part of the time—one of the Psalms, I believe. Instinctively, I began moving toward the doorway that joined the room I was in and the room she was in. It was the voice of that same Aunt Margaret who had spoken to me with so much kindness and sympathy and love in the days just after my mother died. I was barely able to keep from bursting into tears—tears of joy and exaltation.

Jesse didn't, as I have already said, come out and open the door. But at some point, which I didn't mark, he became quieter. Now there were only intermittent sobs and groans. After a while my aunt stopped speaking. She was searching again for his hiding place in there. Presently, Uncle Andrew appeared again. He came over to her and indicated that if she would stoop down she could see Jesse under the desk. He watched her very intently as she squatted there awkwardly before the door.

If it had seemed strange for me to see her running, a few minutes earlier, it seemed almost unbelievable now that I was seeing her squatting there that way on the floor. I watched her and I thought how unlike her it was. I think I know the very moment when she saw her friend Jesse. I could tell her body had suddenly gone perfectly rigid. She looked not like any woman I had ever seen but like some hideously angular piece of modern sculpture. And then, throwing her hands up to her face, she lost her balance. My uncle was quick and caught her before she fell. He brought her to her feet at once and as he did so he called out for assistance—not from me but from Dr. Morley. Dr. Morley brushed past me in the doorway, answering the call.

Even after she was on her feet she couldn't take her hands down from her face for several moments. When finally she did manage to do so, all her high color and all the brightness in her eyes had vanished. As they led her away it was hard to think of her as the same woman who had rested her hand on my sleeve only a little while ago. Had she really wanted to see Jesse as he was this morning? I think she had. But I think the sight of the animal crouched underneath my uncle's desk—and probably peering out at her—had been more than she was actually prepared to look upon. As she was led off by her husband and her doctor, I felt certain that Aunt Margaret had suffered a shock from which she would never recover.

But how mistaken I was about her recovery soon became clear. I waited around until Dr. Morley's men arrived and I watched them go in and take Jesse. Then I wandered through the other display rooms up to the front office, where most of the real paperwork of the firm was done and where my own desk was. The front office was really a part of the front display room, divided from it only by a little railing with a swinging gate. I knew I would find my aunt up there and I supposed I would find her lying down on the old leather couch just inside the railing. I could even imagine how Dr. Morley and my uncle, and probably one of the office girls, would be hovering about and administering to her. Yet it was a different scene I came on. Dr. Morley was seated at my desk taking down information which he said would be necessary for him to have about Jesse. He was writing it on the back of an envelope. Aunt Margaret was seated in a chair drawn up beside him. She seemed completely herself again. Uncle, standing on the other side of the doctor, was trying to supply the required information. But Aunt Margaret kept correcting most of the facts that Uncle Andrew gave. While the doctor listened with perfect patience, the two of them disputed silly points like Jesse's probable age and the correct spelling of his surname, whether it was "Munroe" or "Monroe," and what his mother's maiden name had been. . . . It was hard to believe that either Aunt Margaret or Uncle Andrew had any idea of what was happening to Jesse at that very moment or any feeling about it.

Dr. Morley had Jesse committed to the state asylum out at Bolivar. They locked him up for a while, then they made a trusty of him. Dr. Morley says he seems very happy and that he has made himself so useful that they will almost certainly never let him go. I have never been out there to see him, of course, and neither has Aunt Margaret or Uncle Andrew. But I have dreams about Jesse sometimes—absurd, wild dreams that are not like anything that ever happened. One night recently when I was at a dinner party at my uncle and aunt's apartment and someone was recalling Jesse's devotion to my uncle, I undertook to tell one of those dreams of mine. But I broke it off in the middle and pretended that that was all, because I saw my aunt, at the far end of the table, was looking as pale as if she had seen a ghost or as if I had been telling a dream that *she* had had. As soon as I stopped, the talk resumed its usual theme, and my aunt seemed all right again. But when our eyes met a few minutes later she sent me the same quick, disapproving glance that my mother used to send me at my grandfather's table when I was relating some childish nightmare I had had. "Don't bore people with what you dream," my mother used to say after we had left the table and were alone. "If you have nothing better than that to contribute, leave the talking to someone else." Aunt Margaret's rude glance said precisely that to me. But I must add that when we were leaving the dining room my aunt rested her hand rather firmly and yet tenderly on my arm as if to console and comfort me. She was by nature such a kind and gentle person that she could not bear to think she had hurt someone she loved.

A WALLED GARDEN

No, MEMPHIS IN AUTUMN has not the moss-hung oaks of Natchez. Nor, my dear young man, have we the exotic, the really exotic orange and yellow and rust foliage of the maples at Rye or Saratoga. When our five-month summer season burns itself out, the foliage is left a cheerless brown. Observe that Catawba tree beyond the wall; and the leaves under your feet here on the terrace are mustard and khaki colored; and the air, the atmosphere (who would dare to breathe a deep breath!) is virtually a sea of dust. But we do what we can. We've walled ourselves in here with these evergreens and box and jasmine. You must know, yourself, young man, that no beauty is native to us but the verdure of early summer. And it's as though I've had to take my finger, just so, and point out to Frances the lack of sympathy that there is in the climate and in the eroded countryside of this region. I have had to build this garden and say, "See, my child, how nice and sympathetic everything can be." But now she does see it my way, you understand. You understand, my daughter has finally made her life with me in this little garden plot, and year by year she has come to realize how little else there is hereabouts to compare with it.

And you, you know nothing of flowers? A young man who

doesn't know the zinnia from the aster! How curious that you
and my daughter should have made friends. I don't know under
what circumstances you two may have met. In her League work,
no doubt. She *throws* herself so into whatever work she under-
takes. Oh? Why, of course, I should have guessed. She simply
spent herself on the Chest Drive this year. . . . But my daughter has most of her permanent friends among the flower-minded
people. She makes so few friends nowadays outside of our little
circle, sees so few people outside our own garden here, really,
that I find it quite strange for there to be someone who doesn't
know flowers.

No, nothing, we've come to feel, is ever very lovely, really
lovely, I mean, in this part of the nation, nothing *but* this garden; and you can well imagine what even this little bandbox of a
garden once was. I created it out of a virtual chaos of a backyard
—Franny's playground, I might say. For three years I nursed that
little magnolia there, for one whole summer did nothing but
water the ivy on the east wall of the house; if only you could have
seen the scrubby hedge and the unsightly servants' quarters of
our neighbors that are beyond my serpentine wall (I suppose, at
least, they're still there). In those days it was all very different,
you understand, and Frances's father was about the house, and
Frances was a child. But now in the spring we have what is truly
a sweet garden here, modeled on my mother's at Rye; for three
weeks in March our hyacinths are an inspiration to Frances and
to me and to all those who come to us regularly; the larkspur and
marigold are heavenly in May over there beside the roses.

But you do not know the zinnia from the aster, young man?
How curious that you two should have become friends. And now
you are impatient with her, and you mustn't be; I don't mean to
be too indulgent, but she'll be along presently. Only recently
she's become incredibly painstaking in her toilet again. Whereas
in the last few years she's not cared so much for the popular fads
of dress. Gardens and floral design have occupied her—with
what guidance I could give—have been pretty much her life,
really. Now in the old days, I confess, before her father was taken
from us—I lost Mr. Harris in the dreadfully hot summer of '48

(people don't generally realize what a dreadful year that was—the worst year for perennials and annuals, alike, since Terrible '30. Things died that year that I didn't think would *ever* die. A dreadful summer)—why, she used then to run here and there with people of every sort, it seemed. I put no restraint upon her, understand. How many times I've said to my Franny, "You must make your own life, my child, as you would have it." Yes, in those days she used to run here and there with people of every sort and variety, it seemed to me. Where was it you say you met, for she goes so few places that are really *out* anymore? But Mr. Harris would let me put no restraint upon her. I still remember the strongheadedness of her teens that had to be overcome and the testiness in her character when she was nearer to twenty than thirty. And you should have seen her as a tot of twelve when she would be somersaulting and rolling about on this very spot. Honestly, I see that child now, the mud on her middy blouse and her straight yellow hair in her eyes.

When I used to come back from visiting my people at Rye, she would grit her teeth at me and give her confidence to the black cook. I would find my own child become a mad little animal. It was through this door here from the sun-room that I came one September afternoon—just such an afternoon as this, young man—still wearing my traveling suit, and called to my child across the yard for her to come and greet me. I had been away for the two miserable summer months, caring for my sick mother, but at the sight of me the little Indian turned and with a whoop she ran to hide in the scraggly privet hedge which was at the far end of the yard. I called her twice to come from out that filthiest of shrubs. "Frances Ann!" We used to call her by her full name when her father was alive. But she didn't stir. She crouched at the roots of the hedge and spied at her travel-worn mother between the leaves.

I pleaded with her at first quite indulgently and good-naturedly and described the new ruffled dress and the paper cut-outs I had brought from her grandmother at Rye. (I wasn't to have Mother much longer, and I knew it, and it was hard to come home to this kind of scene.) At last I threatened to withhold my presents until Thanksgiving or Christmas. The cook in the kitchen may have heard some change in my tone, for she came to the kitchen door over beyond the latticework which we've since put up, and looked out first at me and then at the child. While I was threatening, my daughter crouched in the dirt and began to mumble things to herself which I could not hear, and the noises she made were like those of an angry little cat. It seems that it was a warmer afternoon than this one—but my garden does deceive—and I had been moving about in my heavy traveling suit. In my exasperation I stepped out into the rays of the sweltering sun, and into the yard which I so detested; and I uttered in a scream the child's full name, "Frances Ann Harris!" Just then the black cook stepped out onto the back porch, but I ordered her to return to the kitchen. I began to cross the yard toward Frances Ann—that scowling little creature who was *incredibly* the same Frances you've met—and simultaneously she began to crawl along the hedgerow toward the wire fence that divided my property from the neighbor's.

I believe it was the extreme heat that made me speak so very harshly and with such swiftness as to make my words incomprehensible. When I saw that the child had reached the fence and intended climbing it, I pulled off my hat, tearing my veil to pieces as I hurried my pace. I don't actually know what I was saying—I probably couldn't have told you even a moment later—and I didn't even feel any pain from the turn which I gave my ankle in the gully across the middle of the yard. But the child kept her nervous little eyes on me and her lips continued to move now and again. Each time her lips moved I believe I must have raised my voice in more intense rage and greater horror at her ugliness. And so, young man, striding straight through the hedge I reached her before she had climbed to the top of the wire fencing. I think I took her by the arm above the elbow, about here, and I said something like, "I shall have to punish you, Frances Ann." I did not jerk her. I didn't jerk her one bit, as she wished to make it appear, but rather, as soon as I touched her, she relaxed her hold on the wire and fell to the ground. But she lay there—in her canniness—only the briefest moment looking up and past me through the straight hair that hung over her face like an untrimmed mane. I had barely ordered her to rise when she sprang up and moved with such celerity that she soon was out of my reach again. I followed—running in those high heels—and this time I turned my other ankle in the gully, and I fell there on the ground in that yard, this garden. You won't believe it—pardon, I must sit down. . . . I hope you don't think it too odd, me telling you all this. . . . You won't believe it: I lay there in the ditch and she didn't come to aid me with childish apologies and such, but instead she deliberately climbed into her swing that hung from the dirty old poplar that was here formerly (I have had it cut down and the roots dug up) and she began to swing, not high and low, but only gently, and stared straight down at her mother through her long hair—which, you may be sure, young man, I had cut the very next day at my own beautician's and curled into a hundred ringlets.

ALLEGIANCE

"COME IN." And: "Of course I remember you and knew I should the moment your voice came drawling on the wire."

The first one, two, three steps I take across the room are taken with trepidation. And, so to speak, in midair. I am afraid that I shall yield, for even at her age the old creature is still a great beauty. And there is about her, after all, that charm which has long been discredited in my mind.

As she rings for tea I perceive that in her simplest gestures, in her smile, even in her old-lady dress there is that fascination about her which we, who knew her as children, have remembered as her "romantic quality." I discover in an instant that we have been mistaken to suppose her romantic quality was either vulgar ostentation or mere shallow vanity. And now that she is before me I know that I do not remember her, for herself, at all.

"I remember you so well, dear child, in your blue and red rompers and of course those fearful black stockings your mother would have you wear." Now I am in the air again, treading air. I can feel myself recoil at the bare reference to a woman whom she once grievously wronged, draw back at her mention of a sister she cheated in a manner so subtle and base that we have never known nor wished to know its nature, and now never shall.

Here in her little drawing room, the marble mantel lined with her famous figurines, the Japanese screen shielding her diminutive writing desk, and a lampshade dull gold stamped with fleur-de-lis, I feel myself withdraw momentarily to the bosom of a family that has been nursed on hatred of the mistress of this room. The tea is being served, but I feel that there is less reality to the moment and to the noise of the teacups than to many an hour I have sat with the others at coffee pondering a heritage of resentment against this elegant Londoner.

"I remember you better than the others, I should say. You were all of you quiet children, like your mother, but there were occasions when you alone were like my garrulous self. I used to have at my fingertips bright things you had said to me—impudent things about something I wore or something I said. . . . But, alas, alas, I've reached an age at which the incidents of my own childhood and events of my young-ladyhood are a wee bit clearer than those of the dull years since." (I smile to hear her say "dull years," but she thinks I smile because I do not know her age.) "I suspect I'm a bit older than you guess. Your mother and I were sisters, you might say, in fact only. I was a young lady in Nashville the year she was born. I was always more aunt than sister to her. I am more of the generation of your cousin, Ellen Ballenger, who was a sort of double first cousin of ours. To be exact, Ellen was first cousin to Mama and first cousin once removed to your grandfather."

She is pouring the tea now, and this is absentminded talk. I listen but I am thinking all the while of how strange it is to hear old familiar relationships rehearsed so easily in her rather too broad English speech. She seems to have lapsed for a moment into the character of an uninteresting old Britisher recalling certain family ties of her people down in Devon or Dorset. But now she looks up to hand me my tea, saying, "Or do we still say 'first cousin once removed' in Tennessee?"

Her face colors a little as our eyes meet. Then she laughs and nervously she jingles the gold bracelets on her wrist; I observe that life has aged her more than I had at once perceived. For she

has just now become utterly engrossed in the pleasurable reitera-
tion of those old family ties.

But her laughter, which for one second has seemed as remote
a sound as was the look in her eyes abstracted, is now present in
the room again. Her eyes shine again with a light that is expressive and responsive. "How wicked of me to treat you so, to bore
you with tedious things you know by heart. The longer you sit
there the better I do remember you. It's a rather shocking trans-
formation, you'll grant, from red rompers with a scalloped collar
to the olive drab. It was not until I was addressing my note to
you that I pictured you in uniform. Even with the war all about
us here I had not connected events at all. I knew merely that you
were in this country. (Dear old Mr. Gordon enclosed the address
with my last American check.) And so, you see, it was not war-
time sentiment that moved me to ask you here. Further, hadn't I
put myself out on a limb, rather? I was not certain that you
would bother to come." (Yet she had presumed to think I might.
She has thought that one of us might have a change of heart
after many years.) "I was not certain that you would bother to
come, for very often young men haven't much interest in their
kin. Perhaps you have given up something you would like to do
this afternoon only to come here. . . . But there I go playing
the old lady again."

And now I have the sense of being ignored, or of having my
rudeness ignored. I feel an express shame, not of my rudeness,
but of all the uncertainties of my mind as I sit in the presence of
one so self-possessed. The direct and attentive gaze of her eyes is
modest, even shy in a sense, yet she seems as conscious of the
engaging qualities of her personality as of the pleasant effect of
this little drawing room she has arranged with the light now
falling from the west windows across the patterns of the carpet.
While she talks I study the burgundy roosters in the patterns
and once again the figurines of Louis Napoleon and Nell Gwynn
and John Brown with their little china backs reflected in the
mirror over the mantel. She is perceiving that I am "quiet" like
my mother, and she is set now to support the conversation alone.
I hear her. I raise my eyebrows. I nod agreement. I frown. Or I

smile so genuinely that she is silent a moment to enjoy the satisfaction of her jest. I even remark on the irony of something, but my sentence is complete in itself and she has no illusion that I'm going to be a real talker after all. She doesn't try to draw me out. But while she speaks and while I listen I am also thinking that at some point I have betrayed, or at some point I shall betray, someone or something.

I am remembering little notes that my mother used to read aloud, notes placed unanswered on the fire in the parlor at Nashville. Now I can visualize their being penned at this little desk shielded by the Japanese screen. I can picture her counting such notes among correspondence that she must "take care of" on a day when the weather isn't fine. Mere polite inquiries they were into the health of us all with a few chatty words at the end about how early a spring London was enjoying that year or some amusing and endearing household incident—something about her ancient, now dead, but once ever-ailing English husband or about her adored stepchildren. They were notes written in an even hand and there was never any rancor or remorse in them. And there was no reference, ever, to my mother's failure to reply. Their tone presumed it to be simply a matter of temperament. She was a person who *did* write letters, my mother a "quiet" person who *didn't*. But my mother used to say, "It's beautiful, beautiful. Her selfish ends are long since accomplished. Now she develops a sort of mystical, superhuman ignorance of what has been transpiring."

My aunt's figure is thin and erect, though her clothing is draped to conceal her thinness. Presently in the midst of her portrayal of three English types that are to be avoided (if one is to admire Englishmen), I realize that she is not ignoring me or my rudeness or even my innocent silence. These are things that she is coping with. It is only that I am suffering still from the shock of the greater ignorance she pretends to. I am no longer asking how did she dare to presume that I should not return her invitation unopened (as all the other notes since my mother's lifetime have been returned). I am no longer asking how or why; for her manner, her personal appearance, even her little drawing

room all bespeak her confidence in and her concern only for
what is actual. What is more, they express as well her faith in the
actual's being but the sum of a thousand accidents.

And that our meeting is a circumstance that she has ardently
desired and wished to bring about there can be no doubt. I am
certain, further, that she has known it could come about in just
such a form as would allow all the privilege she is now exercising
—namely, the privilege of assuming all such ignorance as should
seem fitting—only by accident or by a series of accidents. In
some corner of her mind there has ever been an awareness that
these accidents might currently be casting themselves one upon
the other. And so it must have appeared to her through the years
that any little message which she could so easily scratch off
might be the last, the efficient accident that the rest of the world
would put down as the cause of our meeting.

"If these were normal times, nothing would please me more
than to offer myself as your guide to England and the English.
But how futile to speak of it even. You are in London on some
terribly official business, no doubt, or on a leave so short that it
will be over before you've got round to half the things you want
to do. Likely you do not even want to understand this country.
You want only to accomplish your mission and get yourself home
again. I have been thinking as we sat here that you might be
wondering how a person could bring herself to know . . . I
know how you silent people are. You have more thoughts than
the rest of us dare suppose. I should hate to have to answer all
the questions in the minds of people who have sat quietly while I
talked on. And if I tried I could answer this one least well of all.
My answer is, I do not know. But you must have observed that
everyone has some aunt or other who has simply pulled out . . .
pulled out on the family with not so much as a by-your-leave. I'm
just another of those aunts that people have. The world's full of
them."

I think: The degree of her long anxiety for the special accidental qualities which would make up the naturalness of our meeting
is patent in the pleasure she takes from its realization.

"What of my own aunts! But you never knew—perhaps never

heard of—the aunts I think of, did you? Yet I remember them so much better than so many people since their time. It is incredible how long people can be dead while their voices and even the moles on their necks are remembered by someone."

I think: The degree of her long anxiety for this meeting without *conditions,* for this easy manner of meeting and her clear vision of the necessity of this ease now seem to me to have been hidden through all the years in the sensible, persistent irregularity of her notes to my mother and later to the individual children. I feel now how right were my mother's claims that this woman could endure anything to gain her ends. For it is as though in her anxiety she has known, too, how unpredictable were her chances.

But are her ends merely this in-person, this final, bold pretense at ignorance of her old wrong against my mother? If this is the depth of the interview's meaning for her, then I am tired of it already. If this is all, then I have satisfied my curiosity about her appearance and her apartments and I am ready to ask for my hat. Yet I do not even steal a glance in the direction of the small chair where my coat and cap are placed. And I ask myself, is it at this point that I betray?

Or was it when I opened her invitation (opened one of the notes our silent pact had forbidden us to do) that I betrayed? Or will it be later when I have listened? She has settled herself now in her chair. She has accepted a cigarette from my case. She is talking of those great-aunts of mine who long ago went off to Washington and St. Louis to live with their husbands, women whom even my mother could hardly have remembered. Her speech is casual, and she appears at first to be rambling through a mixture of recent events and old memories.

Yet withal she now seems quite consciously allowing herself to become thus engrossed in things that she formerly asked my pardon for. She talks of London, and with a twinkle in her eye she speaks of the tediousness of being cut off from the Continent. Whatever are her ends I know that they are somewhere beyond a desire to play her role convincingly to the last. She seems hardly concerned with her role at all. I gasp a gasp that must be audible, because I recognize that she is still depending upon accidents, terrible accidents that are now possible within myself, in my own perceptions. She has the air of having given way to her woolgathering. *After all,* she is thinking, *the part that I can play in making him see is too small for consideration on any level.* As I read her conscious thoughts I am asking myself whether she, not subconsciously but in a consciousness too profound for such a stranger as I to read, can be attributing some magic potency to the mere actuality of this moment, to the actuality of any given moment, even to her faith in the solidness of the precious objects of her drawing room, to the sound of her own voice. If so, then, for her, each moment and indeed everything in the life and body of the world must have in itself a latent magic which might be exploited. I feel that I am in the presence of some newfangled sort of idolater and conjurer. As she speaks I become increasingly aware that she believes it is no matter now what incident or what old wives' tale she may relate, that she considers that whatever words she uses or however her conversation may turn there is but one thing she *can* say and there is no predicting what turn of her mind or speech might be the singular accident that would mean my comprehension.

But I hear only isolated sentences and snatches of sentences.

There are moments when I feel that I have dozed.

Yet I am in no sense drowsy.

Much less do I feel any boredom.

On the contrary it is a sort of literal enchantment I am caught in where all the past and all the future and all occurrences of the exterior world are of no consequence. Even the thing she has said a moment ago or the conclusion she will presently bring out are utterly lacking in any interest for me though her actual words in that split moment when they proceed from her lips consume my whole attention. Sometimes she is speaking of people who figure, or who have figured, in her life. "Mr. Williams always remembered Merle mercifully, I think." I wonder if I have smiled now when I should have frowned. She tells me that some other person she knows has always the air, with strangers, of himself being an angel entertained unawares. This gentleman will smile afterward, she says, and remark that the stranger was kind to him for no reason at all. It is, my aunt thinks, as if to say that he feels there is a perfectly good reason why the stranger should be kind to him if the stranger only knew *who* he is.

This man is probably someone here in London. But presently it seems to be of my own grandmother who has lain for forty years in a remote and neglected graveyard in Tennessee of whom she is speaking. "She was an extremely narrow and provincial woman, but this much must be said in her favor: If she never showed any originality in her housekeeping she was as well never guilty of any superficiality. Things were always easy. She knew what she was about. There was never any silly bustling when guests came, no matter how fine."

Finally her voice stops, and I wish that it had not stopped. It is as though some piece of furniture in the room had suddenly collapsed, even the chair I sit in. I come to my feet without knowing why I have risen. And immediately she rises with the same suddenness. "Perhaps, you would . . ." She hesitates. But she has regained her composure almost before I recognize her loss of it. She turns with all ease, making a gesture toward the marble mantel, and this time I do steal a glance at my things on the fragile chair.

But the cap and the dull-colored coat have lost that quality which meant the probability of my departure. They mean no more than that I am actually here. Yet I realize that it is because I have entertained no thought of leaving just now that I dared turn my eyes to them, and I only wanted to see if there would be any temptation, or rather to see if I had lost all will to go. And so I am conscious again of betrayal and still do not know whether it is a possibility or a fact. My betrayal is like some boundless fear that has really had no beginning in me and can have no end. This room and this old woman and this woman's voice constitute the only certainty. I feel strangely that I must remain until I can identify my guilt or possible guilt with some moment of the visit if not with some object in the room or some trick of her behavior. And so now I say to myself that she has been right, that all experience can be translated into the terms of any one moment of life if one believes sufficiently in the reality of that moment. "Young man, would you be good enough to admire my figurines." Her smile is full of irony. "They are said to be world famous and of inestimable value."

I have hurried to join her before the mantel. I allow her to see that she has remembered correctly my having flashes of garrulousness like her own. I chatter about John Brown and remark endlessly upon the cunningness of the little nigger who stands at his side with John Brown's pink china hand on his coal black head. I reveal my pedantry asking if it was not for Nell Gwynn that all flowers were pulled from some London park. I laugh at the face of Louis Napoleon.

I find suddenly that we are laughing together at the ridiculous sort of dignity which the artist has faithfully, if unknowingly, represented in the delicate figurine of the bourgeois emperor. Our eyes meet in the glass for an instant. Presently I see the whole room reflected there. I see the two of us looking over the heads of the world-famous figurines. I catch the sound of our commingled laughter.

Then we are facing each other again and she is saying, "What if I should ask you to leave now, should ask you to go now and come again to finish our visit some other afternoon, would you think me too insufferably odd and rude? Would you?"

And before I have thought or considered what I am saying, "But I cannot come here again."

At first her countenance seems frozen in an austerity that is totally disarming to me after so much geniality. Her glance is set for a moment on some object in a far corner of the room. It might almost be my own cap and coat, yet I know it is not with an object that she is concerned. Rather, it is the thing I have just said. She is giving its meaning her most serious consideration.

While she does so, I realize the peculiar turn our intercourse has taken. In my voice there has been almost a plea to allow me to remain since I could not come here again. But it was to say: *I have come here and glimpsed the unique sort of power and truth you have discovered or created, but now I wish to remain to disprove its worth.* Perhaps that is how she is interpreting it. Or perhaps she thinks I have been unaffected by the interview and want only to cause her all possible discomfort before I leave.

Yet of course she at last sees the thing as it is. She sees that I spoke before I thought, and laughing she shrouds herself again in her grand ignorance. "Of course you can come back, dear child, if you will. Let's say good-bye and plan on another afternoon."

Having once spoken plainly it is easy to speak plainly again. "Then I must ask you a question. I want to know why you suddenly desire me to go."

· As each moment passes my departure seems to become more difficult for me. I turn with the same abruptness with which I have spoken and go to one of the long windows that overlook the quiet street and park.

There is no sound in the room, and I know that she is still standing there before the mantel. Finally her voice comes groping, yet with confidence in its effect, "Then you do think me rude."

"I don't understand, of course." But I imply that I should listen to explanation. I turn and face her. Our smiles are like smiles in photographs. "You asked your nephew to tea, my dear aunt. I suppose I am only surprised at what a very short teatime you have. I thought you English lingered over tea things."

"See here," she says coming toward me, "there is no great mystery. To be very frank, I have an engagement I had forgotten. I mixed my days. But it is one I intend keeping."

"Certainly it must be important."

"Yes, it's important as an old lady's social engagements go. But if I should describe it you would laugh."

"I should laugh. Yet it is important?"

She drops her eyes. And with her eyelids still closed—broad wrinkled, powdered lids—she says, "I promised someone I'd keep it, you see."

"Oh, it's your word and not the engagement that matters."

"You could understand that?" she asks with her eyes still closed, and I can imagine an echo to her last word "that."

I make my answer with a nod, as though not knowing that her closed eyes mean she cannot see me. But actually I do know that she has not yet my answer; and simultaneously I am filled with disgust for her and with a desire to tiptoe from her presence before she looks up again, for surely this is *it*. Once again I think I am free of the spell of this room. I can almost visualize a pure and self-righteous darkness in which I suspect she is holding herself behind those wrinkled lids. I feel that she has created a terrible war and brought me halfway round the world to prove that she, an old lady in a London apartment, can keep her word in some matter of etiquette. But the harm is not in its being only a small matter of decorum. The harm suddenly appears to be strangely in the altruism, the mere keeping of her word. It is as if her life which she has twisted and formed so willfully has been but a vast circle by which route she has returned to the simple sort of truths that my mother possessed in the beginning. I shall leave now believing what I wished to believe and what this room and this woman have for a time caused me to doubt: that my mother was good because she was simple and unworldly, that my aunt is evil because she is complicated and worldly.

Then in an instant all of my victory is swept from me by the mere opening of her large, handsome, articulate blue eyes. Her last question is now translated and spoken by her eyes. But there is also the further question, "Could you understand more?" And whatever my dull eyes may reply, her lips part and she speaks with new indirectness.

"No. It is not my word. It is something much smaller." A new earnestness has come over her countenance. It is she that has withdrawn from me now. The final accident did not occur. She is no longer hoping that I may see. I know that by "smaller" she means "larger," but beyond that I cannot conceive of what is in her mind. She gives me her hand. As we say good-bye I hear the jingling of her bracelets and observe the barely perceptible twitch at the corner of her mouth.

Now I am outside her door and on the stairs with my military coat over my arm. I wonder, with an insipid smile on my lips, at my own brutality. Have I been a soldier frightening an old lady at teatime? But as I descend the stairs, her face is before me as it was by the window when she raised the wide, wrinkled lids and exposed the brilliant blue of her eyes. I hear again the jingling of her bracelets. And it is then, suddenly recalling now the hard circles of gold rested on the ancient skin drawn over the ungainly wristbone, that I am filled with awe and with a sort of fear as of some fate I might have met at her hands. I feel that I have been in the presence of a withered savage tribeswoman, at the mercy of her absolute authority. But when finally I have passed through the vestibule and out onto the sidewalk and have inhaled gratefully the free air of the cleanswept city street there is no sense of freedom. As I wander in the half-light of evening through the wide thoroughfares and the broad squares of this foreign place, it all seems suddenly as familiar as my mother's parlor; and though my mind is troubled by a doubt of the reality of all things and I am haunted for a while by an unthinkable distrust for the logic and the rarefied judgments of my dead mother, I feel myself still a prisoner in her parlor at Nashville with the great sliding doors closed and the jagged little flames darting from the grate.

THE LITTLE COUSINS

To THE ANNUAL Veiled Prophet's Ball children were not cordially invited. High up in the balcony, along with servants and poor relations, they were tolerated. Their presence was even sometimes suffered in the lower tiers and, under certain circumstances, even down in the boxes. But, generally speaking, children were expected to enjoy the Prophet's parade the night before and be content to go to bed without complaint on the night of the Ball. This was twenty-five years ago, of course. There is no telling what the practices are out there in St. Louis now. Children have it much better everywhere nowadays. Perhaps they flock to the Veiled Prophet's Ball by the hundred, and even go to the Statler Hotel for breakfast afterward.

But I can't help hoping they don't. I hope they are denied something. Else what do they have that's tangible to hold against the grown-ups? My sister and I were denied *every*thing. She more than I, since a boy naturally didn't want so much—or so much of what it was St. Louis seemed to offer us. Having less to complain of myself, however, I undertook to suffer a good many things for Corinna. And she suffered a few for me. We were motherless, and very close to each other at times.

What I suffered for Corinna I suffered in silence. But the

grand thing about Corinna was that she could always find the right words for my feelings as well as her own. The outrage I felt, for example, at our being always taken down to Sportsman's Park to see the Browns play and never the Cardinals left me grimly inarticulate. But Corinna would say for me that it seemed "such an empty glory" to have box seats at the Browns' games. "Any fool had rather sit in the bleachers and watch the Cardinals," she said, "than have the very best box seats to see a Browns' game." She phrased things beautifully. At our house we had always to serve Dr Pep instead of Coca-Cola. Of this Corinna said, "It makes us seem so provincial." But we both knew that with a father like ours we just had to endure these embarrassments. According to Corinna, Daddy was "blind to the disadvantage he put us at"—disadvantage, that is, with our friends at Mary Institute and Country Day. What's more, she had divined at an early age what it was that blinded Daddy: It was always some friend or other of his who owned or manufactured the product imposed on us. We even had Bessie Calhoun because of one of his friends —Bessie, from Selma, Alabama, instead of some stylish, white foreign governess who might be teaching us French or German. "Except for Bessie," Corinna said, "we would be bilingual, like the Altvaders and the Tomlinsons."

The year Corinna and I were finally taken to the Ball, the project was kept a secret from us until the last moment—or practically. I came in from school at five-thirty, and Corinna had got home two hours before that, as usual. At the side door, which Bessie made us use on all days but Sunday in order to save "her floors," Corinna was waiting for me with narrow eyes and pursed lips. "You and I are going to the VP tonight," she said, "but they couldn't permit us the pleasures of anticipation. Isn't that typical?" The news had been broken to her when she came in from school and told Bessie she was going down the block to play. Corinna was already twelve at this time, and though at school she would never deign to associate with girls in the lower grades, out of school she spent most of her time playing with the younger children in our block. The little girls adored her, and I used to watch her sometimes, mothering them and supervising their games. She never seemed happier than then, and she often spoke of the younger children as her "little cousins." This, I suppose, was in fond allusion to all the tales we had listened to from Daddy, and from Bessie, too, about the horde of first, second and third cousins they each had grown up among—Daddy in Kentucky, Bessie in Alabama. At any rate, when Bessie told her she had to stay in and do her homework that afternoon, Corinna wasn't satisfied until she had wrung the reason out of her, and then, of course, she was indignant.

"*Why* didn't you tell me before, Bessie?" she said. "Two other girls in my class were lording it over everybody else today because *they're* going."

"That's it," said Bessie. "I didn't want you lording it over everybody you saw today. That's not the way I'm bringing you up. And I didn't want you being flighty about your lessons."

Corinna knew that Daddy must have told her not to tell us. Or she knew at least that Bessie had got his approval. Yet Bessie always pretended to do everything absolutely on her own authority. And this made life more difficult. This made us forget that she was merely someone hired to take charge of us. It made us try to reason with her about things, made us pretend to be sick sometimes in order to break down her resistance, made us nag at her continually for all kinds of privileges. Bessie's utter disregard for what we considered justice and reason was something else that made us forget who she was, and she never showed any fear of our telling on her or going over her head. Her favorite answer to our "whys" was "Because I said so" or "Because I said to." And if one of us gobbled up his dessert and begged for a share of the other's, Bessie was as apt as not to make the other one share. She was illogical, and she was inconsistent. When we were disobedient, she would hand out terrible punishments—dessertless days and movieless weekends—but then sometimes she would forget, or weaken of her own accord at the last moment. You could not tell about her.

There was her brutal frankness, too. Though she was as blind as Daddy to any need of ours to have our egos bolstered—such as by serving our friends the right drink—and as blind as he to our

deep moral and intellectual failings—failings that we ourselves
were aware of and often confessed to each other—still she never
failed to notice the least sign of vanity in either of us. Corinna
was beginning to worry about her looks, and when she asked
Bessie whether she thought she would grow up to be as beautiful
as a certain Mary Elizabeth Caswell, Bessie said, "Your legs are
too thin. You'll have to do a lot of filling out before you can talk
about that." I was proud of my drawing ability, and I tried to get
Bessie to say she thought I might grow up to be an artist. "Do
you like nature?" she said, and I had to admit what she already
knew: Flowers and trees had little attraction for me. Bessie only
shook her head and gave me a doubting look.

Yet when I was sick in bed with mumps or measles she would
often read my palm, and, among other glories, she saw that I
would be a great musician. I objected that the singing teacher at
school said I couldn't even carry a tune. "What does *he* know
about how you may change if you keep trying? I know how little
teachers know." It was when we were sick that we discovered
Bessie's real talents and saw how indulgent she could be when
she had a mind to. This made us sick a good deal; and pretended
illness was one of our moral failings that Bessie was blind to. I
never knew her to doubt a headache or a stomachache or even "a
funny feeling all over." When we were sick, she played cards
with us, told our fortunes, read to us.

She read to us a lot even when we were well. She had taught
school in Alabama before she came north and went into service,
but it wasn't the kind of stories we were used to in St. Louis
schools that she read to us. She read "Unc' Edinburg's
Drowndin' " and "No Haid Pawn," and her favorites were the
Post stories by Octavus Roy Cohen. When she read us those
stories, she would sometimes throw back her head and laugh and
slap her thigh the way she never did about anything else. We
loved hearing her read, but we didn't ourselves think the stories
were so funny. "Never mind," said Bessie. "*You* don't have to
think they're funny."

In conversation Bessie had only two real subjects, and one of
them was Mary Elizabeth Caswell. Mary Elizabeth was bane of

Corinna's existence. Bessie had brought up Mary Elizabeth to the age of thirteen. When our mother died, Mr. Caswell had sent Bessie over to us—supposedly for only a few days. I was five at the time and Corinna was eight. Mr. Caswell came to our house on several occasions during those first days and had long conferences with Bessie; it was finally decided between them that she would stay with us. Probably Mr. Caswell felt that Daddy's need was greater than his own. Though Mary Elizabeth was motherless, too, it was already known that Mr. Caswell was going to marry again within a few months. Besides, not only was Mary Elizabeth a big girl then, but her mother had been of an old family in the city and there was an abundance of aunts and other female relatives to guide her. And so *we* got Bessie, with the result that Corinna had to "spend her life," as she said, listening to unfavorable comparisons of herself to Mary Elizabeth.

Bessie's other subject was her own family down in Alabama and, more particularly, her half sister, Lilly Belle Patton. Lilly Belle was a saint. Bessie assured us that Lilly Belle was nothing like her, had none of her bad temper and selfish ways, was always doing for others and asked nothing for herself. Lilly Belle was the finest-looking, the smartest, and the best-natured of all Bessie's mama's eleven children. Yet she hadn't insisted on going through high school, the way Bessie had, and she hadn't married. Bessie not only went through school and took to teaching afterward but the money she made teaching she spent foolishly —not on her mama, who was pretty greedy about money anyway, but on first one husband and then another. But Lilly Belle was content to stay at home and help Mama, who was certainly never much help to herself. Lilly Belle took in washing and looked after her little half brothers and sisters, of which Bessie was next to youngest, and even "adopted-like" two orphaned cousins. She was a hard church worker, a beautiful seamstress and laundress, she was the best cook in the whole town of Selma, she kept a garden that was the envy of everyone.

Corinna and I never tired of hearing about Lilly Belle, but for Corinna the most interesting part always was Lilly Belle's courtship. Lilly Belle never felt she could go off and marry while the younger children were still at home to be looked after, and by the time the younger ones were up and gone ("gone to the bad, most of them") Mama was too old to leave at home alone. But Lilly Belle had a faithful suitor, who had been waiting for her through all the years. He was, in fact, still waiting, and Lilly Belle wasn't even engaged to him. Sometimes Bessie had letters from a neighbor friend telling her she ought to make Lilly Belle have pity on Mr. Barker. It seems that on summer evenings he and Lilly Belle kept company sitting together on her front porch. Neighbors would hear their voices over there, and sometimes they would hear Mr. Barker break down and cry as he begged her "at least to get engaged" to him. But Lilly Belle knew what was right; she had taken a vow not even to get *engaged* while Mama lived. Sometimes, too, there would be a letter that Lilly Belle had asked the neighbor friend to write Bessie, warning her that Mama was "low sick." Bessie always "reckoned" Mama was really going this time. And Corinna would be on tenterhooks about it for days. She would try to linger in the mornings till the postman came, and she would rush home from school in the afternoon to see if there was any news. "If Mama goes this time," she would ask, "will Lilly Belle really get engaged to Mr. Barker?" And Bessie would reply, "Of course she will. She hasn't kept him waiting for nothing."

The unfavorable comparisons that Bessie made between herself and Lilly Belle were much more severe than those she made between Corinna and Mary Elizabeth. Yet, quite naturally, Corinna was able to think of Lilly Belle as a heroine of pure romance, whereas she saw Mary Elizabeth as a "pampered, spoiled, stuck-up thing." The worst of it was, Corinna was subject to wearing hand-me-downs from Mary Elizabeth. There was no need for it, of course, but Mr. Caswell and Daddy were that close. Or perhaps Bessie Calhoun was still *that* close to the Caswell family. The dresses would just appear in Corinna's closet and be allowed to hang there for her to ignore until she could resist them no longer. Once she had taken them down and begun wearing them, they became her favorite dresses. She may have managed to forget who it was they had belonged to. Or, without admitting it to me and perhaps to herself, she may have remembered how lovely Mary Elizabeth had looked in them; because Corinna had never lacked opportunity for observing Mary Elizabeth Caswell firsthand. The older girl and Corinna were in the same school together until Corinna was ten. After that, Mary Elizabeth went off to finishing school for two years, but even so she was home for all the holidays, and she and her father and the stepmother would be at our house for meals or we would be at their house. Daddy, during these two years, had begun going about with a very stylish-looking young widow, who was a close friend of Mr. Caswell's second wife. Corinna and I knew this lady then as Mrs. Richards. It was not to be long before she would become our stepmother—a fact that deserves mention only because it explains why our family and the Caswells were now thrown together still more than formerly.

Bessie Calhoun had a clear recollection of every mark Mary Elizabeth ever received in the lower grades at Mary Institute. "Because of Mary Elizabeth," said Corinna, "I have to live in mortal dread of not making the honor roll." At an early age, Mary Elizabeth could cook and sew in a way that promised to rival the arts of Lilly Belle. This information cost Corinna many precious hours that might have been spent with her "little cousins." And because Mary Elizabeth had had a little pansy garden of her own, Corinna was sent "grubbing in the earth" every spring. On the other hand, Mary Elizabeth was almost certainly not the reader that Corinna was, or not the reader of novels— the old best-sellers on the shelves of what had been our mother's sitting room. One day Corinna inquired after Mary Elizabeth's reading habits. Bessie didn't answer right away—something unusual for her. "At your age that child read the Bible, honey." Corinna opened her mouth in astonishment and then she closed it again without saying anything. This was one time when both she and I doubted Bessie's veracity, but Corinna let it pass. There was a limit to what she would undertake. She never raised the question again.

We knew perfectly well why we were being taken to the Veiled Prophet's Ball. This was the year that Mary Elizabeth Caswell was going to be presented. As a matter of fact, Corinna had nagged Daddy about it one Sunday afternoon in the early fall. Since Mary Elizabeth was to be one of the debutantes this year, didn't he think Bessie might take us to watch from the balcony? ("Mary Elizabeth ought to be good for *something* to us," she had said to me in private beforehand.) But Daddy replied, "Don't be silly. You couldn't either of you stay awake that late. You can come downtown and watch the parade from my office the night before. One school night out will be enough." And, of course, we did go down and watch the parade. In fact, we went downtown for dinner with Daddy and Mrs. Richards, and the Caswells and some other grown-ups joined us at the office afterward. They all had a party, with drinks and hors d'oeuvres, while we tossed confetti out the window and watched the floats go by. I hadn't even realized that Mary Elizabeth wasn't present until Mrs. Caswell came over to the window where we were and said, "Mary Elizabeth's out with some of her own crowd, Corinna. But she told me to give you her love and say she would be thinking about you tomorrow night. She's dying for you to see her dress."

Suddenly Corinna leaned so far out the window that I thought she was sure to fall, and I grabbed hold of her.

"Stop it, stupid," she hissed. "Here comes the Prophet's float. The parade's nearly over."

Just below us was passing the last of the countless tableaux representing life in French colonial times and in the days of the Louisiana Territory. We had seen Lewis and Clark, Marquette and Joliet, Indians, fur traders, French peasant girls, river bullies from the days of the keelboat and the pirogue. The parade had begun, for some reason, with Jean Lafitte in the Old Absinthe House at New Orleans, and the final tableau was of Thomas Jefferson signing the Louisiana Purchase. Beyond Jefferson, in his oversized wig and silk knee breeches, I could see the Prophet's float approaching. But I knew that for me the best part of the parade was already over. After so many Indians and fur traders, after the French explorers, after the pirates, the Prophet, with his veil-hidden face and all his Eastern finery, was bound to seem an anticlimax. I stood beside Corinna, hardly watching the royal float go by. As she continued to lean far out over the window ledge, I quietly took hold of the sash of her dress and, without her knowing it, held on to it tightly as long as we remained at the window.

The night of the Ball, we had an early dinner without Daddy. He came in and went up to dress while we were still at the table. After dinner, he sent for us to come to his room, where he said that he wanted us to behave ourselves that night "as never before." He was going out to dinner with the Caswells and Mrs. Richards and some other friends, but he would send the car and chauffeur to fetch us to the Colosseum. He didn't tell us that Bessie wasn't going to accompany us or that we would be sitting with him in one of the boxes downstairs.

And Bessie herself withheld this information till the very last. When it was finally divulged, we had already been so dazzled by another piece of news that the evening before us and these unexpected arrangements seemed of little consequence. When we were both dressed, we went into the sewing room, where Bessie always sat in the evening, to have her look us over.

"How do I look?" Corinna asked.

"You look fine," said Bessie. Then she saw Corinna eyeing herself in the mirror stand, and she added, "But no better than you should."

Corinna went up on her tiptoes and said, "I ought to have on heels."

"Behave yourself tonight, Corinna," Bessie said. "And see that *he* does." She didn't look at me, even. Then leaning back in her chair she said, "I've got something to tell both of you."

"What?" said Corinna.

"I want you to behave yourself next week, too."

"Oh, I thought it was something," said Corinna.

"It *is* something. They've sent for me down home. I'll be gone on the train before you get home tonight."

Corinna stared at Bessie in the mirror. "It's Mama?" she asked, breathless. *"Tell* me, Bessie!"

Bessie nodded. "She's dead. She's been dead for two days. I've just been waiting around here to get tonight over."

Corinna observed a moment of silence. She knew that Mama had been "no pleasure to herself or anybody else" for several years now. Further, she knew that she had never heard Bessie say one good word for her mama, and that no commiseration was expected. But still, the respectful silence would be appreciated and would assure her getting answers to the questions she was bound to ask presently. She sat down on a wooden stool by the mirror and placed her feet, in their patent leather slippers, close together. She sat there smoothing the black velvet skirt over her knees. "Lilly Belle?" she said. "Is she engaged to Mr. Barker yet?"

Bessie nodded again. "She already has Mr. Barker's ring on her finger."

Now it was safe for Corinna to look up. "Will it be a long engagement?" she asked, still restraining herself somewhat.

"I'm going to stay over for the wedding Sunday week."

Corinna sprang to her feet. "Bessie!" she said. "Let me lend you my Brownie so you can bring us some pictures!"

Bessie shook her head. "Never mind about that. Lilly Belle's not going to get herself married to Mr. Barker without some high-type photographer there."

"Bessie, I wish I could go with you! Remember *every*thing."

"When did I forget anything, Corinna? Is there anything I haven't told you about Lilly Belle before this? I'll tell you one thing now. She's going to marry in her mourning, with a black veil to the floor."

Corinna sat down on the stool again, obviously stunned— more by the striking picture in her mind than by the impropriety. But presently she did ask, "Will that be quite proper, though, Bessie?"

"Of course it's proper, if black becomes you like it does Lilly Belle."

Corinna fixed her gaze on the wastebasket in the far corner of the room. "Do you think—" she began, speaking in a tone at once admiring and suspicious. "Do you think maybe she's kept Mr. Barker waiting just so she could marry in black?"

"How can you ask that, Corinna? Do you suppose Lilly Belle's as vain as *you* are?" Then she got up from her chair and said, "It's time for you-all to start downstairs. That car will be here."

It was only after we were out in the upstairs hall that we realized she wasn't going with us. At first, Corinna said she would refuse to go without her. It would be much more fun just to stay at home and talk, she said. "Yes," said Bessie heavily. "I can just see us sending word to your daddy and Mrs. Richards that you've decided to stay home and talk to Bessie."

"Then you'll *have* to come with us," Corinna said. "How can we go by ourselves?"

"Yes, 'have' to come with you," Bessie said. "Can't you just see me in my six-dollar silk sitting down there in the box with you-all and the Caswells." That was the first we knew of where we would be sitting.

We heard Mrs. Richards's voice downstairs; she had convinced Daddy that he couldn't merely have the chauffeur pick us up and have us arrive at the Colosseum by ourselves. And so there Daddy and Mrs. Richards were, waiting for us at the foot of the stairs. As Bessie helped Corinna into her Sunday coat, she said in an undertone, "Behave yourself, Corinna. Don't act silly. Remember this isn't just something gay tonight. I suspect you'll see folks crying. You know, it'll be like a wedding or funeral. There'll be something sad about seeing Mary Elizabeth and all of those other debutantes walking out in their white dresses."

Then we started down, with Bessie still watching from the head of the stairs and Daddy and Mrs. Richards waiting below.

Only a scene as strange and brilliant as that in the Colosseum could have made Corinna forget Lilly Belle altogether. But perhaps the pleasures of anticipation made her begin forgetting in the car. Or it might have been the sight of Mrs. Richards in her furs at the foot of the stairs. I had noticed before that night that with Mrs. Richards Corinna could be counted on to act more grown up than she did with anyone else. As we rode through town to the Colosseum, she and Mrs. Richards conversed, it seemed to me, with wonderful ease. Mrs. Richards had been a Special Maid at the Veiled Prophet's Court when she was a debutante some fifteen years before. She described the excitement of it as though it had been only yesterday—how you waited behind the curtains to hear the herald call out your name, and then how you heard, or imagined you heard, the gasps of surprise from the throngs whose admiring eyes would presently be focused on you as you walked, trembling, the length of the Colosseum, and knelt before the Prophet to be crowned, and then took your place on the dais.

For me, the Colosseum was like the most unreal of dreams. Before that night it had meant to me a wide sawdust arena with metal girders overhead and surrounded by gloomy, often half-empty tiers of seats. It was where I was taken to watch the annual horse show, the radio show, and the Boy Scout Jamboree. Now it had been transformed, by untold yards of bunting and by acres of white canvas on the floor, into a quite cheerful, if rather bathroomy-looking, ballroom. At one end were the thrones of the Prophet and his Queen-to-be, on a raised dais underneath a tasseled canopy, and they were flanked on either side by tiers of folding chairs provided for members of the Court. At the other end were the immense and immaculate white portieres through which the entrances of all persons of the first importance would be made.

After a drill by the Prophet's Guard of Bengal Lancers, the Prophet himself, attired in splendid medieval-Oriental garments and with his face veiled, made his duly ceremonious entrance. I was so bedazzled by the drill of the Prophet's guards and then by the arrival of the pirates and fur traders and Indians I had seen on the floats the night before that I hardly noticed when the Matrons of Honor began filing past our front-row box. These ladies, perhaps forty of them, circled the whole arena and at last took the places reserved for them on the Prophet's left. Even when the debutantes themselves, in white dresses and long white gloves, began to file by, I found it hard not just to sit there peering between them for glimpses of the people in costumes, who now occupied their places in the Court.

It was Corinna who brought me down tc earth and reminded me of where my attention ought to be directed. She didn't do it intentionally, with a nudge or a cross whisper, but by her erratic behavior. She was sitting on the edge of her chair and leaning halfway across my lap trying to see the faces of the debutantes, who were now emerging from a small gateway on our side of the arena. I felt that she ought to wait and see them when they passed before our box.

"Stop," I said, trying to push her from in front of me.

"Oh, hush," she said, not budging.

She and I were in the very front row, and I glanced over my shoulder to see if Daddy had noticed her behavior. I discovered that he, along with everybody else in the box, was beaming at her. I was glad they couldn't see her face, or couldn't see it as well as I could, or at any rate didn't know what her narrowed-eyes-and-pursed-lips expression meant. Everything suddenly became clear to me. I knew what all the adults' smiling indulgence meant. Mary Elizabeth Caswell was going to have a place of honor in the Prophet's Court, and they expected Corinna to be thrilled by this. But I knew what tortures Corinna was suffering. Probably she was wishing I had let her fall out of that window last night. For, after this, how could she hope to measure up to Mary Elizabeth? It was hopeless. Now I began watching the faces of the girls as intently as she.

When the last debutante had passed us, Mrs. Richards leaned forward, smiling, and said to Corinna, "I didn't see Mary Elizabeth, did you?" And somehow, probably just because it *was* Mrs. Richards, Corinna managed to give her a very knowing, grown-up smile. When she turned around and faced the arena, she sat staring straight ahead with a glazed look.

After this came the separate entrances of the four Special Maids, each summoned individually to the Court of Love and Beauty by the Prophet's herald, each making her entrance between the great portieres and walking the length of the arena with measured steps and drawing after her a wide satin train.

How I prayed each time that the next would be Mary Elizabeth!
But already I knew that Mary Elizabeth would be nothing less
than the Queen. Corinna knew it, too. By the time that awful
announcement came, Corinna was even able to turn and smile at
Mr. and Mrs. Caswell.

"His Mysterious Majesty, the Veiled Prophet, commands me
to summon to his Court of Love and Beauty to reign as Queen
for one year . . . Miss Mary Elizabeth Caswell." That was all.
The Queen's subjects came to their feet. Between the white
portieres Mary Elizabeth appeared, arrayed in her white silk coronation gown, its bodice and its wide skirts embroidered all over
with pearls and sparkling beads; her slender arms held gracefully,
if just a little too stiffly, away from her body and encased in pure
white kid so perfectly and smoothly fitted that only the occasional trembling of Mary Elizabeth's hands could suggest there
were real hands and arms beneath; and her hair, her head of
golden blond hair, fairly shimmering under the brilliant lights
that now shone down on her from somewhere up among the
panoplied steel girders. The orchestra, perched in a lofty spot
directly above the portieres, began to play. To the strains of
"Pomp and Circumstance," Mary Elizabeth moved across our
vision, with four liveried pages holding up the expanse of her
bejeweled train—moved across the white canvas floor of the Colosseum toward her throne.

When the brief coronation ceremony was finished, the
Prophet took his Queen's hand and led her out onto the floor for
their dance. After only a few measures, the guards broke their
formation, each of them going to seek the hand of one of the
debutantes as a dancing partner. The Ball had officially commenced.

Very soon, Daddy and Mrs. Richards went out on the floor,
with the Caswells, to congratulate the Queen and to join in
dancing themselves. Corinna and I were urged to come along,
but I rejected the idea even quicker than Corinna did. We would
wait in the box and find a chance to congratulate Mary Elizabeth later.

In almost no time, the floor was crowded with dancers. All but

those who sat in the balcony were free to participate. Corinna
and I sat with our elbows on the rail of the box, staring into the
crowd. It was curious to see the Prophet's guards dancing in
their heavy shoes, and it was most curious to me to see in how
many instances there was a person in costume dancing with
someone in ordinary evening clothes. I was seeking among the
dancers for Mary Elizabeth and the Prophet.

It was Corinna, of course, who spied Mary Elizabeth first.
"There she is," she said in a perfectly flat voice, indicating where
with a tilt of her head, being very careful not to point. "She's not
dancing with the Prophet anymore."

And then I saw her out there, not twenty feet from us, dancing with a dark-haired young man in white tie and tails. Just as I
caught my first glimpse of her, another young man tapped this
one on the shoulder, and she changed partners. She was, as
Corinna might have phrased it, the cynosure of all eyes.

Corinna was on her feet. She cupped her hands to her mouth
and shouted, "Lilly Belle's engaged!"

Mary Elizabeth couldn't hear her above the music. But she
stopped dancing and started toward us, leading her partner by
the hand. The other dancers respectfully made way for her.
When she had come about half the distance, Corinna called out
again, "Lilly Belle's engaged!"

"No!" Mary Elizabeth called back, and her voice and her
radiant countenance expressed astonishment and delight. "Is it
Mr. Barker?"

"None other!" said Corinna in her most grown-up tone. Mary
Elizabeth was hurrying toward us now, and I beheld the spectacle of Corinna and Mary Elizabeth Caswell throwing their arms
about each other. In that moment all was forgiven—all those
splendid accomplishments, and all those unfavorable comparisons: forgiven forever. That which had separated them for so
long had now united them.

"But Bessie didn't tell me!" Mary Elizabeth was saying. "She
was by, this very morning, to have a close-up look at my dress."

"It's gorgeous," said Corinna.

"Isn't it!" And now another embrace.

"She told me just before I left the house," said Corinna. (Told *me*, not *us?* Before *I*, not *we*, left the house? How selfish that sounded.) "The wedding's Sunday week. And Lilly Belle's going to marry in her mourning veil!"

"Oh no! Stop it!" cried Mary Elizabeth, and she and Corinna shrieked with laughter.

"Bessie's taking the train to Alabama late tonight," Corinna said when she had got her breath again.

"Oh, that wonderful Bessie!" said Mary Elizabeth.

"Isn't she splendid!"

"Have you seen her?"

"Seen her?"

"Up there," said Mary Elizabeth, pointing to the balcony opposite us. "I spotted her a while ago and waved to her."

"Why, she didn't tell me she was coming!" said Corinna. "Isn't that typical?"

The two girls tried to locate Bessie again but soon gave it up. Next, I heard Mary Elizabeth introducing us to her partner, referring to us as her two "little cousins," and realized that Bessie must have talked to her about us. She went on to say how brilliant Corinna was in school and how well I could draw and what "perfect lambs" we both were.

I didn't stop searching for Bessie when they did, and I didn't hear what they were saying any longer. My eyes traveled up one row of the balcony and down the next, searching for Bessie's green silk dress. The crowd up there was thinning out; the poor relations and the children and the servants were going home. Bessie had likely hurried off to catch her train. Already I felt that I might never see Bessie Calhoun again.

But I kept looking for her until I could bear my lonely thoughts no longer. I put my arms on the railing before me, hid my face in them, and commenced to sob.

Instantly all attention was turned toward me, but I wouldn't look up or answer questions. In a matter of seconds Daddy and Mrs. Richards arrived.

"What is it, honey?" I heard Mrs. Richards say.

"He's just tired," Daddy said. "He's not used to being up so late. This is what it means, bringing children to something like this."

Then I was led to a seat at the rear of the box, where I wouldn't be so conspicuous. The Caswells had returned, too, now. I heard Mrs. Caswell say, "Poor little fellow," and this evoked fresh tears and deeper sobs.

"What is it, Son?" Daddy said. "You must try to tell me."

Finally I knew I had to say something—something that would sound reasonable to him. I swallowed hard and lifted my face and found Daddy. I don't know whether or not I knew what I was going to say before I said it. What I said was "Bessie's mama is dead."

"How did you know that, Son?" Daddy asked.

"She told me just before I was leaving the house tonight," I said. Then I hid my face and tried to begin crying again, but I couldn't.

"How awful of her!" I heard Mrs. Richards say, threateningly. "How really unspeakably awful!"

I sat with my face in my hands. After a moment I felt some-one's arm go around my shoulder. I didn't know or care whose it was. Probably it was my father's though it may have been Mrs. Richards's, or even Corinna's. Whosoever it was, it didn't have the feel I wanted, and I purposely kept my face hidden until it had been removed.

A LONG FOURTH

FOR OVER FIVE YEARS Harriet Wilson had been saying, "I'd be happier, Sweetheart, if B.T. were not even on the place." Harriet was a pretty woman just past fifty, and Sweetheart felt that she grew prettier as the years went by. He told her so, too, whenever she mentioned the business about B.T. or any other business. "I declare you get prettier by the year," he was accustomed to say. That was how the B.T. business had been allowed to run on so. Once she had pointed out to Sweetheart that he never said she grew wiser by the year, and he had replied, laughing, that it certainly did seem she would never be a judge of niggers. It was while they were dressing for breakfast one morning that he told her that, and she had quickly turned her back to him (which was the severest rebuke she was ever known to give her husband) and began to powder her neck and shoulders before the mirror. Then he had come over and put his hands on her pretty, plump shoulders and kissed her on the cheek saying, "But you're nobody's fool, darling."

Thinking of that had oftentimes been consolation to her when Sweetheart had prettied her out of some notion she had. But really she had always considered that she was nobody's fool and that she certainly was not merely a vain little woman ruled by a husband's flattery, the type her mother had so despised in her lifetime. She even found herself sometimes addressing her dead mother when she was alone. "It's not that I've become one of that sort of women in middle age, Mama. It's that when he is so sweet to me I realize what a blessing that is and how unimportant other things are." For Harriet was yet guided in some matters by well-remembered words of her mother who had been dead for thirty years. In other matters she was guided by the words of Sweetheart. In still others she was guided by what Son said. Her two daughters guided her in nothing. Rather, she was ever inclined to instruct them by quoting Mama, Sweetheart, or Son.

Their house was eight miles from downtown Nashville on the Franklin Pike, and for many years Sweetheart, who was a doctor, had had his own automobile for work and Harriet had kept a little coupe. But after the war began the doctor accepted gas rationing rather conscientiously and went to and from his office on the interurban bus. "We eye-ear-nose-and-throat men don't have to make so many professional calls," he said. Harriet usually walked down to the pike to meet him on the five-thirty bus in the evening.

It was a quarter of a mile from the pike to the house, and they would walk up the driveway hand in hand. Harriet, who said she lived in perpetual fear of turning her ankle on a piece of gravel, kept her eyes on the ground when they walked, and Sweetheart would usually be gazing upward into the foliage of the poplar trees and maples that crowded the lawn and overhung the drive or he would be peering straight ahead at the house, which was an old-fashioned, single-story clapboard building with a narrow porch across the front where wisteria bloomed in June and July. Though they rarely had their eyes on each other during this walk, they were always hand in hand and there was always talk. It was on one of these strolls, not a week before B.T. gave notice, that Harriet last uttered her old complaint, "I've always told you that I'd be happier, Sweetheart, if B.T. were not even on this place now that he's grown up."

"I know." He squeezed her hand and turned a smiling countenance to her.

"I don't think you do know," she said keeping her eyes on the white gravel. "He's grand on the outside, but all of them are grand on the outside. As long as we keep him I'm completely deprived of the services of a houseboy when I need one. When Son and his young lady come I don't know what I'll do. The girls are angels about things, but next week they should be entertaining Son and her, and not just picking up after her. It seems unreasonable, Sweetheart, to keep B.T. when we could have a nice, normal darkie that could do inside when I need him."

Sweetheart began swinging their joined hands merrily. "Ah, oh, now, B.T.'s a pretty darned good darkie, just clumsy and runs around a bit."

Harriet looked up at her husband and stopped still as though she were afraid to walk with her eyes off her feet. "Sweetheart, you know very well it's not that" And making a face she held her nose so acutely that he could feel it in the fingers of the hand he was holding.

"Well, there's nothing wrong that a little washing won't cure." He was facing her and trying now to take hold of her other hand.

"No, no, no, Sweetheart. It's constitutional with him. Last Monday I had him bathe before he came in to help old Mattie move the sideboard. Yet that room was unbearable for twenty minutes after he left. I *had* to get out, and I heard his Auntie Mattie say, 'Whew!' Mattie knows it as well as I do and is just too contrary to admit it. I'm sure that's why she moved into the attic and left him the whole shack, but she's too contrary to admit it."

The doctor threw back his head and laughed aloud. Then for a time he seemed to be studying the foliage absently and he said that he reckoned poor old Mattie loved her little nephew a good deal. "I think it's touching," he said, "and I believe Mattie would leave us in a minute if we let B.T. go."

"Not a bit of it!" said Harriet.

"Nevertheless, he's a good nigger," her husband said, "and we can't judge Negroes the way we do white people, Harriet."

"Well, I should say *not!*" Harriet exclaimed.

Harriet was not a light sleeper but she complained that she often awoke in the night when there was something on her mind. On the last night of June that summer she awoke with a start and saw by the illuminated dial of her watch that it was 3 A.M. She rolled over on her stomach with great care not to disturb Sweetheart who was snoring gently beside her. This waking, she supposed, was a result of her worries about Son's coming visit and the guest he was bringing with him. And then Son was going to the Army on the day after the Fourth. She had been worrying for weeks about Son's going into the Army and how he would fit in there. He was not like other men, more sensitive and had advanced ideas and was so intolerant of inefficiency and old-fashioned things. This was what had broken her sleep, she thought; and then there was repeated the unheard-of racket that had really awakened her.

Harriet grunted in her pillow, for she knew that it was her daughters quarreling again. A door slammed and she heard Kate's voice through the wall. "Oh, Goddy! Godamighty! Helena, won't you please shut up!" She knew at once the cause of the quarrel: Kate had been out this evening and had turned on the light when she came to undress. Poor thing certainly could not pin up her hair and hang up her dress in the dark. Yet it *was* an unreasonable hour. She wondered where the girls ever stayed till such a late hour. They were too old now to be quizzed about those things. But they were also too old to be quarreling so childishly. Why, when Harriet and her sister were their age they were married and had the responsibilities of their own families. What a shame it is, she thought, that my girls are not married, and it's all because of their height. Then Harriet rebuked herself for begrudging them one minute of their time with what few beaux they had.

For there really were so few tall men nowadays. In her own day there had been more tall men, and tall women were then considered graceful. Short dresses do make such a difference, she reflected, and my girls' legs are not pretty. Harriet was not tall herself, but Mama had been tall and Mama was known as one of the handsomest women that ever graced the drawing rooms of Nashville. But the girls were a little taller than even Mama had been. And they were smart like Mama. They read all the same books and magazines that Son did. Son said they were quite conversant. Nevertheless they must behave themselves while Son's friend was here. No such hours and no such quarrels! She did wish that Son had not planned to bring this girl down from New York, for he had said frankly that they were not in love, they were only friends and had the same interests. Harriet felt certain that Son would bring no one who was not a lady, but what real lady, she asked herself, would edit a birth-control magazine? Just then Sweetheart rolled over and in his sleep put his arm about her shoulders. Something reminded her that she had not said her prayers before going to bed, and so with his arm about her she said the Lord's Prayer and went off to sleep.

She forgot to speak to the girls the next day about their quarreling, but on the following day she was determined to mention it. Sweetheart had left for town in his car since he was to meet Son and Miss Prewitt's train that afternoon. Harriet was in the front part of the house wearing a long gingham wrapper and her horn-rimmed spectacles. In one hand she clasped the morning paper and a few of the June bills which had come in that morning's mail. The house was in good order and in perfect cleanliness, for she and the girls and Mattie had spent the past three days putting it so.

These days had been unusually cool with a little rain in the morning and again in the afternoon. Otherwise Harriet didn't know how they could have managed a general housecleaning in June. The girls had really worked like Trojans, making no complaint but indirectly. Once when it began to rain after a sultry noon hour Helena had said, "Well, thank God for small favors." Kate, when she broke her longest fingernail on the curtain rod, screamed a word that Harriet would not even repeat in her mind. But they had been perfect angels about helping. Their being so willing, so tall, and so strong is really compensation, Harriet kept telling herself, for not having the services of a houseboy. They had tied their heads up in scarfs, pulled on their garden slacks, and done all a man's work of reaching the highest ledges and light fixtures and even lifting the piano and the dining room table.

They had spent last evening on the big screened porch in the back, had eaten supper and breakfast there too, so there was not a thing to be done to the front part of the house this morning. In the living room she looked about with a pleasant, company smile for the polished floor and gave an affected little nod to the clean curtains. All she did was to disarrange some of the big chairs which Mattie had fixed in too perfect a circle. Mama used to warn Harriet against being rigid in her housekeeping. "The main thing is comfort, dearest," and Harriet knew that she had a tendency to care more for the cleanliness and order. So she even put the hearthrug at a slight angle. Then she went to the window and observed that a real July sun was rising today; so she pulled-to the draperies and went from window to window shutting out the light till the whole front part of the house was dark.

The girls slept late that morning. They had earned their rest, and Harriet went tiptoeing about the house listening for them to call for the breakfast that old Mattie had promised to serve them in bed. When ten o'clock came she had picked up in her room, given a last dusting to Son's room and to the guest room, and Mattie had swept the screened porch and was through in the kitchen. It was time to go to market. Mattie had much to do that day and it was not planned for her to go marketing with Harriet. But the girls had been such angels that Harriet and Mattie agreed they should be allowed to sleep as late as their hearts desired.

Mattie put on her straw and in Harriet's presence she was on the back porch giving B.T. some last instructions. B.T. was cleaning six frying-size chickens from their own yard. Later he must peel potatoes and gather beans, lettuce, tomatoes, and okra from what was known as the girls' victory garden. He was ac-

knowledged a good hand at many services which could be ren-
dered on the back porch, and his schedule there over the coming
holiday weekend was a full one. "Have you cleaned up the
freezer?" Harriet asked him. She too was standing with her hat
on. She was looking critically at the naked chicken on which his
black hands were operating with a small paring knife. Before he
answered concerning the freezer she had turned to Mattie and
said, "Don't serve the necks tonight, Mattie." Meanwhile B.T.
had crossed the porch and brought back the big wooden bucket
of the ice-cream freezer. The bucket itself had been scrubbed
wonderfully clean, and with eyes directed toward her but focused
for some object that would have been far behind her, B.T. exhib-
ited the immaculate turner and metal container from within. "It
does look grand, B.T.," Harriet admitted.

She was about to depart when she heard one of the girls'
voices through their window across the way. (The rear of the
house was of a U-shape with the big pantries and the kitchen in
one wing and the bedrooms in the other.) Harriet went down
through the yard and looked in the girls' window. She was astonished to find the room in complete order and the girls fully
dressed and each seated on her own bed reading. Harriet's eyes
were immediately filled with tears. She thought of how hard they
had worked this week and with what unaccustomed deference
they had treated her, calling her "Mama" sometimes instead of
"Mother," sometimes even being so playful as to call her
"Mammy." And this morning they had not wanted to be a
bother to anyone. Further, they were reading something new so
that they would be conversant with Son and Miss Prewitt. Kate
jumped from the bed and said, "Why, Mammy, you're ready to
go to market. I'll be right with you." Harriet turned from the
window and called to Mattie to take off her straw, for Miss Kate
was going to market with her.

But she didn't begin to walk toward the garage at once. The
tears had left her eyes, and she stood thinking quite clearly of
this change in her daughters' behavior. She was ashamed of having thought it would be necessary to mention their quarreling
and their late hours to them. Perhaps they had worried as much

as she about Son's getting into the Army, and probably they were as eager to make him proud of his family before Miss Prewitt.

As all of her concern for the success of the visit cleared away she began to think of what a pity it was that Son and Miss Prewitt were not in love. She would have suspected that it might really be a romance except that the girls assured her otherwise. They told her that Son did not believe in marriage and that he certainly would not subject his family and the people of Nashville to the sort of thing he did believe in. This girl was merely one of the people he knew in his publishing business. And thinking again of all Son's advanced ideas and his intolerance she could not but think of the unhappiness he was certain to know in the Army. And more than this there would be no weekly telephone calls for her and perhaps no letters and no periodic visits home. He would be going away from them all and he might just be missing and never be brought home for burial. Her imagination summoned for comfort the warmth of Sweetheart's smile and the feel of his arm about her, but there was little comfort even there.

When they returned from market they found Helena on the back porch peeling the potatoes. "What on earth is Helena doing?" Kate asked before they got out of the coupe. Harriet frowned and pressed the horn for B.T. to come and get the groceries. Then the tall daughter and the short little mother scrambled out of the car and hurried toward the porch. Almost as soon as the coupe appeared Helena had stood up. She took three long strides to the edge of the porch. When her mother and sister drew near, her eyes seemed ready to pop out of her head. Her mouth, which was large and capable of great expansions, was full open. Yet the girl was speechless.

Harriet was immediately all atremble and she felt the blood leaving her lips. To herself she said, "Something terrible has—" Then simultaneously she saw that Helena's eyes were fixed on something behind Kate and herself and she heard old Mattie's broken voice calling to her, "Miss Harriet! Oh, Missie, Missie!"

She turned about quickly, dropping her eyes to her feet to make sure of her footing, and now looking up she saw the old Negro woman running toward her with her big faded kitchen apron clasped up between her clean, buff-colored hands.

The old-fashioned appellative "Missie" told Harriet a great deal. She handed Kate her purse and put out her arms to receive Mattie, for she knew that her old friend was in deep trouble. The Negress was several inches taller than Harriet but she threw herself into her little mistress's arms and by bending her knees slightly and stooping her shoulders she managed to rest her face on the bosom of the white eyelet dress while she wept. Harriet held her so for a time with her arms about her and patting her gently between the shoulder blades and just above the bow knot of her apron strings. "Now, now, Mattie," she whispered, "maybe it's not as bad as it seems. It's something about B.T., isn't it? What is it, Mattie, honey?"

"Oh, oh, oh, he gwine leave."

The voice seemed so expressive of the pain in that heart that Harriet could think only of the old woman's suffering and not at all of the cause. "My poor Mattie," she said.

But her sympathy only brought forth more tears and deeper sobs. "My little nephew is gwine leave his old auntie who raised him up when nobody else'd tetch him." Harriet did not even hear what Mattie was saying now, but she perceived that her own sympathy was encouraging self-pity and thus giving the pain a double edge. And so she tried to think of some consolation.

"Maybe he won't go after all, Mattie."

Saying this she realized the bearing of B.T.'s departure upon the holiday weekend of which this was the very eve. Then she told herself that indeed Mattie's little nephew would not go after all. "He won't go," she said; "I tell you, Mattie, he won't go if I have any power of constraining him." Her blue eyes shone thoughtfully as she watched the two girls who were now making the last of several trips to bring the groceries from the back of the coupe.

"Oh, oh, oh, yes'm he will, Missie. He's gwine Tuesday. It's the war, an' y'can't stop 'm. He gwine work at th'air fact'ry 'cause the draf membuhs don't want 'm much. But iffen he don't work at th'air fact'ry they'll have to take 'im, want 'im or not." And while his auntie was speaking B.T. appeared from the door of the unpainted cabin from which 'Mattie had come. He was still wearing the white coat which he always wore on the back porch, and plainly intended to continue his work through the weekend. He ran over to the car where Kate was unloading the last of the groceries and relieved her of her armful.

Harriet's relief was great. B.T. would be here through Monday! She began to caress Mattie again and to speak softly in her ear. Her eyes and her thoughts, however, were upon B.T. He was a big—neither muscular nor fat, merely big—black, lazy-looking Negro. As he came along the brick walk toward her he kept his eyes lowered to the bundle of groceries. He was what Harriet's Mama would have called a field nigger and had never learned any house manners at all. His face, to her, had ever seemed devoid of expression. He had grown up here on their suburban acreage and had been hardly more than twenty miles distant in his lifetime, but Harriet felt that she had held less converse with him than with any of the men who used to come for short intervals and do the work when B.T. was still a child. He worked hard and long and efficiently here on their small acreage, she knew, and on Saturday nights he usually got drunk down at the Negro settlement and sometimes spent the later part of that night and all day Sunday in the county jail. There had been times when he had stolen pieces of Sweetheart's and Son's clothing off the wash line, and you dare not lose any change in the porch stairs. Sometimes too they would find that he was keeping some black female thing out in the shack for a week at a time, toting food to her from the kitchen. The female things he kept were not Negro women who might have been useful about the place but were real prostitutes from Nashville (who else would have endured the smell there must be in that shack?), and Dr. Wilson was ever and anon having to take him to Nashville for the shots. But all of that sort of thing was to be expected, admitted Harriet, and it was not that which caused her antipathy— over and above his constitutional affliction—toward him. B.T.

was simply wanting in those qualities which she generally found
appealing in Negroes. He had neither good manners nor the
affectionate nature nor the appealing humor that so many niggers have.

As he passed her there at the foot of the porch steps the odor
he diffused had never seemed more repugnant and never so
strong when outside the house. Mattie raised her tear-streaked
brown face, knowing it was B.T. surely more from his odor than
from his footstep, and as he followed the two girls to the kitchen
door she called after him, "B.T., don't leave old Auntie!" Then
she looked at her mistress with what Harriet acknowledged to be
the sweetest expression she had ever beheld in a Negro's countenance. "Miss Harriet," she said as though stunned at her own
thoughts, "it's like you losin' Mr. Son. B.T. is gwine too."

The small white woman abruptly withdrew her arms from
about her servant. The movement was made in one fearful gesture which included the sudden contraction of her lips and the
widening of her bright eyes. "Mattie!" she declaimed. "How
dare you? That will be just exactly enough from you!" And now
her eyes moved swiftly downward and to the porch steps. Without another glance at the woman she had been holding to her
bosom she went up on the porch and, avoiding the kitchen
where the girls were, she went along the porch up into the U of
the house and entered the dark dining room. While she walked
her face grew hot and cold alternately as her indignation rose
and rose again. When she reached her own room in the far wing
of the house she closed the door and let the knob turn to in her
hand. She pulled off her hat and dropped it on her dressing table
among her toilet articles and handkerchief box and stray ends of
gray hair that were wrapped around a hairpin. And she went and
sat down in a rocking chair near the foot of the bed and began to
rock. "Like Son! Like Son!"

The very chair had violence in its rocking motion. Several
times Harriet might have pushed herself over backward but for
lacking the strength in her small legs. Not since she was a little
child had such rage been known to her bosom, and throughout
the half hour of her wildest passion she was rather aware of this.

This evidence of a choleric temperament was so singular a thing for her that she could not but be taking note of herself as her feelings rose and convulsed in their paroxysm. She wondered first that she had refrained from striking Mattie out in the yard and she remarked it humorlessly that only the approaching holiday had prevented her. The insinuation had been sufficiently plain without Mattie's putting it into words. It was her putting it into words that earned Harriet's wrath. The open comparison of Son's departure to that of the sullen, stinking, thieving, fornicating black B.T. was an injury for which Son could not avenge himself, and she felt it her bounden duty to in some way make that black woman feel the grossness of her wrong and ultimately to drive her off the premises. And it was in this vein, this very declamatory language, this elevated tone with which Harriet expressed herself in the solitude of her room. She was unconsciously trying to use the language and the rhetoric of her mother and of the only books with which she had ever had such acquaintance. Between the moments when she even pictured Mattie's being tied and flogged or thought of Mama's uncle who shot all of his niggers before he would free them, and of the Negro governor of North Carolina and the Negro senate rolling whiskey barrels up the capitol steps, of the rape and uprisings in Memphis and the riots in Chicago, between these thoughts she would actually consider the virtue of her own wrath. And recalling her Greek classes at Miss Hood's school she thought without a flicker of humor of Achilles' indignation.

Not the least of the offense was the time that Mattie had chosen. Harriet was powerless to act until this long Fourth of July was over. She meant to endure the presence of that Ethiopian woman and that ape of a man through Sunday and Monday, till her own boy had had his holiday and gone to join the Army. His last visit must not be marred, and she resolved to tell no one—not even Sweetheart—of what had occurred. The holiday would be almost intolerable to her now, and she stopped her furious rocking, and with her feet set side by side on the carpet she resolved to endure it in silence for his sake who was the best of all possible sons. Sweat was running down her forehead, and her little hands hung limp and cold.

People in Nashville had been saying for a week how Son would be missed. More than most boys, even those who had not left Nashville to work in New York or St. Louis, Son would be missed by his family when he went to the Army. People said that he had been a model son while he was growing up. And after his own talents and ability took him away to New York he had been so good about keeping in touch. He had written and telephoned and visited home regularly. That was what the older people remarked. And the young people no less admired the faithfulness and consideration he showed his parents. He had carried all the honors in his classes at school and at the University and had not grieved his parents with youthful dissipation as most Nashville boys do. What the young people thought especially fine was that, being the intellectual sort, which he certainly was, he had been careful never to offend or embarrass his family with the peculiar, radical ideas which he would naturally have. After he left Nashville he never sent home magazines in which his disturbing articles appeared, not even to his sisters who pretended to have the same kind of mind. And finally when the wild stories about his private and semipublic activities began to come back to Nashville and circulate among people, people were not so displeased with these stories as they were pleased to find on his next visit that he behaved as of old while in Nashville.

He was a tall, fair-headed young man, softly spoken, and he dressed conventionally. When he came into his mother's front hall that Saturday afternoon on the second of July he was still wearing the seersucker suit in which he had traveled. Harriet was not at the door to greet him, but as she came from her room she could hear amid the flurry of greetings his polite voice asking in his formal way if she were well. She met him at the door of the parlor and as she threw her arms about him she found herself unable to restrain her tears.

She thought, of course, that her weeping would subside in a moment and she did not even hide her face in her handkerchief.

She tried to speak to him and then pushing him a little aside she tried to say something to the young woman he had brought with him. But the sight of Miss Prewitt there beside Sweetheart seemed to open new valves and it seemed that she was beginning to choke. When she had first seen Son in the doorway his very appearance had confirmed the justice of her outraged feelings this afternoon. When she saw the ladylike young woman in a black traveling dress and white gloves (as an example of his taste), it occurred to her that she had even underestimated the grossness of Mattie's reflection upon him. Her weeping became so violent now and was so entirely a physical thing that it seemed not to correspond to her feelings at all. First she tried to stifle and choke down her tears physically. This failing, she tried to shame herself into composure, thinking of what a vulgar display Mama would have called this. Presently she recognized that her state was already hysteria. Sweetheart rushed forward and supported her, and Son tried to hold one hand which she was waving about.

They walked her slowly to her room speaking to her gently. All the while she was trying at moments to think of the reason for this collapse. It was not—as they would all believe—Son's going into the Army. It could not be simply the scene she had had with her cook that afternoon. Could it be that she had always hated this black, servant race and felt them a threat to her son and her family? Such ridiculous thoughts! Then she was alternately laughing and weeping, and they put her on her bed. Sweetheart attended her and then sat holding her hand till she was absolutely quiet. Later the girls took their turns at sitting with her. All she could remember about Son that afternoon was hearing him say, out in the hall it seemed, "How unlike Mother."

It was late in the evening before they would let her move from her bed or leave her room. But by ten o'clock Sweetheart was convinced that her fretting there in bed was more harmful than a little company up in the front room would be. She declared herself to be quite recovered and after a bit of washing and powdering she presented herself to the four young people who were playing bridge in the parlor.

"Well, well, have a seat," Son said, extending his left hand to her.

His manner was casual, as was that of the others—studiedly so. For they wanted to make her comfortable. Even Miss Prewitt restrained her attentions, pretending to be absorbed in the cards although she was dummy. "The girls have given us a good trimming tonight," she said.

When Miss Prewitt spoke, Harriet observed that she had extremely crooked teeth which had been brought more or less into line probably by wearing bands as a child. Her face was rather plain but her cheeks had a natural rosiness to them and her eyes, though too small, were bright and responsive. She wore no makeup and was redolent of no detectable perfume or powder. And before she sat down in the chair which Sweetheart drew up for her, Harriet had perceived that the girl took no pains with her hair which hung in a half-long bob with some natural wave.

"We're teaching these Yankees a thing or two," Helena said, winking playfully at Kate.

"Will you listen to that?" Miss Prewitt smiled and revealed to Harriet a pleasant manner and an amiable, ladylike nature. "Your daughters keep calling their own brother and myself Yankees. But of course it's partly his fault, for I learn that he didn't write you that I'm from Little Rock, myself, and that I'm on my way home for a visit."

"Isn't that manlike?" Harriet said.

Now Son dropped his last three trumps on the table and proclaimed that that was "game." He suggested that they quit playing, but Harriet insisted that they complete the rubber. Helena began to deal the cards. For a time no one spoke. Harriet pretended to gaze about the room but she could hardly keep her eyes off Miss Prewitt. For though she found her extremely agreeable she perceived that the possibility of any romantic attachment between her and Son was out of the question. The tie between them was doubtless what the girls called an intellectual friendship. In her own girlhood people would have called it Platonic, but then they would have laughed about it. Mama had always said there could be no such relationship between young men and young women. Sweetheart always showed the smutty and cynical side to his nature when such things were discussed. Yet in some matters Son surely knew more than either Mama or Sweetheart. She had of course never, herself, known such a friendship with a man and just now she was really trying to imagine the feelings that two such friends would have for one another.

Until Miss Prewitt had spoken and thus started that train of thought in her mind Harriet had been wondering how dinner came off and whether Mattie served the chicken necks. But now her thoughts had been diverted and her nerves were somewhat relieved. It was she who finally broke the silence. "For Heaven's sake," she said, "let's not be so reserved. You're all being so careful of my feelings that Miss Prewitt will think I have a nervous ailment. My dear, that's the first time in my life I've ever carried on so. You just mustn't judge me by that scene I made. I have no sympathy with women who carry on so."

Then Sweetheart and the children did begin to tease her and make light of her carryings-on. Presently the conversation became animated and she was soon calling Miss Prewitt "Ann" as the girls did. Helena and Kate, she had never seen more cordial to a stranger than to Ann. She had never, indeed, seen them sweeter with one another. It was not until they had played their last card and had shaken hands across the table in acknowledgment of their complete victory that the strangeness of their behavior occurred to Harriet. It had been many a day since they had sat down at the same bridge table, for if they were partners they usually ended by calling each other "stupid" and if they were not partners they not infrequently accused each other of cheating.

Now Harriet felt herself trembling again and she was unable to follow the conversation. After a few minutes she said, "I think what we all need is a good night's sleep." The girls agreed at once, and so did Sweetheart. But Son suggested that he and Ann would like to sit up and talk for a while. Nobody seemed to take exception to this but Sweetheart who gave a little frown and shrugged his shoulders. Then he led Harriet off to their room, and the girls followed inquiring if there was anything they could do for Mother. As Harriet left the parlor she glanced back and observed that Ann's legs were as large and graceless as two fireplugs.

Sweetheart was in bed before her and lay there watching her own preparations at the dressing table. She felt that she was barely able to conceal from him the difficulty she had in rolling her hair and pulling on the net. But when she turned to put off the light she found him fast asleep.

She was standing in the dark for a moment and she heard the voices of Son and Ann out on the porch. Without even considering her action she stepped to the window and listened to their lowered voices.

"She's a very pretty and attractive little woman," Ann was saying, "but from things you had said I was not quite prepared to find her such a nervous woman."

"That's true. But I don't think she really is a nervous woman," Son said slowly. "I believe nobody was more surprised than herself at what happened this afternoon."

"It's not just what happened this afternoon. She was trembling most of the time in the living room tonight."

"I can't imagine what it is. Something seems to have come over her. But there's no visible change. She hasn't aged any. I looked for it in her hair and in the skin about her neck and in her figure." It hardly seemed possible to Harriet that this was Son talking about herself.

"She's certainly past her menopause, isn't she?"

"Oh, certainly. Years ago when I was still in school."

"That's rather early."

"Yes . . . Yes."

"The girls are much more conventional than I imagined, much less independent, more feminine—"

"Something," Son emphasized, "seems to have come over them, too."

"They're too young for any sort of frustration, I suppose."

This whispered but clearly audible conversation caused Harriet to feel herself alienated from all around her. It was Son's disinterested tone and objectiveness. Her mind returned to Mattie. She wondered how she and B.T. would behave through the weekend. And now looking out into the backyard where the moon was shining on the shingled roof of the cabin and through the trees to the porch steps, she considered again the words she had used to Mattie out there this afternoon.

The girls had planned a small party for Monday night, which was July Fourth. It was not to be at the Country Club, where they had always before preferred to entertain, but at the house. But on Sunday night one of Son's old friends named Harry Buchanan had invited the group to supper at the Club. Harry was married and had two small children.

At the breakfast table Sunday morning Helena said to Ann, "We didn't plan anything for last night because we knew you two would be tired from traveling. But we're having a few friends to the house tomorrow night, and tonight the Buchanans"—she hesitated and closed her eyes significantly—"have asked us to supper at the Club. I don't know why some people must entertain at clubs and hotels."

"It all sounds quite festive," Ann said.

"Yes, I'm afraid 'festive' is the word," said Kate. "When people ask you to a hotel or a club, instead of to their home, if the occasion's not 'festive' or 'gala,' what can it be? I don't take such an invitation as a great compliment."

Ann said nothing. Son looked over his pink grapefruit, perplexed. Harriet was completely mystified now by the things her daughters were saying. It sounded like pure nonsense to her although she was pleased to see them in such accord. She could not say that she disagreed with them, but it did sound like nonsense because it was the very reverse of ideas they usually expressed. Perhaps it was because they were growing older and more like herself. "One never realizes when one's children are growing up," she thought. But whether or not she agreed with them in principle she did think it ungracious and unkind of them to speak that way about Son's friend who was entertaining them tonight.

"Kate," she said, "the Buchanans have two small children and their house is so small."

The two daughters laughed. "Dear, dear Mama," Helena said, "you're such a Christian. You wouldn't say anything against *any-body* on Sunday, would you?"

"Let me ask you this, Mama," said Kate. "Would your mother have liked entertaining visitors at a golf club?"

Harriet shook her head. "That was long ago when Mama entertained, and it was not the custom then."

"There you are. We're only thinking as you've taught us to think, Mama, when we think that many of the customs and ways that used to pertain in Nashville were better than what is replacing them."

Harriet asked herself if that was what she had taught them to think. She didn't know she had taught them to think anything. But her only real interest in the matter was the defense of Harry Buchanan whose wife's mother, she presently said, was a dear friend of hers and was from one of Nashville's loveliest families and certainly knew how to "do." Then Helena asked with apparent artlessness what her dear friend's maiden name had been. And the question led to a prolonged discussion between the girls and their mother and even their father of the kinship of various Nashville families. Nothing yet had amazed Harriet more than the knowledge of those kinships and connections which Helena and Kate proceeded to display.

"Why, you two girls," Sweetheart said in his innocence, "are getting to rival your mother in matters of who's kin to who." But Harriet was observing Son and Ann who remained silent and kept their eyes on their food. She herewith resolved that she would make it her special task during the remainder of the visit to avoid such talk since it seemed to cause a mysterious antagonism between the young people.

After breakfast Son and Ann left for a walk about the premises in the company of Sweetheart who wanted to show them his

orchards and his four acres of oats and the old cotton patch
where he had had B.T. put in lespedeza this year. They were also
to see his poultry and the Jersey cow whose milk at breakfast had
tasted of wild onions. He urged Helena and Kate to come along
and show off the vegetable garden where they had worked and
directed B.T.'s labor. But the girls declined, saying that they
were through with outdoor life until the weather was cool again.
Harriet said to herself, "They're perfect angels and don't want to
leave the housework to me this morning."

Later Sweetheart came back to the house and settled himself
on the porch with the Sunday morning paper while Son and Ann
walked down the pike toward the Confederate Monument. Harriet debated the question of going to church. Sweetheart advised
against it in view of her nervous agitation. Then she dismissed
the idea, for she dared not reject Sweetheart's advice in such
matters, though for a while there did linger the thought of how
restful church service would seem. When the straightening up
was done the girls went to their reading again and Harriet made
a visit to the kitchen that she had been postponing all morning.

"Mattie," she said, "do you have everything?" Mattie was
seated at a kitchen table with her back to the swinging door
through which Harriet had entered, and she did not turn
around. The table was in the center of the huge, shadowy
kitchen. Directly beyond the table was the doorway to the back
porch, through which opening Harriet could see B.T. also working at a table.

"I reckon," Mattie answered after a moment. There was no
movement of her head when she spoke. And her head was not
bent over the table. She seemed to be staring through the doorway at B.T. She was seated there on a high, unpainted wooden
stool which she had long ago had B.T. make for her (though she
had complained at the time of having to pay him for it out of her
own stocking), and since B.T. had selfishly made the stool to
accommodate his own long legs, Mattie's stocking feet drooped,
rather than dangled, above her old slippers that had fallen one
upon the other on the linoleum.

She was not wearing her white cap or white serving apron, so there was absolutely no relief to her black dress and her head of black hair. She was the darkest object in the whole of the dark old-fashioned kitchen—blacker even than the giant range stove whereon the vegetables were boiling and in which a fire roared that kept the kitchen so hot that Harriet looked about to see if the windows were open and found them all open but that window where the winter icebox was built on, and she knew Mattie would not open that window while there were so many tomatoes and heads of cabbage and lettuce to keep fresh.

In the kitchen there was only the sound of water boiling. Through the backdoor she could see B.T. in the bright sunlight on the porch and hear the regular thumping of his knife on the table as he chopped a coconut for the ambrosia. He seemed to be unaware of or totally indifferent to Mattie's gaze upon him. Harriet stepped back into the pantry and let the door swing shut, drawing a hot breeze across her face. The two Negroes doubtless had been sitting like that for hours without a word between them. It was a picture she was not able to forget.

Among the family friends the Wilson girls were admired no less than Son though they were considered to have more temperament. (By this it was meant that they occasionally displayed bad temper in public.) They were spoken of as devoted daughters and thoroughly capable and energetic young women. Helena, who was known generally as the blonde Wilson girl though her brown hair was only a shade lighter than Kate's, sometimes taught classes at Miss Hood's school during the winter. She usually substituted, and could teach mathematics, art appreciation, or modern literature to the seniors. During the winter when there were more colds and throat trouble Kate helped with the receiving and secretarial work at Sweetheart's office.

They had large, round, pleasant faces which often seemed identical to strangers. Their voices were considered identical by everyone outside the family, even by close family friends who often remarked that they didn't speak with the vulgar drawl that so many Nashville girls have adopted. Their vocabulary and their accents were more like those of their mother. They pronounced girl as "gull" as all Nashville ladies once used to do. And so it was often shocking to a stranger after hearing their slightly metallic but very feminine and old-fashioned voices to turn and discover both girls were over six feet tall. Their ages were "in the vicinity of thirty," as was Son's, and they too never seemed to have considered matrimony.

As Harriet was returning from the kitchen her ear recognized Kate's familiar touch at the piano. It was by the bass that she could always distinguish the girls' playing; Kate's was a little the heavier but with more variations. She was playing accompaniment to the ballad "Barbara Allen," and presently Helena's straining falsetto could be heard. Then as Harriet passed through the hall she saw through the open front door Son and Ann walking up the straight driveway from the pike. Son wore white linen trousers and a white shirt open at the collar. Ann looked very fresh and youthful in a peasantlike shirtwaist and skirt, though the flare of the skirt did seem to accentuate the heaviness of her legs. They walked over the white gravel beneath the green canopy of the trees and the picture was framed in the semicircle of lavender wisteria that blossomed round the entrance to the porch. The prettiness of it made Harriet sigh. It seemed that her sorrow over Son's going into the Army would not be so great if she could believe that he and Ann were in love. This old house and the surrounding woods and pastures had always seemed to her the very setting for romance. From the time when her girls had first begun to have a few beaux she considered what a felicitous setting the swing on the front porch or the old iron bench down by the fence stile would be for the final proposal; and during her walks with Sweetheart in the evenings she would sometimes look about the lawn trying to fix upon the best spot for a garden wedding. Now the sight of Son and Ann in this pretty frame only reminded her of their unnatural and strange relationship. They were walking far apart and Ann was speaking with deliberation and gesturing as she spoke. But apparently at the first glimpse of Harriet, Ann broke off speaking. And Harriet perceived in an instant that there was at least a trouble of some kind in their relationship. She recollected now that though Son had not been talking he had been shaking his head from side to side as though in exasperation.

Kate was still playing and Helena singing (after her fashion) when they entered the parlor. Son was not long able to restrain his laughter although he had actually pressed his hand over his mouth. When his laughter finally did explode the two girls sprang up from the piano bench. Their mother stood paralyzed, expecting a greater explosion of temper from them. But they only smiled with a shamefaced expression that was utterly artificial. Ann had turned to Son and was remonstrating with him. "I really should think you'd be ashamed," she said.

"Why, he's completely shameless and unchivalrous," Helena said with the same false expression of tolerance and good nature on her face. It was this expression which the faces of both girls were affecting that stunned and mystified Harriet beyond all bounds. She knew now that they were in league to accomplish some purpose. She could see that they were fully prepared for Son's reaction and that it was even desired.

"Hush, Son, you idiot," Kate smiled. Then turning to Ann: "That old ballad is one Mama taught us when we were children. Of course none of us have Mama's music, but we weren't expecting an audience." And finally she addressed her sister, "The only trouble is, Helena, you were not singing the right words—not the words Mama taught us."

"No," Son derided, "you were singing from *The Oxford Book of Verse.*"

"I know," Helena admitted with her feigned modesty and frankness. "But, Mama," she said to Harriet, "sing us your version—the real Tennessee version."

And they all began to insist that Harriet play and sing. At first she would not, for she felt that she was being a dupe to her two daughters. It was for this that the whole scene had been arranged! If she could avoid it she would not assist them in any of their schemings. If there was to be antagonism between her children she was not going to take sides. At breakfast the girls had led her to support their criticism of country-club life and modern ways by bringing in Mama's opinions. Now her singing of an old ballad would somehow support their cause.

But Son and Ann were insisting as well. She looked at Son and he said, "Please do sing." So if her singing was what they all wanted, how could she refuse? Perhaps it would make them forget whatever was the trouble. Besides, Harriet loved so to be at the piano singing the old songs that were fixed so well in her ear and in her heart.

As she sat down before the piano Helena ran to get Sweetheart, for he would never forgive them if Mother sang without his hearing it. She would also get Mattie who loved hearing her mistress sing above all else. Then Helena returned with her father, saying that Mattie would listen from the pantry.

So as Sweetheart took his stand by the upright piano and watched her with that rare expression of alertness in his eyes and as the young people grouped themselves behind her Harriet began to play and sing. Her soprano voice came as clear and fresh as when she was nineteen. When she had finished "Barbara Allen" she followed with other ballads almost without being asked. Anyone listening could tell how well she enjoyed singing the old songs that her grandpa had taught her long ago and how well she remembered the lyrics and the melody, never faltering in the words or hesitating on the keyboard. But her lovely, natural talent was not merely of the music. She seemed actually to experience the mood of each song. And her memory and ear for the soft vowels and sharp consonants of the mountain dialect were such that what was really a precise rendition seemed effortless. All her family and their guest stood round remarking on the sweet, true quality of her voice.

At the dinner table the girls began to talk again of who was kin to whom in Nashville. "Mama," Kate said, "I didn't know till the other day that Miss Liza Parks is Mrs. Frazier Dalton's aunt. She's one of that Parks family who used to live at Cedar Hill."

Harriet could hardly resist saying that Miss Liza was also second cousin to Mr. Bob Ragsdale. But without even looking at

Kate she said, "Now, what interest could that be to Ann? Tell us, Ann, how you liked Sweetheart's little farm."

"Oh, it's a beauty," Ann said. "And his methods are quite modern. He even rotates his crops and paints his barn. Dr. Wilson is certainly no backward Southern farmer. B.T. showed us the garden, and I think B.T. is a wonder."

"He's grand on outside work," Harriet said.

The two girls began to laugh, and Harriet frowned at them.

"Son has told me," Ann whispered to Harriet, for Mattie was passing in and out of the room, "about the poor fellow's peculiarity. He's going away for the Duration, I understand, but when he comes back, why doesn't he try to get a farm of his own and make a real business of it. You can tell he has a genuine love of farming, and he's quite intelligent, isn't he? He ought to—"

"Now, Ann," Son interrupted, "how on earth is a poor Negro just going to reach out and get himself a farm? How can you ask such a question with all your knowledge of conditions?"

"I was thinking that Dr. Wilson would help him. Wouldn't you, Doctor?"

"Yes, of course, if he wanted—"

The girls were laughing together again. "That's just it," Helena said, "*if* B.T. wanted to. But he's a gentleman's nigger, Ann. He worships Daddy, and Daddy couldn't live without him. It's a very old-fashioned relationship, you know what I mean? It's the same with Mother and Mattie." At this point Mattie came in. She was serving the last of the four vegetable dishes. Nobody spoke while she was in the room. The picture of Mattie and B.T. in the kitchen this morning returned to Harriet, and she found herself thinking again of what she had said to Mattie yesterday in the yard. The brooding expression in Mattie's eyes and her repeated glances at Son as she passed round the table suggested anew the hateful comparison she had drawn. But Harriet could not feel such strong resentment now. She told herself that it was because she saw now how great was the real difference between her son and Mattie's little nephew. It was too absurd even to consider. She must have been out of her head yesterday! Her nerves had been on edge. That was the answer. And Mattie had spoken to her about that foul-scented B.T. just when she was grieving most about Son's going into the Army. Today the real pain of that grief had left her. It would doubtless return. But why, she considered, had it left her now? It seemed that his putting on a uniform was as unreal and indifferent a matter to her as the mysterious life he led in New York and his intellectual friendship with Ann Prewitt and this conversation they were having at her table. Last night she had overheard Son and Ann discussing herself as objectively as they were now discussing B.T. and Negro "conditions." Then she rebuked herself and allowed that Son simply lived on a higher plane. She felt that she should be ashamed to understand so little about her son and about her daughters and the antagonism there was between the young people.

When Mattie had left the room Kate said, "Yes, it's quite the same with Mattie and Mama. Yesterday Mattie was upset by some bad news and she came and threw herself into Mama's arms and wept like a child. It seems to me that's what they really are: a race of children, a medieval peasantry. They're completely irresponsible and totally dependent upon us. I really feel that Southern white people have a great responsibility—"

"We are responsible," Ann Prewitt said, "for their being irresponsible and dependent, if that's what you mean, Kate."

"Oh, that's *not* what she means," said Helena. "Their whole race is in its childhood, Ann, with all the wonders and charm of childhood. And it needs the protection, supervision, discipline, and affection that can be given only by Southern white people who have a vital relationship and traditional ties with them. The poor nigs who I feel for are those in Chicago and New York who have no white families to turn to."

Ann was looking to Son to see if he were going to make an argument of this. But Son said only, "What do you think of that, Ann?"

With an aggrieved, shy glance at Son she said, "I think it's a lot of nonsense. But that's only my opinion."

"Well, it's my opinion too," said Son. "The people in the South cannot expect to progress with the rest of the nation until they've forgotten their color line. The whole system has got to be changed. In some strange way it hinders the whites more than the blacks. When B.T. was in the garden with us this morning I felt that this was his home more than mine and that it was because of him that I feel no real tie to this place. Even when we were children it was so. . . . The whole system has got to be changed . . . somehow . . . someway."

"Somehow!" Ann exclaimed. Then she lowered her eyes and seemed to regret having spoken.

"You have a definite idea of how, then?" Helena asked.

"Equality: economic and social."

"You can't be serious," the girls said in one voice.

"Of course, she's serious," Son rejoined. Ann was silent. She appeared to have resolved not to speak again.

"You two are speaking as New Yorkers now," Helena began, "not as Southerners. Didn't it ever occur to you that the South has its own destiny? It has an entirely different tradition from the rest of the country. It has its own social institutions and must be allowed to work out its own salvation without interference."

"Sister," Son laughed, "you're beginning to sound not merely old-fashioned but unreconstructed."

"Then unreconstructed it is," defied Kate with a gallant smile. "Who can say that the Southern states were wrong to fight for their way of life?"

"For slavery, Kate?"

"The Southern master was morally responsible, which is more than can be said for the industrial sweatshopper."

Now Son slapped his hand over his mouth and presently his vehement laughter burst forth. He pushed his chair a little way from the table and said, "Now the cat's out of the bag! I know what you girls have been reading and who you've probably been seeing—those fellows at the University in Nashville. You know what I mean, Ann! Why, Ann, I've brought you into a hotbed of Southern reactionaries. How rich! How really rich this is! Now I know what you girls have been trying to put across. You and all Southern gentlemen and gentlewomen are the heirs and protectors of the great European traditions—and agrarian tradition, I should say. That's what all of this family pride and *noblesse oblige* mean. And Ann here, my comrade, believes that come the Revolution it will all be changed overnight. How rich!"

His laughter was curiously contagious and there did seem to be a general relief among all. "And now, my wise brother," asked Kate, "what do you believe?"

Ann and the two sisters were managing to smile at one another, for Son's derision had united them temporarily. While Son was trying to get his breath Ann leaned across the table and said, "He believes nothing that's any credit to him. He's been reading *The Decline of the West!* A man his age!"

Harriet was utterly dismayed, though she did sense that the incomprehensible antagonism had reached its crisis and that the worst was over. At least the young people understood each other now. But as they were leaving the table she wished, for the first time in many years, that she could be alone for a while this afternoon. She wanted to remember how Son and Helena and Kate had been when they were children—the girls quarreling over scraps from her sewing or playing dolls on the porch and Son begging to go off swimming with B.T. when the creek was still cold in May.

Everybody slept late on the morning of the Fourth of July. Sweetheart was still snoring gently at nine-thirty. He awoke when Harriet started the electric fan. "I'm so sorry, Sweetheart," she said, "but you looked so hot there I thought the fan might help." She was already half dressed, but before she had snapped the last snap in the placket of her dress Sweetheart had put on his clothes and shaved and gone out onto the porch. She smiled as she thought of it; and then she began to hurry, for Son's voice could now be heard on the porch. Besides, there was a lot to be done in preparation for the supper party tonight. Probably the girls were already helping in the kitchen. They were being such angels this weekend!

She was smoothing the last corner of the counterpane when Kate came in.

"I feel like the devil," Kate said. She was wearing her silk negligee and her hair was uncombed and even matted in places.

She was barefooted; and the girls always looked taller to Harriet in their bare feet.

"And you look like the very devil," Harriet said.

"Thanks, dear." She sat down on the bed which Harriet had just now made. She struck a match on the bottom of the bedside table and lit the cigarette which she had brought with her. She patted the bed beside her indicating that Harriet should sit down. Harriet could always tell when the girls had been drinking a good deal the night before by the sour expression which the heavy sleep left on their features. She was long since accustomed to their drinking "socially," and to their smoking but she still did not like the smell of whiskey on them next morning. She pulled up her rocking chair and sat down.

"Mother, I do wish that Helena wouldn't drink so much. She just doesn't know how."

Harriet only shook her head, saying nothing, for Helena would have a similar report about Kate later in the morning. The truce between them was evidently over. "How was the Buchanan's party?" she asked.

"It was pretty nice." Then she shrugged her shoulders. "I want to tell you about Ann."

"What is there to tell?"

"I thought you wanted to hear about the party!" Kate said sharply.

"I do."

"Well listen, that's what I mean—how Ann behaved last night."

"She didn't misbehave?"

"I should say not. She's a perfect little lady, you know. A perfect parlor pink, as we suspected—Helena and I."

Parlor pink meant nothing to Harriet. She turned her face away toward the window to indicate that if Kate persisted in talking the kind of nonsense they talked at the table yesterday she didn't care to listen.

"She holds her liquor well, all right," Kate continued, "but after a few drinks she's not the quiet little mouse she is around here. She talks incessantly and rather brilliantly, I admit. And what I'm getting at is that when she talks Son seems to hang on her every word. He plainly thinks she's the cleverest woman alive."

"What does she talk about?"

"For one thing, she talked about birth control and its implications to Lucy Price who is a Catholic. She was really very funny about the Pope as the great papa who *doesn't* pay." Harriet had no full understanding of birth control itself, much less of its implications. And she knew that she was unreasonably prejudiced against Catholics. Why couldn't Kate talk about Ann without dragging in those things?

"She quotes Marx and Huxley and lots of young British poets. And all the while Son sits beaming with admiration as though she were Sappho or Margaret Sanger, herself."

"Is he in love with her then, Kate, if he does all that?"

"Not at all."

"And Ann herself?"

"Hardly! She's not the type. She never looks at him."

Harriet sighed.

"But there's something between them," Kate said speculatively.

"I suppose intellectual friendships can have very deep feelings."

"Pooh," said Kate.

"Then the girl is in love with him, and he—"

"No, Mother. I don't believe it." But Harriet looked at her daughter with the matted hair and the sleep-creased face and the cigarette with its smoke drifting straight upward into the breathless air. *Her* girls had never been in love. And it isn't their height, she thought, and it isn't their legs. They're like Son, she thought, and it isn't them. She got up from her chair and as she left Kate behind she met Helena at the door. Helena's face and hair and general attire were about the same as Kate's. "Kate's in there," Harriet said and brushed past the daughter who towered above her in the doorway. She went into the parlor to draw the draperies before the sun got too warm.

The day grew warm. You could almost hear the temperature rising if you stood still a minute. Harriet was so busy about the house that she thought it her activity that made her perspire. But now and then she would step out to the porch and slip on her spectacles to look at the thermometer. "What an awful day," she would say to Sweetheart who was sleeping in his chair.

The girls remained in their room until afternoon. Once or twice Harriet heard them speaking irritably to one another. When they finally appeared Helena turned on the radio in the parlor and Kate sat on the porch. They would show no interest in the coming party. They sulked about as though they had been disappointed or defeated in something.

"Quit buzzing around, Mother," Kate said. "There are only a dozen or so people coming and it's supposed to be informal."

"Oh, Goddy, I never saw so much commotion over a cold supper," Helena said.

Ann tried to help, but Harriet said, "There's nothing left to do. I just have to cut the melon balls and everything will be ready."

Later Sweetheart and Son went off to Nashville to pick up the whiskey at the hotel. Ann went along to make her Pullman reservations, for she was taking a train at one A.M. She said she had to be in Little Rock the next day.

Most of the guests parked their cars in the backyard alongside B.T.'s shack or in front of the garage. As they arrived Son went out into the yard to greet them or welcomed them on the screened porch. Supper was served buffet style, and Sweetheart brought everybody two or three drinks before they began to eat. "We want you to have an appetite," he would say.

The guests were, for the most part, Son's old school friends and their wives. There were two young men of sufficient height to escort the girls from room to room. And there was a young professor from the University and his wife who had taught at Miss Hood's School with Helena. Son was most cordial to this couple, introducing himself to them in the yard since Helena was not present when they arrived. The young professor (he explained that he was really only a teaching fellow) wore a small mustache and a dark bow tie with his linen suit. He was very timid and spoke only a few words in the course of the whole evening.

While dressing for the party Harriet observed in the mirror that her face showed the strain she had been under. She spread extra powder under her eyes and applied more rouge than was usual for her. When she had finished her toilet she removed all her personal things from the dressing table, opened a new box of powder, and brought from the closet shelf an ivory hand mirror and comb and brush. The ladies were going to use this as a powder room. From the closet shelf she also brought four small pillows with lacy slipcovers which she arranged on the bed.

She was arranging the pillows when Son knocked at her door. He entered with his own large glass in one hand and a small tumbler for her in the other. "It's mostly ginger ale," he said, "and I thought it would cool you off. It's right hot tonight."

It is this moment, she thought, that I've been waiting for through the whole weekend. And in this moment she banished all the despair that had been growing in her feelings toward Son and the girls. The insufferable insolence with which Mattie had treated her today also seemed as nothing. He has come to tell me what is in his heart. Or at least he has come so that we may have a few minutes alone before he leaves for the Army tomorrow. She glanced up at the childhood pictures of him which with pictures of the girls and a few of Mama and Papa and of Sweetheart covered one wall of her room. She pointed to a picture taken when he was thirteen wearing a skullcap on the back of his head and a sleeveless sweater. "That's my favorite," she said. "I began to notice a new look in your eyes when you were that age."

Son looked at the picture. Then his eyes roved indifferently over the other pictures there. "Well," he said, "I'd better go out and see that the girls are not sticking hat pins in Ann just to see how she reacts. Or at least not miss seeing it, myself, if they do."

The guests were beginning to leave by eleven-thirty. Harriet was sitting in a straight chair on the front porch. She had been sitting there in the dark for an hour with her hands folded in her lap. Sweetheart was slumped down among the pillows on the swing near by, asleep. The party had all been vague to Harriet, like a dream of some event she dreaded. After Son left her standing alone before the gallery of pictures in her room she was hardly able to go into the house and meet the guests. There were no tears and no signs of nervous agitation. Rather, she felt herself completely without human emotion of any sort as she lingered there in her room for a long while. When finally she did go forward and take her place by the buffet in the dining room, she pretended to be preoccupied with the food so that the guests would not notice how little concern she had for them. There were things she had planned to watch for this evening; but those things had become trivial and remote.

Early in the evening most of the party was gathered in the parlor and much of the conversation referred to things that had been said and done last night. Harry Buchanan urged Ann to express her views on something, but Ann declined. Several times Son was asking Ann what she thought about this or that, and always it seemed that Ann spoke two or three monosyllables which were followed by silence. Conversation between Son and the young professor did not materialize, and the girls did not try to draw him out as Harriet had expected. Ann and the professor were once heard talking about the "fragrance" of the wisteria. Helena took her tall, stooped young man to sit on the screened porch. Kate took hers to the chairs on the lawn. Now and then the two beaux appeared in the house on their way to the pantry with tall, empty glasses. Nothing could stir Harriet from her torpor, not even the information that in the middle of the evening B.T. had put on his hat and gone off to the settlement or to Nashville.

When she realized that the guests were beginning to go, she placed her hand on Sweetheart's knee and said, "People are leaving, Sweetheart." He followed her into the hall and the two of them stood smiling and nodding and shaking hands of guests amid the hubbub of giddy and even drunken talk about Son's going into the Army. As the last of the automobiles pulled away, backing and turning in the gravel before the garage with its headlamps flashing on B.T.'s shack and on the house and then on the trees and the white gravel of the driveway, someone called back, "Good-bye, Private Wilson!"

Harriet stood on the screened porch after the headlamps had gone round the house leaving the yard in darkness. While she was there she saw the light go off in the kitchen. The backdoor closed, and presently Mattie's dark figure moved sluggishly across the yard to the shack. There was no window on the near side of the little cabin, but when Mattie had put on the light inside, Harriet could see a square of light which a small window threw on a thick, green mint bed over by the fence. "She's going to wait up for B.T.," Harriet said. And now she went through the house and into the warm kitchen to see in what state Mattie had left things.

The dishes were not washed but they were stacked neatly on the table and in the sink. The backdoor was locked, and Harriet unlocked it so that Mattie could come in that way to go to her bed in the attic room above the kitchen. "Poor thing is so distracted she locked herself out," she said. She stood with her hand on the knob for a minute, for she wanted to go out and see Mattie. She could not bring herself to go.

When she came into the parlor she found that Ann had changed to her traveling dress. Helena and Kate were sprawled in two of the large chairs. Sweetheart was standing by the fireplace talking about train schedules to Little Rock. Ann was seated on the piano bench with her feet close together and her small delicate hands folded in her lap. Harriet had crossed the room and was taking her seat beside Ann when Son entered with the luggage.

"It's not quite time to go," Son said. He set the two bags by the hall door and drew up an odd chair. Harriet had taken one of Ann's hands between her own and was about to make a little farewell speech when Ann spoke.

She was looking into Harriet's face but as she spoke she turned her eyes to Son. "He thinks I have not behaved well tonight."

"Oh, for Heaven's sake, Ann," Son said, turning in his chair and crossing his legs. Kate and Helena visibly collected their sprawled persons and looked attentively from Ann to Son.

"He does, indeed," said Ann. She stood up and walked to the mantel and stood at the other end from Sweetheart. "Very badly. He always thinks a person behaves badly who doesn't amuse him. He cares nothing for anything I say except when I'm talking theory of some kind. He was very willing to bring me here before your friends to express all manner of opinion which they and you find disagreeable while he behaves with conventional good taste. He even discouraged me bringing the proper clothes to make any sort of agreeable appearance. Yet see how smartly he's turned out."

Son had now ceased to show any discomfort. He was watching Ann with the same interest that the girls showed. He was smiling when he interrupted her, "You are really drunk, Ann. But go on. You're priceless. You're rich. What else about me?"

"Nothing else about you," she said, undismayed. "But about me, now . . . We have had a very beautiful and very Platonic friendship. He has shown a marvelous respect for my intelligence and my virtue. And I, alas, have been so vulgar as to fall in love with him." She turned to Sweetheart who stood with his hands hanging limp at his sides and his mouth literally wide open. "It's a sad story, is it not, Doctor?" The doctor tried to smile.

Son rose from his chair saying, "Now it *is* time we go." And he and Ann left the room in such a hurry that Harriet was still seated when she heard them step out onto the porch. Then she jumped from her place on the piano bench and began to follow them.

But she had only reached the doorway to the hall when one of the girls said, "Mother, can't you see how drunk that gal really is?" As she stopped there in the hall her eyes fell on the mahogany umbrella rack where Sweetheart kept his seven walking sticks. She counted the sticks and it seemed that there were only six of them. Then she counted them again and found that all seven were in their places. She counted them several times over, and each time there were still seven sticks in the rack.

Harriet was on her knees at her bedside. She had already repeated the Lord's Prayer twice but still was unable to think of the meaning of the words as she began it the third time. Her elbows were pressing into the soft mattress, and though the room was in darkness her eyes were closed. She was repeating the prayer slowly, moving her lips as she pronounced each word, when the fierce shout of a Negro woman seemed to break not only the silence but even the darkness. Sweetheart had sprung from the bed and put on the light. Harriet remained on her knees and watched him go to the closet shelf to get his pistol. "It's Mattie," she said. "It's Mattie screaming!"

"No, it's not Mattie," she said. "I don't think it was a scream either." Sweetheart turned his eyes to her with a suddenness that struck her dumb for a moment. When she was able to speak she said, "It's one of those women B.T. has." But the doctor had understood her before she spoke again and in his white pajamas had already disappeared into the darkness of the hallway.

His hearing had been keen enough to detect that it was a Negro's voice. But his ear was not so sensitive as Harriet's. She was the only one in the house who knew that Mattie was waiting in the shack, and the shout came distinctly from that quarter; but her ear was not deceived for an instant. She raised herself from her knees and faced her two daughters who had come to her door. She knew as well now as they would know when they were told a few minutes later what scene was taking place in the low doorway of that cabin. In her mind she saw the very shadows that were then being thrown on the green mint bed.

The first shout was followed by other distinct oaths. Now Mattie's and B.T.'s voices could be heard mixing with that of the third Negro. So Harriet knew too that there had not yet been a cutting. "Hurry, Sweetheart," she called in a voice that hardly seemed her own. The girls stood watching her, and she stood motionless listening for every sound. Presently there came amid the voices the crunching sound of gravel under the wheels of her own coupe. Son was returning home from the depot. She pushed herself between the girls and went to the window in their room. From there she could see that the incident was over. Sweetheart and Son stood in the bright light from the headlamps of the automobile. They stood talking there for several minutes, and then Son came toward the house and Sweetheart went into the shack.

Son came into her room where she and the girls were waiting. His face was pale, but he was smiling. "It's not really anything," he said. "B.T. had brought one of his lady friends home, and his auntie would not receive her. I think his auntie even struck her. The lights of the car scared her off into the woods, and B.T. followed. Dad's bringing Mattie into the house."

Harriet put on her robe and went through the house to the kitchen. She waited there a long while watching the light in the shack. Finally Sweetheart appeared on the stoop. He stood there in his white pajamas for an endless time speaking into the doorway in such a quiet voice that she could not hear him. When he did turn and see her at the kitchen he left the shack and came to her at once.

"You'll have to talk to Mattie," he said. "She doesn't want to come in the house, but of course she'll have to. That pair just might come back tonight."

Harriet gazed at him blankly for a moment and then closed her eyes. "I can't go," she said.

"Harriet? You'll have to go, love. I'll go with you and wait at the door. The poor creature needs you."

"Did she ask for me?"

"No. She didn't think to. She's in a terrible state. She doesn't talk."

"Did you tell her I was coming?"

"Yes," he said, "and that's the only thing that made her even look at me."

Harriet turned away and moved toward the dining room. When he called to her she was at the swinging door and she said, "I'm going to dress."

"You've no need to dress," he said. He came round the kitchen table and stopped a few feet from her. She had never known him to speak to her in private from such a distance. "Harriet, why should this be so hard for you?"

There was no sympathy in the question, and actually he did not seem to want an answer to this precise question. He seemed to be making a larger and more general inquiry into her character than he had ever done before. She dropped her eyes to the floor and walked hurriedly by him to the backdoor. She paused there and said, "Wait here."

Mattie was seated on a squat, ladder-back chair whose short legs had the look of being worn away through long usage. Her brown hands were resting on the black dress over each knee. A dim bulb hung on a cord almost at waist level, and the gray moths that flitted around it were lighting on Mattie's head. Harriet came in and stood directly before her. When she first tried to speak she felt that she was going to be nauseated by the awful smell of B.T., a stench that seemed to be compounded of the smell of soiled and moldy clothing and the smell of condensed and concentrated human sweat. She even glanced about the room half expecting to find B.T. standing in one of the dark corners. "Mattie," she said at last, "I was unkind to you Saturday. You must not hold it against me."

Mattie raised her eyes to her mistress, and there was neither forgiveness nor resentment in them. In her protruding lower lip and in her wide nostrils there was defiance, but it was a defiance of the general nature of this world where she must pass her days, not of Harriet in particular. In her eyes there was grief and there was something beyond grief. After a moment she did speak, and she told Harriet that she was going to sit there all night and that they had all better go on to bed in the house. Later when Harriet tried to recall the exact tone and words Mattie had used—as her acute ear would normally have allowed her to do—she could not reconstruct the speech at all. It seemed as though Mattie had used a special language common to both of them but one they had never before discovered and could now never recover. Afterward they faced each other in uncommunicative silence for an indefinite time. Finally Harriet moved to the door again, but she looked back once more and she saw that besides the grief and hostility in Mattie's eyes there was an unspeakable loneliness for which she could offer no consolation.

When she told Sweetheart that Mattie still refused to leave the shack he sat down on the porch steps and said that he was going to keep watch for a while. She didn't try to dissuade him, and he said nothing more to her as she put her robe about her shoulders and went inside.

In her room she tried to resume her broken prayers. Then she lay on the bed with the light still burning and she longed to weep as she had done when she first saw Son in the doorway. Not a tear would come to her eyes. She thought of all the talking that Son and the girls had done and she felt that she was even beginning to understand what it had meant. But she sadly reflected that her children believed neither what Ann Prewitt nor what the professors at the University were offering them. To Harriet it seemed that her children no longer existed; it was as though they had all died in childhood as people's children used to do. All the while she kept remembering that Mattie was sitting out in that shack for the sole purpose of inhaling the odor in the stifling air of B.T.'s room.

When Sweetheart finally came she was on her knees again at her bedside. She heard him put out the light and let himself down easily on the other side of the bed. When she opened her eyes it was dark and there was the chill of autumn night about the room.

RAIN
IN THE HEART

WHEN THE DRILLING was over they stopped at the edge of the field and the drill sergeant looked across the flat valley toward the woods on Peavine Ridge. Among the shifting lights on the treetops there in the late afternoon the drill sergeant visualized pointed roofs of houses that were on another, more thickly populated ridge seven miles to the west.

Lazily the sergeant rested the butt end of his rifle in the mud and turned to tell the squad of rookies to return to their own barracks. But they had already gone on without him and he stood a moment watching them drift back toward the rows of squat buildings, some with their rifles thrown over their shoulders, others toting them by the leather slings in suitcase fashion.

On the field behind the sergeant were the tracks which he and the twelve men had made during an hour's drilling. He turned and studied the tracks for a moment, wondering whether or not he could have told how many men had been tramping there if that had been necessary for telling the strength of an enemy. Then with a shrug of his shoulders he turned his face toward Peavine Ridge again, thinking once more of that other ridge in the suburban area where his bride had found furnished rooms. And seeing how the ridge before him stretched out endlessly north and south he was reminded of a long bus and streetcar ride that was before him on his journey to their rooms this night. Suddenly throwing the rifle over his shoulder, he began to make his way back toward his own barrack.

The immediate approach to the barrack of the noncommissioned officers was over a wide asphalt area where all formations were held. As the sergeant crossed the asphalt, it required a special effort for him to raise his foot each time. Since his furlough and wedding trip to the mountains, this was the first night the sergeant had been granted leave to go in to see his wife. When he reached the stoop before the entrance to the barrack he lingered by the bulletin board. He stood aimlessly examining the notices posted there. But finally drawing himself up straight he turned and walked erectly and swiftly inside. He knew that the barrack would be filled with men ready with stale, friendly, evil jokes.

As he hurried down the aisle of the barrack he removed his blue denim jacket, indicating his haste. It seemed at first that no one had noticed him. Yet he was still filled with a dread of the jokes which must inevitably be directed at him today. At last a copper-headed corporal who sat on the bunk next to his own, whittling his toenails with his knife, had begun to sing:

> *"Yes, she jumped in bed*
> *And she covered up her head—"*

Another voice across the aisle took up the song here:

> *"And she vowed he couldn't find her."*

Then other voices, some faking soprano, others simulating the deepest choir bass, from all points of the long room joined in:

> *"But she knew damned well*
> *That she lied like hell*
> *When he jumped right in beside her."*

The sergeant blushed a little, pretended to be very angry, and began to undress for his shower. Silently he reminded himself that when he started for town he must take with him the big volume of Civil War history, for it was past due at the city library. *She* could have it renewed for him tomorrow.

In the shower too the soldiers pretended at first to take no notice of him. They were talking of their own plans for the evening in town. One tall and bony sergeant with a head of wiry black hair was saying, "I've got a strong deal on tonight with a WAC from Vermont. But of course we'll have to be in by midnight."

Now the copper-headed corporal had come into the shower. He was smaller than most of the other soldiers, and beneath his straight copper-colored hair were a pair of bright gray-green eyes. He had a hairy potbelly that looked like a football. "My deal's pretty strong tonight, too," he said, addressing the tall soldier beside him. "She lives down the road a way with her family, so I'll have to be in early too. But then you and me won't be all fagged out tomorrow, eh, Slim!"

"No," the tall and angular soldier said, "we'll be able to hold our backs up straight and sort of carry ourselves like soldiers, as some won't feel like doing."

The lukewarm shower poured down over the chest and back of the drill sergeant. This was his second year in the Army and now he found himself continually surprised at the small effect that the stream of words of the soldiers had upon him.

Standing in the narrow aisle between his own bunk and that of the copper-headed corporal, he pulled on his clean khaki clothes before an audience of naked soldiers who lounged on the two bunks.

"When I marry," the wiry-headed sergeant was saying, "I'll marry me a WAC who I can take right to the front with me."

"You shouldn't do that," the corporal said, "she might be wounded in action." He and the angular, wiry-headed sergeant laughed so bawdily and merrily that the drill sergeant joined in, hardly knowing what were the jokes they'd been making. But the other naked soldiers, of more regular shapes, found the jokes not plain enough, and they began to ask literally:

"Can a WAC and a soldier overseas get married?"

"If a married WAC gets pregnant, what happens?"

"When I get married," said one soldier who was stretched out straight on his back with his eyes closed and a towel thrown across his loins, "it'll be to a nice girl like the sergeant here's married."

The sergeant looked at him silently.

"But wherever," asked Slim, "are *you* going to meet such a girl like that in such company as you keep?"

The soldier lying on his back opened one eye: "I wouldn't talk about my company if I was you. I've saw you and the corporal here with them biddy-dolls at Midway twiest."

The corporal's eyes shone. He laughed aloud and fairly shouted. "And *he* got *me* the date both times, Buck."

"Well," said Buck, with his eyes still closed and his hands folded over his bare chest, "when I marry it won't be to one of them sort. Nor not to one of your WACs neither, Slim."

Slim said, "Blow it out your barracks bag."

One of those more regularly shaped soldiers seemed to rouse himself as from sleep to say, "That's why y'like 'em, ain't it, Slim? Y'like 'em because they know how?" His joke was sufficiently plain to bring laughter from all. They all looked toward Slim. Even the soldier who was lying down opened one eye and looked at him. And Slim, who was rubbing his wiry mop of black hair with a white towel, muttered, "At least I don't pollute little kids from the roller rink like some present."

The naked soldier named Buck who was stretched out on the cot opened his eyes and rolled them in the direction of Slim. Then he closed his eyes meditatively and suddenly opened them again. He sat up and swung his feet around to the floor. "Well, I did meet an odd number the other night," he said. "She was drinking beer alone in Connor's Café when I comes in and sits on her right, like this." He patted his hand on the olive-drab blanket, and all the while he talked he was not looking at the other soldiers. Rather his face was turned toward the window at the end of his cot, and with his lantern jaw raised and his small, round eyes squinting, he peered into the rays of sunlight. "She was an odd one and wouldn't give me any sort of talk as long as I sit there. Then I begun to push off and she says out of the clear,

'Soldier, what did the rat say to the cat?' I said that I don't know and she says, 'This pussy's killin' me.'" Now all the other soldiers began to laugh and hollo. But Buck didn't even smile. He continued to squint up into the light and to speak in the same monotone. "So I said, 'Come on,' and jerked her up by the arm. But, you know, she was odd. She never did say much but tell a nasty joke now and then. She didn't have a bunch of small talk, but she come along and did all right. But I do hate to hear a woman talk nasty.".

The potbellied corporal winked at the drill sergeant and said, "Listen to him. He says he's going to marry a nice girl like yours, but I bet you didn't run up on yours in Connor's Café or the roller rink."

Buck whisked the towel from across his lap and drawing it back he quickly snapped it at the corporal's little, hairy potbelly. The drill sergeant laughed with the rest and watched for a moment the patch of white that the towel made on the belly which was otherwise still red from the hot shower.

Now the drill sergeant was dressed. He combed his sandy-colored hair before a square hand mirror which he had set on the windowsill. The sight of himself reminded him of her who would already be waiting for him on that other ridge. She with her soft, Southern voice, her small hands forever clasping a handkerchief. This was what his own face in the tiny mirror brought to mind. How unreal to him were these soldiers and their hairy bodies and all their talk and their rough ways. How temporary. How different from his own life, from his real life with her.

He opened his metal footlocker and took out the history book in which he had been reading of battles that once took place on this campsite and along the ridge where he would ride the bus tonight. He pulled his khaki overseas cap onto the right side of his head and slipped away, apparently unnoticed, from the soldiers gathered there. They were all listening now to Slim who was saying, "Me and Pat McKenzie picked up a pretty little broad one night who was deaf and dumb. But when me and her finally got around to shacking up she made the damnedest noises you ever heard."

With the book clasped under his arm the drill sergeant passed down the aisle between the rows of cots, observing here a half-dressed soldier picking up a pair of dirty socks, there another soldier shining a pair of prized garrison shoes or tying a khaki tie with meticulous care. The drill sergeant's thoughts were still on her whose brown curls fell over the white collar of her summer dress. And he could dismiss the soldiers as he passed them as good fellows each, saying, "So long, Smoky Joe," to one who seemed to be retiring even before sundown, and "So long, Happy Jack," to another who scowled at him. They were good rough-and-ready fellows all, Smoky Joe, Happy Jack, Slim, Buck, and the copper-headed one. But one of them called to him as he went out the door, "I wouldn't take no book along. What you think you want with a book this night?" And the laughter came through the open windows after he was outside on the asphalt.

The bus jostled him and rubbed him against the civilian workers from the camp and the mill workers who climbed aboard with their dinner pails at the first stop. He could feel the fat thighs of middle-aged women rubbing against the sensitive places of his body, and they—unaware of such personal feelings —leaned toward one another and swapped stories about their outrageous bosses. One of the women said that for a little she'd quit this very week. The men, also mostly middle-aged and dressed in overalls and shirt-sleeves, seemed sensible of nothing but that this suburban bus somewhere crossed Lake Road, Pidgeon Street, Jackson Boulevard, and that at some such intersection they must be ready to jerk the stop cord and alight. "The days are getting a little shorter," one of them said.

The sergeant himself alighted at John Ross Road and transferred to the McFarland Gap bus. The passengers on this bus were not as crowded as on the first. The men were dressed in linen and seersucker business suits, and the women carried purses and wore little tailored dresses and straw hats. Those who were crowded together did not make any conversation among themselves. Even those who seemed to know one another talked in whispers. The sergeant was standing in the aisle but he bent over now and again and looked out the windows at the neat bungalows and larger dwelling houses along the roadside. He would one day have a house such as one of those for his own. His own father's house was the like of these, with a screened porch on the side and a fine tile roof. He could hear his father saying, "A house is only as good as the roof over it." But weren't these the things that had once seemed prosaic and too binding for his notions? Before he went into the Army had there not been moments when the thought of limiting himself to a genteel suburban life seemed intolerable by its restrictions and confinement? Even by the confinement to the company of such people as those here on the bus with him? And yet now when he sometimes lay wakeful and lonesome at night in the long dark barrack among the carefree and garrulous soldiers or when he was kneed and elbowed by the worried and weary mill hands on a bus, he dreamed longingly of the warm companionship he would find with her and their sober neighbors in a house with a fine roof.

The rattling, bumping bus pulled along for several miles over the road atop the steep ridge which it had barely managed to climb in first gear. At the end of the bus line he stepped out to the roadside and waited for his streetcar. The handful of passengers that were still on the bus climbed out too and scattered to all parts of the neighborhood, disappearing into doorways of brick bungalows or clapboard two-storied that were perched among evergreens and oak trees and maple and wild sumac on the crest and on the slopes of the ridge. *This* would be a good neighborhood to settle down in. The view was surely a prize— any way you chose to look.

But the sergeant had hardly more than taken his stand in the grass to wait for the streetcar, actually leaning a little against a low wall that bordered a sloping lawn, when he observed the figure of a woman standing in the shadow of a small chinaberry tree which grew beside the wall.

The woman came from behind the tree and stood by the wall. She was within three or four steps of the sergeant. He looked at her candidly, and her plainness from the very first made him want to turn his face away toward the skyline of the city in the valley. Her flat-chested and generally ill-shaped figure was clothed with a baglike gingham dress that hung at an uneven knee length. On her feet was a pair of flat-heeled brown oxfords. She wore white, ankle-length socks that emphasized the hairiness of her muscular legs. On her head a dark felt hat was drawn down almost to her eyebrows. Her hair was straight and of a dark color less rich than brown and yet more brown than black, and it was cut so that a straight not wholly greaseless strand hung over each cheek and turned upward just the slightest bit at the ends.

And in her hands before her the woman held a large bouquet of white and lavender sweet peas. She held them, however, as though they were a bunch of mustard greens. Or perhaps she held them more as a small boy holds flowers, half ashamed to be seen holding anything so delicate. Her eyes did not rest on them. Rather her eyes roved nervously up and down the car tracks. At last she turned her colorless, long face to the sergeant and asked with an artificial smile that showed her broad gums and small teeth, "Is this where the car stops?"

"I think so," he said. Then he did look away toward the city.

"I saw the yellow mark up there on the post, but I wasn't real sure," she pursued. He had to look back at her, and as he did so she said, "Don't that uniform get awful hot?"

"Oh yes," he said. He didn't want to say more. But finally a thought of his own good fortune and an innate kindness urged him to speak again. "I sometimes change it two or three times a day."

"I'd sure say it would get hot."

After a moment's silence the sergeant observed, "This is mighty hot weather."

"It's awful hot here in the summer," she said. "But it's always awful here in some way. Where are you from?"

He still wanted to say no more. "I'm from West Tennessee."

"What part?" she almost demanded.

"I'm from Memphis. It gets mighty hot there."

"I oncet know somebody from there."

"Memphis gets awfully hot in the summer too."

"Well," she said, drawing in a long breath, "you picked an awful hot place to come to. I don't mind heat so much. It's just an awful place to be. I've lived here all my life and I hate it here."

The sergeant walked away up the road and leaned forward looking for the streetcar. Then he walked back to the wall because he felt that she would think him a snob. Unable to invent other conversation, he looked at the flowers and said, "They're very pretty."

"Well, if you like 'em at all," she said, "you like 'em a great lot more than I do. I hate flowers. Only the other day I say to Mother that if I get sick and go the hospital don't bring any flowers around me. I don't want any. I don't like 'em."

"Why, those are pretty," he said. He felt for some reason that he must defend their worth. "I like all flowers. Those are especially hard to grow in West Tennessee."

"If you like 'em you like 'em more than I do. Only the other day I say to my Sunday School teacher that if I would die it'd save her a lot of money because I don't want anybody to send no flowers. I hate 'em. And it ain't just these. I hate all flowers."

"I think they're pretty," he insisted. "Did you pick 'em down there in the valley?"

"They was growing wild in a field and I picked them because I didn't have nothin' else to do. Here," she said, pushing the flowers into his hands, "you take 'em. I hate 'em."

"No, no, I wouldn't think of taking your flowers. Here, you must take them back."

"I don't want 'em. I'll just throw 'em away."

"Why, I can't take your flowers."

"You have 'em, and I ain't going to take 'em back. They'll just lay there and die if you put them on the wall."

"I feel bad accepting them. You must have gone to a lot of trouble to pick them."

"They was just growing wild at the edge of a field, and the lady said they was about to take her garden. I don't like flowers. I did her a favor, and you can do me one."

"There's nothing I like better," he said, feeling that he had been ungracious. "I guess I would like to raise flowers, and I used to work in the garden some." He leaned forward, listening for the sound of the streetcar.

For a minute or two neither of them spoke. She shifted from foot to foot and seemed to be talking to herself. From the corner of his eye he watched her lips moving. Finally she said aloud, "Some people act like they're doing you a favor to pay you a dollar a day."

"That's not much in these times," he observed.

"It's just like I was saying to a certain person the other day, 'If you are not willing to pay a dollar and a half a day you don't want nobody to work for you very bad.' But I work for a dollar just the same. This is half of it right here." She held up a half dollar between her thumb and forefinger. "But last week I pay for all my insurance for next year. I put my money away instead of buying things I really want. You can't say that for many girls."

"You certainly can't."

"Not many girls do that."

"I don't know many that do."

"No sirree," she said, snapping the fingers of her right hand, "the girls in this place are awful. I hate the way they act with soldiers downtown. They go to the honky-tonks and drink beer. I don't waste anybody's money drinking beer. I put my own money away instead of buying things I might really want."

The sergeant stepped out into the middle of the road and listened for the streetcar. As he returned to the wall, a Negro man and woman rode by in a large blue sedan. The woman standing by the wall watched the automobile go over the street-car tracks and down the hill. "There's no Negro in this town that will do housework for less than two and a half a day, and they pay us whites only a dollar."

"Why will they pay Negroes more?" he asked.

"Because they can boss 'em," she said hastily. "Just because they can boss 'em around. I say to a certain person the other day, 'You can't boss me around like a nigger, no ma'am.'"

"I suppose that's it." He now began to walk up and down in front of her, listening and looking for the streetcar and occasionally raising the flowers to his nose to smell them. She continued to lean against the wall, motionless and with her humorless face turned upward toward the car wire where were hanging six or eight rolled newspapers tied in pairs by long dirty strings. "How y'reckon them papers come to be up there?" she asked.

"Some of the neighborhood kids or paperboys did it, I guess."

"Yea. That's it. Rich people's kids's just as bad as anybody's."

"Well, the paperboys probably did it whenever they had papers left over. I've done it myself when I was a kid."

"Yea," she said through her nose. "But kids just make me nervous. And I didn't much like bein' a kid neither."

The sergeant looked along one of the steel rails that still glimmered a little in the late sunlight and remembered good times he had had walking along the railroad tracks as a child. Suddenly he hoped his first child would be a boy.

"I'll tell you one thing, soldier," the woman beside him was saying, "I don't spend my money on lipstick and a lot of silly clothes. I don't paint myself with a lot of lipstick and push my hair up on top of my head and walk around downtown so soldiers will look at me. You don't find many girls that don't do that in this awful place, do ya?"

"You certainly don't find many." The sergeant felt himself blushing.

"You better be careful, for you're going to drop some of them awful flowers. I don't know what you want with 'em."

"Why, they're pretty," he said as though he had not said it before.

Now the blue sedan came up the hill again and rolled quietly over the car tracks. Only the Negro man was in the sedan, and he was driving quite fast.

"How can a nigger like that own a car like that?"

"He probably only drives for some of the people who live along here."

"Yea. That's it. That's it. Niggers can get away with anything. I guess you've heard about 'em attacking that white girl down yonder."

"Yes . . . Yes."

"They ought to kill 'em all or send 'em all back to Africa."

"It's a real problem, I think."

"I don't care if no man black or white never looks at me if I have to put on a lot of lipstick and push my hair up and walk around without a hat."

The sergeant leaned forward, craning his neck.

"I'm just going to tell you what happened to me downtown the other day," she persisted. "I was standing looking in a store window on Broad when a soldier comes up behind me, and I'm just going to tell you what he said. He said he had a hotel room, and he asked me if I didn't want to go up to the room with him and later go somewhere to eat and that he'd give me some money too."

"I know," the sergeant said. "There's a mighty rough crowd in town now."

"But I just told him, 'No thanks. If I can't make money honest I don't want it,' is what I told him. I says, 'There's a girl on that corner yonder at Main that wants ya. Just go down there.' "

The sergeant stood looking down the track, shaking his head.

"He comes right up behind me, you understand, and tells me that he has a room in a hotel and that we can go there and do what we want to do and then go get something to eat and he will give me some money besides. And I just told him, 'No thanks. There's a girl on that corner yonder at Main that wants ya. Just go down there.' So I went off up the street a way and then I come back to where I was looking at a lot of silly clothes, and a man in a blue shirt who was standing there all the time says that the soldier had come back looking for me."

The sergeant stretched out his left arm so that his wristwatch appeared from under his sleeve. Then he crooked his elbow and looked at the watch.

"Oh, you have *some* wait yet," she said.

"How often do they run?"

"I don't know," she said without interest, "just every so often. I told him, y'see, if I can't make money honest I don't want it. You can't say that for many girls." Whenever his attention seemed to lag, her speech grew louder.

"No, you can't," he agreed.

"I save my money. Soldier, I've got two hundred and seven dollars in the bank, besides my insurance paid up for next year." She said nothing during what seemed to be several minutes. Then she asked, "Where do your mother and daddy live?"

"In West Tennessee."

"Where do you stay? Out at the camp?" She hardly gave him time to answer her questions now.

"Well, I stay out at camp some nights."

"*Some* nights? Where do you stay other nights?" She was grinning.

"I'm married and stay with my wife. I've just been married a little while but we have rooms up the way here."

"Oh, are you a married man? Where is she from? I hope she ain't from here."

"She's from Memphis. She's just finished school."

The woman frowned, blushed deeply, then she grinned again showing her wide gums. "I'd say you are goin' to take her the flowers. You won't have to buy her any."

"I do wish you'd take some of them back."

The woman didn't answer him for a long time. Finally, when he had almost forgotten what he had said last, she said without a sign of a grin, "I don't want 'em. The sight of 'em makes me sick."

And at last the streetcar came.

It was but a short ride now to the sergeant's stop. The car stopped just opposite the white two-story house. The sergeant alighted and had to stand on the other side of the track until the long yellow streetcar had rumbled away. It was as though an ugly, noisy curtain had at last been drawn back. He saw her face through an upstairs window of the white house with its precise cupola rising ever higher than the tall brick chimneys and with fantastic lacy woodwork ornamenting the tiny porches and the cornices. He saw her through the only second-story window that was clearly visible between the foliage of trees that grew in the yard.

The house was older than most of the houses in the suburban neighborhood along this ridgetop, and an old-fashioned iron fence enclosed its yard. He had to stop a moment to unlatch the iron gate, and there he looked directly up into the smiling countenance at the open window. She spoke to him in a voice even softer than he remembered.

Now he had to pass through his landlady's front hall and climb a crooked flight of stairs before reaching his rooms, and an old-fashioned bell had tinkled when he opened the front door. At this tinkling sound an old lady's voice called from somewhere in the back of the house, "Yes?" But he made no answer. He hurried up the steps and was at last in the room with his wife.

They sat on the couch with their knees touching and her hand in his.

Just as her voice was softer, her appearance was fairer even than he had remembered. He told her that he had been rehearsing this moment during every second of the past two hours, and simultaneously he realized that what he was saying was true, that during all other conversations and actions his imagination had been going over and over the present scene.

She glanced at the sweet peas lying beside his cap on the table and said that when she had seen him in the gateway with the flowers she had felt that perhaps during the time they were separated she had not remembered him even as gentle and fine as he was. Yet she had been afraid until that moment by the window that in her heart she had exaggerated these virtues of his.

The sergeant did not tell her then how he had come into possession of the flowers. He knew that the incident of the cleaning woman would depress her good spirits as it had his own. And while he was thinking of the complete understanding and sympathy between them he heard her saying, "I know you are tired. You're probably not so tired from soldiering as from dealing with people of various sorts all day. I went to the grocery myself this morning and coming home on the bus I thought of how tiresome and boring the long ride home would be for you this evening when the buses are so crowded." He leaned toward her and kissed her, holding her until he realized that she was smiling. He released her, and she drew away with a laugh and said that she had supper to tend to and that she must put the sweet peas in water.

While she was stirring about the clean, closet-like kitchen, he surveyed in the late twilight the living room that was still a strange room to him, and without lighting the table or floor lamps he wandered into the bedroom, which was the largest room and from which an old-fashioned bay window overlooked the valley. He paused at the window and raised the shade. And he was startled by a magnificent view of the mountains that rose up on the other side of the city. And there he witnessed the last few seconds of a sunset—brilliant orange and brick red—beyond the blue mountains.

They ate at a little table that she drew out from the wall in the living room. "How have I merited such a good cook for a wife?" he said and smiled when the meal was finished. They stacked the dishes unwashed in the sink, for she had put her arms about his neck and whispered, "Why should I waste one moment of the time I have you here when the days are so lonesome and endless."

They sat in the living room and read aloud the letters that had come during the past few days.

For a little while she worked on the hem of a tablecloth, and they talked. They spoke of their friends at home. She showed him a few of their wedding presents that had arrived late. And they kept saying how fortunate they were to have found an apartment so comfortable as this. Here on the ridge it was cool almost every night.

Afterward he took out his pen and wrote a letter to his father. He read the letter aloud to her.

Still later it rained. The two of them hurried about putting down windows. Then they sat and heard it whipping and splashing against the window glass when the wind blew.

By the time they were both in their nightclothes the rain had stopped. He sat on a footstool by the bed reading in the heavy, dark history book. Once he read aloud a sentence which he thought impressive: "I have never seen the Federal dead lie so thickly on the ground save in front of the sunken wall at Fredericksburg." This was a Southern general writing of the battle fought along this ridgetop.

"What a very sad-sounding sentence," she said. She was brushing her hair in long, even strokes.

Finally he put down the book but remained sitting on the stool to polish his low-quartered military shoes. She at her dressing table looked at his reflection in the mirror before her, and said, "It's stopped raining."

"It stopped a good while ago," he said. And he looked up attentively, for there had seemed to be some regret in her voice.

"I'm sorry it stopped," she said, returning his gaze.

"You should be glad," he said. "I'd have to drill in all that mud tomorrow."

"Of course I'm glad," she said. "But hasn't the rain made us seem even more alone up here?"

The sergeant stood up. The room was very still and close. There was not even the sound of a clock. A light was burning on her dressing table, and through the open doorway he could see the table lamp that was still burning in the living room. The table there was a regular part of the furnishing of the apartment. But it was a piece of furniture they might have chosen themselves. He went to the door and stood a moment studying the effect she had achieved in her arrangement of objects on the table. On the dark octagonal top was the white lamp with the urn-shaped base. The light the lamp shed contrasted the shape of the urn with the global shape of a crystal vase from which sprigs of ivy mixed with periwinkle sprang in their individual wiriness. And a square, crystal ashtray reflecting its exotic lights was placed at an angle to a small round silver dish.

He went to the living room to put out the light. Yet with his hand on the switch he hesitated because it was such a pleasing isolated arrangement of objects.

Once the light was out he turned immediately to go back into the bedroom. And now he halted in the doorway again, for as he entered the bedroom his eye fell on the vase of sweet peas she had arranged. It was placed on top of a high bureau and he had not previously noticed it. Up there the flowers looked somehow curiously artificial and not like the real sweet peas he had seen in the rough hands of the woman this afternoon. While he was gazing thus he felt his wife's eyes upon him. Yet without turning to her he went to the window, for he was utterly preoccupied with the impression he had just received and he had a strange desire to sustain the impression long enough to examine it. He kept thinking of that woman's hands.

Now he raised the shade and threw open the big window in the bay, and standing there barefoot on a small hooked rug he looked out at the dark mountains and at the lines and splotches of lights in the city below. He heard her switching off the two small lamps at her dressing table. He knew that it had disturbed her to see him so suddenly preoccupied, and it was as though he tried to cram all of a whole day's reflections into a few seconds. Had it really been the pale flowers that had impressed him so? Or had it been the setting of his alarm clock a few minutes before and the realization that after a few more hours here with her he must take up again that other life that the yellow streetcar had carried away with it this afternoon? He could hear the voices of the boys in the barrack, and he saw the figure of the woman by the stone wall under the chinaberry tree.

Now he could hear his wife moving to switch off the overhead light. There was a click. The room being dark, things outside seemed much brighter. On the slope of the ridge that dropped off steeply behind the house the dark treetops became visible. And again there were the voices of the boys in the barrack. Their crudeness, their hardness, even their baseness—qualities that seemed to be taking root in the very hearts of those men—kept passing like objects through his mind. And the bitterness of the woman waiting by the streetcar tracks pressed upon him.

His wife had come up beside him in the dark and slipped her arm about his waist. He folded his arms tightly about her. She spoke his name. Then she said, "These hours we have together are so isolated and few that they must sometimes not seem quite real to you when you are away." She too, he realized, felt a terrible unrelated diversity in things. In the warmth of her companionship, he felt a sudden contrast with the cold fighting he might take part in on a battlefield that was now distant and almost abstract.

The sergeant's eyes had now grown so accustomed to the darkness inside and outside that he could look down between the trees on the slope of the ridge. He imagined there the line after line of Union soldiers that had once been thrown into the battle to take this ridge at all cost. The Confederate general's headquarters were not more than two blocks away. If he and she had been living in those days he would have seen ever so clearly the Cause for that fighting. And *this* battlefield would not be abstract. He would have stood here holding back the enemy from the very land which was his own, from the house in which she awaited him.

But here the sergeant stopped and smiled at himself. He examined the sergeant he had just imagined in the Confederate ranks and it was not himself at all. He compared the Confederate sergeant to the sergeant on the field this afternoon who had stood a moment puzzling over the tracks that twelve rookies had made. *The sergeant is I,* he said to himself desperately, *but it is not that morning in December of '62 when the Federal dead were lying so thick on the ground.* He leaned down and kissed his wife's forehead, and taking her up in his arms he carried her to their bed. *It is only a vase of flowers,* he remarked silently, rhetorically to himself as his wife drew her arms tighter about his neck. *Three bunches from a stand of sweet peas that had taken the lady's garden.* As he let her down gently on the bed she asked, "Why did you look so strangely at the vase of flowers? What did they make you think about so long by the window?"

For a moment the sergeant was again overwhelmed by his wife's perception and understanding. He would tell her everything he had in his mind. What great fortune it was to have a wife who could understand and to have her here beside him to hear and to comprehend everything that was in his heart and mind. But as he lay in the dark trying to make out the line of her profile against the dim light of the window, there came through the rainwashed air outside the rumbling of a streetcar. And before he could even speak the thoughts which he had been thinking, all those things no longer seemed to matter. The noise of the streetcar, the irregular rumble and uncertain clanging, brought back to him once more all the incidents of the day. He and his wife were here beside each other, but suddenly he was hopelessly distracted by this new sensation. The streetcar had moved away now beyond his hearing, and he could visualize it casting its diffused light among the dark foliage and over the white gravel between the tracks. He was left with the sense that no moment in his life had any relation to another. It was as though he were living a thousand lives. And the happiness and completeness of his marriage could not seem so large a thing.

Impulsively, almost without realizing what he was doing, he sat up on the other side of the bed. "I wasn't really thinking about the flowers," he said. "I guess I was thinking of how nicely you had arranged things on the living-room table."

"Oh," she said, for by his very words *I guess* it was apparent that she felt him minimizing the importance of his own impressions this evening and of their own closeness. In the dark he went to the small rocking chair on which his clothes were hanging and drew a cigarette from his shirt pocket. He lit it and sat on the edge of the little rocker, facing the open window, and he sat smoking his cigarette until quite suddenly the rain began to fall again. At the very first sound of the rain he stood up. He moved quickly to the window and put out his cigarette on the sill near the wire screen. The last bit of smoke sifted through the wire mesh. The rain was very noisy among the leaves. He stumbled hurriedly back through the dark and into the bed where he clasped his wife in his arms.

"It's begun to rain again," she said.

"Yes," the sergeant said. "It's much better now."

PORTE COCHERE

CLIFFORD AND BEN Jr. always came for Old Ben's birthday. Clifford came all the way from Dallas. Ben Jr. came only from Cincinnati. They usually stayed in Nashville through the following weekend, or came the weekend before and stayed through the birthday. Old Ben, who was seventy-six and nearly blind—the cataracts had been removed twice since he was seventy—could hear them now on the side porch, their voices louder than the others', Clifford's the loudest and strongest of all. "Clifford's the real man amongst them," he said to himself, hating to say it but needing to say it. There was no knowing what went on in the heads of the other children, but there were certain things Clifford did know and understand. Clifford, being a lawyer, knew something about history—about Tennessee history he knew, for instance, the difference between Chucky Jack Sevier and Judge John Overton and could debate with you the question of whether or not Andy Jackson had played the part of the coward when he and Chucky Jack met in the wilderness that time. Old Ben kept listening for Cliff's voice above the others. All of his grown-up children were down on the octagonal side porch, which was beyond the porte cochere and which, under its red tile roof, looked like a pagoda stuck out there on the side lawn. Old Ben was in his study.

His study was directly above the porte cochere, or what his wife, in her day, had called the porte cochere—he called it the drive-under and the children used to call it the portcullis—but the study was not a part of the second floor; it opened off the landing halfway up the stairs. Under his south window was the red roof of the porch. He sat by the open window, wearing his dark glasses, his watery old eyes focused vaguely on the peak of the roof. He had napped a little since dinner but had not removed his suit coat or even unbuttoned his linen vest. During most of the afternoon, he had been awake and had heard his five children talking down there on the porch—Cliff and Ben Jr. had arrived only that morning—talking on and on in such loud voices that his good right ear could catch individual words and sometimes whole sentences.

Midday dinner had been a considerable ordeal for Old Ben. Nell's interminable chatter had been particularly taxing and obnoxious. Afterward, he had hurried to his study for his prescribed nap and had spent a good part of the afternoon dreading the expedition to the Country Club for supper that had been planned for that evening. Now it was almost time to begin getting ready for that expedition, and simultaneously with the thought of it and with the movement of his hand toward his watch pocket he became aware that Clifford was taking his leave of the group on the side porch. Ah yes, at dinnertime Clifford had said he had a letter to write before supper—to his wife. Yet here it was six and he had dawdled away the afternoon palavering with the others down there on the porch. Old Ben could recognize Cliff's leave-taking and the teasing voices of the others, and then he heard Cliff's footsteps at the bottom of the stairs. In a moment he would go sailing by Old Ben's door, without a thought for anyone but himself. Old Ben's lower lip trembled. Wasn't there some business matter he could take up with Cliff? Or some personal matter? And now Cliff's footsteps on the stairs—heavy footsteps, like his own. Suddenly, though, the footsteps halted, and Clifford went downstairs again. His father heard him go across the hall and into the living room, where the carpet silenced his footsteps; he was getting writing paper from the desk there. Old Ben hastily pulled the cord that closed the draperies across the south window, leaving only the vague light from the east window in the room. No, sir, he would not advertise his presence when Cliff passed on the landing.

With the draperies drawn, the light in the room had a strange quality—strange because Old Ben seldom drew the draperies at night. For one moment, he felt that his eyes or his glasses were playing him some new trick. Then he dropped his head on the chairback, for the strange quality now seemed strangely familiar, and no longer strange—only familiar. It was like the light in the cellar where, long ago, he used to go fetch Mason jars for his great-aunt Nell Partee. Aunt Nell would send for him all the way across town to come fetch her Mason jars, and even when he was ten or twelve, she made him whistle the whole time he was down in the cellar, to make certain he didn't drink her wine. Aunt Nell, dead and gone. Was this something for Clifford's attention? Where Aunt Nell's shacky house had been, the Trust Company now stood—a near-skyscraper. Her cellar, he supposed, had been in the space now occupied by the basement barbershop—not quite so deep or so large as the shop, its area without boundaries now, suspended in the center of the barbershop, where the ceiling fan revolved. Would this be of interest to Cliff, who would soon ascend the stairs with his own train of thoughts and would pass the open door to the study without a word or a glance? And whatever Cliff was thinking about—his law, his gold, or his wife and children—would be of no real interest to Old Ben. But did not Clifford know that merely the sound of his voice gave his father hope, that his attention gave him comfort? What would old age be without children? Desolation, desolation. But what would old age be with children who chose to ignore the small demands that he would make upon them, that he had ever made upon them? A nameless torment! And with his thoughts Old Ben Brantley's white head rocked on his shoulders and his smoked glasses went so crooked on his nose that he had to frown them back into position.

But now Clifford was hurrying up the stairs again. He was on the landing outside the open study door. It was almost despite himself that the old man cleared his throat and said hoarsely, "The news will be on in five minutes, if you want to listen to it." Then as though he might have sounded too cordial (he would not be reduced to toadying to his own boy), "But if you don't want to, don't say you do." Had Cliff seen his glasses slip down his nose? Cliff, no less than the others, would be capable of laughing at him in his infirmity.

"I wouldn't be likely to, would I, Papa?" Cliff had stopped at the doorway and was stifling a yawn as he spoke, half covering his face with the envelope and the folded sheet of paper. Old Ben nodded his head to indicate that he had heard what Cliff had said, but also, to himself, he was nodding that yes, this was the way he had raised his children to talk to him.

"Just the hourly newscast," Old Ben said indifferently. "But it don't matter."

"Naw, can't make it, Papa. I got to go and write Sue Alice. The stupid woman staying with her while I'm away bores her pretty much." As he spoke, he looked directly into the dark lenses of his father's glasses, and for a brief second he rested his left hand on the doorjamb. His manner was self-possessed and casual, but Old Ben felt that he didn't need good sight to detect his poor son's ill-concealed haste to be off and away. Cliff had, in fact, turned back to the stairs when his father stopped him with a question, spoken without expression and almost under his breath.

"Why did you come at all? Why did you even bother to come if you weren't going to bring Sue Alice and the grandchildren? Did you think I wanted to see you without them?"

Clifford stopped with one foot on the first step of the second flight. "By God, Papa!" He turned on the ball of the other foot and reappeared in the doorway. "Ever travel with two small kids?" The motion of his body as he turned back from the steps had been swift and sure, calculated to put him exactly facing his father. "And in hot weather like we're having in Texas?"

Despite the undeniable thickness in Clifford's hips and the

thin spot on the back of his head, his general appearance was still youthful; about this particular turning on the stairs there had been something decidedly athletic. Imperceptibly, behind the dark glasses, Old Ben lifted his eyebrows in admiration. Clifford was the only boy he had who had ever made any team at the University or done any hunting worth speaking of. For a moment, his eyes rested gently on Cliff's white summer shoes, set wide apart in the doorway. Then, jerking his head up, as though he had just heard Cliff's last words, he began, "Two small *kids?* (Why don't you use the word *brats?* It's more elegant.) I have traveled considerably with five—from here to the mountain and back every summer for fifteen years, from my thirty-first to my forty-sixth year."

"I remember," Cliff said stoically. Then, after a moment, "But now I'm going up to my room and write Sue Alice."

"Then go on up! Who's holding you?" He reached for his smoking stand and switched on the radio. It was a big cabinet radio with a dark mahogany finish, a piece from the late twenties, like all the other furniture in the room, and the mechanism was slow to warm up.

Clifford took several steps toward his father. "Papa, we're due to leave for the Club in thirty minutes—less than that now—and I intend to scratch off a note to my wife." He held up the writing paper, as though to prove his intention.

"No concern of mine! No concern of mine! To begin with, I, personally, am not going to the Club or anywhere else for supper."

Clifford came even closer. "You may go to the Club or not, as you like, Papa. But unless I misunderstand, there is not a servant on the place, and we are all going."

"That is, you are going after you scratch off a note to your wife."

"Papa, Ben Jr. and I have each come well over five hundred miles—"

"Not to see me, Clifford."

"Don't be so damned childish, Papa." Cliff was turning away

again. Old Ben held his watch in his hand, and he glanced down at it quickly.

"I'm not getting childish, am I, Clifford?"

This time, Clifford's turning back was not accomplished in one graceful motion but by a sudden jerking and twisting of his shoulder and leg muscles. Behind the spectacles, Old Ben's eyes narrowed and twitched. His fingers were folded over the face of the watch. Clifford spoke very deliberately. "I didn't say *getting* childish, Papa. When ever in your life have you been anything but that? There's not a senile bone in your brain. It's your children that have got old, and you've stayed young—and not in any good sense, Papa, only in a bad one! You play sly games with us still or you quarrel with us. What the hell do you want of us, Papa? I've thought about it a lot. Why haven't you ever asked for what it is you want? Or are *we* all blind and it's really obvious? You've never given but one piece of advice to us, and that's to be direct and talk up to you like men—as equals. And we've done that, all right, and listened to your wrangling, but somehow it has never satisfied you! What is it?"

"Go on up to your letter-writing; go write your spouse," said Old Ben.

The room had been getting darker while they talked. Old Ben slipped his watch back into his vest pocket nervously, then slipped it out again, constantly running his fingers over the gold case, as though it were a piece of money.

"Thanks for your permission, sir." Clifford took a step backward. During his long speech he had advanced all the way across the room until he was directly in front of his father.

"My permission?" Old Ben said. "Let us not forget one fact, Clifford. No child of mine has ever had to ask my permission to do anything whatsoever he took a mind to do. You have all been free as the air, to come and go in this house. . . . You still are!"

Clifford smiled. "Free to come and go, with you perched here on the landing registering every footstep on the stairs and every car that passed underneath. I used to turn off the ignition and coast through the drive-under, and then think how foolish it was, since there was no back stairway. No back stairway in a house this size!" He paused a moment, running his eyes over the furniture and the other familiar objects in the shadowy room. "And how like the old times this was, Papa—your listening in here in the dark when I came up! By God, Papa, I wouldn't have thought when I was growing up that I'd ever come back and fuss with you once I was grown. But here I am, and, Papa—"

Old Ben pushed himself up from the chair. He put his watch in the vest pocket and buttoned his suit coat with an air of satisfaction. "I'm going along to the Club for supper," he said, "since there's to be no-un here to serve me." As he spoke, he heard the clock chiming the half hour downstairs. And Ben Jr. was shouting to Old Ben and Clifford from the foot of the stairs, "Get a move on up there."

Clifford went out on the landing and called down the steps. "Wait till I change my shirt. I believe Papa's all ready."

"No letter written?" Ben Jr. asked.

Clifford was hurrying up the second flight with the blank paper. "Nope, no letter this day of Our Lord."

Old Ben heard Ben Jr. say, "What did I tell you?" and heard the others laughing. He stood an instant by his chair without putting on a light. Then he reached out his hand for one of the walking canes in the umbrella stand by the radio. His hand lighting on the carved head of a certain oak stick, he felt the head with trembling fingers and quickly released it, and quickly, in three strides, without the help of any cane, he crossed the room to the south window. For several moments, he stood motionless at the window, his huge, soft hands held tensely at his sides, his long body erect, his almost freakishly large head at a slight angle, while he seemed to peer between the open draperies and through the pane of the upper sash, out into the twilight of the wide, shady park that stretched from his great yellow-brick house to the pike. Old Ben's eyes, behind the smoked lenses, were closed, and he was visualizing the ceiling fan in the barbershop. Presently, opening his eyes, he reflected, almost with a smile, that his aunt's cellar was not the only Nashville cellar that had disappeared. Many a cellar! His father's cellar, round like a dun-

geon; it had been a cistern in the very earliest days, before Old
Ben's time, and when he was a boy, he would go around and
around the brick walls and then come back with a hollow sound,
as though the cistern were still half full of water. One time, ah—
Old Ben drew back from the window with a grimace—one time
he had been so sure there was water below! In fright at the very
thought of the water, he had clasped a rung of the ladder tightly
with one hand and swung the lantern out, expecting certainly to
see the light reflected in the depths below. But the lantern had
struck the framework that supported the circular shelves and
gone whirling and flaming to the brick floor, which Ben had
never before seen. Crashing on the floor, it sent up yellow flames
that momentarily lit the old cistern to its very top, and when
Ben looked upward, he saw the furious face of his father with the
flames casting jagged shadows on the long, black beard and high,
white forehead. "Come out of there before you burn out my
cellar and my whole damn house to the ground!" He had
climbed upward toward his father, wishing the flames might en-
gulf him before he came within reach of those arms. But as his
father jerked him up onto the back porch, he saw that the flames
had already died out. The whole cellar was pitch-black dark
again, and the boy Ben stood with his face against the whitewashed brick wall while his father went to the carriage house to
find the old plow line. Presently, he heard his father step up on
the porch again. He braced himself for the first blow, but instead
there was only the deafening command from his father: "Attention!" Ben whirled about and stood erect, with his chin in the
air, his eyes on the ceiling. "Where have you hidden my plow
lines?" "I don't know, sir." And then the old man, with his
coattails somehow clinging close to his buttocks and thighs, so
that his whole powerful form was outlined—his black figure
against the white brick and the door—stepped over to the doorway, reached around to the cane stand in the hall, and drew out
the oak stick that had his own bearded face carved upon the
head. "About face!" he commanded. The boy drew back his toe
and made a quick, military turn. The old man dealt him three
sharp blows across the upper part of his back. . . . Tears had

run down young Ben Brantley's cheeks, even streaking down his neck under his open collar and soaking the neckline binding of his woolen underwear, but he had uttered not a sound. When his father went into the house, Ben remained for a long while standing with his face to the wall. At last, he quietly left the porch and walked through the yard beneath the big shade trees, stopping casually to watch a gray squirrel and then to listen to Aunt Sally Ann's soft nigger voice whispering to him out the kitchen window. He did not answer or turn around but walked on to the latticed summerhouse, between the house and the kitchen garden. There he had lain down on a bench, looked back at the house through the latticework, and said to himself that when he got to be a grown man, he would go away to another country, where there would be no maple trees and no oak trees, no elms, not even sycamores or poplars; where there would be no squirrels and no niggers, no houses that resembled this one; and, most of all, where there would be no children and no fathers.

In the hall, now, Old Ben could hear, very faintly, Ben Jr.'s voice and Laura Nell's and Katie's and Lawrence's. He stepped to the door and looked down the dark flight of steps at his four younger children. They stood in a circle directly beneath the overhead light, which one of them had just switched on. Their faces were all turned upward in the direction of the open doorway where he was standing, yet he knew in reason that they could not see him there. They were talking about him! Through his dark lenses, their figures were indistinct, their faces were blurs, and it was hard for him to distinguish their lowered voices one from another. But they were talking about him! And from upstairs he could hear Clifford's footsteps. Clifford, with his letter to Sue Alice unwritten, was thinking about him! Never once in his life had he punished or restrained them in any way! He had given them a freedom unknown to children in the land of his childhood, yet from the time they could utter a word they had despised him and denied his right to any affection or gratitude. Suddenly, stepping out onto the landing, he screamed down the stairs to them, "I've a right to some gratitude!"

They were silent and motionless for a moment. Then he could hear them speaking in lowered voices again, and moving slowly toward the stairs. At the same moment he heard Clifford's footsteps in the upstairs hall. Presently, a light went on up there, and he could dimly see Clifford at the head of the stairs. The four children were advancing up the first flight, and Clifford was coming down from upstairs. Old Ben opened his mouth to call to them, "I'm not afraid of you!" But his voice had left him, and in his momentary fright, in his fear that his wrathful, merciless children might do him harm, he suddenly pitied them. He pitied them for all they had suffered at his hands. And while he stood there, afraid, he realized, or perhaps recalled, how he had tortured and plagued them in all the ways that his resentment of their very good fortune had taught him to do. He even remembered the day when it had occurred to him to build his study above the drive-under and off the stairs, so that he could keep tab on them. He had declared that he wanted his house to be as different from his father's house as a house could be, and so it was! And now he stood in the half-darkness, afraid that he was a man about to be taken by his children and at the same time pitying them, until one of them, ascending the steps switched on the light above the landing.

In the sudden brightness, Old Ben felt that his senses had returned to him. Quickly, he stepped back into the study, closed the door, and locked it. As the lock clicked, he heard Clifford say, "Papa!" Then he heard them all talking at once, and while they talked, he stumbled through the dark study to the umbrella stand. He pulled out the stick with his father's face carved on the head, and in the darkness, while he heard his children's voices, he stumbled about the room beating the upholstered chairs with the stick and calling the names of children under his breath.

THE SCOUTMASTER

THAT YEAR all the young people in Nashville were saying, "Don't tell me that, old dear, because it makes me *too* unhappy." It was *the* answer to almost anything that could be said.

You could hear Virginia Ann saying it to her beaux in the parlor up in front. She had her own special way of saying it and would sometimes give new emphasis to the irony by saying "too, too, too unhappy" or by beginning with "Please, please don't tell me that." Whenever she said it loud enough for Father to hear her all the way back in the sitting room, he would say that he could not bear to hear her using that expression, though he said he didn't know why he could not. "I can't abide it," he would say. "That's all there is to it."

In the hall there was a picture of Father at the age of six, still wearing what he called his kilts but large enough to be holding the reins of a big walking horse on the back of which was seated Uncle Jake. My Uncle Louis, too, in his first pants, was in the picture. He was seated on the grass underneath the horse's belly with his arms about the neck of a big airedale. (But Uncle Louis had died of parrot fever when he was only twelve.) Virginia Ann would show the picture to her beaux as they were leaving at night. It was always good for a laugh, especially if it was a new beau that had just met Father or Uncle Jake, who was living at our house then. "Really," she would say, harking back to the thing that all the young people had said last year, "I think that picture is *truly* a sugar." And she would point out Father's long curls and the lace on the hem of Uncle Jake's dress. Father would say that he could not abide that expression either.

I used to hear Uncle Jake asking Father very gently why he was so "hard on" Virginia Ann and asking if he didn't know that all "modern girls" were like that. And I would sit and wonder why he was so hard on her. Father would say sometimes that he couldn't explain it even to himself.

Mother found just as much fault with Virginia Ann, but she never worried about explaining what it was that was wrong. She would tell Uncle Jake and Aunt Grace (who was not Uncle Jake's wife but Mother's own sister, staying with us then after her divorce from Uncle Basil)—she would tell them that as each of her children passed seventeen she intended either to give them up as a bad job or, if they didn't all turn out as Virginia Ann had, to sit back and rest on her laurels. Yet Mother's groans were as loud as Father's when they heard Virginia Ann greeting her date at the front door with "Well, well, well, if it isn't my country cousin!" I would turn my eyes to her and Father as soon as I heard Virginia Ann say this, for I knew it was one of the things they could not abide.

Aunt Grace was never gentle with people the way Uncle Jake was. She would tell Mother and Father that they were real fools to be so critical of Virginia Ann, who she said was one of the brightest, cleanest girls she had ever known. Hadn't this daughter of theirs had the finest average in her junior class? And wasn't she studying practical things even in high school (business administration, accounting, shorthand!)? Father and Mother would nod and smile. Father would be put in such a grand good humor by Aunt Grace's admiration of his daughter that he would begin to tease her about some unmarried man or other in their acquaintance. Or he would take off his spectacles and smile benevolently at her as she ranted, she now making a show of her outspokenness: Wasn't Virginia Ann's behavior with her beaux

above all suspicion? she would ask. Certainly she was one of the
few young girls who never—Never once! Aunt Grace could
vouch for it. *She* had the girl's confidence—never stepped outside the front door to say good night to her date.

"Poor Grace!" Father and Mother would sit for a long while
after one of these outbursts and lament the hard lot that had
been Aunt Grace's. Uncle Basil was such a hopeless ne'er-do-
well, really a drunken scoundrel whose vanity and social ambi-
tions had been his ruination; and yet they believed that deep in
her heart Grace loved him still. And that was going to make it
hard for her ever to marry again. How sad it was. She was still a
comparatively young woman. "Today women of thirty-eight are
looked upon as quite young, you know," one of them would say.

And, for all she had been through, they agreed, Aunt Grace
showed her years remarkably little. Who would ever have
guessed that she was actually only five years younger than dear,
sweet Jake? She had a certain girlish prettiness about her that
would always deny her age.

Yet it wasn't that Uncle Jake's own sad life told on him ("No
one has ever borne such sadness as his with so fine a spirit"), but,
Father explained, Jake had had a motherless daughter to raise
and to nurse through a fatal illness at the age of nineteen, and
that had kept him old-fashioned. Even if this motherless daughter of his had not been a prig and a fanatic—His daughter had
died at nineteen from a skin disease she had caught in her social
work. Her name had been Margaret, but he had always called
her "Presh" for "precious"—even if she had not been such a
one, Uncle Jake would have remained old-fashioned, Father explained, because just raising a child did that for one.

Aunt Grace stayed with us for six weeks after she had gotten
her divorce. The morning that she left for her job in Birmingham I came and sat beside her on the porch swing. She pulled
me up close to her and beckoned to Brother to come and sit at
her other side. "I've stayed here on you forever," she said to
Mother and Father who were seated about the porch with Virginia Ann and Uncle Jake, "and these two rascals are not the

least of my reasons for it." Simultaneously she pressed Brother
and myself so tightly to her that we found ourselves face to face,
each with a cheek lying against the blue linen cloth of the suit
she and Virginia Ann had been sewing on for a week. Brother
had just reached the age to join Uncle Jake's Boy Scout troop,
and it occurred to me that if Aunt Grace was so very young
Brother would soon be old enough to marry her himself. I looked
into his eyes to see if he were going to cry about her going away.
But he was looking back at me with a grin on his face. Presently
he stuck out his tongue, curled it up on each side till it looked
like a tulip, and before I could pull away from Aunt Grace's
embrace he had blown a spit bubble in my face.

A fight ensued right across Aunt Grace's lap. It was a furious,
noisy scuffle and it left the new linen skirt in a hundred creases
and wrinkles. Yet Aunt Grace's good humor remained unruffled.
And as Uncle Jake's large and gentle hands pulled us apart I
caught a quick glimpse of my aunt's face. Her head was thrown
back, as to avoid the blows. Her soft creamlike complexion
seemed to have just a little more color than usual. Her big blue
eyes, matching her blue hat and her blue suit, were squinted as
they always were when she laughed. Between her bursts of laughter she was saying, "Look! Look! Look at the little demons. See
them! I wish you could see their eyes flashing."

It was Brother and I that Aunt Grace took with her in the
taxi. All of the grown-ups had, of course, wanted to go with her
to the station. Uncle Jake had even brought his car from the
garage, and Father's car always stayed in front of the house. But
she would let neither of them drive her to the depot. She would
not even let Virginia Ann—who tried with Aunt Grace to make
a joke about the parting though there were certainly tears caught
in the long lashes of her small brown eyes—Aunt Grace would
not even let her go along. They were both very gay, but Aunt
Grace's gaiety had so much more unity and was so much more
convincing and contagious that you hardly noticed Virginia
Ann's.

When the taxi came she made everyone but the children say
good-bye to her on the porch. Brother and I helped the driver

take her luggage to the cab, and we waited in the backseat while she walked down the front walk with her arm about our sister's waist. Just before they reached the cab they even skipped for a few steps and sang without any special tune, "Look out, Birmingham, here comes the widow from Nashville, Tenn-tenn-tennessee."

They stopped a minute at the car door and we heard Virginia Ann saying, "I'll keep you posted on my progress with you-know-who and such stuff. It'll be, 'Dear Miss Dix, I care deeply for someone who . . .'"

"Oh, he'll come around," Aunt Grace said. "I know the type —silent, serious, indifferent."

"I'll write you all about it."

"You write me, Virginia Ann. But, Virginia Ann, here's one parting piece from your Aunt Grace before she goes: Let the boys be fools about you. Don't you ever be the fool. *Don't* be a little fool for any boy."

Virginia Ann blushed and then laughed in a high, excited voice. Aunt Grace laughed too, and they kissed each other goodbye.

It was my and Brother's first ride in a taxicab, and we were going to ride the streetcar home, a thing which we had not done many times unless accompanied by Father. I sat gazing first at the noisy meter, then at the picture of the driver on his license that hung beside the rearview mirror. We rode for several blocks through the streets lined with the two-story residences, each approximating a square or oblong shape, each roofed with tile or slate or painted shingle, each having a porch built of the same solid materials appended to the front or the side of the house, each with a yard big enough for perhaps one, two, or three trees, every last one of these houses with features so like those of my father's house that they failed to rouse any curiosity in me. And so finally I turned and simply looked at Aunt Grace.

She was just then peering over the cardboard hatbox that she held most carefully on her lap, trying to see the time by her tiny wristwatch. Her white-gloved forefinger and thumb pushed the glove of the other hand from a white silk cuff (a dainty yet full cuff extending below the blue sleeve of her suit coat) and she was bending cautiously over the big round box to get a view of the dial. I climbed to my knees and myself peered over to the face of that little white gold ornament. When I saw that the tiny black hands actually told the correct time of day I experienced a breathtaking amazement.

But I raised my eyes to Aunt Grace's face, and no longer did it seem that the watch was the cause of my amazement. I felt myself growing timid in her presence, for she had become a stranger to me. The hatbox, the watch, the white gloves, the absurdly full silk cuffs, the blue linen suit on which she had labored so long and so painstakingly, and even the tiny brown bows on her white shoes all took on a significance. The watch seemed to have been but a key. And all of those things that once indicated that Aunt Grace was one sort of person now indicated that she was quite another sort. She was not the utterly useless if wonderfully ornamental member of the family. In the solid blueness of her eyes I was surely on the verge of finding some marvelous function for her personality. (I would have said my mother's function was Motherhood and my father's, Fatherhood.) I was about to find the reason why there should be one member of a boy's family who was wise or old-fashioned enough to sit with Mother and Father and discuss the things they could not abide in Virginia Ann and yet who was foolish or newfangled enough to enjoy the very things that Virginia Ann called "the last word." But it was precisely then that the cab stopped before the entrance to the dirty limestone railroad depot, and Uncle Basil stepped up and opened the automobile door.

I hopped out onto the sidewalk and Brother after me, he taking the small suitcase and I the cardboard hatbox which I held by a heavy black ribbon that was tied in a bow knot above the side of the box. Aunt Grace followed us straightening her straw hat with her left hand, clasping her white purse under her right arm. She and Uncle Basil began to talk as though they were strangers making pleasant conversation. It seemed that Aunt Grace did not cease her chatter and her excited laughter from the time she left the taxi until we saw her on the train.

Uncle Basil's very presence was itself shocking, but I was even more astonished to find him unchanged in appearance. Actually I must have recognized him by his smart attire—his plaid coat and white trousers—for it had been fully a year since he had been to our house. I had expected dissipation to show not only in his face but in his dress as well. He paid the taxi driver over Aunt Grace's protests and summoned a Negro redcap to take all the luggage. Brother and I followed them into the station.

We followed them under the high, vaulted ceiling of the lobby and into the station yard. All the while Aunt Grace's laughter could be heard above the hum of people whom, one and all, I imagined to be taking their final farewell of one another. When we were in the station yard her laughter seemed to reach even a higher pitch.

Finally we were waiting beside the sleeping car into which the redcap had taken Aunt Grace's luggage. Brother and I studied the black wheels and the oily brakes underneath the car. The conductor in blue called, "Ullaboward." I looked up and saw Uncle Basil speaking with an expression on his face that was half serious and half playful. Aunt Grace stopped laughing just long enough to say something that made him blush. She told him not to tell her *that*, because it made her too, too unhappy. Then she turned from him to us and stooping down, she put her arms around Brother and me and kissed us again and again. "Put these two rascals on the streetcar, will you, Basil?"

When she stepped into the dark vestibule of the sleeping car I saw a bit of the lace that hemmed her "slip" showing from beneath her blue skirt. I felt that it was more like the wide lace on Mother's petticoats than the little strips on Virginia Ann's. The train began to move, and she was still in the vestibule looking over the conductor's shoulder. Presently she began to laugh as she waved to us. I suddenly turned my face so as not to see the enormous spread of her smile, but for several seconds it seemed that I could hear the sound of her strange, high laughter above the noise and commotion of the train.

Uncle Jake used afterward to repeat the witty things that Aunt Grace had said when she was staying with us. Oftentimes when the clock on the mantel of the upstairs sitting room chimed he would remind the other members of the family— sometimes only with a smile—of what Grace used to say about the quarter-hourly chiming. "Remember what Grace used to say, 'I'd as soon have someone come and knock on my door every fifteen minutes of the night and say, "Fifteen minutes have passed," as have that clock in a house of mine.'"

He would talk about what a happy nature Aunt Grace had. Whenever Mother said that she worried about how Aunt Grace was getting on in Birmingham with her new job, he would say that Aunt Grace would always be happy, that she was one of those fortunate people who have a special faculty for happiness. He would sometimes recall the songs that she and Virginia Ann had sung together when they washed dishes on Sunday night. They were the only popular songs he had ever seemed to catch on to. He would speak of her as the "Sleepy Time Gal," for she had called herself that whenever she came down to breakfast later than the rest of the family or whenever she went up to bed earlier. You could hear her on the stairs singing in a voice that mimicked the blues singers we heard on the radio:

> . . . *you're turning night into day* . . .
> *My little stay at home, play at home,*
> *eight o'clock sleepy time gal.*

At night especially her voice seemed to drift through the whole house like a wisp of smoke. Sometimes before bed she and Virginia Ann would don their most outlandishly faded and ragged wrappers and with cold cream on their faces and with their hair in a hundred metal curlers they would waltz about the bare floor of the upstairs hall singing. They would sing "I'd Climb the Highest Mountain" or "Three O'Clock in the Morning." But the song that Uncle Jake said he could not help liking best of all was called "Melancholy Baby." Mother and Father said it was no better than other new songs. Father would say, "I think maybe it's even a little *more* suggestive, Jake, than the usual run." But Uncle Jake said that it had more of the old-time feeling in it and that it put one in a mood the way music was supposed to do. So he would sit and listen while Virginia Ann accompanied herself and Aunt Grace on the piano:

> *Every cloud must have a silver lining.*
> *Wait until the sun shines through.*
>
> *So smile, my honey dear,*
> *While I kiss away each tear,*
> *Or else I shall be melancholy too.*

Yet it wasn't Aunt Grace alone that Uncle Jake remembered kindly. He had a good word even for Uncle Basil, if it was only to say, "Basil has a way with him that you can't help liking."

Whenever Father and Mother were out for dinner Uncle Jake was likely to spend the whole meal talking to us about our good fortune at having such splendid parents. "Your father," he'd say, "puts all of his brothers and sisters to shame, and your mother is certainly the choice of her mother's brood. . . . There is no finer woman in the South than your mother, and no businessman in town is respected more than your father. . . . I declare I don't know any other parents these days who live as much for their children as yours do. It's always looked to me like they each learned secrets of happiness from their parents that none of the rest of us did. . . . You children are their whole life, and you ought to remember that."

After such a speech not one of us was able to speak. Virginia Ann's eyes would always fill with tears. And one evening Uncle Jake went so far as to say that Mother and Father were just the sort of parents that his and Father's own had been and that he sometimes woke in the night and wept at the realization that his parents were actually dead and that he could never, never make amends to them for the little worries he had caused them.

And that night Virginia Ann did burst right out crying. She wept in her napkin and I thought she sounded like a little kitten begging to get out of the cellar or to get in the house when it was raining. I almost cried myself to think of poor Uncle Jake in his room crying, and I vowed that I should not postpone making amends to my own mother and father even till the next morning.

(I waited, in fact, all that evening in the living room for them to come in, lying on my stomach before the fire. But I dropped off to sleep with my eyes set on the orange glow of the coals, and when I awoke it was morning. I was in my bed with Brother where Uncle Jake had placed me.)

Whenever all the family were at the table Uncle Jake would often talk of the saintly nature of Uncle Louis who had died at the age of twelve from parrot fever. Neither he nor Father could remember ever having heard Uncle Louis speak an uncivil word or remember his misbehaving on any occasion. Once their father —the two of them would recall—had come through the strawberry patch behind the old house on the Nolansville Pike and found Uncle Jake and Father playing mumble-the-peg while Uncle Louis did all the berry picking. And when Uncle Louis saw his father stripping off his belt to give his brothers a whipping he ran to him and told him that he, the eldest brother, was to blame for not making them work and that he should receive the punishment. My grandfather had turned and walked to his house without another word.

Whenever Father and Uncle Jake talked about that incident Father would say that Grandfather walked away in disgust. But Uncle Jake would say that he walked away toward the house in order that they should not see how moved he was by Uncle Louis's brotherly love and spirit of self-sacrifice.

Father was not as tall as Uncle Jake when they were standing, but that was only because Uncle Jake had such long legs. When we were seated at the table they seemed to be of the same height. Each had an extremely high forehead and a pointed chin that Uncle Jake said they had got from their mother's people. Nothing could hold my interest more keenly in those days than watching them sit together at table after dinner when Mother and Virginia Ann had gone into the living room. Sometimes they would only sit and smoke in silence. Sometimes they would talk about the old times.

One night when they had talked about the Negroes who had worked their father's farm, about Cousin Lucy Grimes who turned Catholic and later went completely crazy, and about the meanness of their Uncle Bennett who lost his leg at the Battle of Stones River, they turned again to the subject of Uncle Louis's native sweetness. While they talked, I looked across the table from one to the other trying to discover why they did not really look alike since their individual features were so similar. I felt that they actually did look alike and that I was just blind to it in some way. The only differences that I could see were not ones of my own observation but differences that I had heard Mother point out now and again: Uncle Jake had lived outdoors so much with his hunting and fishing and his other activities with the Boy Scouts that his skin was considerably rougher than Father's, who had no real life but in his office and in our house. Too, Uncle Jake's hair was still a hard, young, brown color whereas Father's was full of pleasant gray streaks. Yet withal there was a softness or gentleness about Uncle Jake's eyes and about the features of his face that were not to be found in Father's kind but strong countenance.

After dinner Mother would always switch off the principal light as she left the dining room, and the men's talking was done in softer illumination from the side wall lamps.

Brother had gone one night and climbed into Father's lap, I was sitting beside Uncle Jake, and I leaned my head over on his knee. It seemed that the lights were lower than usual that night, and the Negro cook in her white serving apron seemed to take longer than ever in removing the dishes. She kept reaching over me to clear the dishes from my and Uncle Jake's places, and once she told me to sit up and quit being a bother to my Uncle Jake. But he, without turning his eyes from Father, laid his hand lightly across my chest to hold me there; and the cook went off to the sideboard shaking her head. Uncle Jake had not spoken for a long while. He had sat smoking his white-bowled pipe and listening to Father, but I could tell now by the twitching at the corner of his mouth that he was finally about to speak. When his lips parted and he simultaneously removed the pipe I remarked the long distance between the point of his chin and his eyes and noticed that the eyes themselves were set far apart and were rather popped, I thought, from this upside-down view.

Addressing Father as "Brother"—a thing he did only when they were reminiscing—he began to speak of Uncle Louis. He lifted his eyes to the ceiling, and from where I lay it seemed that he had rolled his eyeballs far back into his head; and I noticed the strange animal-like moisture of his upper lip. "Brother," he said, "I was playing with Louis one day under the mulberry tree at the end of the side porch. We had a couple of pillboxes that old Dr. Pemberton had given us and we had caught two of the caterpillars that fell from the mulberry tree. With some black thread from Mama's basket we were hitching the poor fuzzy worms to the little boxes and then filling the boxes with sand to see how heavy a load the caterpillars could manage. But Louis quite accidentally pulled the thread so tightly about the middle of one of them that he cut the little fellow half in two. Then he looked at me silently across the two pieces of worm. And, mind you, after several seconds he scrambled to his feet and ran the length of the porch to where Mama was sitting with her sewing in her lap.

"I followed hot on his heels and stood by watching him as he fell on his knees and hid his face in her sewing. Pretty soon when he began to weep and shake all over—more like a girl than a boy —Mama thought he had hurt himself on the scissors or a needle and she jerked him up from her lap. He could not speak for his sobbing, and when I had told Mama that he had only cut a little worm half in two with a piece of thread, she drew him to her, smiling and patting his head tenderly. When at last he was able to speak he said, 'I killed the little caterpillar, Mama, and he'll never, never come back to life.' "

Uncle Jake was stirring unconsciously in his chair as he spoke, and I raised up from his lap and peered across the tablecloth into Father's face. His mouth literally hung open, and he said, "Why, Jake, I've never heard you tell that before."

Uncle Jake replaced his pipe between his teeth and chewed on it. He said, "Brother, I never had much heart for telling it, because it happened the same summer he caught the fever." And in a few minutes he got up and went over and unlocked the door to the porch that nobody ever used. Before he went out

Father called him in a very stern voice, but he went out anyway and sat on the porch for a long time by himself, still smoking his pipe. In the living room I asked Father if he supposed Uncle Jake was thinking about Uncle Louis. He said he supposed he was thinking about Aunt Margaret his wife who had died so many, many years ago and about their daughter who had been a prig and a fanatic. Mother said that Father should not talk that way before the children.

Virginia Ann had innumerable beaux. It used to seem on Sunday afternoons that all the young men in Nashville had flocked to our house, some for but a few minutes' visit, others to make an all-afternoon stay. Father called them the Arabs and the Indians. The Arabs were the timid or sulky boys who stayed a short while and then moved silently on to some other house. The Indians were those bold ones who, he said, camped or squatted on his property for the eternity of a whole Sunday afternoon.

Father really did seem to despise the Indians. But it was the Indians who were Uncle Jake's delight. He would sit and talk to them while Virginia Ann gave her attention to those whose devotion had not been proved. And when they all had finally gone, he never failed to pretend that he was worried because Virginia Ann would not choose what he called a steady from among them. He would stop Virginia Ann as she was straightening up the parlor or perhaps by the newel post at the foot of the stairs and, rolling his eyes speculatively, he would enumerate the good and bad qualities of each of those he considered potential steadies.

Virginia Ann would listen, pretending, like himself, to be in dead earnestness. I could not have told that they were not speaking their literal thoughts had it not been for the pompous gestures Uncle Jake made with his hands whenever he was making fun and for the broad smile that broke upon Virginia Ann's face whenever Uncle Jake mentioned the devotion to herself which some young Indian had confided in him.

It was at the dinner table one night in the presence of all the family that Uncle Jake began to describe a conversation he had

had with Bill Evers. He began by professing to believe that Bill Evers was the beau whom Virginia Ann should choose as her steady. The things he was saying were so much of the kind he had so often said to her about other young men that I did not really listen at first. I only remarked the mock seriousness in the tone of his voice and saw him batting his eyes as he concealed a smile behind his coffee cup. Several times I watched him bring his cup up in rather a hurry to his lips and, as often before, I studied the wide gold band on the fourth finger of his left hand. Uncle Jake had large hands, and I thought, as I studied them, of how much softer to the touch they were than one could imagine from their rough appearance.

It was likely the word "revolver" that finally made me listen to what he was actually saying about that particular one of the Indians. "Yes, Bill Evers tells me," he said, "that he is never afraid anywhere on the darkest night or in the wildest country as long as he has his revolver." And Uncle Jake each time he pronounced "revolver" would roll it out magnificently.

Virginia Ann's face suddenly blossomed into a broad smile that showed her lovely white teeth and revealed perhaps here and there on her teeth little splotches of orange-red paint that Mother said she applied "so liberally" to her lips.

Then Uncle Jake reported several of the incidents wherein Bill Evers had felt himself more secure for having his revolver by his side. Once he had been camping in the Baxter Hills. Another time he had been hunting along Duck River and had met a couple of old moonshiners whom Bill had described as "very much intoxicated." Whenever Uncle Jake was quoting Bill directly he would deepen his voice and roll his r's, and for some reason this made Virginia Ann blush. It was, of course, because Bill was the only one of her beaux that really had a man's voice. And it seemed that Uncle Jake by deepening his voice was referring to that fact rather too persistently and somehow indelicately. Possibly I was the first to feel that Virginia Ann was no longer feigning that sober expression that had settled on her face now. I was watching her when Uncle Jake said, "Bill Evers is never afraid so long as he has his revolver by his side. 'My revolver,' Bill told me, 'is my best friend and just let any fellow take care who meddles with me when I have my revolver by my side.' "

Without warning, Virginia Ann sprang from the table weeping, not like a kitten but like a wounded animal out in the woods in the Baxter Hills. She ran from the dining room crying, "Oh, you're too cruel. You're heartless."

Uncle Jake seemed unable to move or speak. He looked helplessly from Father to Mother whose faces registered nothing but half-amused surprise. Then he pushed back his chair and hurried clumsily after Virginia Ann calling, "Child . . . Child." Brother and I slipped automatically from our chairs to follow as curious witnesses to the spectacle, but Mother and Father, who were now looking at one another, smiling and shaking their heads sadly, turned quickly to us and commanded us to return to our seats.

"Poor Jake," Father said, "always has to pay for what fun he has in life."

Mother continued to take an occasional sip from her white coffee cup. Finally she sighed, "Poor Jake. I'm sure he hadn't suspected how things are."

Father raised his eyebrows. After a moment he shook his head emphatically and said that Mother was reading things into this incident. "The girl's just tired tonight," he said. "She doesn't give a snap for the boy."

Mother shook her head with equal emphasis. "No. Grace told me before she left." She replaced her cup in its saucer but continued for several seconds to hold to its handle with her thumb and forefinger. "I must say, I thought Bill Evers had long since passed out of her head. There *was* a time when young girls confided such prolonged crushes in their mothers."

From somewhere in the front part of the house we could hear Uncle Jake's voice apologizing and entreating. Eventually we began to hear Virginia Ann reassuring him. And I recalled then how in front of the church one Sunday, after services, I had been tugging at Uncle Jake's hand, trying to pull him away from a crowd of men who were talking foxhound and bird dog. My eyes, as I tugged, were on an old Negro man who was selling bags of peanuts on the street corner. I saw that the vendor was closing the lid to the primitive cart that he pushed and was preparing to move to another corner. I tugged at Uncle Jake's hand and turned to beg him to come along. But upon turning my eyes to him I saw that he had somehow managed to slip my hand into that of a strange man; and he and all the others were standing about laughing at me.

With a violent jerk I had broken loose and had run off down the street in a beastly rage. When Uncle Jake finally caught me he held me and knelt on one knee before me imploring humbly that I forgive him (instead of cajoling as most men would have done). And silently I began to blame myself for not having realized that the hand I had been pulling on had a hardness and coarseness about it that should have distinguished it from that of my gentle uncle's.

"Poor Jake." Mother used to say that Father was "an omnivorous reader," and I would say myself when I was nine or ten that she and he were both "omnivorous talkers" when they were alone together. They talked about everything and everyone under the sun. They didn't talk especially kindly or unkindly about people, but I felt that in the years of their married life they had certainly left nothing that came into their heads unsaid. I was sometimes surprised to overhear them speak with such detachment of Virginia Ann or Brother or Uncle Jake. "Poor Jake," Father would say, "he's really incapable of being very realistic about his dealing with people. His real calling, his real profession is, you know, that of the Scoutmaster. It's during those Thursday night meetings with the boys that poor Jake fulfills himself. I always knew that he'd never make a great go of it in business, and sometimes when he tells me that he should have held on to the homeplace and farmed it, I can barely keep from telling him that somebody would have gotten it away from him and that he would have ended up as the tenant, forever recollecting the good old days, y'know, when it was our own." Mother would say that she didn't understand how he had done even as good a job of raising poor Presh as he did.

"Presh's religious mania, it's always seemed to me," Mother would say, "began as very much the same sort of thing as Jake's nostalgia. It was all tied up with notions of her mother's existence in Heaven. Toward the last her social work consisted mostly of preaching to those wretched poor people in East Nashville about her mother in Heaven. She could just not be bothered with any real view of things."

Father would speculate concerning Uncle Jake's fate and what it might have been if his wife had not died when Presh was only half grown: "If only Margaret, herself, had lived to make him and Presh a home, he might not have forever been looking to the past and being so uncritical of things in the present. He might have taken hold of himself." Here Mother would disagree. Men's natures weren't changed by circumstances, she contended. And the discussion would continue thus long after my interest had lagged.

At last I would hear Mother saying, "My Love, you simply have those age-old illusions of the male about Character and Fate. You've never really been Christianized." To which Father's favorite reply was: "I think you mean I've never been Calvinized." Or he would say, "The female is the cynic of the species."

Then if it were bedtime they would go about the house together locking-up, shutting-down, turning-off, putting-out, arranging everything for the night. And I would hear them in their bedroom still talking as they undressed and went to bed.

Father would never help us celebrate the Fourth of July. He said that it was because Vicksburg had fallen to the Yankees on the Fourth. And Uncle Jake would stand behind him and say he was exactly right, though Uncle Jake would, himself, come and help us set off the firecrackers in the backyard.

But Mother, as she and Father sat playing Russian bank on the screened porch, would denounce Father as a hypocrite and remind him that he had some excuse or other for not celebrating any of the holidays in hot weather. He simply could not abide hot weather. Nothing could stir him to action from Decoration Day till after Labor Day in September. But after that it was very different. Mother would say that a week before Thanksgiving he began to develop holiday spirits that were continuous through Easter. Yet she, in turn, could not abide the cold weather; and *that*, Father maintained, was responsible for her "scaring up" such a religious point of view about Christmas and New Year's. Except for the Thanksgiving football game they would stay home on holidays reading or playing cards or maybe receiving a few friends or kinspeople. And the next day you could hear Mother on the telephone telling the woman who took her orders at the grocery, "We had a very quiet holiday at home, which is after all a more fitting way to spend such a day. . . . The children were in and out with their friends, so it was quite gay for us. . . . I think such days, after all, should be a time for the family to be together. . . . Yes, a time for us to count our blessings."

Uncle Jake never failed to comment upon the old-fashionedness of holidays at our house. When Aunt Grace had once accused Mother and Father of being together too lazy to face any kind of weather and had said that each of them was the other's worst enemy—socially—he had come forward most earnestly in their defense. He said that their mutual sacrifice of practically all social life for the sake of the other's comfort amounted to no less than "a symbol of unity."

"Besides," he said, "it's not as though they were denying themselves the sort of social gatherings that there were in and around Nashville a generation ago."

Aunt Grace had expressed her delight at this with several seconds of laughter so violent that she finally choked. With her face still very red, her eyes watery, and her voice hoarse she said, "How perfectly wonderful, Jake!" Then she leaned toward him, narrowing her eyes till they were two dark slits in her fair complexion, and said, "But you might be surprised, Jake, at what really grand old times some of the married set do have at their 'social gatherings' today."

Uncle Jake merely nodded soberly.

Aunt Grace laughed again, but carefully now so as not to choke. "I know what you mean," she added with a wink that had a little self-consciousness about it. "Look at what it 'done done' to me."

Uncle Jake blushed and remained quite serious for a moment. But he could not long resist the persistent, infectious laughter. He smiled genially and softly repeated the phrase which he must have thought good—"A symbol of unity."

It would sometimes be irksome to Virginia Ann that Mother planned all of the meals around Father's special tastes. Rarely did an evening meal come to our table, for instance, without there appearing on the menu either turnip salad or string beans cooked in ham fat. Aunt Grace had amused Virginia Ann mightily at breakfast one morning by her response to Mother's complaint against the drudgery of planning meals. She had pulled a small daisy from the centerpiece and offered it to Mother saying, "All you have to do is pluck off the petals repeating, 'Turnip greens—Beans. Turnip greens—Beans.' And so on till you get the answer." Virginia Ann had already made this something of a sensitive subject with Mother who now only closed her eyes and pressed down imaginary creases in the tablecloth with her small hand.

Father seemed no more amused than Mother by the suggestion for deciding the menu and he chose that as the signal for him to down the last of his coffee, pull his napkin loosely through his napkin ring, and go into the living room to look for the morning paper.

Uncle Jake, too, rose from his chair. But he reached out and took the daisy from Aunt Grace's hand and said slyly, "It's not a bad suggestion, Grace. But you don't understand that she's just telling her fortune the way clever women have always done. She pulls the petals not saying, 'He loves me. He loves me not,' but saying, 'He loves me. He loves me.' "

Aunt Grace laughed appreciatively. "Jake, how perfectly wonderful."

But when the men had gone to work, Virginia Ann, being a little out of humor that morning, said again that she could not see why Mother had always to put Father's tastes before those of the children. Mother turned to her and spoke finally, "If you don't know why, Daughter, then let me tell you: Some fine day each of my children will have a husband or a wife or some other

equally absorbing and wonderful interest in life that will take
them away from me. And so some fine day I shall have only your
father's tastes to cater to. I don't want there to be any doubt in
his mind on that fine day that he always came first at my table. I
don't like the prospect of two old souls' turning from loneliness
to one another because their children have left them."

"Well spoken," said Aunt Grace soberly. But presently she
began to laugh and said that she was reminded of the limerick,
"There was an old lady of Romany whose husband ate nothing
but hominy," and Virginia Ann and Mother began to laugh too
because her laughter was so infectious.

In Nashville Thanksgiving Day might be quite warm. It might
be almost a sluggishly summerlike day, and sometimes we'd find
that the freakish iris in the flower bed beside the porch had a few
pale, bedraggled blossoms left. But, too, there will be years when
it will snow at Thanksgiving time in Nashville, and everyone will
be thinking so much about the problems of Christmas ahead
that they have but little heart for even the football game.

Uncle Jake always went duck hunting on the weekend before
Thursday so that there'd be duck to serve with the spiced round
for Thanksgiving dinner. On Thanksgiving morning he went
quail hunting. Dinner was usually kept waiting on him, for
Mother would say that they were, after all, his ducks. But if he
was very late, the tension would sometimes become unendur-
able, and Mother would go through the dining room, push open
the swinging door a little way, and call to the cook mournfully,
"Well, we'll just have to go ahead without Mr. Jake." It seems to
me now that he always came in as Father was carving the ducks.
Father would go on carving the roasted fowl before him while he
admired the dead partridges that Uncle Jake brought out of the
large patch pockets of his khaki hunting coat. Father would stop
a minute with his knife still placed in a joint of the duck and
watch Uncle Jake's big fingers feeling through the soft, dark
feathers over the dead bird's breast. Once I wondered momentarily whether or not I'd be able to eat my meal after seeing the
poor dead partridge with the blood on its speckled neck.

But there is no aroma more affecting to the palate than that of just-carved roast duck. When the steaming slices of dark meat and drumstick were placed in front of me I had no more thoughts of the dead birds that we would eat the following Sunday. I inhaled the delicious odor of the duck, I listened to the warm, eager voices around the table, and soon I would look up to see Uncle Jake returned now in his navy blue smoking jacket and with his hands washed whiter and cleaner than I ever saw them on ordinary days.

But before Uncle Jake came there would be tension, because the Thanksgiving football game began at two o'clock. And Father and Mother, no matter the weather, did attend the Thanksgiving football game. Presumably they had long ago established this as the one really feasible outing of the year because fall weather was neither too hot nor too cold. There was also the fact that at some time in the remote past Father had been a left tackle on the University team, and Mother had come there to watch his superb tackling and blocking. Actually, too, the football game was just as necessary to Uncle Jake's happiness on that day as was his quail hunting.

All of the grown people went to the Thanksgiving game. Virginia Ann had been going almost as far back as I could remember. Finally the year arrived when even Brother was to be allowed to go with the family; and the question was naturally raised, since I was only two years younger than he, as to whether or not I too should be allowed to go.

I should certainly have been taken along that day had I not shown real indifference to it. But it was considered on the whole well enough to leave me behind since Brother would be responsibility enough for Uncle Jake on this, his favorite holiday. Further, this year Virginia Ann was planning to attend, not with the rest of the family, but with Bill Evers. And this, strangely enough, involved me.

When Brother told me that Bill Evers was her "date" for the game, I did not quite understand what he meant. For several months she had been going to movies and to dances with Bill

Evers, but it just happened that I had never before noticed this use of the word "date."

Mother must have seen the puzzled expression on my countenance. She put her hand on the top of my head and explained, "Brother means that Bill Evers is going to escort Virginia Ann to the football game." It did not occur to her that "escort" meant no more to me than "date." She allowed a faint smile to play across her face that seemed to tell me that other considerations than the weight of Uncle Jake's responsibility had brought her to agreeing to leave me alone on Thanksgiving afternoon. Presently she addressed these remarks to Father and Uncle Jake: "As we used to say in the country, Bill Evers is going to carry her to the game today. And if I know Virginia Ann's beaux, he'll not come for her till after we've left for the game. Boys today don't seem to have any respect for the girls, the way they keep them waiting."

"It used to be the boys that were kept waiting," Father said. "It's really the girls' own fault. They don't require anything of them."

"It never enters Virginia Ann's head," Mother said, "whether or not promptness is a virtue in young men."

"Well, well," Uncle Jake said rather sadly yet with the obvious intention of softening the remarks being directed against his niece, "customs change. Everything changes."

Mother gazed about the room as though she were keeping most of her thoughts to herself. At last she absently put her hand on my head again and said that Uncle Jake was quite right, that everything changes. "But, in any event, my lamb here will act as chaperon when Mr. Evers does arrive today. How is the weather out, Jake?"

A cold unexpected rain fell that afternoon.

They had all observed the gray overcast sky before they left, but none of them could predict what sort of weather would result.

The rain that fell, not a downpour or a mist but a fitful and wind-driven rain, was of such an uncertain character that I could not tell whether or not it would bring the family home early.

But the wind and rain together did bring them home. The wind that sprayed the rain against the pane of the bedroom window seemed to have blown them all into the front hall at once. Or, rather, it seemed to have blown them all through the hall and into the living room where Virginia Ann and Bill Evers had for the past half hour kept a silence that I felt I could not endure another second, a silence utterly unnatural in a house where someone had always before been talking and talking.

"How dare you! You get out of here you common dog." Father's voice burst upon the quietness.

Then everyone seemed to be talking at once. Mother uttered something as near to a scream as she had ever been known to utter, "Virginia Ann, I want you to get yourself upstairs, out of your father's sight."

"Get out of here and never let me catch you on my premises again."

"How could you take such an advantage?"

Uncle Jake spoke too, but what he said was inaudible from where I stood in the doorway to my and Brother's room. But the sound of their voices in the house once more had filled me with confidence, had filled me with a sense of relief now. Father's first indignant commands were the relief and the proof I'd been waiting for. All my feelings of shock and fear and resentment were gone. I could enjoy the wonderful satisfaction that Father and Mother and Uncle Jake and even Brother had been driven home by the rain to make a reality of something that I felt had been frightening because of its unreality.

I had gone to the kitchen soon after the front door had closed behind the family when they left for the game. I had waited there, watching the cook dash the pots and pans about in her great haste to get away on Thanksgiving afternoon. The doorbell finally rang, and the cook and I heard Virginia Ann in the front hall saying to Bill Evers, "Hello, Cousin." The cook ceased her noisy business long enough to listen to Virginia Ann's chatter and to smile over it. She shook her head and, using Virginia

Ann's own language, she told me that that sister of mine had a dandy line with her boyfriends.

And from thereout the cook didn't seem to be making such a racket with the utensils she was cleaning. In a few minutes she reached her brown hand through the gray, soapy water and opened the drain of the sink. She stacked those dishes that she had not washed on the draining board and said that they would just have to go till tomorrow. Then she gathered her hat and her coat and umbrella and asked me to lock the backdoor behind her. "I got to make haste," she said.

When I had locked the door I gave one glance to the dirty dishes and began to move toward the dining room. But at the sound of the voices of Virginia Ann and Bill Evers I stopped in the middle of the kitchen floor. It hadn't occurred to me that those two did not leave for the football game immediately after his arrival, and I was restrained from going into the front part of the house by a sudden wave of timidity. I stood a moment studying the black and white squares of linoleum about my feet. I observed now the bread crumbs in one spot and the grease splotch in another. I saw on the long table beneath the window a crockery bowl filled with water in which pieces of cake batter floated. A large spoon lay beside it on the table, and beneath the spoon a little puddle of water had settled on the white oilcloth. I was so sensible of the general mess in which the cook had left the kitchen and of the displeasure it would cause Mother when we should come to the kitchen to fix sandwiches tonight that I could not bear to think of being confined here any longer.

Yet I waited. If they didn't leave soon they'd certainly be late for the game. It had not yet begun to rain and so there was no question in my mind as to whether or not they would go. They would go, and they would go soon. I had merely to wait.

I waited. Still there was only the sound of their voices. I listened for the noise of footsteps. But there was none. As I waited with growing impatience I remarked how strange it was to hear a man's voice that was not Father's and a woman's voice that was not Mother's sounding on and on in our living room. Finally it seemed to be only Bill Evers's voice that I heard. Whenever

Virginia Ann did speak, her voice had a sweetness about it that I had never heard and that almost brought tears to my eyes.

After a while my impatience grew naturally into resentment. But as the temptation to invade their privacy increased, so did my timidity.

I decided of a sudden that I was hungry.

I went to the big white refrigerator and opened its door. It had never before been so completely stocked with edibles. And the cook in her haste to be away had apparently crammed every perishable in sight into the box without thought or care for arrangement or accessibility.

A long stalk of celery fell out on the floor at my feet. I stooped to pick it up, and as I rose I found myself looking directly in on the heap of dead quail.

At that moment I heard, or thought I heard, Virginia Ann's voice calling my name. I remained staring at the dead birds for a moment. They were stacked one upon the other in their bloody, feathery deadness in the same shelf with the respectable skeletons of the roast ducks. I resolved not to move until I had heard Virginia Ann calling again. Then I should oh so gladly shut that door on the unwelcome sight of the birds and all that food for which I knew now I felt no hunger.

But when presently she called my name again, I could not make good my resolution. I stood holding the refrigerator door half open. She had called me, there was no doubting, but there was in her voice a note of caution. There was too evident a careful gauging of her volume. She plainly did not intend to disturb me if I were safely asleep or were safely out of earshot. And now that she had called me twice without answer, how could I ever answer? It was then that I determined to creep up the little flight of steps that went up from the kitchen (and joined the front stair on the landing) and to go and wait in my room. After I reached the small square bedroom with its overlarge pieces of mahogany furniture and metal bedstead I heard not another sound; and I had waited in the silence there until I thought I could endure it not another instant.

After Father had shut the front door behind Bill Evers, I heard Virginia Ann's footsteps on the stair. I hurried to the double bed that Brother and I shared and threw myself across it, but with my face toward the doorway. Presently she passed along the hallway, her hair disheveled, her turbanlike navy blue hat in her hand. I watched her indistinct daytime shadow that followed her along the plain wall of the hallway one second after she was out of sight.

In a little while Uncle Jake and Brother came upstairs. Brother came in the room and pushed his cap back on his head as he usually did when he came in the front door downstairs. Uncle Jake stopped in the doorway. I raised myself on my elbows and pretended to yawn. Uncle Jake said to me, "Tonight's Scout meeting night and we want you to go with us as our visitor." It was more command than invitation and I said, "Yes, sir."

"You two get yourselves a nap," he said, and as he moved away he pulled the door closed behind him.

Brother went to the closet and pulled out his Scout suit. I sat up on the side of the bed. Thursday night is Scout night, I said to myself. He and Uncle Jake would be going to Scout meeting the same as on any other Thursday. This made it all quite real now. A sort of joy took possession of me. I saw that Brother, in his way, was quite as disturbed as I by what had happened. Father had already expressed his rage as he entered the house. Mother I could hear talking and weeping intermittently in Virginia Ann's bedroom. I felt somehow that I could hear Aunt Grace saying to Virginia Ann, "You're a fool. You're a real little fool."

Brother was scrutinizing his uniform, brushing his shirt, loosening the knot of his kerchief. He would not look at me. Finally, without raising his eyes, he said, "You weren't asleep. Did you or didn't you go down and spy on them?" I made no answer. Now for some reason I felt myself blushing. I had no mind to answer him, I cared not whether he thought I had crept down the steps and spied on them or had remained in our room sleeping. Though I had not done so, I felt momentarily that I had. I could hardly remember whether I had or had not. But that was no matter. Actually I seemed to have forgotten Virginia Ann and Bill Evers. I was concerned only with Brother's eagerness to get into his uniform and be gone to the Boy Scout meeting. For I saw that he was trying to interest himself in other things. He hung his khaki trousers and shirt on a chair and began to move toward the bed. When he had lain down beside me he said, "Well, they were only necking, but they sure were *at* it." It had not occurred to me to imagine what they might have been doing. I rolled over on my back and looked up at the blank ceiling. I did not know exactly how to imagine what they might have been doing. And I couldn't imagine why I had been left at home this afternoon since I was not rebuked for my failure as a chaperon. A sense of my own ignorance overshadowed all my other dark feelings. Yet it did seem that all my elders, who knew so much, were no less surprised than I by Virginia Ann.

When Uncle Jake woke us from our nap he was dressed in his khaki Scout clothes. It was dark outside, and he had turned on the light and gone back into the hall to bring in a tray of sandwiches and two glasses of milk. Brother dressed himself in his khakis, and we ate.

Brother kept trying to make Uncle Jake talk about things pertaining to the Scouts. The only thing Uncle Jake said was, "If you'll apply yourself you'll be the first Eagle in our troop."

"I'm going to," Brother said. "I'm going to if it takes every single afternoon of the week." He was still trying to think of *other things*, I reflected.

When we went downstairs we found Mother and Father back in the sitting room playing casino. Virginia Ann was looking on. Father was winning and he pretended to be very proud and boastful of his score. He called us around to look at his hand and observe how cleverly he played it. But when he had called, "Cards," and the last hand was played, Mother had much the larger stack and all but one of the spades. So now she derided him for his boasting. Father pretended to want to talk of other things. "I believe," he said with feigned formality, "I say I believe, my dear wife, that you said you had a letter from your sister Grace yesterday. What did she say? Do tell me about it."

And Mother did commence to tell him all about the "nice, fat, long, happy" letter.

So we left the house amidst a new burst of conversation between Mother and Father, and I felt a gladness that I was not going to be in the house tonight. It would have meant being there alone with Virginia Ann. For just as Mother and Father had not invited her or anyone else to join their game they would not really have allowed anyone to join their conversation.

On the way to the Scout meeting, sitting in the front seat of the automobile between my uncle and my brother, I thought of the letter from my Aunt Grace. If she had been there that afternoon I knew that she would have said, "Virginia Ann, you're a real little fool." And I did not long to see her tonight, for she would have been singing in the kitchen and in the hall, full of the sort of cheer that was in the letter, the exaggerated sort of cheer she had shown the day she left for Birmingham.

The Scout meeting was held in an unused servants' room above the garage of one of Uncle Jake's hunting friends. As we walked up the shadowy drive to the garage we could see the light already burning in the room upstairs, and several of the other Scouts were at the window. But when we came into sight just below the window I saw them leave the window hurriedly as though they were in school and the teacher was arriving.

We went into the garage and began to climb the steep, dark stairs. When we were about halfway to the top I suddenly reached forward and grasped Uncle Jake's hand. He held my hand firmly and led me to the top step. And I wondered what might have become of me tonight if it had not been for Uncle Jake.

Presently we entered the bright room and found all of the boys sitting erect on straight wooden benches that lined three walls of the bare room.

"Good evening, boys," Uncle Jake said. The sound of his voice sent a chill up my spine. I felt goose bumps on the backs of my hands. The light in the room was bare and sharp and sent a long blue-black shadow of Uncle Jake's figure against the wall.

The boys answered in a chorus of high tingly voices.

Then Uncle Jake directed me to sit down beside Brother on one of the benches, and he went to the table in the center of the room.

As my eyes moved automatically from one face to another of those boys seated on the benches I was aware that every single face was a familiar one. They were boys whom I had seen with Brother either at school or in Sunday School. Yet tonight in their Scout suits, they were total strangers. Whenever one of them met my gaze there was no communication between us. Rather, our eyes seemed to rub against each other in the cold room.

Though I was unable to follow the procedure of the meeting I did at first try to stand up and to raise my hand when the other boys did. And I even moved my lips when the oath was recited, feeling a kind of elevation by the lists of adjectives. But it was while I saw Uncle Jake's lips pronounce the words "loyal, brave, trustworthy, clean, reverent" that it seemed that he too was becoming a stranger.

After that I made no effort to understand what was being done or said. I simply watched my kind and gentle Uncle as he became more and more another stranger to me, losing himself in the role of the eternal Scoutmaster. It was later, just before the meeting was over (when the plans for Saturday's hike were completed), that I braced myself with the palms of my hands flat on the seat beside me; and while my heart pounded so that I imagined those around me would hear or feel it, I watched Uncle Jake as he stood by his table speaking to the Boy Scouts. I realized now that Father had been right. This was Uncle Jake fulfilling himself. And to fulfill one's self was to remove one's self somehow beyond the reach of my own understanding and affection. It seemed that the known Uncle Jake had moved out of his body just as Aunt Grace had moved out of hers when she sang and laughed and as the Mother and Father whose hands I liked to have placed gently on the top of my head left their bodies whenever they excluded all the world from their conversation.

To the exclusion of all the world Uncle Jake was now become a Scoutmaster. I felt myself deserted by the last human soul to whom I could turn. He, rather, had turned and hidden himself in something more serious than laughter and song and more relentless than even persistent, endless, trivial conversation with a chosen mate. He stood before us like a gigantic replica of all the little boys on the benches, half ridiculous and half frightening to me in his girlish khaki middy and with his trousers disappearing beneath heavy three-quarter woolen socks. In that cold, bare, bright room he was saying that it was our great misfortune to have been born in these latter days when the morals and manners of the country had been corrupted, born in a time when we could see upon the members of our own families—upon our own sisters and brothers and uncles and aunts—the effects of our failure to cling to the teachings and ways of our forefathers. And he was saying that it was our duty and great privilege, as Boy Scouts, to preserve those honorable things which were left from the golden days when a race of noble gentlemen and gracious ladies inhabited the land of the South. He was saying that we must preserve them until one day we might stand with young men from all over the nation to demand a return to the old ways and the old teachings everywhere.

TWO LADIES
IN RETIREMENT

SOME NASHVILLE WIT had once said, "When I look at Miss Betty Pettigru, I'm reminded of an old, old baby." Others thought she looked more like the Home-Run King himself. She was a short, plump woman, not fat but with an individual plumpness to all her limbs and to her torso, her breasts, her hands, and even to the features of her moon-shaped face. She was a lady well known in Nashville, during a period of twenty-five years, for her Sunday-night parties and for her active role in the club life of the city. Miss Betty's face and figure and her parties and her active role seemed so much a part of Nashville that hardly anyone could believe it when, in the spring of 1926, word finally got around that she was definitely going to move away and go to live in St. Louis.

At first they all said, oh, it would be merely another of her protracted visits to St. Louis, and she would come back talking of nothing but her little nephews, who, of course, weren't really her little nephews at all. She was only going for another stay with some of that Tolliver family she was kin to. Miss Betty's enemies were particularly skeptical. "Miss Betty Pettigru leave Nashville? The scene of all her victories? Nonsense! Never!" And they kept asking what on earth made her even talk of leaving. "I think I'm going to St. Louis to watch my irresistible nephews grow up," she said. "But you know me. Womanlike, I seldom know my own mind or what my reason is for doing anything."

By everyone, her talk of leaving Nashville was considered "completely and entirely absurd." But then it came out in the Sunday paper that Miss Betty Pettigru had sold her house on West End Avenue—came out not on the society page but in the real-estate section—that convinced everybody. Soon they learned that she had actually sold her lovely big limestone house, disposed of all but a few pieces of her furniture, and had left for St. Louis in the company of her cousin and close companion of many years, Mrs. Florence Blalock. In Nashville, it seemed the end of an era!

During ten years, Miss Betty and Mrs. Blalock had been paying visits together to their St. Louis relatives, the James Tollivers. Their visits were frequent and long, yet as guests they had always had to have their stockings "rinsed out" by the maid and their breakfasts brought to their rooms, and had to be given little parties, which had been made up of mothers and aunts of the Tollivers' friends. At last, and quite unexpectedly, too, they had been told by Mr. James Tolliver himself that their visits were a bad length. Either they should come for shorter visits or they should come and live the year around as members of the household. Miss Betty had burst into tears on the spot—from pure shock, as she said afterward. James Tolliver, a very gentle and businesslike man of about forty, had tried immediately to relent. But there was no relenting once such a thing was said, and the decision had to be made.

How could anyone who had followed Miss Betty's social career imagine that she would make the choice in favor of St. Louis? The answer, of course, was that nobody but her cousin Mrs. Blalock could. Mrs. Blalock remembered the warmth with which Miss Betty had welcomed her into her house thirty years before, how she commenced calling her Flo Dear at once, how she talked of the longing she had always felt for a sister whom she could love. And, what was more, Flo Dear remembered how

Miss Betty's kindness and generosity toward her continued even after she realized that her poor cousin could not supply the sort of family affection that she craved. Flo Dear knew that at the Tolliver fireside it would be a different story.

To the Tolliver boys, it seemed that Auntie Bet and Flo Dear had always lived in St. Louis and occupied those two rooms at the end of the upstairs hall. Before the two ladies had resided in the Tollivers' house six months, the boys would speak of something that had happened during last year's visit as though their "aunts" had already been living with them then, and they would have to be reminded that it was otherwise.

It wasn't long before the boys' aunts seemed to feel, with the boys, that they had always lived there. Reaching back into the days of their visits for anecdotes, they managed to vest each of the three little boys with a highly individual character. There was little Jimmy, who had a natural bent for arithmetic and knew his multiplication tables before he ever went to school a day. They stood in awe of his head for figures and wondered what it would be like to have a scientist in the family. They said proudly that they hated to think of what out-of-the-way opinions he might come to hold. Jimmy's birthday came on January 8, and when he was "just a little fellow," he had figured out that if Christmas comes on a Sunday, then so must New Year's Day, and so must the eighth day of January, and then he had calculated how many times in his life Sunday was bound to ruin those three best days of the year. His aunts marveled at him. He was the second boy and in some ways the brightest. Vance was the oldest, and about him they said, "He is a very sober child, so respectful—and beautifully mannered." As for little Landon, they felt that one could not help adoring him, because of his sweet, dreamy nature and because he was the baby.

Vance was certainly the best mannered. But not their favorite. They had no favorite. Miss Betty and Flo Dear were impartial, utterly and completely. If one of Mr. Tolliver's business friends said to them, "Tell me about your little nephews; I understand you're very fond of them," they would hardly know where to begin. Finally Flo Dear might say, "Well, Vance is the oldest."

"Yes, Vance is getting so grown up it frightens me," Miss Betty would add, as though she had been with him every minute since he was born.

All in all, the move to St. Louis gave Miss Betty Pettigru just the new start in life that it seemed to promise. She and her cousin had a small circle of acquaintances among the mothers and aunts of the Tollivers' friends, but they seldom went anywhere or saw anyone except the members of their own family. Almost at once, Flo Dear had set up her drawing board in her room (she practiced the ancient art of blazonry), and very soon had completed a Tolliver coat of arms, which was hung in the library. Before long, she was accepting commissions from various friends of the Tollivers. Miss Betty assumed just as many household duties as Amy Tolliver would allow her to. But Amy, despite her easygoing nature, was too efficient and farseeing a family manager to leave an opening for trouble in that quarter. Miss Betty, in the end, was left free during almost all her waking hours to be of service to her little nephews. It was the new start in life she hoped for, and yet, almost upon her arrival, there began an unfortunate episode that threatened to demolish all this happiness. Within a matter of weeks after the two ladies were installed a terrible competition for the boys' favor developed between Miss Betty and Vennie, the Tollivers' aging cook.

At first glance, it would seem that Miss Betty had all the advantages in the struggle with Vennie. She lived in the same part of the house as the boys did; she ate at the table with them, was treated with respect by their parents, was at their service any and every hour of the day, not excluding Saturday or Sunday, when her chaperonage and financial backing were needed for excursions to the ice-skating rink or to the amusement parks and movie houses. Plainly, she was willing to throw into the battle the entire fortune old Major Pettigru, her father, had left her. She even went so far as to replace the town car she had sold upon leaving Nashville with a sea-green touring car, whose top could be put back in pleasant weather, and she added half again to the houseboy's salary in order that he might look after the car and Flo Dear and the boys on their expeditions.

Vennie's advantages were different, but they were real ones and were early recognized by Miss Betty. Vennie lived in a basement. She had not just a room there but an apartment, complete with an outside entrance, living room, kitchen, et cetera. One reached it by descending from the back hall to a long, narrow, poorly lit passage flanked by soapy-smelling laundry rooms, a tightly locked wine cellar, and the furnace room and coal bin. Her quarters were at the end of the passage. Miss Betty was destined never to go there, but in her mind she carried a picture of it that was as clear and accurate as if she had once occupied the rooms herself. The clearness was due to her knowledge of other such quarters she had visited in years gone by, but the accuracy of detail was due to the accounts her little nephews supplied. Landon told about the pictures on Vennie's walls: pictures of Negro children in middy blouses and other absurdly old-fashioned clothes you never thought of Negroes as wearing, pictures of Negro sergeants and corporals who had actually gone to France in the Great War (they all wore spectacles and looked, somehow, very unlike Negroes), pictures of Landon's mother and father and of other white people Vennie used to work for, in Thornton, and pictures of those other white people's children. Jimmy told about the horn on Vennie's old-timey phonograph and about the player piano and how it stretched and tired your legs to pedal it. Vance never said much about how things looked down there, but he talked about Vennie's "magic stove." Nothing cooked on the gas stove upstairs ever tasted like things cooked on that little coal range in Vennie's kitchen. And not one of the boys had failed to mention the dark scariness of the passage and how safe and bright Vennie's place always seemed when you got there.

Vennie's cooking, naturally, was a big advantage, but not such a serious one in itself. Auntie Bet could treat the boys to all manner of good things to eat when they went out. And what sort of handsome presents might she not have made them if it had been permitted! But it wasn't permitted, and Miss Betty didn't have to be told but once by Mr. James Tolliver that Christmas was the time—and the only time—when boys should receive expensive presents like bicycles and motor scooters. Amy and James were quick to shake their heads accusingly at her if one of the boys came back from Forest Park Highlands with even just a toy pistol he had won in a chance game. But when a three-layer chocolate cake was discovered in the lower compartment of the sideboard, and there was every reason to think other cakes had been kept there before and partaken of at will by the boys, despite all the rules against eating between meals, no more than a teasing, jovial finger was shaken at Vennie. Miss Betty protested that it really ought to be stopped, because Vance already had hickeys all over his face from so many sweets between meals. "But what can one do?" replied James Tolliver, shrugging his shoulders. "Vennie's like somebody's granny, and since the world began, grannies have been hiding cooky jars for young 'uns."

Certainly James Tolliver would not have made that casual remark if he had known the pain it would cause Miss Betty. It came on a day when the boys had been repeating to her some of the stories they liked to hear Vennie tell, stories about the old times at Thornton and in the country along the Tennessee River where it flows north up from Mississippi. How Uncle Wash got lost in the snowy woods and slept in a hollow log for two nights, and how Mr. Ben Tolliver found him there and thought he was "dead and maybe murdered." How little Jane Pettigru fell down the old well and Vennie's blind dwarf brother, whose name was Pettigru, too—Jules Pettigru—was the only one small enough to be let down on a rope to bring the baby out. Vennie's stories and her way of telling them were surely her greatest advantage. Or, at least, it was the thing that most unnerved Miss Betty and made her feel useless to her little nephews. Occasionally, she had heard Vennie telling some old anecdote to the whole Tolliver family. Vennie would take her stance just inside the dining-room door, arms akimbo, her head thrown back, and wearing a big smile that grew broader and broader until she finished the story in a fit of laughter. Her stories were mostly about the Tolliver family and the Tolliver Negroes, about the wondrous ways they were always rescuing each other from dangers great and small, usually ending with some fool thing a field hand Negro had said, or with Mr. Jeff Tolliver quoting the law to a pickaninny who had snatched an apple from the back porch. The really bad thing was that Miss Betty so often recognized Vennie's stories, remembered hearing other versions of them in her youth. Yet she could not tell the stories herself, or even think of them until something Vennie had told the boys reminded her. Sometimes she would recall a very different version of a story Vennie had told, but the boys were not impressed by Auntie Bet's corrections.

When the very first newness of Miss Betty's "treats" wore off, there would be times when she got all dressed and ready to take the boys somewhere and found that they were down in the basement with Vennie. Instead of sending for them, she would go to her room in a fit of depression, asking Flo Dear to tell the boys she had a headache and they would go another day.

James and Amy Tolliver were apt to say of almost anyone, "He is a genuine, intelligent, thoroughly sane person and has a fine sense of humor." They said something of the sort about Miss Betty and Flo Dear, and added that they were also "characters," which was the final term of approval. Amy especially was inclined to think everyone had a fine sense of humor. She herself saw what was funny in any situation and was wonderfully responsive to other people's humor, frequently inspiring them to say something quite beyond their ordinary wit. She would laugh heartily at things the two aunts said, though at least half the time James would say afterward that he didn't think she had been supposed to laugh. But Amy would reply, "Why, Flo Dear has a fine sense of humor," or "You don't do the boys' Auntie Bet justice, James."

No one was funnier to Amy than her own servants. She was forever laughing either at them or with them about something. But whereas many a Southern woman in a Northern city will get to be on rather intimate terms with her Southern servants, Amy never did. To some extent, she treated them with the same mixture of cordiality and formality that she used with her next-door neighbors. She nearly always liked her servants but never hesitated to "send them on their merry way" when there was reason to. "There are no second chances in Amy's service," her husband once said. "One false step and you are cast into the pit."

"Oh stuff!" said Amy. "This house serves as a sort of immigration office for Tennessee blacks in St. Louis. We bring them up here and train them, and when they leave us, they always go to something better. You *know* that's so."

James laughed and said, "Only old Vennie is a permanent fixture here, I guess."

"Ah, have no illusion about that," said Amy. "Vennie's time is bound to come. And when it does, we'll be liberated from a very subtle tyranny. When Vennie is gone, I tell you, the turnover among the others won't be nearly as fast."

It seemed too funny for words when the current maid and houseboy could not get used to the fact that Flo Dear and Miss Betty were no longer to be regarded as guests. Despite all Amy could do, Emmaline would put only company linen on their beds, and every few mornings she would slip upstairs with their breakfasts on a tray. One morning, in an effort to put a stop to that, the two ladies came marching down the stairs carrying their trays, and they proceeded, amid general hilarity, to transfer their breakfast dishes to their regular places at the table. Emmaline was called in to witness it, and Bert, the houseboy, was also present. The two Negroes laughed more heartily than even the little boys at the two aunts' clowning. Amy seemed almost hysterical. "I laughed so hard I thought I was going to have hysterics," she said afterward.

But Miss Betty said, "The only signs of hysteria I saw were in Bert and Emmaline. They seemed downright scared to me." Half an hour later, when she went upstairs, she didn't stop a second in her own room but passed right on through it and through the bathroom into Flo Dear's room. Flo Dear had preceded her upstairs by some fifteen or twenty minutes and was already at work at her drawing board. Miss Betty knew that her cousin hated being interrupted, but what she had to say could not wait. "I am now convinced," she announced, "that all this politeness is that old Vennie's doing."

Flo Dear raised her eyes and stared at Miss Betty. "It is now plain to me," said Miss Betty, "that Bert and Emmaline are taking orders from two mistresses."

Presently Flo Dear gave three quick, affirming little nods and said, "Yes, you're probably right. But you and I must not give them still two more mistresses." She and Miss Betty looked into one another's eyes for a moment, and then Miss Betty turned and retreated into the bathroom, closing the door behind her.

Yet very soon Bert and Emmaline began to have small pieces of change thrust into their hands at the oddest moments—when Bert forgot to put the pillow in Miss Betty's chair at table or when Emmaline put frayed and faded towels in the ladies' bathroom. Within a few weeks, the difficulty with the two younger servants was past.

Miss Betty's three "nephews" went to a school on Delmar Boulevard, only a few blocks from home. School was out at one o'clock on Wednesdays, and it was their privilege that day to bring home as many as four guests to lunch. Since Wednesday also happened to be Emmaline's day off, it was Vennie's privilege not only to cook but to serve the meal to the boys. It was a privilege and an advantage of which she made the most. By a ruling of Vance's, none of the white adults were allowed to be present at the meal, and Vance often directed what menu should be used. He always saw to it that Landon asked the blessing at that meal, and there was no horseplay whatsoever at the table. Vennie served in a black uniform with white cap and apron, and she never said a word until spoken to by Vance. But Vance, seated at the head of the table with his black hair slicked down on his head, the part glistening like a white scar, would faithfully begin addressing remarks to Vennie when dessert was about over. He did it in just the manner that his father did it whenever Vennie appeared at the evening meal, and Vennie responded with the same show of modesty and respect. "Oh, come on,

Vennie," Vance would say. "Tell us about Uncle Wash's fight with the bear when they were laying the railroad to Texas."

Vennie would demur, saying, "Those boys don't want to hear my old-nigger talk." But finally she would be brought around by the insistence of all the boys, and never were her tales so exciting as then, and never so full of phrases like "plantation roads" and "ol' marster" and "befo' freedom." While she talked, Vance would sit winking at the other boys, just as his father would do. Vennie's favorite way of beginning was to say, "Now, every Tolliver, black or white, know this story and know it be true." It was a convincing way to begin and usually removed all doubt from the minds of her listeners. But on a Wednesday in the fall after the boys' aunts had come there to live, one long-faced little friend of Jimmy's stopped Vennie with the question "How do you mean 'black or white'? Are there black Tollivers?"

"What do you think my name is?" Vennie asked, annoyed by the interruption.

"Your name is Vennie."

"My name's Vennie Tolliver," Vennie said. Her name indeed was Tolliver, since she had once been married to one of the Negro Tollivers at Thornton. The Negro Tollivers, like the Negro Pettigrus and Blalocks, had kept the name of their former masters after emancipation, and most of them had continued in service to the Tollivers. But Vennie's husband, like Flo Dear's, had long before "disappeared off the face of the earth."

The four luncheon guests all broke into laughter because they thought Vennie was joking. Landon and Jimmy laughed, too. But Vance began to blush. His whole face turned red; even the part in his hair changed color. Vennie looked at him a moment in bewilderment, and then suddenly she began to laugh herself. "Didn't you-all know I was kin to Vance?" she said in a shrill voice, which normally was rather deep and hoarse, grew clearer and higher. "Course it ain't really the truth, 'cause I 'uz only *married* to a sort of cousin of his. But I'm his old Auntie Vennie, all right. Ain't that so, Cousin Landon?"

Landon smiled sweetly and said he guessed it was so. Vennie never did tell her story that day. Under her breath she kept laughing so hard that she couldn't have told if she had tried. And the boys—all but Vance—kept giggling until they finished their dessert and left the table.

Worst of all for Vance was the laughter that night from the grown people. Landon told all about it at the dinner table, right where Vennie could hear every word of it. Vance at first managed to smile halfheartedly, but in the midst of all the talk and laughter he observed that there was no shade of a smile on his Auntie Bet's face. His own halfhearted smile vanished, and he and Auntie Bet exchanged a long look, which—in Vance's mind, at least—may have constituted some sort of pledge between them.

It was Vance, with his sense of what the grown-ups liked, who had invented the pet name Auntie Bet, and he would have said Auntie Flo, except that Flo Dear had discouraged it. Instead, she had asked the boys just to call her Flo Dear, the way their Auntie Bet did. She was ever considerate of Miss Betty's prerogative as a blood relation, despite all of Amy and James's impartiality. In her consideration, she went so far as to try to accept Miss Betty's views of every important thing that happened in the house. When the first complaints against Vennie were made to her by Miss Betty, she tried to admit their justice, while at the same time minimizing their importance. She imagined she saw seeds of Miss Betty's ruin in the struggle, and events pointed more and more in that direction.

By Miss Betty's "ruin" she didn't mean that Vennie would remain and Miss Betty would go; she knew that Vennie would finally be sent away, but Miss Betty's ruin would lie in her very condescension to this struggle and in the means she would use to dispose of Vennie. If only Flo Dear could delay action on Miss Betty's part, then soon enough Vennie would be discharged for reasons that wouldn't involve anyone else, because Flo Dear knew, without listening at the hot-air register in the shut-off cardroom downstairs, that if Vennie entertained and cooked on her magic stove for the boys in her basement rooms, she also entertained and cooked for a large number of those colored people, or their like, whose pictures hung on her walls, and the food, of course, all came out of Amy's kitchen. She knew there would be a last time for Amy's saying, "My grocery bills are outrageous! I don't understand where the leak is. That is, I'm not sure yet."

Miss Betty's complaints were not all of indirect thrusts through the boys and the other servants, for after Bert and Emmaline had been neutralized, Vennie began, herself, a series of personal affronts. If Miss Betty crossed the threshold of the kitchen, she put down whatever she was doing and retired to the basement. If the two were about to meet in the narrow hall or on the stairs, Vennie would turn back and manage to get out of sight before Miss Betty could call her. Miss Betty did try to call to her sometimes, or at least to speak to her—there was a period when she imagined it was not too late to make friends and join forces with her adversary—but Vennie would have none of it. At last, Miss Betty trapped her one day in the pantry and said, "Why don't you and I plan a surprise dessert for the family tonight? You make us a cake—one of your good devil's food cakes—and I'll set us up to a wonderful new sort of ice cream they're making at a place I know out on De Baliviere."

Vennie rared back and her voice became shrill: "I been making the ice cream since before you-all came here, and I'll be making it when you and her's both gone."

When Flo Dear heard about this, her heart went out to Miss Betty in a way it seldom did. But she was also frightened by the look in Miss Betty's eyes. Ruin seemed inevitable at that moment—spiritual ruin, or, more specifically, spiritual *relapse*. Flo Dear's life in Nashville had been as quiet as Miss Betty's had been active. She knew that some people in Nashville had called her "Miss Betty Pettigru's silent partner." She had overheard people speaking of her that way, but she had said to herself, "I live this way because I have *chosen* to live this way." It was true that if she had wished, she could have shared all of Miss Betty's activities, for that was what Miss Betty had once hoped she would do. But the choice had been made long before she came to live on West End Avenue. She didn't herself pretend to know when she had made the choice, but it was made before she ever married Tolliver Blalock and became a part of his huge family connection. In the big country family that she was born into, they had always told her she was by nature a mouse, to which she had replied (silently), "If I am a mouse, at least I am a principled mouse." But when she was twenty-two and already considered an old maid, she had been swept off her feet by Tolliver Blalock, the black sheep of his family and widely known as a rascal with women. He had left her after only two months, "disappeared off the face of the earth," leaving his hat and coat on the bank of the Tennessee River, more as a sign that he would never return than as any real pretense that he had drowned. As his widow, Flo Dear was taken to the bosom of the Tolliver-Pettigru-Blalock connection as no other in-law ever was. For years, she lived with first one of her in-laws and then another. They quarreled over who was to have the privilege next. Apparently there had never been a mouse in any of those families, or at least not a *silent* mouse, and they delighted in how she would sit and listen to what *any* of them said. She listened, and listened especially to the old ones, and then, one day, thinking it would help her forget for a while the loneliness and humiliation she felt in the bosom of her husband's fine family, she sat down and wrote out all she had heard about their splendid history. As much as anything, it was to clear her head of the stuff. The manuscript was discovered and she became known as the finest living authority on the history of the Tollivers, Blalocks, and Pettigrus. After ten years of this life in the vicinity of Thornton, there came a letter to her from Miss Betty Pettigru, whose wealthy old father had taken her up to Nashville in the vain hope of finding her a suitable husband. Miss Betty was then seeking membership in the Colonial Dames of America and she wanted Flo Dear's help in that cause. It ended, of course, by Flo Dear's moving up to Nashville.

Searching through Nashville libraries for proof of Miss Betty's eligibility, Flo Dear found her true vocation, discovered the one passion of her life. It happened in a single moment. She was standing—tiny, plain, dish-faced creature that she was—in the dark and towering library stacks of what is surely the mustiest, smelliest, dirtiest, ugliest of state capitol buildings in the Union. In her pawlike little hands she held a book whose faded title she was trying to read on the mildewed binding. Presently, she opened the book with an impatient jerk. It came open not at the title page but at the plates of two brightly emblazoned fifteenth-century escutcheons. They were the first coats of arms Flo Dear had ever seen, and the beauty of their joyful colors seemed suddenly to illuminate her soul and give her a first taste of the pure joy of being alive. Needless to say, the joy and inspiration she received from her discovery made the matter of talent an unimportant one. In practically no time at all, she became a modern master in the art of blazonry, and by the time she left Nashville, thirty years later, there was hardly a nice house in town on whose walls a piece of her work was not hung.

Flo Dear's work became the absorbing interest of her life. Yet it wasn't entirely her fault or her work's fault that she and Miss Betty could not become "as close as sisters." At first, Flo Dear was guilty of suspecting Miss Betty of disingenuousness. She could not see why Miss Betty made over her so and she felt that she was being "cousined" to death. Outside her profession, Flo Dear soon got so she could not abide the word "cousin." She felt that if she allowed it, Miss Betty would smother her with confidences. More than her time, somehow her small supply of energy seemed to disappear when she listened to her cousin. She simply could not afford the intimacy and dependency that was being asked of her.

There was more explanation than this: When old Major Pettigru was on his deathbed, he had said to Miss Betty, who was his only child, "It's a shame and a scandal, Bet. Since I brought you to Nashville, you've expended your time making a place for yourself among strongheaded women while you ought to have been making your place in the heart of some gentle, honest man." He had said that to her in the presence of two doctors and a nurse, and so almost immediately it had become known all over town. To most people it was an amusing story, but not to Flo Dear. She felt, exactly as Major Pettigru had, that Miss Betty had expended foolishly not merely her time but her invaluable, marvelous energy as well. Perhaps, with her unprepossessing appearance and her lack of small talk, finding a husband was not feasible for Miss Betty, but something—surely *something*—better than a life of social climbing could be found. It was worse than a shame and a scandal in Flo Dear's eyes; it was a sin. She had never told Miss Betty in so many words, but she knew that Miss Betty acknowledged in her heart that she was right. Else why had Miss Betty always made a point of matching every social victory with some act of charity? When she succeeded in having Mrs. John O'Neil Smith impeached as madam president of the Corrine Society (for having sat down to dinner with the president of a Negro college), she immediately gave a formal luncheon for the homeliest, least eligible debutante of the season. After she had blackballed every candidate for membership in the West End Book Club until the other members accepted an ambitious but illiterate satellite of her own, she paid a formal call on a notorious lady in town and went about saying that she, for one, thought that that lady's "adopted" child looked nothing in the world like its foster mother. Surely, in Nashville, Miss Betty's life had been all sin and expiation, but with never a resolution to sin no more.

"They have big get-togethers down there," Vance said.

"Big get-togethers?" said Miss Betty.

"Yes, ma'am. Sometimes there's a whole crowd and sometimes not so many. We used to always listen to them through the radiator in here, till we got tired of it. Listen! That's Vennie's cousin who works out at the Florisant Valley Club. He's from Thornton, too, and used to work for us. Listen to them! They think they're whispering now. But you can hear them just as plain."

"Yes, you can almost hear them breathing," said Auntie Bet.

"And they can't hear you at all unless you really holler."

Vance and his Auntie Bet were in the cardroom, behind the drawing room. It was a room that Amy kept shut off, because she and James were not cardplayers and it was only another room for Bert to keep clean. It was a tiny room, and the furniture had been left there by the former occupants. There was a built-in game cabinet with a dozen different size pigeonholes and compartments, and a "stationary card table," and some chairs. It all went with the house, the former occupants had said.

It was a Sunday afternoon and Vance and Auntie Bet were playing checkers. He had come back from a long walk in the park and had found her arranging some flowers in a vase on the hall table. When he invited her to go with him to the cardroom and have a game of checkers, she looked at him wonderingly, because she could tell that he had something on his mind. When they began to play, it occurred to her that perhaps the boys weren't supposed to play games like checkers on Sunday. And in the *cardroom*, too. Then she began to notice the Negro voices coming through the hot-air register in the corner of the room. She was so distracted by her thoughts and by those voices that almost before she knew it, the game was over and she was badly beaten.

"Oh, you weren't even trying, Auntie Bet," said Vance.

She smiled—or, rather turned up the corners of her mouth self-consciously. "I tried, but I got to listening to the Negroes' voices in the radiator," she said. "We must be right above Vennie's living room." And then Vance told her about the get-togethers down there.

"It's rather eerie, isn't it?" she said. "I mean how we can hear their voices and they can't hear ours."

Vance began arranging the checkers for a new game. "Sometime," he said, not looking at her, "you might just come in here —you and Flo Dear, that is—when Jimmy and Landon and I are down in Vennie's rooms." He raised his eyes and said in a grave, reflective tone of voice, "Auntie Bet, that Vennie says the darnedest things to us children. You should just hear her."

"Why *what*, Vance?" But before he could answer, Miss Betty had suddenly understood what sort of plot he was suggesting, and she abruptly got up from the table.

Vance instantly grew pale. "What's the matter, Auntie Bet?"

"Nothing's the matter, my darling," she said. "But I—I left half my flowers out of water." She was opening the door into the drawing room, but she glanced back at Vance and saw him still sitting with the checkerboard before him and with the bare light of the overhead lamp shining on his black hair, which looked rather too soft and too thick for a boy, and on the mottled complexion of his forehead, on the widespread nares of his nose. And silently Miss Betty Pettigru was saying to the oldest of her three Tolliver nephews, "Poor wounded, frightened child! What thoughts have you had of me? What thoughts?"

As she passed through the hall, she was surprised to see that she had indeed left some of her flowers lying on the big console table. She had bought them at a florist's on the way home from church that morning but had waited till Vennie left the kitchen to select her vase and arrange them. She snatched the flowers from the table and went upstairs.

In her room, she dropped the flowers in her wastebasket and, without taking off her daintily pleated dress, she lay down across the bed. This time, she was not pacing the floor after fifteen or twenty minutes. She was still lying there when Flo Dear called her to go down to supper.

As she lay on her bed this Sunday afternoon, she thought of the life she had left in Nashville. Her life there had never in her eyes been one of sin and expiation. It had just been life, plain and simple, where you did what good things you could and what bad things you must. As she looked back, it seemed that it had been hard for her to decide to leave Nashville only because it had meant facing the fact of the worthlessness of the goal she had set herself many years before—the goal set *for* her, really, by circumstances and by her personal limitations. What else could she have done with her life? She had not asked to be born in the days when Victoria was queen of England, when Southern womanhood was waited upon not by personal maids but by personal slaves. She had not asked to be born the unbeautiful, untalented heiress of a country family's fortune, or to grow up to find that the country town that gave that fortune its only meaning was decaying and disappearing, even in a physical sense. The men of her generation, and of later generations, had gone to Nashville, Memphis, Louisville, and even St. Louis, and had used their heads, their connections, and their genteel manners to make their way to the top in the new order of things. And wasn't that all *she* had done, and in the only way permissible for a Miss Pettigru from Thornton? Once the goal was defined, was it necessary that she should be any less ruthless than her male counterparts? In her generation, the ends justified the means. For men, at least, they did. Now, at last, Miss Betty saw how much like a man's life her own had been. She saw it in the eyes of the wounded, frightened child. She saw how it was that every day of her adult life had made her less a woman instead of more a woman. Or less somebody's old granny instead of more somebody's old granny. Wrong though it seemed, the things a man did to win happiness in the world—or in the only world Miss Betty knew—were of no consequence to the children he came home to at night, but every act, word, and thought of a woman was judged by and reflected in the children, in the husband, in all who loved her. "If only Flo Dear had not been so embittered before she even came to my house," Miss Betty thought miserably, "maybe my instincts would not have died so dead."

She had done nothing to bring on Vennie's dismissal, and yet Vance had seen that she was capable of doing that something and had thought she might enter into a conspiracy with little children in the house of her kinspeople. If he condemned old Vennie for saying things to "us children" that she ought not to say, what thoughts must he have of *her?* All was lost, and in the morning she would go—not back to Nashville but perhaps to Thornton itself.

Flo Dear knocked on Miss Betty's door from the hall. "It's almost supper time," she said.

"Well, I'll be along soon," Miss Betty answered, not suggesting that Flo Dear open the door and come in.

"It's Bert's Sunday on," Flo Dear reminded her, "and Amy and James are going out to dinner."

Its being Bert's Sunday on meant that Bert would prepare and serve the cold supper and that someone must check closely to see that he washed the lettuce for the salad and that the table was set properly. Amy and James's going out to dinner meant that the check on Bert would be Miss Betty and Flo Dear's responsibility.

Flo Dear inferred from Miss Betty's being alone for so long in her room that there had been another incident. She had heard Miss Betty come upstairs an hour earlier, and although she had put down her book, her mind had wandered more than once from the subject of heraldic symbolism to all the incidents of recent weeks. Miss Betty had managed to make it plain enough to her, in the way she reported the incidents, that Vennie's antagonism was directed equally at both of them. It was really Flo Dear, wasn't it, Miss Betty had asked her one day, that Vennie had made fun of to the boys and their Wednesday guests? During all their thirty years together, Flo Dear felt, this was the first deliberate unkindness Miss Betty had shown her. Yet she interpreted it as a "sign of nerves." It was so unreasonable that she could not really resent it. It was as though Miss Betty expected *her* to do something about Vennie. Even in Nashville, Miss Betty had never tried to involve *her* in her petty wars with womankind. She stood outside Miss Betty's door now, shaking her head and saying to herself, "Well, it can't go on. It can't go on. We must leave. We must leave Amy and James and their children to their peace. If we can't go back to Nashville, we—or I—can go back to Thornton." But the very thought of that prospect made Flo Blalock clasp her hands and shudder inwardly. Spending her last days among the remnants of the Tolliver-Blalock-Pettigru clan! Moving from garrulous house to garrulous house! She, the pitiable woman whom one of them had wronged. She hurried along the hall, past the room where Amy and James were dressing, down the stairs, and into the dining room to see how things were going with Bert. The light was on, but there were not even place mats on the table yet. "I declare," she whispered, "that Negro Bert is not worth his salt." She went into the pantry and into the kitchen, but one of the gas jets of the stove was burning, though no pot or pan was on the stove, or even a coffeepot.

And then, through the backdoor and vestibule, she heard Bert's footsteps on the cement driveway. She stepped to the backdoor and saw him, in his white coat, coming through the twilight from the garage—the old carriage house, where he had his room, in the coachman's loft. She could see that he saw her, and that he hesitated. "What's the matter, Bert?" she asked.

He came on up the steps. He was a tall, brown-skinned Negro and walked with a peculiar gait. Amy said he picked his feet up slewfoot and put them down pigeon-toed. As he came inside the door, he pretended to laugh. "You know what I done, Miss Flo? When I left out of here, I aimed to turn off the stove, but I turned off the light instead." He switched on the light and went to the table where the coffeepot and the open coffee can were sitting.

"And now you've left the light on in your room." She was still looking out toward the garage.

"Is I now?" He was filling the coffeepot.

Flo Dear was trembling. When she spoke, she hoped her voice would sound like Miss Betty's or Amy's or James's, or Vennie's, or *anybody's* but her own. "Somebody's out there, Bert, who hasn't any business out there. Is that so, Bert?"

Bert put the coffeepot on the stove and then looked at Miss Flo, but not in his usual simple big-eyed way. "Yes, ma'am, they is. It's Vance."

Flo Dear couldn't find the words she wanted, but she continued to stare at Bert, and she knew that even with just a stare she was taking a hand in things. And now Bert, too, knew that she was taking a hand, and when he saw that, every last bit of foolishness seemed to go out of his face.

"I'm just going to tell you about it, Miss Flo," he said. "Vance came down here in the kitchen and he was crying around and wanted to talk to me. He said he had hurt Miss Betty's feelings and wouldn't never git over it, and he was scared to talk to his daddy or Miss Amy about it. He wanted to go out yonder to my old rooms to talk with me, so I just taken him on out there, Miss Flo, and he and me had it all out. He'll be along in the house directly."

Flo Dear sat down on a chair beside the table. "Tell me how he hurt Miss Betty's feelings, Bert."

Bert, looking right into Miss Flo's eyes, stood before her and told her how Vance had got Miss Betty to go in the cardroom and all they had said there and finally how Miss Betty wouldn't really listen to Vennie and her company and wouldn't "be conniving with any little old Vance."

When he had finished, Flo Dear made no move to go. "You begin setting the table, Bert," she said. "I want to just sit here awhile."

Amy and James came downstairs in evening clothes. They were going first to a cocktail party and then to a large supper party honoring the debutante daughter of two of their friends. They knew that Miss Betty always liked to see them when they were "dressed," particularly if they were going out among people whom she considered "prominent in an important way."

Amy went to the dining-room door to see if the two ladies were in there. Bert was just beginning to set the table. "You're late getting started with that, Bert," she said.

"Yes'm, ain't I, though? I got behind." He was all big-eyed simpleness again.

"Well, have you gotten Mr. James's car out?"

"Yes'm, it's at the side."

"Hasn't Miss Betty or Miss Flo come down?"

"Miss Flo's back here," he said, and he dashed off toward the kitchen. Amy stood watching the swinging door until Flo Dear appeared.

"How lovely you look, Amy," said Flo Dear, coming into the dining room. "Nothing so becomes you as green, Amy." Compliments from her were rare but not unheard of. Such compliments on Amy's appearance were Miss Betty's prerogative, but now and then, when Miss Betty was not present, Flo Dear would say something like this.

"Why, I thank you, Flo Dear," Amy said. "A compliment from you really sets me up. You're not the wicked flatterer Aunt Betty is."

"She's just more articulate than I, Amy."

"Pooh," said Amy, turning back into the hall. "Where is she, anyway?"

"Here she comes from upstairs now," James said. He was standing near the foot of the stairs, his derby on his head, his overcoat over one arm and Amy's white *lapin* wrap over the other.

"Take off your hat in the house, James," Amy said. "What will your aunts think of you?"

"It's time we're going," James said, holding up Amy's wrap for her.

"Do wait and let me see Amy's dress," called Miss Betty from the stairs, rather spiritlessly.

The others looked up at her. "Aunt Betty, you don't sound like yourself," Amy said.

"I've been taking a nap," she said. "You look lovely, Amy. It's a stunning dress."

Amy's dress was of a dark green silk, with a long waist, a very low back, and a hemline just at her knees. Her hair was not bobbed, but tonight she had it arranged in a way that made it at first glance look so.

"She looks sixteen, doesn't she?" said Flo Dear.

Suddenly Amy called out, "Boys! Boys! We're going!"

Landon and Jimmy came racing down from upstairs, and in a moment Vance appeared in the doorway from the dining room, looking solemn and dejected. Miss Betty went to him and put an arm about his shoulders.

"If you boys behave and mind your aunts," James Tolliver said, getting into his coat, "I'll take you to East St. Louis with me next Saturday. I'm going out to see old Mr. Hendricks at the stockyards."

Jimmy was standing on the bottom step of the stairs. Partly, no doubt, because he didn't like to go to East St. Louis but mostly because he wished to satisfy his thirst for scientific truth, he asked, "Why do you say 'our aunts' when Flo Dear is not our aunt or even related to us and Auntie Bet isn't really our aunt, either?"

Jimmy's mother and father looked at him as though he had spoken an obscenity. "Jim, are you asking to be punished?" his father said. "Do you want me to take you upstairs in my dress clothes and punish you?"

Amy dropped her velvet evening bag on the console table and sat down in one of the high-backed hall chairs. This was her usual way of saying she wouldn't go somewhere until the boys stopped misbehaving. It was also a way of emphasizing her speechlessness. After a moment, she said, "Just what do you mean by that, James? What earthly power made you ask that?"

Flo Dear glanced at Miss Betty and saw that she had managed to catch Vance's eye and was shaking her head at him warningly. Jimmy was blushing and carefully avoiding the eyes of the aunts. He kept looking first at his mother and then at Landon. After a moment, Landon, who was always the one most moved by his mother's threats, said to Jimmy, "Go ahead and tell, Jimmy. It's just Vennie, and she always says she doesn't care who you tell." Then, turning to his mother, he said, "Vennie's always saying we aren't a bit of kin to Flo Dear, and not much to Auntie Bet. And she thinks they ought not to live with us unless they are close kin."

But Jimmy still had not told when his father pulled the derby off his head and was saying, "You boys—all of you—get upstairs to your rooms and get up there quick."

The three boys were upstairs and in their rooms almost before their father had taken off his overcoat. He removed the coat with great care and folded the sleeves and the collar as though he were about to pack it in a traveling bag. Then he handed it and his derby to Amy.

"Oh, James," said Miss Betty in a hoarse whisper, "don't punish the boys."

"I'm not going to punish the boys," he said. "I'm going downstairs before I leave this house and give Amy's notice to Vennie."

"No," Miss Betty said, "don't do that, James!"

But Amy said, "Tell her she needn't ever come up in the house again."

"I'll meet you at the car, Amy," he said to her, and as he went out through the dining room, he called back, "I'll tell Bert to stay in the house all evening, till we come home."

When he was gone, Amy tried to smile. "I don't know why he couldn't wear his overcoat to fire Vennie," she said. "A sign of special respect, I suppose."

Miss Betty, wearing a dazed expression, said, "This won't do, Amy. It just won't do."

"Oh, it'll do fine, Aunt Betty," said Amy. "Don't you think I know what's been going on in my own house? It was James who had to be shown. He has been Vennie's protector since long before this business. And Emmaline and Bert both gave me notice a week ago; I've been sick about it. Why, for a houseboy, you just can't beat that simpleminded Bert. No, my dears, Vennie's days of usefulness in this house are past. Her superannuation is long overdue."

Supper for Miss Betty and Flo Dear and the boys was delayed for three quarters of an hour that Sunday night. Bert was an eternity getting the food on the table, but none of them was hungry, and so it did not matter. Not long after their parents were out of the house, Vance and his brothers came downstairs and into the living room, where the two aunts were sitting together. But before the boys came down, Flo Dear and Miss Betty had exchanged a few words, and each had had a great many thoughts that were not exchanged, at least not in words.

They were seated directly opposite each other on either side of the fireplace, in two little Windsor chairs that were the only uncomfortable chairs in the room. Last embers of the usual Sunday fire were smoldering in the wood ashes between the andirons. When first they sat down, there was a long silence, with each of them staring into the embers, watching an occasional flame spring up and then die almost at once. Miss Betty's small, pudgy nose seemed swollen and her eyes were two glazed buttons. She sat with her feet placed far apart, her ankles looking swollen like her nose, and on her knees her hands rested, the ten fingers spread out like so many wrinkled little sausages. Flo Dear sat crossing and uncrossing her narrow ankles, fingering the buttons that ran from the high neck to the waist of her dress, and blinking her eyes at the fire.

At last, without changing her expression or moving a muscle of her body, Miss Betty said, "We should go on back to Nashville, I think, Flo Dear, or maybe to Thornton." She wanted to tell Flo Dear that she had had no hand in Jimmy's outburst, but it would be useless and somehow not entirely truthful to say that. Yet at the very moment she was saying that they must leave and thinking that they must, she was also thinking that if they could stay, if they could only stay, she might, with her new insight, begin to be of some use to the Tolliver boys. After all, they were rich children, just as she had been a rich child, and the world was still changing, preparing people for one thing and giving them another. And poor little Vance—what problems would be his! Not excelling in his schoolwork, certainly not good-looking, with only that one terrible talent that she, too, had—the talent for observing what things the world valued and making the most of *that*.

But she knew that she could not spend the last years of her life with Flo Dear sitting there so straight in the Windsor chair, accusing her with every crossing of her slim ankles and every blinking of her narrow eyes.

All that Flo Dear said before the boys came down was "We must do whatever seems the right thing to you and the best thing for the boys." From this, Miss Betty took hope. She detected a new softness in Flo Dear's voice. It was a softness that must have come from Flo Dear's own reassessment of things. Whether it was the thought of Thornton or her thoughts in the dark kitchen or the knowledge that Miss Betty had been truly hurt by Vance's proposal, something was making her question her old judgments of Miss Betty Pettigru. It seemed to her that perhaps to do anything at all in the world was to do wrong to *someone*. She thought of Vennie and of what would become of her now. Perhaps it was fair and just that Miss Betty should have the affection the boys gave to Vennie. Perhaps Vennie had nieces and nephews of her own. She could go and live with them or with some of her many friends. There must be many of her relatives who loved and needed old Vennie. And yet perhaps she didn't really have a family of her own. Or perhaps none of them would find her so lovable and attractive when she no longer had this good job and could make them presents and cook them meals on her little coal range. But already Flo Dear could hear Vance and Jimmy and Landon coming down the stairs into the hall.

When the boys came into the living room, with their hair combed and wearing fresh shirts, Miss Betty and Flo Dear stood up and greeted their nephews as though it were after long months of separation. And the boys seemed equally glad to see their aunts. There was even kissing and hugging, and there were some tears shed. Supper was still not on the table, and though Miss Betty complained about Bert's being "so mortally slow," Flo Dear did not say again that he wasn't worth his salt. Instead, she gathered the three boys about her chair and commenced explaining to them, as no one else in the world was so well qualified to do, just exactly what her family connection was to them, and in even greater detail she described the blood ties that existed between them and their Auntie Bet. There was a certain hollowness in her voice, and as she spoke she stared somewhat vacantly into the dying embers of the Sunday fire. The boys, however, did not notice any of this. They listened attentively to the facts she was presenting, as though they were learning life's most important lessons.

For a while, Miss Betty watched this scene with tears in her eyes. But then she went and lay down on the sofa. It would be no more protracted visit to St. Louis; she was here for life. And when, finally, Bert announced supper, Vance had to go and touch Auntie Bet's hand to wake her from a deep, dreamless slumber.

THE DEATH
OF A KINSMAN

CAST OF CHARACTERS
Robert Wade
Margie, his wife
Aunt Lida Wade
Miss Bluemeyer, their housekeeper
Myra Willis, family servant
Lennie, upstairs maid, Myra's niece
Paris, houseboy, Myra's nephew
The Wade children
    James
    Nancy
    Alfred
    Charles William
    Lida Sue

SCENE I

It is long before daybreak, but in the Wade house lights have been put on in the halls and in the pantry and in the upstairs sitting room and in nearly every room in the whole house and on the side porch as well. Nobody has been left sleeping. The curtain rises on

*the scene in the upstairs hall. It is a rectangular room running the
entire width of the stage. On the wall beyond the balustrade
which guards the descending stairs is an enormous mirror. Doors
to the bedrooms are at either end of the hall. A door at the
extreme right in the back wall opens into the service hall where
there is presumably another stairway. The door at the head of the
stairs (left, back) leads to the bedroom of Mr. and Mrs. Wade.
The general effect is that all of the wall space, except that beyond
the stairwell, is taken up by the doorways. The elaborate door
facings and the oak balustrade and the pilasters at the four corners
of the stairwell indicate that the house is one of those mansions
put up in Midwestern cities during the early part of the present
century. The floor is not carpeted, but is partly covered by two
large rugs. The one on the left is a handsome, though worn and
faded, Oriental rug. On the right is an obviously new imitation of
the same thing, with extremely bright colors and a general effect
of silkiness. The end of the hall to the left (and front) is furnished
as an upstairs sitting room. There are several upholstered chairs, a
footstool, a small table and lamp. The only other furnishings are a
table and chair at the right (front) corner of the balustrade. The
table is an old-fashioned card table, the typical Southern antique,
and the chair a ladder-back imitation antique with a cushion on
the seat. On the table are an electric clock, a modern French-style
telephone, and an ultramodern desk lamp which, except for the
dimly lit table lamp, is the only light burning as the curtain rises.*

*Simultaneously two Negro maids enter from doors at opposite
ends of the hall. One is a tall, thin, stooped woman with a good
deal of gray in her hair. The other is a somewhat more than plump
young woman. Both are black. They advance hurriedly toward the
middle of the room until simultaneously children's voices call
from the rooms they have just quitted.* "Myra, where are my good
socks? What did you do with . . ." "Lennie, where's the brush I
put . . ." *The two women halt, exchange first exasperated
grimaces and then indulgent smiles, and return to the children.
Aunt Lida Wade appears from one of the doors at the left. Her
thin white hair is in rollers and she is attired in a cinnamon-
colored kimono. As she enters she is addressing her great-niece*

Nancy over her shoulder: "No, I don't know which dress you mean, Nancy, but it must be one of those in the back hall closet." Nancy's eleven-year-old whine can be heard from within: "You know the one, Aunt Lida; the one with the long sash." Aunt Lida answers in an impatient but conciliating voice, "I'll see. I'll see." She closes the door behind her and moves across the stage taking the small, practiced ladylike steps of a long-legged woman who would naturally move with great strides. She goes into the service hall, closing the door behind her. Now quick footsteps are heard on the dark stairway, and presently a Negro houseboy, wearing an unbuttoned white jacket, dashes up into the hall. He places a pair of highly polished brown shoes by the door at the head of the stairs and turns at once to descend the stairs. Seeing the dark stairwell before him, he inadvertently reaches out and flicks the light switch on the wall beside him. The light does not come on, and grinning at himself he says, "Ah, shoot!" Meanwhile, the older Negro woman has entered from a door at the right; she addresses him contemptuously, "Ain't fix 'at even yit, have you, Paris?" His grin broadens into a big, silly smile, showing a mouth full of gleaming white teeth. "I cain't fix it, Aunt Myra." He puts his hand on the rail and disappears from the stairway. Now Aunt Lida enters from the service hall with three of Nancy's dresses over her arm. She passes Myra, who is moving slowly toward the head of the stairs.

AUNT LIDA: What an hour of the day to be gotten up, eh, Myra?

MYRA: Ain't it the truth, Miss Lida? An' him not on this place more'n three times in ten year.

AUNT LIDA: But he was the only relative any of us have in Detroit, Myra.

MYRA: Not much kin. An' getting all them chillun up.

AUNT LIDA: I don't see why the children should be gotten up, but you know Mr. Robert.

MYRA: I know white folks.

AUNT LIDA: Listen here, don't you talk about white folks to

me, Myra Willis. If it were *your* Cousin Harry, you'd be off work for a week. *(She has now opened the door to Nancy's room.)*

MYRA *(at the head of the stairs, looking down into the darkness; still addressing Aunt Lida)*: Nobody ain't fix 'at light yit.

AUNT LIDA: Mr. Robert said he would do it today.

MYRA: He say.

AUNT LIDA: I know, I know. *(Closing the door behind her.)*

Mr. Wade opens the door of his own room to fetch his shoes. Myra looks over her shoulder at him.

MR. WADE: Morning, Myra.

MYRA: It's still night to me. An' this here light ain't fix yit.

MR. WADE: By George, it's not. You tell Paris to bring the ladder up, and we'll fix it right now.

MYRA: Now? This now? At five o'clock in the mornin'? *(He picks up his shoes and closes the door.)*

MR. WADE: Lord God.

Miss Bluemeyer, the housekeeper, enters from the service hall. She is a large woman dressed in navy blue with tiny white ruffles at the collar. Her hair, cut like a man's has obviously not been combed this morning, and she is still wearing her flat-heeled bedroom slippers. She is carrying a small tray with one cup of coffee and a silver sugar and cream set.

MISS BLUEMEYER: Are you in a great rush, Myra?

MYRA: Not me.

MISS BLUEMEYER: Then I would like to see you a minute, please. About something.

MYRA: Yassum.

Meanwhile, the housekeeper strides across the hall and knocks at the door at the head of the stairs.

MRS. WADE *(from within)*: Just a minute! Who is it?

MISS BLUEMEYER: It is I. . . . Miss Bluemeyer.

Mrs. Wade opens the door. She is an extremely small woman of about forty. Her long brown hair falls about the shoulders of her negligee. She is pregnant.

MRS. WADE: Oh, I'm *so* obliged to you, Miss Bluemeyer. You know that I'm not a bit of good till I've had my coffee. I'll just bet you had to make it yourself.

MISS BLUEMEYER: I did, Misses Wade. But that's all right, I made a cup for myself too.

MRS. WADE: Isn't it a hideous hour? *(Beginning to close the door.)*

MISS BLUEMEYER: Yes, it is, but I am awfully sorry about your cousin.

MRS. WADE: Yes, it is sad of course. He was very old, you know, and we knew him very little, really.

MISS BLUEMEYER: I see.

Mrs. Wade closes the door, and Miss Bluemeyer turns to Myra. With a movement of her head she indicates that Myra should follow her. Then she crosses the stage and seats herself at the telephone table. Myra follows and stands before Miss Bluemeyer, with her hands folded and resting against her white apron.

MISS BLUEMEYER *(smiling intimately and a little sadly):* Myra, tell me, did you ever know their Cousin Harry?—Mr. Wilson, that is.

MYRA: Yassum, oh, yassum. *(Casually.)* My sister Cora used to work for his own sister, Miss Jamie, in Nashville, way back yonder. Most of them Wilsons is dead though. He muss be the lass of 'em, I reckon.

MISS BLUEMEYER: That is not what I mean, Myra. I know that all of you knew one another back in Tennessee, but that is ten years or more—

MYRA: Yassum, we been in Deetroit ten year. Now, the two oldest chillun was born'd in Tennessee, but—

MISS BLUEMEYER: That is not what I mean, Myra. I mean—that is, I have been keeping house for Misses Wade nearly a year now and had never heard Cousin Harry's name—Mr. Wilson, that is to say—mentioned until his stroke a few weeks ago.

MYRA: No'm. He never come aroun' here much. He warn't congenial with 'em, that's all.

MISS BLUEMEYER: I . . . I did not mean to imply that there was more to it, Myra. I only mean that they are such wonderful people to feel so responsible for a person they hardly know.

MYRA *(quickly):* Yes'm, but he *war* kin to 'em.

MISS BLUEMEYER: Yet he never came to see them.

MYRA: It warn't because he warn't invited. *(Resentfully.)* He didn't care nothin' bout kinfolks. Stuck off to hisself and worked down in the depot up here. He was jess—*(Breaks off suddenly, and begins again with an entirely different tone.)* Well, anyhow, he 'uz kin to 'em, and the only one here kin to 'em. That's all.

MISS BLUEMEYER: I did not mean to be prying, you understand, Myra. It is only that it seems odd that they should make such to-do over a man they knew so slight.

MYRA: He didn't have no money, sho God.

MISS BLUEMEYER: That, Myra, is not what I meant.

MYRA: I don't know what you been meanin', Miss Bloomer, but he's daid an' he war kin to 'em.

From the left the voice of Charles William, aged five and a half, is heard calling, "Myra! Myra!" A door is thrown open and a towheaded little boy rushes into the hall with his shoestrings flopping about.

CHARLES WILLIAM: Myra, Alfred won't tie my bows!

MYRA *(who has turned around and advanced several steps in his direction):* I'll buss his back wide op'n.

CHARLES WILLIAM: You tie 'em, Myra.

MYRA *(already on her knees before him):* Come here, chile.

CHARLES WILLIAM: Is Cousin Harry Wilson dead, Myra?

MYRA: Sho.

CHARLES WILLIAM: Was he eighty-three years old?

MYRA: Course he was, C.W.

CHARLES WILLIAM: Still?

MYRA: He'll be eighty-three from here out, C.W.

CHARLES WILLIAM *(obviously comforted, he places his hand on the head bent over before him):* I love you, Myra.

Myra lifts her dark oval face and grins broadly at him. He whispers to her, "You haven't got your teeth in, Myra." She bends with laughter as Charles William runs back to his room. During their conversation Miss Bluemeyer examines her wristwatch and the electric clock very closely. She dials a number on the telephone and says after a moment, "Will you repeat that? Will you repeat that?" She dials the number again and then sets her watch and moves the hand of the clock a fraction of an inch. When Charles William is gone, she says:

MISS BLUEMEYER: Myra—

MYRA *(rising and moving toward the dark stairs):* I got go fetch Paris an' the ladder for Mista Robert. This here light!

MISS BLUEMEYER: You *could* use the back stair, Myra.

MYRA: Not me. Not them straight-up-and-down steps. *(She goes down the steps.)*

Miss Bluemeyer rises and strides toward one of the doors at right. Aunt Lida Wade opens the door from Nancy's room, left, and the two women face each other in silence a moment. "Oh," says Aunt Lida, "I thought you were my nephew, Mr. Wade." Miss Bluemeyer makes her exit, and Aunt Lida remains a moment to giggle girlishly. Then she withdraws into Nancy's room again and closes the door. Lennie enters from door at right and moves sluggishly across the hall to head of stairs. Aunt Lida opens her door again and says, "Oh, I thought you were my nephew, Mr. Robert." Lennie answers, "No'm, it's jess me." Aunt Lida closes her door again, but before Lennie has begun to descend the stairs Mr. Robert Wade, master of the house, opens the door to his room and steps into the hall. Mr. Wade is six feet, three inches in height. His hair and his small mustache are dark. The belt to his silk dressing robe is tied, but the robe is not brought together in front; and so his dark trousers and white shirt and his bow tie may be seen. He wears usually a pouty expression on his face and has little to say except when giving directions or explaining some matter to his family.

MR. WADE: Lennie, a full half hour ago I sent word for Paris to bring me the ladder.

Lennie makes no answer but fairly dives down the dark stairwell. Her feet on the steps make a frightful racket. Aunt Lida opens her door again.

AUNT LIDA: Well, now, did you ever? No wonder the women in the house have been insulted when I mistook their steps for yours. How do you do it?

MR. WADE: That was Myra's little niece descending the stair. *(He walks around to the front balustrade and leans out over the stairs to peer up at the fixture.)* And, incidentally, my wife's cousin is dead.

AUNT LIDA *(matter-of-factly):* Poor Harry. You ought, in all conscience, to have made him come live with us years ago, Robert.

MR. WADE: He wouldn't live with his own sister, much less us. He had an allergy to the very idea of blood relations. *(Turning to Aunt Lida.)* You know, one of the few times I saw him he asked me how I could stand living under the same roof with you.

AUNT LIDA: I'm sure he did. And he told me that he left Tennessee to get away from his own flesh and blood, and that you and Margie and your young 'uns had to pursue him up here. *(They laugh merrily.)*

While they talk, the top of a ladder rises from the stairwell.

AUNT LIDA: But we ought to have gotten him to come here and live, somehow.

MR. WADE: He'd have been miserable here, Aunt Lida. And he'd have made us more than miserable. He wouldn't have fitted in.

AUNT LIDA: Pooh! That's why it would have been all right. *(She whispers.)* When I selected Miss Bluemeyer for Margie's housekeeper I was careful to choose someone who wouldn't fit in. If she were congenial with us, her presence here would be an intrusion. That's why my presence is an intrusion, don't you see?

MR. WADE: Tut-tut, Auntie. *(Pronounced "ontee.")*

The head and shoulders of Paris have now appeared from the top landing where he is setting up the ladder. The ladder leans backward and forward, backward and forward, and Paris can be heard panting and grunting.

AUNT LIDA: Oh, but what I say about Miss Bluemeyer is really pretty true, Robert. She's always happy when we're sad, and sad when we're happy; and that's right convenient. This morning, for instance—Well, notice for yourself.

MR. WADE: Aunt Lida, you're just awful! The poor woman.

AUNT LIDA: Why, I'm crazy about her. She's perfect. And have you seen her this morning? She's mourning your Cousin Harry, as none of us would think of doing—poor old codger's got his blessed relief at last—and, Robert *(rolling her eyes thoughtfully)*, she never even saw him once, did she? Once even? No! . . . But if she were showing the kind of relief that we feel for him, it *would* be kind of bad, now. You see!

MR. WADE: Oh, what difference does it make that she's— *(Breaking off.)* What *in* the devil?

He whirls about. Paris, having steadied the ladder and climbed uneasily to the top of it, has been sitting there tapping first his lip and then his forehead with his finger, trying hard to think of something, then with a stupid but still speculative expression on his face he has reached down and brought up a long broom with the handle of which he has now bent forward and poked (between the balusters) the back of Mr. Wade's knee. Mr. Wade's knee bends slightly. He whirls about, saying, "What in the devil." Paris jerks back the broom, gives a short, hysterical laugh, and splutters out:

PARIS: Mista Robert!

MR. WADE: What in the name of sin do you mean by that, boy!

PARIS *(solemnly)*: Somehow, I couldn't call yo name, Mista Robert, why you reckon? Couldn't think of it till you whull aroun' an' say, "What *in* de debil?" *(Catching Mr. Wade's exact intonation.)*

MR. WADE *(leaving Aunt Lida, who stands in open-mouthed wonder and amazement at Paris's behavior, and going round the balustrade to the head of the stair)*: Come down off that ladder! Did you bring the screwdriver and the bulb?

PARIS: I brung the screwdriver, Mista Robert.

MR. WADE: Well, go "brung" me a big bulb and a dust rag from the pantry.

Paris disappears from the ladder and down the stairs. Mr. Wade has now come down the stairs to the landing and climbed to the top of the ladder. The ladder shakes violently, and Aunt Lida cries out in a voice unlike her rather deep speaking voice:

AUNT LIDA: Robert, mind; do be careful, honey!

MR. WADE: Careful, hell! *(He clambers down the ladder.)* Paris! Paris, you come hold this ladder for me!

At the sound of Aunt Lida's voice doors from both right and left and from the back are opened. Now the children come one by one to the head of the stairs and watch their father who is climbing the ladder again. The two older children come first and watch their father in silence; they are Nancy, from left, and James, from right—aged eleven and twelve, respectively. Quick on James's heels come Charles William who is five and a half, and behind him Alfred, aged nine, still wearing the "niggery" stocking cap he sleeps in. Then the fifth child, Lida Sue, the youngest of all, comes chattering. No one can understand what she says, for she has been slow learning to talk and now at four she stammers and lisps alternately. When the doors to the children's rooms opened, the door to their parents' room, at the head of the stairs, opened also; and Mrs. Wade, having glanced at her husband and smiled at Aunt Lida, has turned back into her room, leaving the door open. Her hair is now pinned up, and she wears a maternity dress. She can be seen moving about the room, making up the bed, etc. During the conversation that follows, Lida Sue, instead of watching her father, as she has sat down to do, allows her attention to be distracted by the glimpse she has had of her mother, and lying back on the floor and rolling on her left side she watches her mother's movements in the room. Aunt Lida, still wearing her cinnamon-colored kimono, has moved away from the balustrade on which the children are now leaning. She stands, arms akimbo, in the center of the hall with the back of her head of sparse, uncombed gray hair to the audience.

AUNT LIDA (*to Mrs. Wade in a loud voice*): Margie, he's taking the whole business apart, screw by screw.

MRS. WADE (*from the bedroom*): It's the only way to do it, Aunt Lida.

AUNT LIDA: He has poor Paris holding the ladder, who ought to be down setting the table.

MRS. WADE: There's plenty of time. (*Still from the bedroom.*)

AUNT LIDA: I should say plenty of time. The greatest plenty. There was no earthly reason in his getting the whole house up at this hour.

MRS. WADE: No sense, I admit. *(Only slight interest.)*

AUNT LIDA: And did you ever in your life hear of a man's choosing such a time for such a job?

MRS. WADE: Never in my life. *(Complete indifference.)*

AUNT LIDA: I've been after him for weeks to do it, myself, and I know you have. There's really no earthly reason why Paris shouldn't learn to take down a chandelier. Otherwise, let's take him back to Tennessee and bring Mamie's brother up here. Or let Paris learn to drive, and bring Sellars in the house. Sellars's too old to drive, anyway. *(She pauses. All of this is being delivered in a shaky but resonant voice that Mrs. Wade and possibly even the servants in the kitchen can hear.)* Sellars can do anything if you show him once. But the main thing, though, is the time for such a job, the unheard of hour of the morn. . . .

MR. WADE *(interrupting with a booming voice, his early morning hoarseness adding to the onomatopoeic effect):* Thunderation, Aunt Lida!

Aunt Lida seems only to have been waiting for this; immediately she dismisses from her mind the problem of the light fixture and all of this business in the hall. She raises her little right forefinger to her chin and frowns meditatively, trying to recollect for what she has originally come into the hall. Then of a sudden she turns and goes out the door leading to the service hall.

MR. WADE: Now, you see, children, this is not a very simple undertaking. Each of the glass sections must be removed separately, and for each there are three screws. Observe: one at the top and one on each side. Now, this protector must be broken down into its five component parts, and to do this you must understand the real structure of the fixture. Mind, now. *All* of the five pieces must be removed before the bulb—because of its large size—can be inserted. Once the bulb is in, each piece must be dusted and cleared of all dead bugs, lint, dust, trash, et cetera before being replaced.

Mr. Wade works in silence for several moments. Then suddenly the light shines brightly above the stairwell. Mr. Wade, atop the ladder in a white shirt and a polka-dot bow tie with a sprinkling of dust on his black mustache, is a bright figure of enchantment for the five children who all fix a charmed gaze upon him, like five little green-eyed kittens. The spell is so absolute that they are momentarily blind and deaf to the sudden hilarious commotion on the part of Paris. This lantern-jawed houseboy, whose complexion is a dull copper color, who is supposed to be giving support to the unsteady ladder, has become so convulsed by laughter that he has thrown his whole weight against the ladder. One stern word of rebuke from Mr. Wade, however, makes Paris jump back from the quivering ladder.

MR. WADE: Get away from this ladder, you idiot!

Paris runs up the steps until he is in plain view of the audience. He continues to cavort about, twisting and bending his body, completely unable to restrain himself, giggling and pointing to the mirror on the wall beyond the stairs. All the while he is sputtering, "Look-a-there! Look-a-there!" and pointing to the mirror. Mr. Wade sits uneasily atop the ladder, staring at Paris in exasperation. As Paris runs up the steps, the children by the balustrade all turn their faces toward him but move not a muscle in their bodies.

PARIS: Do y'see what I see, Mista Robert? Look-a-there, Mista Robert.

Slowly the five children move their eyes from the houseboy to the mirror opposite them. Then Mr. Wade, steadying himself on the ladder, looks in the mirror too. What he sees there are the eight brown-stockinged legs of the four older children and the row of brown balusters interspersed with the legs.

PARIS: I thought them posts was movin'! They's jest alike—all of them legs and all them little stair posts, Mista Robert. In the mirror they all seem alike—posts and legs. Same size an' same color. *(His words are interrupted now and again by his own giggling.)*

Mr. Wade's mustache twitches involuntarily, and his eyes narrow into little slits. Then he looks into the mirror for the first time. Recognizing the ridiculous likeness of the legs to the balusters, he tosses back his head and laughs aloud. And the children one by one, even down to Lida Sue, who has picked herself up from the floor, join in the laughter. Their mirth has just reached its peak when Miss Bluemeyer, the housekeeper, appears from left. Her short hair is now combed, and she has exchanged her slippers for a pair of oxfords. She advances toward the head of the stairs without showing any interest in the cause of their mirth. She passes the children with a tolerant smile, affecting to be absorbed in her own thoughts. When she reaches the head of the stairs, Lida Sue and Paris step to one side; and Lida Sue reaches for the Negro man's hand, which she holds until the housekeeper has passed. Miss Bluemeyer descends the first three of four steps and then stops as she addresses Mr. Wade.

MISS BLUEMEYER: If you will pardon me, Mr. Wade, I would like to try to get by. I am going to run down and see how breakfast is going.

MR. WADE: Good morning, Miss. Isn't that a sight up there in the mirror?

MISS BLUEMEYER *(glancing briefly in the general direction of the glass):* Oh, yes, isn't it? *(She takes another step as she speaks.)* I was going to say—*(She begins, but finding Mr. Wade's eyes fastened on her she hesitates.)* If you will pardon me, Mr. Wade, I must ask you to let me pass. *(Fearlessly, courageously.)*

MR. WADE *(sternly):* I suggest that you use the back stairs since we haven't quite finished operations here, Miss Bluemeyer.

Miss Bluemeyer gazes defiantly at Mr. Wade for a moment, then at Paris and Lida Sue, then at the four children who are lined up along the balustrade and who, like sheep, have drawn closer together, their slight movement having been almost imperceptible to the audience.

MISS BLUEMEYER *(utterly without expression, as though answering a question about the day of the week or the title of a book):* Good morning, kiddies. *(Presently she retreats to the head of the stairs, at which point she stops to address Mr. Wade again.)* I was going to say that when Paris has put away the ladder, it will be time to set the table for breakfast. That is, if you have an early breakfast in mind, Mr. Wade.

MR. WADE: I had an early breakfast in mind, Miss Bluemeyer, for there is a busy day ahead for us all.

MISS BLUEMEYER *(in a sympathetic stage whisper):* The funeral won't be until tomorrow, I presume, Mr. Wade?

MR. WADE: Well . . . there'll be a little service in the undertaker's chapel today. I'm taking the body back to Tennessee on the train tonight.

MISS BLUEMEYER: I see . . . I see. *(In a gentle voice, full of sentimentality.)* He must have been a fine old man—Mr. Wilson. The few times I saw him he seemed very, very polite. I imagine to ladies, especially, being Southern.

MR. WADE: I suppose so. . . . Yes, I suppose he was. *(He turns his attention back to the light fixture for a moment, and then as though only now realizing what she has said he turns again to her with a little jerk of his head.)* Did I understand you to say you had seen him? But I didn't know you had ever seen our cousin, Miss Bluemeyer.

MISS BLUEMEYER: Oh, really? *(Significantly, as though perceiving that there had been some conversation about her not having seen Mr. Wilson.)*

MR. WADE: Yes, indeed . . . really. *(With parts of the fixture in his hands he goes down several rungs of the ladder, then jumping nimbly off onto the stairs and coming up into the hall he hands these pieces to Paris. Miss Bluemeyer has meanwhile moved past the children and as far as the telephone table in the direction of the door to the service hall.)* I don't recall Mr. Wilson's having been to see us since you came, Miss Bluemeyer.

MISS BLUEMEYER: That is quite right.

MR. WADE *(his usually direct manner exaggerated somewhat):* Miss Bluemeyer, I think you are behaving and speaking in a mighty strange manner.

MISS BLUEMEYER: I am sorry if that is your opinion, Mr. Wade.

MR. WADE: Well, I think . . .

MISS BLUEMEYER: Remember, I am not one of the servants, Mr. Wade, not one of your servants.

When Mr. Wade came up into the hall, all of the children turned about and faced him and Miss Bluemeyer; and now he turns and gives them a "look" which sends them off quietly but quickly to their rooms, the older ones leading the younger. Paris, who has until this time been standing on the stairs with the parts of the light fixture in his hands, now moves down toward the ladder, ascends it, and begins hurriedly and skillfully to reassemble the fixture.

MR. WADE: I am aware that you are not one of the servants, and I am not speaking to you as such. In fact, I don't mean to provoke any unpleasantness this morning.

MISS BLUEMEYER *(repentantly, mournfully):* And I am truly sorry to have been any bother this morning, Mr. Wade—this morning of all mornings. The truth is I used to see Mr. Wilson elsewhere. I never met him, you understand.

MR. WADE: I see. But you never mentioned having seen him to my wife or my aunt?

MISS BLUEMEYER: I didn't know the family would be interested that I had seen him. You understand, he lived a door from a lady with whom I am great friends.

MR. WADE: I see, I see.

MISS BLUEMEYER: He was a solitary figure, Mr. Wade, and this friend of mine had noticed him. She is an invalid, you understand, and when I was staying with her she would sometimes look out the window and say, "There goes that old Mr. Wilson. He seems to be an independent sort like us, Madge." That is all there was to it, Mr. Wade, and I used to notice him quite often.

MR. WADE: But this happened when you were staying with your invalid friend?

MISS BLUEMEYER: Yes. You will think it is odd, I know, but that was before I even came here, Mr. Wade.

MR. WADE: I was thinking just that. And when was it you first made the connection between your Mr. Wilson and our Cousin Harry Wilson? That is, when did you discover that the old man you watched from your friend's window was my wife's cousin?

MISS BLUEMEYER: Only the shortest time ago, Mr. Wade, only a few weeks. Only when I happened to mention to this friend of mine that Misses Wade's only relative in Detroit had had a stroke. "What is his name, Madge?" she asked me. I told her his name and she said, "Why, Madge, that must be the same old Mr. Wilson I have pointed out to you. They tell me *he's* had a stroke," she said. It quite struck me at the time, Mr. Wade, that it was quite a coincidence, but I didn't want to bother the family at the time in their grief with idle, outside talk.

MR. WADE: Of course not. I'm sure you didn't. And it was very considerate of you.

A pause, during which Mr. Wade straightens his tie and casts his eyes about the room as though trying to decide how this conversation should be concluded.

MISS BLUEMEYER: If you would not think it was too odd, Mr. Wade, would you mind telling me to what funeral home the remains will go?

MR. WADE: Why! *(Taken aback.)* Of course I wouldn't mind. To Lewis Brothers, I believe.

MISS BLUEMEYER: Lewis Brothers, you say? I don't believe I have heard of . . . ?

MR. WADE: No, it's a small, uh, shop, uh, concern on the other side of town. But the Lewises were from Tennessee, from my mother's county, and my aunt thought it would be—uh—nice.

MISS BLUEMEYER: I see . . . yes . . . Well I *do* thank you, Mr. Wade. *(Turning quickly to Paris, as though to change the subject.)* Paris, you can set the table now!

She walks rapidly toward the door to the service hall. As she reaches for the doorknob, the door opens and Aunt Lida enters with still another dress for Nancy, a black one. Paris has meanwhile reassembled the light fixture. Mr. Wade turns toward him and exclaims in genuine surprise at Paris's achievement, "Say!" Simultaneously Mrs. Wade enters from the door to her room.

MR. WADE: Boy, how did you know how to put that thing together?

PARIS *(giving one glance at Mr. Wade)*: I had to do somepn to make myself scass. I thought you gwine eat 'at woman alive, way you come down off 'at ladder.

AUNT LIDA: What in the world do you make of it, Margie?

MRS. WADE: What do you think, Aunt Lida?

The two women have met in the center of the stage, in front of Mr. Wade, and by first addressing each other, instead of Mr.

Wade whose conversation has roused their interest, they reveal their mutual sympathy and understanding and their slight regard for any interpretation which Mr. Wade might put upon his own conversation.

MR. WADE *(having completely forgotten the episode with Miss Bluemeyer)*: Margie! Aunt Lida! Look what Paris has learned! *(Paris sits beaming atop the ladder.)*

AUNT LIDA *(paying no attention to him)*: Did you hear every word of what she said?

MRS. WADE: I think so.

AUNT LIDA: I could hear every word. She said she had watched him from her friend's window even before she came here. All through his sickness she has known he was the man she and her cripple friend watched. She *is* a weird one, now, I'll tell you.

MRS. WADE: It's a curious picture, isn't it—those two lonely women watching that lonely old man. Why hasn't she spoken of it, do you suppose?

MR. WADE: Margie! Aunt Lida! This is a great day. This is important. This is a turning point in Paris's life, in the life of us all. He has learned to put that fixture together. Now he can have a try at the chandelier downstairs. *(When the women continue to take no notice of him, Paris begins to descend the ladder.)*

AUNT LIDA: It's from sheer perversity that she hasn't mentioned it, poor creature. She seems to delight in dreary "solitary figures." And I suppose we mustn't begrudge her her greatest pleasure.

Paris has now disappeared down the ladder, and as the ladder is seen being slowly lowered from view, Mr. Wade begins to show interest in what the women are saying.

MR. WADE: Now, Auntie, a while ago it was her sheer perversity that made Miss Blue so suitable for our household. You know, I think you are downright vicious about that "poor creature."

AUNT LIDA: Why, I'm not at all, Robert Wade!

MR. WADE: Indeed, you are. You seem to have developed a

special voice, a special expression, a special vocabulary for talking about her.

MRS. WADE: That's nonsense, Robert. How could you accuse Aunt Lida of being vicious about *any*body, *ever?*

AUNT LIDA: There, you see.

MRS. WADE: A fine way your house would be in if it weren't for Aunt Lida. And your children, and your wife, and yourself!

MR. WADE *(waving his hands before his face):* I didn't mean to start such a furor. I wasn't serious. That is, it's not a very serious crime of Aunt Lida's. That Bluemeyer is a strange duck. Anybody can see that.

AUNT LIDA: Now who's being cruel? I am interested in all people, Robert, and am not without sympathy for . . .

MR. WADE: But this seems a very special—You have a wonderful interest in the ways and doings of all your friends and especially in your family, in us particularly *(indicating this household, by a gesture).* A kindly, gentle, womanly interest. You have a real knowledge of people, too. You know us better than we know each other. You are a wonderful, wonderful woman, Aunt Lida, and we couldn't live without you. But *(holding up one finger)* I still maintain that regarding Miss Blue—

AUNT LIDA: Her name is not . . .

MRS. WADE: Robert! What nonsense!

AUNT LIDA: And at such an hour. *(Unruffled.)*

When interrupted, Mr. Wade turned and began walking toward the door to his room. Now he hesitates at the doorway.

MR. WADE: Has my blue serge come back from the cleaner's, Aunt Lida?

AUNT LIDA: It'll be back today, Robert.

Mr. Wade goes into his room and closes the door. Mrs. Wade moves to the front of the stage and sits down in one of the upholstered chairs, at left.

MRS. WADE: Where are the children, Aunt Lida?

AUNT LIDA *(calling, in a voice almost as deep as Mr. Wade's):* Chill-drun!

Doors on both sides of the stage open. The children peer out at their Aunt Lida.

AUNT LIDA: Come say good morning to your mama-dear.

The children run across the stage to Mrs. Wade, all hugging and kissing her at once, saying, "Good morning, Mama-dear. How pretty you are, Mama." Mrs. Wade kisses each of them, pushing the older ones slightly aside in order to lean over and kiss little Lida Sue who says, "P-p-puhty muh-muh." Aunt Lida watches approvingly. Presently she says:

AUNT LIDA: Not one of you has noticed how charming your mama-dear has done up her beautiful hair this morning.

MRS. WADE: Aunt Lida, I declare! *(Smiling and shaking her head.)*

All of the children go behind her chair and admire her coiffure, Nancy lifting Lida Sue up to where she can see.

JAMES: It's all plaited and fixed.

NANCY: It's fixed in a bun. It's charming, Mama-dear.

ALFRED: How long is it now, Mama-dear?

MRS. WADE: Too long, too long. I'm going to cut it again before . . .

CHILDREN: No, no, no.

AUNT LIDA *(coming forward):* We won't let her cut that beautiful hair, will we, children? . . . Nancy, let me fix your sash. It's all twisted.

MRS. WADE: It's impractical. Especially now. It will be too much trouble.

AUNT LIDA: Nonsense. We'll take turns arranging it for you. We'll never let her cut this beautiful hair, will we, children?

CHILDREN: Never, never.

MRS. WADE: I'll do as I like about my hair, thank you, all. You'll someday all be sorry for spoiling me so. I'll be the spoiledest of spoiled women. I'll cut off all my hair and wear a ring in my nose, just to show you I can if I want to.

The children are delighted and they scream with laughter. "No, no, we won't let you, we won't let you."

MRS. WADE: I will. And I'll wear tow sacks for dresses and old tennis shoes with the toes cut out. I'll wear a stocking cap like Alfred's.

The children laugh again and chant, "No, never. No, never. No, never."

AUNT LIDA: Turn around, Charles William. I do believe you've managed to get your bottom rompers on backward again.

CHARLES WILLIAM: I like 'em.

AUNT LIDA: Stand still, child. *(She has got down on one knee and begun unbuttoning his little pants. Without more words about it, she makes him step out of his pants; she turns them around and puts them on properly. Meanwhile, Charles William continues to gaze at his mother.) (Addressing the children as she buttons up Charles William.)* We're going to keep Mama-dear the ornament of this household, aren't we? She ought to let us get her a personal maid, instead of a housekeeper.

MRS. WADE: One day you'll all be sorry. And I can hear you mumbling behind my back about *she.*

AUNT LIDA: Take off that stocking cap, Alfred. You'll be bald before you're in long pants. *(Alfred hesitates, turns his face away and gazes at the wall, pouting.)* Take it off, Alfred, I said. *(He snatches off the cap, revealing a flat pompadour with every hair in place, and continues to stare at the wall, right.)* Look at him pouting, children. Stick a pin in his cheeks and they'd pop like a balloon. *(The children laugh; even Alfred gives up pouting and laughs with them.)* Margie, every one of your children has a different way of pouting while being reprimanded. Only a slightly different way, however, for they are all gazers. Alfred here gazes at a blank wall. James likes to gaze up at the ceiling. *(She mimics each as she describes his form of gazing. The children and Mrs. Wade laugh appreciatively after each piece of mimicry.)* Nancy is a window gazer. Charles William is a hand gazer, or a plate gazer, if we're at the table.

JAMES: What about Lida Sue, Aunt Lida?

AUNT LIDA *(still on one knee after buttoning Charles William's pants, she turns to Lida Sue, who is nearby):* Why, she's the fearless type who stares a hole right through you and makes you feel that you couldn't possibly be right. *(She places her hands on Lida Sue's shoulders and stares, with a ridiculous frown. Lida Sue and the other children laugh hysterically. But Mrs.*

Wade has become aware of the presence of Miss Bluemeyer who has entered several moments before from the service hall with Mrs. Wade's breakfast on a tray. Mrs. Wade watches the housekeeper whose eyes are fixed on Aunt Lida. During that moment Mr. Wade, now wearing his suit coat, enters from the bedroom.)

MR. WADE *(observing all that is taking place):* Is there breakfast for the rest of us downstairs, Miss Bluemeyer?

MISS BLUEMEYER: Yes, there is, Mr. Wade.

MR. WADE: Then let's break up this dog and pony show, what say? Breakfast, children! James! Nancy!

The children go frolicking to the head of the stairs and disappear down the steps. Aunt Lida has got to her feet and turned about so quickly that she catches Miss Bluemeyer's gaze still upon her.

AUNT LIDA: Is my petticoat showing, Miss Bluemeyer?

MISS BLUEMEYER: No, Miss Wade, not that I can see.

AUNT LIDA: Then, what is it, please? You were staring so, I thought something must be wrong. *(She pretends to examine her dress.)*

MISS BLUEMEYER: I beg your pardon.

MR. WADE *(coming forward; cordially):* Ah, that's a mighty fine-looking breakfast a certain person's going to get this morning. *(Taking the tray from Miss Bluemeyer.)* Ah, look-a-here. I believe they've got you on double rations, Margie.

MRS. WADE *(clearing the coffee table that Aunt Lida has pushed before her):* Well, I should think so.

Miss Bluemeyer, continuing to scrutinize the group until the very last, has finally retreated down the front stairs. Aunt Lida goes and looks over the balustrade into the stairwell. Mr. and Mrs. Wade observe her action and exchange glances.

MR. WADE: Now, Aunt Lida! What is it? What's the matter? If that woman bothers you so, why don't you give her her walking papers?

MRS. WADE: Don't talk so, Robert. Don't make a mountain out of a molehill.

AUNT LIDA: No, dear. He's right. This is more than a molehill. When I looked over the bannister just now I could see Miss

Bluemeyer. She was running her hand through her hair, like this, and clenching her other fist with all her might. *(She comes to the front of the stage and speaks, as to herself, while Mr. and Mrs. Wade look on in wide-eyed amazement.)* That poor, embittered creature! My God, my God, when I looked down that stairwell I felt that I had been given a quick glimpse of a soul suffering the tortures of hell. *(Turning to Mrs. Wade.)* And it's our happiness that is her hell, mind you, Margie. She can't abide the sight of our family happiness. Particularly not this morning when one of her sort—a man who reveled in his own bitterness and despised all those who tried to make his life a less lonesome, a less dreary business—lies dead in an undertaker's parlor. She cannot endure the presence of our happiness. Particularly not mine. *(Now angrily.)* Can you tell me how the good Lord can endure the existence of such a mean and jealous being in His world? She watched me there on my knees fondling those children, and it filled her with nothing but resentment and hatred. *(Quietly again.)* No, you are right, Robert. She shall have her proverbial walking papers the moment you and the corpse of our Cousin Harry are safely on the night train to Tennessee.

MR. WADE: Aunt Lida, what a tirade! What a fit of temper! And at such an hour of the morning! Who ever heard of making such an important decision before breakfast?

Aunt Lida stares blankly at Mr. Wade for a moment; then she turns her face slowly from him to the audience. She is not smiling and she makes no answer. She doesn't seem to have heard what he said.

SCENE II

The curtain rises on a second scene in the upstairs hall. It is the evening of the same day. One table lamp is lit, front and left, and as the curtain rises Miss Bluemeyer switches on the desk lamp, seats herself, and begins dialing a number on the telephone. She is alone in the hall. The Wade family is still at dinner. During the late afternoon a funeral service has been held in the undertaker's chapel.

MISS BLUEMEYER *(speaking into the telephone):* Merton? It's Bluemeyer speaking. Quite well, thank you. And you? Oh, that's too bad. *(Pause.)* Well, let me tell you . . . *(Pause.)* Ah, that's too bad, Merton. *(Pause.)* I want to tell you . . . *(Pause.)* Well, have you taken something? *(Pause.)* Merton, I want to tell you . . . *(Impatiently.)* Of course I am interested in how you feel, but you said yourself for me to call you when they got back. Yes they have been back a couple of hours, Merton. . . . No. . . . Why, I mean exactly this: When I talked to you a few hours ago, when they had just left for the funeral home—all but Misses Wade. She didn't go; she took her nap—I said to you then, you remember, they were sure to guess whose flowers they were. Yes, I know you thought so too, Merton, and that is not what I am calling to tell you. We both knew they would, and I have already heard all about it, but not the last of it, I am afraid. This is what I mean: I dreaded, as you said you dreaded for me, that they would come home all sentimentalized and would gush over me with their thanks. The thing I was afraid of, Merton, was that they would think I was playing up to them. . . . Don't rush me, Merton. I will tell you the whole story right now if there is time. They are all at dinner now, you see, and if I am interrupted I will call you back from the kitchen phone when the Negroes have gone to bed. . . . I *am* going to get on with it, Merton. Don't be rude to your best friend. On the card I sent with the flowers, you remember, I had the young man write, "From Two Friends." Well, when *she* came back with the rest of the family, from the funeral, she had our card tucked in her little gray glove. I was downstairs in the side hall, you understand, when they came in, and she just stopped beside me for a minute as though she were thinking of something. Then she slips the card out, like she was a magician—she had that air, Merton, that I should be surprised where she got it—and says in a deep, businesslike voice, "Many thanks, Miss Bluemeyer, and thank the other friend for the family of the bereaved." Bereaved, indeed! They spent breakfast poking their sly fun at the child Nancy for wanting to wear a black dress. . . . No, that is all there was to it, Merton. No, not a question about who the other friend was. No,

not another word, not from any of them. . . . No, I didn't
want their thanks any more than you. .What I mean is they have
hardly spoke another word to me since, except about the usual
things. Dinner was just awful, and I left just now without dessert. I couldn't have eat it, and the children carrying on so as if
nobody had ever passed away, much less a poor lonesome old
man. But the grown-ups are all hopping mad, I can tell you.
Mad, you understand, because we had the presumption to send
flowers to somebody who was their relation. Wouldn't you think
she would understand, though, Merton, how it is. . . . Of
course, she does, and she is ashamed. If *he* had been one of those
who care to fawn over their relations, as *she* has! Anybody who
has so little pride and independence, indeed! Of course, I know
you know, but . . . *(Hearing someone on the stairs.)* Well, that
will be all. Thank you. Good-bye, Merton. *(Sotto voce.)* Of
course, I am not angry. Somebody's . . . Yes. Good-bye, Merton.

*Mr. and Mrs. Wade are ascending the stairs, arm in arm. Miss
Bluemeyer moves toward her room, at right. Lennie enters from
door to service hall, right and back.*

MISS BLUEMEYER *(just before entering her room)*: Lennie,
you need not turn down my bed tonight. I have some patterns
spread out.

LENNIE: Yehs'm.

*Miss Bluemeyer closes the door behind her. Lennie enters the
boys' room through the other door, right. Mr. and Mrs. Wade
come forward and take seats in the sitting-room end of the hall,
extreme left. They have been talking quietly as they came up the
stairs and crossed the hall. Now their words become audible.*

MR. WADE: The children couldn't have behaved better. I
think even Lida Sue would have behaved all right if I had taken
her.

MRS. WADE: I still feel a little as though I should have been
there. Mama always felt so sorry for Cousin Harry. She used to
say he was offish and surly even as a child. He never *was* happy.

MR. WADE: God! Eighty-three years of it! . . . Well, did
you wire Cousin Lula what time I arrive with the body?

MRS. WADE: Oh, I wired her this morning. They'll want to have a little service in Nashville, I'm sure.

MR. WADE: Oh, I'm *sure* they will. And I suppose I'll have to attend that too?

MRS. WADE: Darling, I hope you will. It'll mean so much to them.

MR. WADE: I know. I know. And it won't be nearly so bad without Aunt Lida there.

MRS. WADE: Did she really behave badly?

MR. WADE: Well, I don't suppose the undertakers noticed, and there was nobody else to notice it. But as soon as they brought in that big wreath—it was a tremendous thing *(he holds his hands out to indicate the size)*—she took herself up to where they set it by the coffin and looked at the card.

MRS. WADE: And just what did the card say?

MR. WADE: "From Two Friends."

MRS. WADE *(smiling):* Isn't that incredible?

MR. WADE: And a strange expression came over Aunt Lida's face that didn't leave it until after we were home. She sat through the whole service as stiff as a broom and didn't sing a word of either hymn.

MRS. WADE: She was obviously making her plans. I doubt if Miss Bluemeyer will still be on the place as late as noon tomorrow.

MR. WADE: Do you think she'll let her stay the night?

MRS. WADE: Aunt Lida ought to restrain herself. The woman is merely peculiar. I wish you would talk to Aunt Lida about it before you go, Robert.

MR. WADE: *You* will have to talk to her, Margie. She has never been known to take a man's advice on anything but money matters.

MRS. WADE: Aunt Lida's a mighty clever woman.

MR. WADE: Be serious, dear. There's more in this than meets the eye.

MRS. WADE: Speak for your own eye, Robert.

MR. WADE: Then, what is it? I know I am a mere unimaginative man, but . . .

MRS. WADE (*casually, as she settles herself in her chair*): You make us out awfully ugly, honey—Aunt Lida and me.

MR. WADE: And how do you two make me out?

MRS. WADE: I really think you are coming to believe literally in our womanly contempt for mankind. I think you're good for lots more than breadwinning, my love. Our contempt is only skin deep. It's only a tiresome old joke that makes life easier for two women under the same roof.

MR. WADE: I wish it made it easier for three. . . . Tell me, then, what is it you see in this business that I don't see? What is it about Miss Bluemeyer's queerness that disturbs Aunt Lida so? Are we only detecting the first signs of old age in her?

MRS. WADE: It has nothing to do with old age. It is simply that someone has entered the field who won't play the game according to Aunt Lida's rules.

MR. WADE: What sort of nonsense is that? You and Aunt Lida are forever . . .

MRS. WADE: Robert Wade, stop linking me with your aunt as though there were no difference between us.

MR. WADE: Then her age . . .

MRS. WADE: I'm not speaking of the difference in our ages. Don't you really know that your wife and your maiden aunt are two quite different people? (*Hotly.*) If you haven't perceived *that* in thirteen years, how can you hope to comprehend the niceties of a problem between your maiden aunt and an old-maid house-keeper?

MR. WADE: What in the devil are you getting so worked up about?

MRS. WADE: Worked up! I say!

MR. WADE: Have you and Aunt Lida been quarreling, too?

MRS. WADE: Have we . . . ? (*Quietly.*) God in heaven, give me strength. For the ten years we have been in Detroit, Robert Wade, your Aunt Lida and I haven't had a cross word; and now you ask me calmly, have we been quarreling!

MR. WADE: And why is that such an outlandish question?

MRS. WADE: Don't you really know why it is? And don't you really know why Aunt Lida and I have such smooth sailing? It's because we have arranged our lives as we have. It's because Aunt Lida and I have played our roles so perfectly, as we've always seen them played in Tennessee: She, the maiden aunt, responsible and capable! I, the beautiful young wife, the bearer of children, the reigning queen! *(She laughs, and Mr. Wade jumps to his feet, obviously alarmed.)* Why, suh, sometimes ah can almos' heah the darkies acroonin' in the quawtuhs! *(Her laughter is now definitely hysterical.)*

MR. WADE: Margie, I won't have you flying off like this!

MRS. WADE *(coming to her feet)*: I may fly off further than you think. *(Then she bursts into tears and throws her arms about his neck, weeping on his shirtfront.)* Robert, forgive me. You know I adore Aunt Lida. *(But she continues to weep.)*

MR. WADE *(putting his arms around her)*: There, darling. Of course you do.

As he eases her into her chair again, Miss Bluemeyer throws open her door and hurries across the stage.

MISS BLUEMEYER: Oh, the dear thing! She has been such a brave lady up until now. It has been a very sad day for her, and I feel . . .

MR. WADE *(seated on Mrs. Wade's chair arm with his arms still around her; to Miss Bluemeyer)*: Hold on, ma'am. You're mistaken.

MISS BLUEMEYER: Indeed, I have been very much mistaken. Grief has strange ways, Mr. Wade. Let me get her a cup of coffee.

She turns and strides toward the door to the service hall. Suddenly she faces Lennie who has been observing events from the door to the boys' room.

MISS BLUEMEYER: Lennie, bring Misses Wade a cup of coffee.

LENNIE: Yehs'm, but she's jess having a nachal spell.

MISS BLUEMEYER: A natural spell?

LENNIE *(impatiently)*: She's six months gone, Miss Bloomer. *(She goes to fetch the coffee.)*

MISS BLUEMEYER: She's . . . ? Oh, of course.

The housekeeper glances quickly in the direction of Mr. and

Mrs. Wade, and her glance is met by Mr. Wade's glare. She turns and makes a hurried exit into her own room. Aunt Lida's voice is heard on the stairs, and the three children come romping up the steps ahead of her.

MRS. WADE *(completely recovered):* How silly of me.

MR. WADE: That Bluemeyer woman *is* morbid, Margie.

MRS. WADE: You mustn't worry yourself about her, Robert. What time does your train leave?

AUNT LIDA *(crossing from head of stairs to sitting room):* Robert, I told Paris to bring up your Gladstone. Isn't that what he should take, Margie?

MRS. WADE: I think so, Aunt Lida.

AUNT LIDA *(standing, hands clasped loosely before her):* You feel like packing for him, don't you, Margie?

MRS. WADE: There, you see, Robert!

AUNT LIDA: See what, Margie?

MR. WADE: Yes, what?

MRS. WADE: *He* knows very well what.

Charles William has now climbed on his mother's knees. Alfred is tugging at his father's hand. Lida Sue is walking round and round Aunt Lida.

AUNT LIDA: You children run and play.

ALFRED: Can we play in your room, Aunt Lida?

AUNT LIDA *(severely):* Yes, we don't touch one thing on my dresser. *(They scamper away to Aunt Lida's room, left.)*

MRS. WADE: I've made a little scene since we came upstairs, Aunt Lida. I've had a good cry and everything.

AUNT LIDA: Are you feeling right tired, honey?

MRS. WADE: I guess I am. I must be awfully tired, for I was protesting Robert's linking our names so eternally.

MR. WADE: Jealous of you, Aunt Lida!

AUNT LIDA: Pshaw! It *is* tiresome of you, Robert.

MRS. WADE: And what I was just now pointing out to him was an example of how well we know our roles and how clearly defined are our spheres of authority. *(Turning to Mr. Wade.)* Aunt Lida saw to it that your bag should be brought up, but she would leave the packing of it to me.

AUNT LIDA *(in good nature):* Now, if I am to be embarrassed by your referring to your private conversations about me, be good enough to explain what set you off on the subject.

There is a moment's silence.

MR. WADE: We were trying to fathom the reasons for your sudden strong feelings against the housekeeper.

There is another moment of silence. Aunt Lida puts her hand self-consciously to her string of pearls. Lennie enters from service hall with coffee.

AUNT LIDA: Oh, I see.

MRS. WADE *(uncertain of what she is going to say):* Robert . . .

AUNT LIDA: Put the tray on the table here, Lennie. Are you right sure you want to drink coffee at this hour of the night, Margie?

MRS. WADE: Come to think of it, I guess I won't.

AUNT LIDA: Leave it there, Lennie, and I'll drink it.

LENNIE: Yehs'm. *(She goes into the girls' room, left.)*

AUNT LIDA: What time is your train, Robert?

MR. WADE: I've got just about an hour. *(Looking at watch.)*

AUNT LIDA: Then you'd better set about packing. Margie's plainly not up to it.

MR. WADE *(rising from chair):* You're dead right.

MRS. WADE: Do you mind?

MR. WADE: Not a bit, honey. *(He goes into his bedroom.)*

Aunt Lida sits down in the chair that Mr. Wade was occupying a few minutes before. With her foot she draws a footstool in front of her and rests her feet on it. She rests her head on the chairback and with her elbows raised she interlocks her fingers and places her hands over her eyes.

AUNT LIDA: Margie, I'm right tired, myself.

MRS. WADE: Poor dear, I know you are. It's been an awful strain on you, Aunt Lida.

AUNT LIDA: What has, Margie?

MRS. WADE: Oh, all of Cousin Harry's illness, with me in this condition, and the funeral today especially.

AUNT LIDA: Margie, I hope you don't ever think I underestimate you.

MRS. WADE: How so?

AUNT LIDA: I mean your powers of perception and understanding.

MRS. WADE: I'm a simple, artless little mother-woman from upper Middle-Tennessee.

AUNT LIDA: And I, I am a pore relation, a maiden aunt from the Cumberland Plateau. *(They laugh, and Aunt Lida removes her hands from before her eyes.)*

AUNT LIDA: That's how your Cousin Harry saw us in the very end, you know.

MRS. WADE: That's how we *are* to the very end, isn't it, Aunt Lida?

AUNT LIDA: I don't know, Margie. It's sometimes hard, isn't it?

MRS. WADE: Aunt Lida, it's great fun mostly. And what else is there better, with the given circumstances? When I was a girl I used to think . . .

AUNT LIDA: Yes, and so did I, even I, even then. But what chance has a person? It's like throwing away money, the horrid stuff. Yet it's the coin of the realm, and you'd best use what you have of it.

MRS. WADE: But I also thought . . .

AUNT LIDA: Ah, and so did I. But that part was harder for me, not being the pretty little thing.

MRS. WADE: Now, Aunt Lida, I was always told at home that you were a mighty attractive young girl.

AUNT LIDA: Well, as your husband's great-aunt Rhody Baird from East Tennessee used to say of herself *(in the voice of a crone)*, "Like any other, I had my little lovyer. Hee-he-he—hee." And let me tell you I made them step and fetch for me; but I used to hate myself. Sometimes I hate myself now and think that your Cousin Harry was right about it all. People like him, and like her *(pointing with her thumb in the direction of Miss Bluemeyer's room)* make it hard. They point an accusing finger.

MRS. WADE: I know what you mean.

AUNT LIDA: Yes, I thought you did. And that's how we began this conversation.

Mr. Wade appears at the door of his room.

MR. WADE: Aunt Lida, does Paris think I'm not leaving till tonight?

AUNT LIDA *(rising from chair):* I told that boy . . .

MR. WADE *(seeing Lennie as she comes out of the girls' room):* Never mind, Aunt Lida. Lennie, you tell Paris to get up here with my Gladstone!

LENNIE *(stepping into the hall):* Yehsuh, he's on the back stair, wipin' it. You wouldn't-a tetched it the way it wuz.

AUNT LIDA *(to Mrs. Wade):* Lennie always has to add her nickel's worth.

LENNIE: Aw, Miss Lida, I got beds to tunn back.

AUNT LIDA: Girl, that sounded to me just this side of uppity. I'll have to speak to *your* Aunt Myra.

LENNIE: Wull, there's uppitier niggers than I in this house.

MR. WADE *(coming forward):* By George, this isn't getting me my Gladstone.

At this moment Paris enters from the service hall, and Lennie turns toward Aunt Lida's room. Simultaneously Myra appears on the stairway with a stack of clean, highly starched rompers and dresses for the smaller children piled high in her arms. She is mouthing over her shoulder at James and Nancy who are behind her, "Wull, make hase! Come ohn by me if y'aim to come, and mine these here close." Nancy and James brush past her and gallop up the few remaining steps before her. Each carries a large walking cane with a crook handle. Meanwhile, Mr. Wade addresses Paris the length of the hall, "Paris, is that the bag Miss Lida told you to bring me?" Paris replies, "Yessuh, it the Gladstone." And Aunt Lida is saying to Lennie whom she has called back from her room, "You can leave my bed; the children are playing in there. And if you're going to change Miss Margie's sheets tonight, get Nancy to help you. I want her to learn to look after things."

MR. WADE *(still to Paris, who has stopped in his tracks at the far end of the hall):* It's a Gladstone, I'll grant you. It's the one Miss Margie's papa took to the Tennessee Centennial in 1896.

AUNT LIDA *(turning toward Paris):* What's this about the Gladstone?

MR. WADE *(to Aunt Lida):* Do you think I'm going to travel with that old carpetbag? Did you tell Paris . . . ?

AUNT LIDA: I *did* not!

MRS. WADE *(whose attention has been attracted by the noise of the children, James and Nancy, behind her—looking over her shoulder to Myra):* Myra, the clothes look lovely. Come let me see them.

MYRA: Yassum. 'At James come mighty nigh spillin' 'um "lovely close."

JAMES: I did not, Myra. It was Nancy.

AUNT LIDA: Don't contradict Myra, James.

LENNIE: Come ohn, Nancy.

AUNT LIDA: Paris, you march right back down there and get the new Gladstone.

MRS. WADE *(holding up one of Lida Sue's dresses):* They're positively lovely, Myra. Look, Aunt Lida! Of course, these ruffles here ought to be pressed over this way.

NANCY: Aunt Lida, I know how to turn back an old bed! Don't make me do it tonight, Aunt Lida. James and I want to roll back the big rug yonder and play slide-on-the-rag-rug.

MR. WADE: You *are not* going to play that game while I'm in this house. Do as your Aunt Lida says; and James, put that walking cane down and come help me pack.

PARIS: I don't know which-a-one you mean, Miss Lida.

AUNT LIDA *(stepping nearer to Mrs. Wade and examining the dress she holds up):* Of course, it should be over that way. I told you so, explicitly, Myra; and you knew how I wanted it. *(Suddenly laughing.)* Myra Willis, admit it! You just liked it better this way.

MYRA *(bending forward and laughing):* Aw, Miss Lida, ain't you a sight.

PARIS: I don't know which-a-one you mean, Miss Lida.

NANCY: Aunt Lida, don't make me . . .

MR. WADE: For God's sake, tell him the right one, Auntie.

LENNIE: She ain't comin', Miss Lida.

MRS. WADE: Aunt Lida . . .

AUNT LIDA *(raising her voice):* Now, see here, all of you . . .

At this moment Aunt Lida realizes that Miss Bluemeyer is standing in the open doorway to her room, right. Since Mr. Wade came from his room saying, "Does Paris think I'm not leaving till midnight?" she has been standing there, watching.

MISS BLUEMEYER: Mr. Wade.

MR. WADE *(furiously):* Yes—ma'am!

MISS BLUEMEYER: I will see that you get the right luggage. *(Taking a step in the direction of door to service hall.)* Come with me, Paris.

AUNT LIDA: That won't be necessary, Miss Bluemeyer. Paris knows the suitcase we mean now.

PARIS *(quickly):* Yessum, I suhtnly do.

He hurries through the service hall doorway, closing the door after him. At the same moment Lennie takes Nancy's hand and pulls her into her parents' room. "Come ohn, Nancy!" As they are closing the door, James rushes after them, pushing his way through the half-closed door and then closing it after him. Miss Bluemeyer begins walking slowly across the hall toward Aunt Lida who watches her intently.

MRS. WADE *(pushing the child's dress at Myra and nodding her head significantly toward the girls' room):* Here, Myra. *(Half-whispering.)* Robert, you will miss the train if you don't hurry.

MR. WADE: By George, yes! *(Looking at his watch.)*

Paris now runs up the stairs with a yellow-brown Gladstone bag. Myra goes into the girls' room.

PARIS: Here, Mista Robert. *(He sets the bag down at the head of the stairs.)*

MR. WADE *(striding in the direction of Paris):* Tell Sellars to bring the car round.

PARIS: Sellars waitin' in the potecoshay.

Paris glances at Miss Bluemeyer, who has now reached the center of the hall, and runs down the stairs. Mr. Wade goes into his room and closes the door. Miss Bluemeyer suddenly turns about face and hastens to her room, leaving the door ajar.

MRS. WADE *(in alarm):* Aunt Lida!

AUNT LIDA *(reassuringly, in her deepest voice):* She's only going to fetch her hat and coat. She's quitting. She's not going to stay the night.

MISS BLUEMEYER *(enters with a light coat thrown over her left arm, a handbag in her left hand, and a soft felt hat in her right hand; with the latter she gesticulates rather wildly as she speaks in a loud masculine voice):* No, not another hour in the house with such as you. *(Striding the length of the hall to face Aunt Lida.)* My conscience would burn me out before morning.

AUNT LIDA *(sternly, calmly):* Just leave us your address, Miss Bluemeyer. We'll send your things tomorrow.

MISS BLUEMEYER: Send 'em or not, Miss Wade, as you like. Do I care if I never see them again? Not one thing that will remind me . . .

MRS. WADE *(rising from the chair):* Good night, Miss Bluemeyer! *(Miss Bluemeyer turns submissively and goes to the head of the stairs.)*

AUNT LIDA: Wait a moment.

MRS. WADE: No, Aunt Lida!

AUNT LIDA: Miss Bluemeyer, can't you calm yourself sufficiently to tell me what you have to say in a civilized manner? You and I will never see each other again, and you might be glad someday that you told me. *(Miss Bluemeyer laughs ironically.)*

MRS. WADE: Good *night,* Miss Bluemeyer.

MISS BLUEMEYER: No, Misses Wade, I will stay a bit. *(She returns to the group of chairs.)* I want to talk to you about your husband's aunt.

MRS. WADE *(turning her back and taking several steps in the direction of her room):* I have no interest in what you may say. Good night.

MISS BLUEMEYER: Ah, shame, Misses Wade. You who are so kind to your husband's aunt ought to be kind to other lonesome beings in this world. *(Mrs. Wade stops and turns halfway round.)*

Doesn't it seem maybe that's what is wrong with all the family folderol your sort go in for?

AUNT LIDA: It was not to hear your criticism of my niece that I called you back, Miss Bluemeyer.

MISS BLUEMEYER: It was not to criticize her I am staying. . . . *(Mr. Wade enters with his Gladstone. He pulls the door to behind him and stands listening.)* Misses Wade, I have a thing or two to say. . . .

MRS. WADE: If those things concern my aunt . . .

AUNT LIDA: Miss Bluemeyer, I asked you to stop a moment because I thought you had something to say about our late cousin, Mr. Wilson.

MISS BLUEMEYER *(suddenly, with emotion):* Mr. Wilson! Mr. Wilson! Your *cousin*, Mr. Wilson! *(Then speaking in a hoarse monotone, obviously making a conscious effort at self-restraint.)* Can you not hear yourselves? Aunt! Niece! Nephew! Father! Son! Daughter! Cousin! *Cousin!* I can see the poor old fellow now tramping past Merton's window to the lunchroom or going up the corner with a little package of laundry under his arm.

AUNT LIDA: Are you accusing us of unkindness to Cousin Harry?

MISS BLUEMEYER: Not to Cousin Harry, but to Mr. Wilson.

MR. WADE: I thought it had been definitely established that Cousin Harry *was* . . .

AUNT LIDA: Your distinction isn't quite clear, Miss Bluemeyer.

MISS BLUEMEYER: Oh, it is clear enough!

AUNT LIDA *(calmly):* If only you could calm yourself. I do think you may have a point to make.

MRS. WADE: Aunt Lida, this whole interview is uncalled-for. . . . Even if you have no respect for our family, Miss Bluemeyer, remember that one near to us has died this day. We simply do not understand each other. Please say no more and go.

MISS BLUEMEYER: Do we not understand each other, Misses Wade? I understand a good deal of how this family business works. It makes a woman safe and sure being related this way and that way to everybody around her. And it keeps you from having to bother about anybody else, since they are not "kinfolks." I understand how it works, for I was one of nine, and I saw the women in my family making the most of it too. And I might have done the same, but I was a queer sort who couldn't make herself do it.

AUNT LIDA: Is that all, Miss Bluemeyer?

MISS BLUEMEYER: Not quite all. For a solid year I have watched you here giving directions and making this house your own. And I have seen it right along that you are really the same as I in lots of your feelings, Miss Wade, that you are really lost and alone in the world, but you would not have it so, you just wouldn't. All along I have seen you are really a brainy woman and yet to see you here saying the things you say and playacting all the time! And then when the old man Wilson was dying, you, like the rest of 'em, talked of nothing but that he was kin, kin, kin. You have mocked and joked all this day and gave him a funeral only because he was a kinsman.

MR. WADE: Miss Bluemeyer.

MISS BLUEMEYER: I am going now, Mr. Wade. *(She goes to the head of the stairs where he is standing by the door.)* Good-bye, Mr. Wade.

MR. WADE: Good-bye, ma'am. And believe me, to us all our Cousin Harry was just a poor, lonely old man that we would have befriended if he had let us.

MISS BLUEMEYER: I know your feelings are good, Mr. Wade. But you are a man. For a man it is easier. *(She goes down the stairs. There is a moment's silence when each of the three persons present seems to be concerned with his own thoughts.)*

MRS. WADE: What could have so embittered a person?

MR. WADE: Why, the woman's crazy, and naturally Aunt Lida was the first to make it out. How long have you known she was insane, Aunt Lida?

AUNT LIDA: I don't know.

MR. WADE *(taking several steps forward, slowly)*: What do you mean?

MRS. WADE: She means that she doesn't know when she realized it.

MR. WADE: By the way she said it, I thought she meant she wasn't sure she was crazy.

MRS. WADE *(taking his arm):* Oh, could a sane person possibly have been so critical and questioning of a happy family life?

AUNT LIDA: Robert, aren't you going to miss your train?

MR. WADE: By George! Well, aren't the children going to tell me good-bye?

AUNT LIDA *(calling):* Chill-drun!

Mr. Wade kisses Miss Wade.

MR. WADE: So long, Auntie.

AUNT LIDA *(casually):* Toodle-oo. Hurry back, Robert.

The children have now appeared in the doorways from Aunt Lida's room and their parents' room. "Yes, ma'am!" "What, Aunt Lida?"

AUNT LIDA: Tell your daddy good-bye. *(Slowly letting herself down into the chair.)*

NANCY: Oh, of course!

JAMES: Sure!

All of the children rush toward their father to be kissed. As he bends and stoops to kiss each of them, he is saying, "Good-bye, Alfred. Good-bye, Nancy. Good-bye, Lida Sue. Good-bye, James. Good-bye, Charles William." But Mrs. Wade is watching Aunt Lida, who, as the curtain falls, sits with her hands over her face, as before.

FOR THE BEST IN PAPERBACKS, LOOK FOR THE 🐧

In every corner of the world, on every subject under the sun, Penguin represents quality and variety – the very best in publishing today.

For complete information about books available from Penguin – including Pelicans, Puffins, Peregrines and Penguin Classics – and how to order them, write to us at the appropriate address below. Please note that for copyright reasons the selection of books varies from country to country.

In the United Kingdom: For a complete list of books available from Penguin in the U.K., please write to *Dept E.P., Penguin Books Ltd, Harmondsworth, Middlesex, UB7 0DA*

In the United States: For a complete list of books available from Penguin in the U.S., please write to *Dept BA, Penguin, 299 Murray Hill Parkway, East Rutherford, New Jersey 07073*

In Canada: For a complete list of books available from Penguin in Canada, please write to *Penguin Books Canada Ltd, 2801 John Street, Markham, Ontario L3R 1B4*

In Australia: For a complete list of books available from Penguin in Australia, please write to the *Marketing Department, Penguin Books Australia Ltd, P.O. Box 257, Ringwood, Victoria 3134*

In New Zealand: For a complete list of books available from Penguin in New Zealand, please write to the *Marketing Department, Penguin Books (NZ) Ltd, Private Bag, Takapuna, Auckland 9*

In India: For a complete list of books available from Penguin, please write to *Penguin Overseas Ltd, 706 Eros Apartments, 56 Nehru Place, New Delhi, 110019*

In Holland: For a complete list of books available from Penguin in Holland, please write to *Penguin Books Nederland B.V., Postbus 195, NL–1380AD Weesp, Netherlands*

In Germany: For a complete list of books available from Penguin, please write to *Penguin Books Ltd, Friedrichstrasse 10 – 12, D–6000 Frankfurt Main 1, Federal Republic of Germany*

In Spain: For a complete list of books available from Penguin in Spain, please write to *Longman Penguin España, Calle San Nicolas 15, E–28013 Madrid, Spain*

A CHOICE OF PENGUIN FICTION

Monsignor Quixote Graham Greene

Now filmed for television, Graham Greene's novel, like Cervantes' seventeenth-century classic, is a brilliant fable for its times. 'A deliciously funny novel' – *The Times*

The Dearest and the Best Leslie Thomas

In the spring of 1940 the spectre of war turned into grim reality – and for all the inhabitants of the historic villages of the New Forest it was the beginning of the most bizarre, funny and tragic episode of their lives. 'Excellent' – *Sunday Times*

Earthly Powers Anthony Burgess

Anthony Burgess's magnificent masterpiece, an enthralling, epic narrative spanning six decades and spotlighting some of the most vivid events and characters of our times. 'Enormous imagination and vitality . . . a huge book in every way' – Bernard Levin in the *Sunday Times*

The Penitent Isaac Bashevis Singer

From the Nobel Prize-winning author comes a powerful story of a man who has material wealth but feels spiritually impoverished. 'Singer . . . restates with dignity the spiritual aspirations and the cultural complexities of a lifetime, and it must be said that in doing so he gives the Evil One no quarter and precious little advantage' – Anita Brookner in the *Sunday Times*

Paradise Postponed John Mortimer

'Hats off to John Mortimer. He's done it again' – *Spectator*. A rumbustious, hilarious new novel from the creator of Rumpole, *Paradise Postponed* is now a major Thames Television series.

Animal Farm George Orwell

The classic political fable of the twentieth century.

A CHOICE OF PENGUIN FICTION

Maia   Richard Adams

The heroic romance of love and war in an ancient empire from one of our greatest storytellers. 'Enormous and powerful' – *Financial Times*

The Warning Bell   Lynne Reid Banks

A wonderfully involving, truthful novel about the choices a woman must make in her life – and the price she must pay for ignoring the counsel of her own heart. 'Lynne Reid Banks knows how to get to her reader: this novel grips like Super Glue' – *Observer*

Doctor Slaughter   Paul Theroux

Provocative and menacing – a brilliant dissection of lust, ambition and betrayal in 'civilized' London. 'Witty, chilly, exuberant, graphic' – *The Times Literary Supplement*

July's People   Nadine Gordimer

Set in South Africa, this novel gives us an unforgettable look at the terrifying, tacit understanding and misunderstandings between blacks and whites. 'This is the best novel that Miss Gordimer has ever written' – Alan Paton in the *Saturday Review*

Wise Virgin   A. N. Wilson

Giles Fox's work on the Pottle manuscript, a little-known thirteenth-century tract on virginity, leads him to some innovative research on the subject that takes even his breath away. 'A most elegant and chilling comedy' – *Observer* Books of the Year

Last Resorts   Clare Boylan

Harriet loved Joe Fischer for his ordinariness – for his ordinary suits and hats, his ordinary money and his ordinary mind, even for his ordinary wife. 'An unmitigated delight' – *Time Out*

A CHOICE OF PENGUIN FICTION

Stanley and the Women   Kingsley Amis

Just when Stanley Duke thinks it safe to sink into middle age, his son goes insane – and Stanley finds himself beset on all sides by women, each of whom seems to have an intimate acquaintance with madness. 'Very good, very powerful . . . beautifully written' – Anthony Burgess in the *Observer*

The Girls of Slender Means   Muriel Spark

A world and a war are winding up with a bang, and in what is left of London all the nice people are poor – and about to discover how different the new world will be. 'Britain's finest post-war novelist' – *The Times*

Him with His Foot in His Mouth   Saul Bellow

A collection of first-class short stories. 'If there is a better living writer of fiction, I'd very much like to know who he or she is' – *The Times*

Mother's Helper   Maureen Freely

A superbly biting and breathtakingly fluent attack on certain libertarian views, blending laughter, delight, rage and amazement, this is a novel you won't forget. 'A winner' – *The Times Literary Supplement*

Decline and Fall   Evelyn Waugh

A comic yet curiously touching account of an innocent plunged into the sham, brittle world of high society. Evelyn Waugh's first novel brought him immediate public acclaim and is still a classic of its kind.

Stars and Bars   William Boyd

Well-dressed, quite handsome, unfailingly polite and charming, who would guess that Henderson Dores, the innocent Englishman abroad in wicked America, has a guilty secret? 'Without doubt his best book so far . . . made me laugh out loud' – *The Times*

A CHOICE OF PENGUIN FICTION

Trade Wind   M. M. Kaye

An enthralling blend of history, adventure and romance from the author of the bestselling *The Far Pavilions*

The Ghost Writer   Philip Roth

Philip Roth's celebrated novel about a young writer who meets and falls in love with Anne Frank in New England – or so he thinks. 'Brilliant, witty and extremely elegant' – *Guardian*

Small World   David Lodge

Shortlisted for the 1984 Booker Prize, *Small World* brings back Philip Swallow and Maurice Zapp for a jet-propelled journey into hilarity. 'The most brilliant and also the funniest novel that he has written' – *London Review of Books*

Village Christmas   'Miss Read'

The village of Fairacre finds its peace disrupted by the arrival in its midst of the noisy, cheerful Emery family – and only the advent of a Christmas baby brings things back to normal. 'A sheer joy' – *Glasgow Evening Times*

Treasures of Time   Penelope Lively

Beautifully written, acutely observed, and filled with Penelope Lively's sharp but compassionate wit, *Treasures of Time* explores the relationship between the lives we live and the lives we think we live.

Absolute Beginners   Colin MacInnes

The first 'teenage' novel, the classic of youth and disenchantment, *Absolute Beginners* is part of MacInnes's famous London trilogy – and now a brilliant film. 'MacInnes caught it first – and best' – *Harpers and Queen*

The Age of Reason   Jean-Paul Sartre

The first part of Sartre's classic trilogy, set in the volatile Paris summer of 1938, is itself 'a dynamic, deeply disturbing novel' (Elizabeth Bowen) which tackles some of the major issues of our time.

Three Lives   Gertrude Stein

A turning point in American literature, these portraits of three women – thin, worn Anna, patient, gentle Lena and the complicated, intelligent Melanctha – represented in 1909 one of the pioneering examples of modernist writing.

Doctor Faustus   Thomas Mann

Perhaps the most convincing description of an artistic genius ever written, this portrait of the composer Leverkuhn is a classic statement of one of Mann's obsessive themes: the discord between genius and sanity.

The New Machiavelli   H. G. Wells

This autobiography of a man who has thrown up a glittering political career and marriage to go into exile with the woman he loves also contains an illuminating Introduction by Melvyn Bragg.

The Collected Poems of Stevie Smith

Amused, amusing and deliciously barbed, this volume includes many poems which dwell on death; as a whole, though, as this first complete edition in paperback makes clear, Smith's poetry affirms an irrepressible love of life.

Rhinoceros / The Chairs / The Lesson   Eugène Ionesco

Three great plays by the man who was one of the founders of what has come to be known as the Theatre of the Absurd.

FOR THE BEST IN PAPERBACKS, LOOK FOR THE

PENGUIN MODERN CLASSICS

The Second Sex   Simone de Beauvoir

This great study of Woman is a landmark in feminist history, drawing together insights from biology, history and sociology as well as literature, psychoanalysis and mythology to produce one of the supreme classics of the twentieth century.

The Bridge of San Luis Rey   Thornton Wilder

On 20 July 1714 the finest bridge in all Peru collapsed, killing 5 people. Why? Did it reveal a latent pattern in human life? In this beautiful, vivid and compassionate investigation, Wilder asks some searching questions in telling the story of the survivors.

Parents and Children   Ivy Compton-Burnett

This richly entertaining introduction to the world of a unique novelist brings to light the deadly claustrophobia within a late-Victorian upper-middle-class family . . .

Vienna 1900   Arthur Schnitzler

These deceptively languid sketches, four 'games with love and death', lay bare an astonishing and disturbing world of sexual turmoil (which anticipates Freud's discoveries) beneath the smooth surface of manners and convention.

Confessions of Zeno   Italo Svevo

Zeno, an innocent in a corrupt world, triumphs in the end through his stoic acceptance of his own failings in this extraordinary, experimental novel which fuses memory, obsession and desire.

The House of Mirth   Edith Wharton

Lily Bart – beautiful, intelligent and charming – is trapped like a butterfly in the inverted jam jar of wealthy New York society . . . This tragic comedy of manners was one of Wharton's most shocking and innovative books.

A Confederacy of Dunces John Kennedy Toole

In this Pulitzer-Prize-winning novel, in the bulky figure of Ignatius J. Reilly, an immortal comic character is born. 'I succumbed, stunned and seduced . . . it is a masterwork of comedy' – *The New York Times*

The Labyrinth of Solitude Octavio Paz

Nine remarkable essays by Mexico's finest living poet: 'A profound and original book . . . with Lowry's *Under the Volcano* and Eisenstein's *Que Viva Mexico!*, *The Labyrinth of Solitude* completes the trinity of masterworks about the spirit of modern Mexico' – *Sunday Times*

Falconer John Cheever

Ezekiel Farragut, fratricide with a heroin habit, comes to Falconer Correctional Facility. His freedom is enclosed, his view curtailed by iron bars. But he is a man, none the less, and the vice, misery and degradation of prison change a man . . .

The Memory of War and Children in Exile: (Poems 1968–83) James Fenton

'James Fenton is a poet I find myself again and again wanting to praise' – *Listener*. 'His assemblages bring with them tragedy, comedy, love of the world's variety, and the sadness of its moral blight' – *Observer*

The Bloody Chamber Angela Carter

In tales that glitter and haunt – strange nuggets from a writer whose wayward pen spills forth stylish, erotic, nightmarish jewels of prose – the old fairy stories live and breathe again, subtly altered, subtly changed.

Cannibalism and the Common Law A. W. Brian Simpson

In 1884 Tod Dudley and Edwin Stephens were sentenced to death for killing their shipmate in order to eat him. A. W. Brian Simpson unfolds the story of this macabre case in 'a marvellous rangy, atmospheric, complicated book . . . an irresistible blend of sensation and scholarship' – Jonathan Raban in the *Sunday Times*

Bedbugs   Clive Sinclair

'Wildly erotic and weirdly plotted, the subconscious erupting violently into everyday life . . . It is not for the squeamish or the lazy. His stories work you hard; tease and torment and shock you' – *Financial Times*

The Awakening of George Darroch   Robin Jenkins

An eloquent and powerful story of personal and political upheaval, the one inextricably linked with the other, written by one of Scotland's finest novelists.

In Custody   Anita Desai

Deven, a lecturer in a small town in Northern India, is resigned to a life of mediocrity and empty dreams. When asked to interview the greatest poet of Delhi, Deven discovers a new kind of dignity, both for himself and his dreams.

Collected Poems   Geoffrey Hill

'Among our finest poets, Geoffrey Hill is at present the most European – in his Latinity, in his dramatization of the Christian condition, in his political intensity . . . The commanding note is unmistakable' – George Steiner in the *Sunday Times*

Parallel Lives   Phyllis Rose

In this study of five famous Victorian marriages, including that of John Ruskin and Effie Gray, Phyllis Rose probes our inherited myths and assumptions to make us look again at what we expect from our marriages.

Lamb   Bernard MacLaverty

In the Borstal run by Brother Benedict, boys are taught a little of God and a lot of fear. Michael Lamb, one of the brothers, runs away and takes a small boy with him. As the outside world closes in around them, Michael is forced to an uncompromising solution.

FOR THE BEST IN PAPERBACKS, LOOK FOR THE 🐧

KING PENGUIN

The Beans of Egypt, Maine Carolyn Chute

Out of the hidden heart of America comes *The Beans* – the uncompromising novel about poverty and of what life is like for people who have nothing left to them except their own pain, humiliation and rage. 'Disturbingly convincing' – *Observer*

Book of Laughter and Forgetting Milan Kundera

'A whirling dance of a book . . . a masterpiece full of angels, terror, ostriches and love . . . No question about it. The most important novel published in Britain this year' – Salman Rushdie in the *Sunday Times*

Something I've Been Meaning to Tell You Alice Munro

Thirteen brilliant and moving stories about women, men and love in its many disguises – pleasure, overwhelming gratitude, pain, jealousy and betrayal. The comedy is deft, agonizing and utterly delightful.

A Voice Through a Cloud Denton Welch

After sustaining a severe injury in an accident, Denton Welch wrote this moving account of his passage through a nightmare world. He vividly recreates the pain and desolation of illness and tells of his growing desire to live. 'It is, without doubt, a work of genius' – John Betjeman

In the Heart of the Country J. M. Coetze

In a web of reciprocal oppression in colonial South Africa, a white sheep farmer makes a bid for salvation in the arms of a black concubine, while his embittered daughter dreams of and executes a bloody revenge. Or does she?

Hugging the Shore John Updike

A collection of criticism, taken from eight years of reviewing, where John Updike also indulges his imagination in imaginary interviews, short fiction, humorous pieces and essays.